Hit The Road, Frank

Brian Ford

Published in 2013 by FeedARead.com Publishing – Arts Council funded

A CIP catalogue record for this title is available from the British Library.

For those I met along the way.

And for Tom Paxton, Bob Dylan, Chuck Berry, Jim Webb and all those who showed me the way.

Respect and apologies to Leonard Cohen, whose work I love, but who I thought might be too much for Frank on a dark Manitoba night.

"You can travel on ten thousand miles and stay right where you are"
Harry Chapin, 1974

Thanks to Redgraphite Design for the cover
www.redgraphite.co.uk

With love and gratitude to Jackie

And for Alexandra, the future

Chapter One: Talkin' New York

Saturday August 3rd 1974.   Texas

My mouth was dry enough already. The crazy woman had left me standing by the road and disappeared in a cloud of dust, leaving me with the midday sun for company. An improvement for sure, but it must have been a hundred degrees with no hint of shade. It could have been a hundred and twenty for all I knew. Coming from England means I'm not exactly an expert on judging the mercury when it gets to running wild like that. I was a little hung over, though not in too bad shape, and the two lane desert road was a state highway which should have seen me all the way to El Paso without any problems. An hour later it was hotter still, and not a single motor vehicle had passed in either direction. I was already thinking that I might do what every hitchhiker will do only as a last resort, and take a ride going back the other way if that's what came along first. Go back to the Rockin' R to drink beer and make a new plan. Thinking of the beer made my mouth even drier. Then I saw the snake crawl out from behind a rock.

The crazy woman had picked me up on the outskirts of Del Rio. I had slept late, and woke to find myself a little frazzled, but no more than that. The sun was making a mockery of the thin excuse for a curtain while a primitive air conditioner gurgled to little effect. The walls of the motel were made of tin. It was time to move on.

I bought two bottles of Gatorade from the tiny store, and stood out on the highway. I drank them both straight down and a minute later I felt more than slightly drunk again. Maybe that's one of the secret qualities of tequila, you dilute to taste. God knows there was still plenty of it kicking around my system. That's when she picked me up. At first she didn't seem that crazy, just stupid, which is not the same thing at all.

"England, huh? I'll tell you the place I've always wanted to go, Paris, France."

The woman was in her late thirties, overweight, not drastically so, but not flattered by baggy khaki shorts, white tennis shirt and blue cap. A large black Labrador was stretched languidly across the back seat of the beat up old Ford.

"Well if you go to Paris, you can visit London as well. It's only two hundred miles away."

"Paris, France is in England? I didn't know that."

I quickly realised that attempting any kind of geography lesson would be on the pointless side of futile.

"I'm gonna kill that Lucy Carmichael, I'll tell you that."

Silence reigned for an uneasy thirty seconds. I pretended I never heard it, hoping that she in turn might think she never said it, but her eyes were off the road and fixed on me in a manner most downright suspicious.

"Do you know her?"

I could have looked her straight in her crazed eyes and told her the God's honest truth, which is that I know but two people in the whole state of Texas, and Lucy Carmichael most assuredly isn't one of them. Instead I stared at the road ahead and slowly and steadily moved my head from side to side.

"No, I don't. Never heard of her."

I could see the wheels of her mangled mind going round and round, and they were surely telling her that the handsome stranger was more than likely old Lucy's bosom pal.

See that gun in the back?"

I'd never seen a double barrelled shotgun in real life, but there on the back seat next to the dog was what I would imagine to be one.

The snake was at least four feet long, light brown with black stripes. The stripes had a barbed pattern, like they were saying don't mess with me. The snake was on the other side of the road, but it wasn't a wide road, just a regular old two lane blacktop. It may just have been the reflection of the Texas sky, but I could have sworn the snake had blue eyes. Bright, shining blue eyes. Its belly was slithering across the rock hard ground, but its head was lifted from the ground and it was looking at me, looking straight at me with the bright blue shining eyes. I was transfixed by the eyes but I was trying to concentrate on the tail. If I know one thing about snakes, and if I do, it is only the one thing, it's this. When that tail starts shaking and rattling, then you're a goner.

People ask me sometimes, how can you just take off and jump into a stranger's car? I tell them that it's how you find the best in people, even more so when you're in another country. Some of the greatest kindness I've ever been shown came from people I didn't know from Adam. On the other hand, the law of averages tells you that you will meet the occasional weirdo, and one day, if you do it long enough, you will surely run into the psychopath who has been lying in wait for you since the day you were born. Logic and a cool head are what you need. Nobody is going to be crazy enough to shoot you when they are driving. They can pull over to the side of a deserted road, pull out the gun and tell you to get out the car, and you can refuse. They want brains all over the dash and forensic on the upholstery? Logic and a cool head will get you out of any number of tricky situations.

The snake doesn't know logic. The snake only knows rattle and bite, and leaving you to die beneath the unforgiving Sun. I started walking. Almost imperceptibly the snake increased its slither. It made no move to cross the road, but I knew it was following me. I wanted to run, but that would have been tantamount to signing my own death warrant. I could see the hills of Mexico in the distance and I wished I was there, wished I was anywhere.

I had dreamed of Texas ever since Ma bought me a cowboy outfit when I was six. Not for the first time I thought of something she used to say. Be careful of what you wish for, son. One day you just might get it.

Three weeks earlier. New York City

I'm on the front table at Max's with my new friend Robyn and her friend Shannon. I've just lit up my third straight Disque Bleu. I brought twenty packs with me for consumption in the big cities. Everywhere else I can slum it with Marlboros or smoke other peoples. Most definitely smoke other peoples.

Shannon is blonde, Monroe gorgeous and out of my league. Robyn is in my league, she's five feet tall, pretty if a little mousy, and she likes me. Robyn seems to know everybody here, which makes me feel as if everyone knows me, the New York City me that is, the street smart butterfly which emerges when you trade the Piccadilly line for the D train.

The girls both pass on my French smokes. Shannon seems vaguely disturbed to find that there are cigarettes out there that she has never heard of. She says she can't get off unless it's her own brand, and takes a long draw on her Winston as if to reassure herself that all is well with the world. Robyn chain smokes Kools. Robyn appears convinced that nothing that isn't readily available below 14th Street can possibly be of any value, which I think is a kind of a closed way of thinking for an artist, but she doesn't see the contradiction. I don't come from any kind of street with numbers in it, but I'm an exception. I'm from London. I'm automatically cool.

A guy gets on the stage and speaks into the microphone just above us.

"Will you please welcome an old friend, Al Caplan."

Al takes the stage and greets the audience, most of whom appear to know him personally. Robyn and Shannon both get a cursory nod, and I could almost swear that I get one too. So why wouldn't I? Sure I know Al. I've been in New York all of twenty six hours.

Eight hours earlier.

The White Horse Tavern on Hudson Street. Dylan Thomas drank here. It seems he was quite a regular until one night he fell off his barstool after seventeen whiskies to go not so gently into the good night, and a-carousing no more. It may have been seventeen, but then it could have been thirty six, depending on who's telling the tale. Seamus the bartender points out his photo on the wall. Seamus is from Dublin. He maintains that it's well known that the Welsh can't hold their drink, and that he once saw Brendan Behan in the Palace Bar, and Behan drank more whiskey than that, and a pint of stout to go with each one.

"They both ended up dead." I point out, like I'm being helpful or something.

"Ah sure they did, but Behan had more fun getting there" he replies.

"Thomas was a miserable Welsh bastard and no mistake."

Seamus then recites a poem about a pint of plain being your only man, or some such.

"That's Seamus's party piece", says a pretty if slightly mousy girl perched on the bar stool next to me.

"What's he do for an encore?"

"You don't want to know, believe me. So what brings you to the Village?"

I'm kind of expecting that one.

"Big white bird out of the sky. Do you want to know how I find America?"

"You turn left at Greenland? I've seen that movie a hundred times. Can I get you a beer?"

"Is the Pope a catholic?"

Three beers later and we're getting along just fine. Robyn's an artist. She lives in a walk up brownstone on Jones Street. I'm not exactly sure what a walk up brownstone is at this point, but it sounds impressive enough to me. She drinks vodka and grapefruit. She could be twenty she could be thirty two, which gives a one in three chance of her being younger than me, and a chance of about one in four thousand that we share the same birthday. I don't ask. I get good points for being from London, and bonus points for being called Frank. It's such a New York name apparently.

"You part Italian?"

"Irish, sort of. Not Irish like Seamus though. My mum was Irish."

The old man too, if you go back far enough.

"He'll be Irish when it suits him, like half of them across the water", chips in our friendly bartender, and here's me thinking they are supposed to be discreet.

"What do you prefer, Frank or Frankie?" asks Robyn while simultaneously lighting up a Kool and getting another round in. This is my kind of girl.

"Grandmother calls me Francis. Ma called me Frankie. You can call me Mr Downes."

"Call me what you want but don't call me late for dinner."

Guy standing at my shoulder. Thirties, Jewish afro, black leather waistcoat. Thick shades that look like they don't get removed too often. Robyn jumps up to give him a kiss on the cheek. I can feel that this guy carries some kind of status. They exchange some New York tittle tattle and then I get introduced.

"This is Frank from England, and this is my friend Al Caplan."

I feel like I've already absorbed some of this New York coolness, for want of a better word, so I shake and say hello as if I might know who he is or I might not. In fact I know full well who Al Caplan is. Well known sideman, to those in the know anyway, and I remember hearing one of his solo albums once, and pretty good it was too. So we've got a bohemian artist chick, a poetry reciting barman and a rock star all hanging out on a Wednesday afternoon with little old me. Welcome to New York.

Al is clutching a mandolin which he has just bought on Bleeker Street. He's playing a solo gig tonight at Max's Kansas City. The Dolls played there, and the Velvets played there way back when. I've been hanging out in the London clubs since I was sixteen, but I still get a little buzz at the prospect of going to Max's, which it turns out I am, as Robyn has got a table reserved for herself and her friends, of which it seems I am now one. Show time is eleven. We arrange to meet at ten thirty. I'll be on the guest list.

Cue to make a move. Apart from some British Airways processed plastic I haven't eaten for two days, and I'm thinking that if I have another beer I might start talking too much and bore Al. I may have been in town just a few hours, but I think I know already that boredom is the ultimate sin in this city, maybe the only one.

"See you later man" I tell Al, a little self- consciously.

Robyn squeezes my arm in a way that makes me think she really wants me to be there.

"You'll be there, right?"

"Sure I will. I wouldn't miss it."

I wander through the Village, and get a slice of pizza on MacDougal and then another on Bleeker. Suddenly I'm tired. I catch the Subway back to the Iroquois and book an alarm call for nine. Nine pm, that is.

Confidence is one thing I'm seldom short of, but for a moment at London Airport I felt as though I was ten years old and the first grown up I saw in a uniform would more than likely send me home. Don't be silly son, you can't go to New York, have you been watching too much Kojak or something? But no, I got my boarding pass and breezed into the departure lounge same as if I was going anywhere else. I don't mind admitting I was still wrapped a little tight. Yes I'm from the big city, and I've served my apprenticeship on the road from Berlin to Marrakesh and all points in between, but New York seemed a little scary even for me. A few days would be enough, and then I'd hit out to the great blue yonder, the big country where I could lose myself and find the world.

There was a boy of about seventeen sitting next to me, and he seemed like a pretty good kid, although I was more interested in the clouds and the occasional patch of ocean than any conversation. In true British fashion we didn't really talk much until we were about an hour away from landing. He was a posh lad, but he seemed all right. His dad was a big deal in some finance house on Wall Street, and the kid, who went by the name of Conrad, went to boarding school in England and visited in the holidays. He told me that he never went out after seven at night when he was in New York, because anyone who does gets mugged for sure. Thanks Conrad, that really makes me feel good. Conrad is concerned that I don't have an address for my landing card.

"Use my address. I can't invite you back because my Dad got fed up with people staying, but you can use the address. It's not like they check, but you do need one."

Sounds OK to me. East 68th Street, my imaginary home. The next thing I knew the plane was tilting, and I looked out the window to see the city reaching up towards me. Looking down on Manhattan I felt like I was seventeen myself, and was being threatened with seduction by a rampant divorcee. Excited but very, very nervous. Then we were briefly over water again, before we touched down and taxied to the terminal zone. Conrad passed me a piece of paper while we were waiting for the seat belt sign to go off.

"I've got an idea. Go to this hotel and say you have a reservation.

13

When they can't find it tell them it was booked by Mr Schumann's office. My Dad's company are called First European, they're major customers. They'll think their reservations staff screwed up. You're a graduate trainee fresh from the London School of Economics. Only thing is, you need to be gone by Friday morning. Friday is when the accounts come over the telex machine. I've helped out in my Dad's office so I know how it works."

I checked the address. Iroquois Hotel. 44th Street. Sounds good.

"Isn't that sort of ripping your Dad off?" I inquired.

Conrad gave me a thin smile.

"He can afford it, believe me. Anyway, serves him right for being an arsehole and not letting my friends stay over. Don't worry about it."

It occurred to me that if I was Conrad's Dad I wouldn't be too keen on every Tom, Dick and Frankie taking up residence in my evidently rather posh gaff either, but I was grateful for the spiel nevertheless. Conrad breezed through passport control as I would expect him to, but then so did I, my Upper East Side address working a treat. I got three months admission no questions asked, not even how much money I've got with me, which was one I was expecting. I've got quite a lot thank you, should you ask, but that's a story for another day. I've got one piece of luggage, old fake leather overnight or at best weekend bag, which has seen service for three months at a stretch more than once. Old faithful rolled off that carousel sure enough, but I felt duty bound to stick around and help Conrad with what turned out to be a mountain of stuff. We stacked a trolley and wheeled it through a disinterested customs hall into arrivals, where Conrad had a chauffeur waiting for him, no less. The guy was in uniform, hat, the full works.

Conrad told me apologetically me that he would give me a lift but it could cause problems, know what I mean. Sure, I say, you've done enough already. He thrust another note into my hand.

"Give me a ring sometime" he said, and then he was gone.

Sure I'll phone you Conrad, you're seventeen and you don't go out after seven o'clock. It crossed my mind that Conrad might be queer, boarding school and all that. Not that I care, if the kid's done me a favour. Unless he was bullshitting me it looks like I've got myself a complementary hotel for three nights, which would be what I call getting off to a flyer. He seemed too much of a serious kind to be putting me on, but I want to get there as quickly as possible just to make sure. There were signs for buses, but there are times when only a cab will do, and this was one of them. Anyway, this is New York. I've seen enough films to know that cabs and the subway rule, and the natives don't go riding around on buses too much.

Darkness had fallen by now, and the balmy night hit me for all of the ten seconds it took to reach the cab rank.

"First time in New York?" asked my driver.

"I'm on business. I come here all the time."

No thanks pal, I don't want a tour of the city, I don't want any tourist detours, and I don't even want to talk to you. I just want to look out of the window and take it all in. Anyway, I do come here all the time, if only in my head. Now the dream is a reality. I'm in New York. I'm in America. Finally made it, Ma. I'm Frank Downes, that's who I am.

So I had felt a little uneasy at the airport, both of them, although there was never any real danger of me losing my bottle, but all the old confidence was back as I strode up to the hotel reception. I even had to keep my natural insouciance in check. I'm supposed to be a graduate trainee and I would imagine they would be the keen type. I'm not too sure what a graduate trainee should look like, but I imagine it's not a lot like me. Sure enough, the clerk didn't admit that there wasn't a booking and just asked who made the reservation. I just had to say the magic words and I'm in. Thanks Conrad, you're a little star.

The room wasn't quite as luxurious as I had hoped, but it would do well enough, thank you. It even had a kitchenette attached, though I can't see it being used while I'm around. I should have been tired, but the adrenaline had kicked in and I needed a drink, just one or two to help me sleep. I was out on the sweaty street for all of two minutes before I found a bar and sunk three Jack Daniel's on the rocks. Then it was back to the room to try and sleep, with the air conditioner whirring and my mind spinning, and New York City not pausing for breath outside my hotel door.

I have to say Al is pretty good. I knew him as this legendary session man, but he can sing, he's got some good songs of his own, and he can play the hell out of his acoustic twelve string. He takes his new mandolin out of the case and plays something by Sleepy John Estes. Some wise ass enquires why he's still got the price tag on the mandolin.

"Well I'm Jewish, what do you expect?"

I'm loving Al, and I'm digging just being here. Robyn and Shannon seem oblivious to much of anything other than their own conversation, and Al gets snappy with them at one point.

"If you wanna carry on like you're at a fuckin' ball game, why don't you go and do that?"

"Blow it out of your ass, Al."

Nice one Shannon, very upmarket.

"Whaddayou think I am, a fuckin' one man band?"

And so on and so on. Al is gone by one thirty, but it appears the night is still young in Max's. Come three am and nobody is leaving, but I think I will. Robyn grabs my arm with the same intensity she did earlier, and asks me to meet her at the White Horse in the afternoon. I haven't mentioned that I'll be gone by the weekend. No one has asked me.

I'm hardly tired, I didn't get up till nine pm, but I felt it was the right time to go. I know it's not recommended at this time of night, but I walk all the way uptown to 44th Street. I want to breathe in as much of the energy as I can. From a doorway I hear the metallic sound of a switchblade springing open. For a second I'm fucking paralysed, but I manage to turn my head to see a black guy leaning back with a can of coke from which he's just pulled the ring top. You're from London Frank, you don't need to be paranoid. As I approach 42nd Street, beautiful black prostitutes in hot pants congregate looking like the Supremes about to sing 'Come See About Me' or 'Stop in the Name of Love', even. At Four a.m. 42nd Street is as crowded as Oxford Street on a Saturday morning. Punters coming in and out of porno cinemas, dope dealers trading openly on the sidewalk, beggars asking for money, girls calling me honey. Two blocks later and I'm home free. I'm not even going to think about trying to sleep, so I put the TV on and find Danger Man, Ma's old favourite. We used to watch it together on Sunday nights when I was a kid. God bless you, Ma. You've got your own Danger Man now, or would have if you were still around. Let's hope he doesn't end up a Prisoner.

Thursday morning I've got a date with a big green lady. I've seen sidewalks, I've got a sore neck from looking up at buildings, I've seen the subway, and I've seen the Village. It's time to see some sights. The cloud cover hanging just above the skyline rules out the Empire State, so today I shall pay my respects to the lady with the torch.

On the ferry it feels like I'm surrounded by people from everywhere except New York, which makes sense. I mean, I've never been to the Tower of London, never thought about it. The boats that brought people over from Europe would have been even more crowded, and it must have been a long uncomfortable voyage. At this point my knowledge of America has been learned strictly from Mark Twain, John Steinbeck, John Ford, John Wayne, James Stewart, Marlon Brando, Woody Guthrie, Bob Dylan, Marshall Dillon, Davy Crockett, Chuck Berry, Lou Reed, Robert Johnson, Leadbelly and Mississippi John Hurt. Oh, and maybe Lonnie Donegan. Now there's a hell of a lot there, but it still leaves some gaps. Leaning on the rail of this ferry I couldn't tell you when the Statue of Liberty was built or by whom, though I suspect I will soon find out. I know enough to know that it was there at the turn of the century, when the poor huddled masses came in their millions, looking to make their dreams come true and create a life for themselves. Put down some roots. My Granny had cousins who left Connemara and put down roots so strong they were never heard from again. Now I'm living a dream simply by being here, but I'm not poor. I've got a money belt stuffed with ill gotten gains. I don't intend to put down any roots either. That's why I'm here, I tear them up before they're even planted. I can still fancy that I can feel what they felt when they clapped eyes on that lady with the torch beckoning them on in like a great green usherette. Welcome. People who had never felt welcome anywhere, except in their own front parlours, and maybe not even there, some of them.

Built in Paris. Shipped to New York, reconstructed and unveiled in 1886. One hundred and fifty one feet high. 1886 doesn't seem that long ago standing here on the island. My Dad's ma used to live in a house that must have been older than that. This is a young country. We've got stuff that goes back to ten sixty six and beyond.

I feel that mixture of superiority and melancholy detachment I always do when I'm on my own and around tourist traps. I didn't know the statue was hollow. It feels like something of a violation, but I climb the stairs anyway, and look out over to the New York Island. This Land is Your Land. It feels like my land too. And I've only just begun.

On the ferry back, two blonde Canadian girls of about eighteen ask me to take their picture. I frame their happy innocence with a backdrop of grey water and all-knowing city. Another time and place, say on an Inter Rail train through Europe, I would have invited myself into their company and doubtless been most gratefully received, but today I keep my own counsel. Back in Manhattan I wander up from Battery Park through the financial district and continue along towards Hudson

17

Street. I have a sudden hankering to sink a few beers and chew the fat with Seamus. On Liberty Island I had surrounded myself with ghosts and shadows, and it had dawned on me that I must surely have relatives here, grandchildren of those who sailed away and never looked back. What could be better than to spend a few hours swapping banter with a horny handed son of Erin, larger than life and twice as ugly.

As it happens, it's Seamus's day off. Robyn is sitting at the bar on the same stool she occupied yesterday.

"Hey, I've just come in to use the pay phone so I could call you" I lie.

She looks at me a little quizzically.

"Well I've just saved you a dime, you better buy me a drink."

"What you got for a dime?"

The new bartender gives me a look that suggests that this is a question he is regularly asked for real.

"If you don't mind me asking, when do you work, Robyn?"

"Mornings, usually"

"Mornings, sure. I bet you never get up before noon."

"Well today you would win your bet, but I don't go to Max's that often."

"And does your painting pay the rent?"

"Sure!" Then a slight pause. "How do you pay your rent?"

"Well at the moment I don't have any."

"So what's your plan?"

"My plan is not to have any plans."

Sounds good, but I do have a plan, half a plan anyway. I know I'm never going to jump through any hoops for this chick, but I like her well enough, and I don't want to give her too much bullshit, although the fact that old habits die hard means that a certain amount is unavoidable. So I tell Robyn the plan, which is to leave tomorrow.

That thing of grabbing my arm again.

"You only just got here! You've hardly seen anything yet. Stay with us for a while. Stay as long as you like."

Well what can I say? The highway is calling me, but it can wait a week, maybe longer. So I say yes, I would love to stay with you for a while, Robyn.

Robyn has to be somewhere; I have to be at her place tomorrow before nine thirty, which suits me fine, as I'm still a little anxious about getting rumbled by the hotel.

A brisk squeeze of the arm and she's gone. I remain at the bar nursing another cold one. Decision time. I could still skip and no harm done. I mean, that's what I always do, save for the no harm done. I can't quite figure Robyn out yet. I don't get the feeling that she really wants a piece of me, but those moments when she grabs my arm tell me there's something there. As for me, I haven't got the serious hots for her, but I wouldn't say no. I realise this puts her in a not very exclusive club. So, why the hell not? After all, that Port Authority Bus Station is just a few miles downtown.

By the time I get back to the Iroquois I don't feel like doing much of anything other than making the most of my elegant solitude. Watch baseball, alien, unfathomable, and strangely captivating, while I'm getting my stuff ready for the morning, which doesn't exactly take long. Then the best night's sleep I've had for a long time, only interrupted by a dream about Danger Man.

I'm at the desk bright and early at eight thirty. I have decided that if there is any misunderstanding over the bill I will just pay it. I'm not exactly short, though I don't particularly want to advertise the fact to people I meet, and I don't want to risk being thrown out of the country almost as soon as I've got here for the sake of a few bucks. I needn't have worried, I just sign on the dotted line and I'm out, sweet as a nut. If I had been skint Murphy's law would have made sure it was a different story. I take the subway to West 4th Street and walk through the Village towards Robyn's place. Turning into Jones Street I now realise what a brownstone is, and I am soon to discover what a walk up is, too. Robyn looks pleased to see me.

"I've got to go uptown today. Make yourself at home. Fix a sandwich, watch TV if you want. I'll be back later and make up a bed for you in my studio"

I make a sandwich as instructed, though the cheese in Robyn's refrigerator has seen better days and the bread isn't much better. I don't think she eats at home too often. I watch the morning news. Strange to be watching television in the day. They're big on news here. I'll buy a paper at home, but I have to admit to seldom working back further than the racing page, so all I hear usually are the hourly bulletins on Capital. I'd heard vaguely about this Watergate thing, though I couldn't tell you what it's about. They're certainly well into it here. The thing I had heard about was this heiress Patricia Hearst who got kidnapped and then joined her captors. Her current whereabouts are a mystery. Not too many people know where I am either. The difference is that there's a whole country looking for this chick, and two, possibly three people, who might be curious about me, and one of those might not be that interested anyway.

The morning news gives way to ridiculous game shows which are followed by unwatchable soap operas. Robyn hasn't provided me with a key but I'm getting a little stir crazy so I shut the door firmly behind me and trust to luck, which is running pretty well so far, that I will catch up with her later. I wander the Village for a while. Some of it seems like a mixture of present day Soho and Ladbroke Grove, and some of it appears to be resolutely hanging on to nineteen sixty seven. Washington Square, a sea of acoustic guitars, chess boards, beards and the odd tell-tale whiff of a jazz cigarette, falls firmly into the latter.

I stop by an old ale house somewhere over towards the east side on 7th Street. The bar looks like it's older than Columbus, and the beer is fine, but this Friday afternoon finds it full of students and young executives, so I don't hang around too long. Back on the street it's getting hotter though it's still cloudy. I make my way back towards the West Side and the White Horse where I expect to meet a more like minded clientele. Robyn is waiting for me. Well she's here, it's a fair bet she would be here anyway, but it feels like she's waiting for me, and right now that's a nice enough feeling. There's a plan for this evening. I was hoping there would be.

"Friday night is pizza night. We booked a table for five. That's me and Shannon, and our friends David and Neil and you're coming too, right?"

"Yeah, sure."

She looks at me like she's reading my mind.

"You don't need to worry about David and Neil. You're safe with us."

Safe with us? So what does that mean? I'm sure I'll find out before long.

I find out. David is about as stereotyped as its gets. Works in the theatre, set designer, camp as a row of tents. Neil is darker, comparatively taciturn, works in a bar that doesn't open till eleven. I'm not particularly versed in these things, but I assume him to be the dominant male. This is going to be our dinner and his breakfast. We meet at a bar on Bleeker a few doors down from the pizza joint and drink Margaritas. This is a new one on me, although I don't let on. Something I could get used to, as well. I flash the Disque Bleu, and find that my two new acquaintances react a lot more enthusiastically than Robyn and Shannon, which pleases me in one way, but means my stock is further diminished.

"Don't pass those around if you get to Texas" says Neil, "They'll think you're gay for sure."

"All those cowboys down there are faggots anyway" says David.

"They hate themselves because of it, and they hate everyone else as well."

Shannon is her charming self.

"David, you're full of shit. You've never been to Texas. In fact I doubt you've even been to New Jersey."

"Well why would anyone in their right mind want to go to New Jersey, let alone Texas? I've been to Montreal. I think Frank should go there instead of going west. I would be pretty sure he could get these cigarettes in Montreal. You can get almost anything up there. Almost anything. Manhattan is the only place you can get absolutely everything. Except French cigarettes."

David takes that as his cue to help himself to another one. I make a mental note to switch to Marlboros as soon as I get off this island. Mention of New Jersey leads Neil to mention that he's trying to unload tickets he's been given for a club called The Bottom Line tomorrow night. Some guy from the shore called Springsteen is playing, and it's supposed to be a hot ticket but Neil's got to work.

My turn. "The shore? You mean the guy lives on the beach?"

The margaritas are kicking in, and for some reason I find this really funny.

Neil explains it to me like I'm seven years old.

"The shore is just what they call the coast down there. To us the coast is west. East we say the shore."

"Springsteen. Is he Jewish?" asks Robyn, and I look at her and it occurs to me that she might be Jewish herself.

"I don't think so" says Neil. "I think he might be Italian."

Shannon knocks the whole idea on the head because she saw the guy at Max's last year and he sucked. One guy on his own strummed a guitar and mumbled into the mike. She can't believe he's got a gig at the Bottom Line. Even more damning, he comes from Jersey, and the only good thing that ever came out of Jersey is the Turnpike.

My turn again. "Well just a minute there. I happen to know for a fact that Frank Sinatra comes from New Jersey."

Now David is really animated.

"No, no, no, you don't get it. Sinatra's from Hoboken. That's just the other side of the river, just a little accident of geography. It's no different to coming from Brooklyn. Sinatra is New York through and through. This guy is strictly hicks from the sticks. Don't even think about it."

That particular subject firmly put to bed, it's now time to go and eat.

I love a restaurant. Ever since I had my own money I would always rather go out and eat than go to a club. A lot of my friends find that weird, but that's the way I am. It's not that I'm a gourmet, or even particularly fussy about what I eat, it's the surroundings, the service, and the glow you get from a quality cognac after a good meal. In a night club there's always someone who can dance better than me or with a better haircut, but in a good restaurant I feel at home. Something else I'll tell you, chicks love it. If things go well, which they usually do, you can hear their knickers hit the floor before the dessert trolley comes round.

I'm hungry. All I've eaten today is the meagre ration I scraped from Robyn's fridge about thirteen hours ago, and that scarcely counts as food at all. The place is heaving. Waiters in red and black run around with the biggest pizzas I have ever seen. Just what the doctor ordered. The deal is that you share, which is something I've never been big on, but even I couldn't tackle one of these babies on my own. Me and Neil dig in to the pepperoni, while the girls share one that has too much green stuff on it for my liking, and David picks at a vegetable lasagne. The feast is washed down with carafes of robust red, which keep on coming.

The conversation had sparkled in the bar, but we're all more or less defeated now, temporarily anyway. I wouldn't relish a night's work after putting that away, but Neil disappears into the night with his faithful Sancho Panza in tow. David picked up the check. It appears he's worth a few bucks. So then there were three. I would just love it if Shannon said goodnight and made her exit, but I know full well that she won't. She and Robyn chatter away the short walk back to the apartment, and for the first time I feel slightly excluded. When we get inside Robyn puts on Transformer, the album Lou Reed recorded in Willesden, just a few miles from the Downes family home, and Shannon rolls a joint. Ah, the dreaded drug! Four days out and my first encounter with the old Mary Jane. To tell you the truth, I can take it or leave it. Sure I'll take a puff to be sociable, but I've always found it over rated, and the whole ritual and paraphernalia thing that goes with it a crashing bore. So on this occasion I would rather leave it, but it would be rude to say no, even though it always leaves my throat really dry after drinking, and I've already got that contented glow that only wine on a very full stomach is truly capable of providing.

To my relief it is just the one. I'm already starting to drift away when I hear them both bid me goodnight. Robyn makes her way into her bedroom followed by Shannon, who gives her a little nudge in the back as they go through the door. My brain is three parts closed down by now, but I've still got just enough grey cells working to realise two things. One, that I'm as thick as two planks, and two, the truth about Robyn and Shannon. I let the last track play out, put it back in its sleeve, turn off the stereo and tiptoe into the studio where a single bed has been neatly made up. Goodnight ladies. Suck that lemon dry.

I sleep deep and I sleep long. My sleep patterns have been erratic since I got here, although to be fair, circumstances had dictated that they were erratic for quite some while before that. I wake up feeling good, if a little thirsty. I'm also very horny, like I always am in the morning when the alcohol is still coursing through my veins. There are no clocks in Robyn's studio. I fish for my watch and find that it's a quarter to twelve. What's more, it feels like a quarter to twelve. I'm finally on New York time. I head for the bathroom wearing just my underpants, reckoning that no one is likely to get too excited by the sight of me. I needn't have bothered as there's nobody home. There's a note on the table.

"Stuff to do. See ya later. This is your key."

Sure enough, there is my key. It's not exactly the key to the highway, but it's useful. In the shower I try thinking of Robyn and Shannon and whatever they do, but it doesn't really work for me so I think of Julie, loyal Julie who would give everything to please me.

Not only am I back in sync with the clock, but I've regained my appetite. I hadn't really thought of food too much since I got here, living on bar snacks and slices of this and that, but last night got the old juices flowing. I thought I wouldn't need to eat for a week after that, but now I'm hungry again. I don't even bother to look in the fridge, but head down to 7th Avenue and stop by a diner for a 99c breakfast which doesn't disappoint, and take advantage of the unlimited coffee refills. I think of Robyn and friend, and I have to struggle to suppress my laughter. The waitress thinks I'm smiling at her, and obligingly gives me more coffee. The joke's on you for once Downes, the first girl you try your hand with in the States and she bats for the other team. The chaps at home would be spluttering into their

23

pints if they knew. It all seems to make sense now, but at the same time she does make it clear that she likes me. Maybe she just likes me, if you know what I mean. Unusual, but in this instance it is something which could suit me very well. If there was another guy involved it would be different, but clearly there isn't. It means I can distance myself a little, come and go as I please, especially now I have a key, and sling my hook when I'm ready, which will be fairly soon. The waitress is smiling at me but I don't need conversation right now, so I leave her a quarter and make my exit. Well, its twenty five per cent, that's generous enough. She wasn't a bad looker either, so I reserve the right to return another time.

The sun has now burst through for the first time since I've been here. I look uptown and then down, and see the city transformed. Skyscrapers which were camouflaged grey to match the sky now shine sparkling white and silver against the clear blue. I take a wander. Rule one in this town is never to look at a map when you're on the street, but I don't see anyone on the avenue, so I sneak a furtive look and head down towards Little Italy and Chinatown. The sidewalks seem almost deserted. Back home, Saturday is always the big day of the week. Not here it would seem, not in this part of town anyway. It's hot now and getting hotter. Maybe the thing to do here is either to get out of town or stay in the shade.

The Italian quarter is smaller and quieter than I expected. I'm looking for mommas hanging washing from upstairs windows and calling to each other across the street in dialect. I'm half expecting, in fact I'm hoping, to see wise guys in sharp suits sitting in restaurants eating vongole, and facing open doors while the accordions play. Looks like I'm twenty, maybe thirty years too late. There are restaurants on Mulberry Street, but only a few of them are open this lunchtime, and a glance through the window reveals the same kind of crowd you would find on Bleeker. Only a Catholic church, which instantly radiates the feeling that people actually use it, gives any real indication of its heritage. Chinatown is busier and on the surface appears more open about what it is, but it still only seems to cover a few blocks. I look at some set menus in the windows which appear to be outrageously cheap, and resolve to come back some time when I've skipped breakfast. Going further south I soon realise that I am on the outskirts of the wasteland which is a financial district at the weekend. I head west, and then north at the bottom of Hudson Street, which I know by now is a long street, but one that always takes me where I want to be.

By the time I reach the top of Hudson it's just after three pm. Back home we would have been turned out on the streets by now. Lloyd George introduced afternoon closing during the First World War to get the women back to the munitions factories on time. To my way of thinking the more sensible thing would have been to provide canteen facilities and not allow them to leave the factory during their shift. Instead of that the ladies could still knock back their gin at a penny a tot, and they were then free to go back and make shells for the poor bastards at the front, a task for which you might think a degree of precision would be useful. It was a few years after that when Americans woke up one morning to find they couldn't get a drink at any time of the day or night, not legally anyway. Reason eventually prevailed, but back in the U.K. we are still saddled with the legacy of one sober Welshman. So I'm thinking on all this, and before I know it I'm at the door of The White Horse, which saw off prohibition, and also saw off one decidedly unsober Welshman.

This afternoon it's about half full. It seems like a different crowd. The girls aren't in. Seamus is behind the bar, but he seems subdued by his own standards, preferring to spend the time not spent serving customers reading the Irish Times rather than reciting poetry. He pours a pint, and pushes it towards me with a nod and no further comment. I take his lead, and picking up a copy of the New York Times, grab an unoccupied table. The newspaper must weigh about ten pounds. I give thanks that none of the good citizens of Acton had this on order when I was doing my paper round ten years ago. Another job I had for all of a week; too early, too cold and dark, and altogether too much hassle for ten shillings a week.

This Watergate thing takes up pages and pages. Politicians in high office have been telling lies, and the evidence appears to suggest that the biggest liar of them all is none other than the President of the United States himself, Richard Milhous Nixon. Looking at the picture of this sweaty, shifty looking man makes me wonder why this is any kind of story at all. Tricky Dicky. Would you buy a used car from this man? Tin soldiers and Nixon coming. So why does everyone seem so surprised now? Maybe the details will gradually unfold before me during the coming weeks. Maybe they won't. Maybe out in the great blue yonder people write their own history. Somewhere there's a world where people don't need the New York Times or serious looking old men in suits on the CBS News to tell them how things are.

And that is the kind of world I'm looking for.

I stay in the pub far longer than I intended. When I do step back out on the street it is already getting dark, but it seems even hotter than it was earlier, and I'm happy but weary. I head down through the Village, stopping to pick up a pepperoni slice before I return to the apartment. It appears that no one has been home since I left earlier. Robyn's note is still on the table.

I'm glad to be alone. It suddenly hits me that apart from asking for beer and food I haven't conversed with a soul all day. Even if I didn't realise it before, that's exactly the kind of day I've been in need of for a long time. I just didn't expect that I would eventually find it in the city that never sleeps.

The paucity of Robyn's fridge comes in sharp contrast to the Aladdin's cave of oils, creams, potions and many other mysterious things which fight for space on her bathroom shelf and which I prefer to leave well alone. I mask the taste of beer, pizza and way too many Disque Bleu with some mouthwash that could fool me in to thinking I had lived on peaches for a week if I didn't know better. Then I go straight to the studio and hurriedly get between the sheets before anybody can disturb my damn near perfect day.

Chapter Two: Keys To The Highway

I'm looking down a rainy street and I see Teresa standing outside a church. It's one of those churches you find in cities that has no churchyard, and you walk straight in off the street. Teresa says nothing, but her eyes are locked on me, pulling me towards her. As I walk towards her I realise the church is the one in Little Italy. When I reach her I see that Gino is with her. Gino seems shrunken since I last saw him, his hair and moustache grey and bedraggled. He's wrapped in his familiar old brown overall, but he appears to be almost lost in it. The Gino I remember always looked like a millionaire even though he was the scruffiest man in London. Teresa still doesn't speak, but her eyes remain fixed on me, revealing sadness, accusation and resignation in equal measure.

Gino speaks. "I'm very disappointed in you, Frank. Very disappointed"

Gino must have said that to me a thousand times when I worked for him, and it was always forgotten in five minutes, but this time he speaks with a weariness that sounds as if it comes from the core of his very soul. He shuffles down the street and the two of us follow in silence. Then I notice Gino's brand new Volvo. Teresa gets in the front and I get in the back, but her eyes continue to hold mine through the rear view mirror. We glide silently through streets that I don't recognise, until I realise this has to be a dream because we have stopped at the lights outside North Acton tube station. Anyway, Gino's dead. I know now that I can leave the dream behind if I concentrate hard enough, but part of me wants to get out of the car and catch the tube to Ma's house. I thought I had some choice, but that was an illusion too. Teresa's gaze holds me prisoner. The car moves noiselessly forward. Now I know where we are, and I know where we are going.

Gino pushes open the gate and leads us in single file up the tiny pathway. Teresa follows him, and I bring up the rear, free from her eyes for a moment. Now I never want the dream to end. Gino has a key, which can't be right, but it doesn't matter. The three of us are now standing in Ma's front room. She's not in her usual chair but she's sitting at the dining table. Her usual chair is occupied by Julie. Now it's Julie who is looking at me. Her eyes are hazel green but the look is the same as Teresa's. Ma just looks puzzled. So she should. She's dead too. Gino and Teresa sit down on the small sofa. I stand rooted on the small piece of available carpet in front of the fireplace. Nobody speaks. We stay like this for some dreamtime that cannot be measured. Then there's a knock on the door.

There are one or two sensory experiences better to wake up to than the smell of bacon frying, but only one or two. It takes me a few seconds to realise where I am, and when I do I'm even more confused, because I know I'm in Robyn's apartment, and Robyn's apartment and food don't have too much interaction. Another knock on the door.

"Hey Frankie. Get up! We fixed you breakfast!"

I get out of bed, put on my jeans, and dig a fresh t-shirt from my bag. Six days away, and I'm going to need to get some laundry done soon. I emerge to find the table neatly laid with juice, cereal and fresh rolls.

"I didn't think you girls ate at home."

"Sunday mornings we do" pipes up Robyn, who emerges from the kitchen bearing eggs, bacon, pancakes and coffee, which she places on the table in front of me. The pancakes are shop bought, and the coffee is instant, but all in all it is a very creditable effort, a nice surprise, and an extremely civilised way to start the day.

"You're coming to Coney Island with us today" says Shannon, skipping any kind of good morning. This is phrased as a matter of fact rather than as a question, and without any discernible enthusiasm. Robyn is more animated.

"You're coming, right? David's coming too, oh and Shannon's friend, Patti."

So more than one question to be addressed there. David, but not Neil? I'm curious but no way am I going to ask. I didn't mind Neil, but I don't want anyone to think that I might like Neil, if you get my drift. And who's Patti? Is she a straight friend? Or is there some kind of triangle deal going on here? And if she's straight, is she nice? Is she like Shannon? Shannon, as I may have mentioned, is stone gorgeous, although without the personality, and as I discovered the other night, the necessary sexual inclination, to match. Too many imponderables for this early in the day, so I reply, yes, I'd love to come to Coney

Island. I volunteer to wash up which causes some confusion, until I discover that to wash up Stateside means to wash yourself up, like a wash and brush up. You hear people say they are going to go home from work, wash up and then go out, which sounds kind of sweet. Washing up, they call doing the dishes. This conversation takes up about twenty minutes, as Robyn seems reluctant to admit there is a world existing more than a mile and a half away from the Village, and Shannon could care less, so the concept of linguistic differences is more than a little difficult for them to deal with.

"As someone once said, England and the United States are two countries divided by a common language."

Shannon is impassive. Robyn at least has the curiosity to ask who the someone was.

"It was me. Just now."

"Oh."

I think it may have been Oscar Wilde, but I wouldn't put money on it. What I would put money on is that Seamus will surely know. So anyway, I do the dishes, although I would have been less eager to volunteer if I had known that there was no washing up liquid. Still, you can't have everything. Then I wash up.

David is supposed to be here at twelve, which gives us an hour to kill. Shannon puts on Diamond Dogs. I'm in to it, but it's one of those records I like to listen to in the dark. Aladdin Sane would be my Sunday morning Bowie album of choice. Like every girl whose flat I have ever been in, Robyn has a very small record collection. Zeppelin, Mott the Hoople and Humble Pie all feature. There's the first Lou Reed as well as Transformer, but apart from that, everything seems to be English. No black music, no New York groups, and nothing before 1971, so there's no Beatles, but there is Band On The Run and Imagine. Goat's Head Soup is here, but not Exile on Main Street. Nothing featuring Al I notice, and no female artistes, which is a little surprising, all things considered. Considering where she lives, what she does, and who she knows, I'm thinking that Robyn is decidedly unhip.

I'm expecting David to be late, which is probably total stereotyping on my part, but he is bang on time. No mystery about Neil's non-appearance, he doesn't get home from his club till gone eight. Sees less daylight than Dracula does our Neil. Shannon's friend lives in Brooklyn, so we are going to meet her there. Coney Island is in Brooklyn and is New York's seaside resort. Brooklyn is in Brooklyn, but is still part of New York. What I've always thought of as New York is actually Manhattan, which is one of the five boroughs that make up the city. Brooklyn and the Bronx I know, the others are Queens, which I have vaguely heard of somewhere, and Staten Island, which I haven't. Harlem is not a borough but is part of Manhattan, which surprises me, and Hell's Kitchen, which I assumed was in the Bronx, is also in Manhattan, just a few blocks west of where I was staying at the Iroquois. You live and learn. Staten Island is an island but Coney Island isn't. So there you go. Frankly I'm amazed that the girls can bring themselves to ever leave the Village, but Sunday seems to have its own rules.

We take the subway. For Coney Island you take the D train to Stilwell Avenue, right at the end of the line. The train emerges above ground somewhere in residential Brooklyn. Family houses, their wooden frames witness to secrets and dreams as they are everywhere. I'm still unsettled by my dream. You can cross an ocean but your dreams will take you back in an instant. I think for a minute of a song I heard on the radio before I left that really hit home, but the phone rang or something so I never caught the title or the singer.

'Sometimes I get this crazy dream where I just take off in my car, but you can travel on ten thousand miles and stay right where you are.'

I don't have a car, but I do have a dream, and it looks like it's following me.

David is telling the girls about a small problem he has. In fact he's telling the whole carriage if they're interested. Seems like he drank too much red wine the other night, which led to a severe stomach upset, which in turn brought on a really bad haemorrhoid attack. Now he doesn't want to go on the beach because he is worried that he might get sand in his Preparation H. I've been in the country less than a week but I already know what this stuff is because they advertise it in on TV every fifteen minutes. The cultural differences are coming thick and fast. I have never known anyone who would admit to having this particular condition, much less tell the whole world about it. If I was in different company David's concern about his Farmer Giles would provide much mirth, but as it is I maintain a dignified silence and continue to look out the window.

We continue on through the Brooklyn suburbs until a giant rollercoaster rears up as if from nowhere, and we're here.

Robyn turns to me and smiles. "Patti should be waiting for us outside Nathan's. You'll like her, she's really sweet."

I now see that Patti is either coming along for my benefit or I'm there for hers, and neither prospect excites me too much. I know from experience that sweet can be used to cover a whole host of sins in however many dialects of the English language as there may be.

"So is Nathan's a bar?" I ask hopefully.

This causes amusement all round. They don't expect me to know what this place is, but it's still funny to them that some people in the world haven't heard of it.

"Nathan's is a hot dog joint" David explains patiently. "You never been, you're in for a real treat. This is what the world does on a Sunday. If you're rich you go up to your holiday home in the Hamptons. Everyone else, you come to Coney Island and eat at Nathan's."

The last time I ate a hot dog was off a stand at the White City dog track and it proved to be a serious mistake, but I'm confident that this will be in a different league.

Patti is waiting for us outside Nathan's. She may well be a sweet girl, but she would certainly seem to have a sweet tooth and a liking for hot dogs as well, as she is already digging in to one. The girl is big. She is wearing a pair of jeans that look as though she may have made them herself out of mailbags, and which do nothing to disguise her more than ample posterior. Robyn introduces us, and she mumbles something unintelligible through a morass of sausage, onions, ketchup, and mustard.

"I'm sorry?"

She speaks again, and this time I understand her, as the hot dog has now been swiftly dispatched to her expansive bread bin.

"Are you a bloke?"

"I guess so"

"That's so neat! We had an English girl in our school for a while, and all she talked about was blokes. It's so cool."

"Well there you go."

I wouldn't say I'm lost for words exactly, but the only ones that come to mind are along the lines of what's bigger, your IQ or your waist size, and I am determined to be on my best behaviour today.

The hot dog is magnificent, and I'm not even that hungry after my surprise breakfast. I wouldn't say that the perfect hot dog is as difficult to achieve as the perfect pizza, but this is definitely the hot dog equivalent of what we ate Friday. Patti obviously thinks so, as she fills her face with another one. All the questions that Robyn is either too cool or not interested enough to ask me, she asks me. How old I am, what do I do, why am I here, and on and on. I tell her old I am. The rest is bullshit. I'm sort of prepared for being asked what I do. I suppose accountant would be the closest to the truth, although I'm not a real accountant, not having any qualifications in that line. I was a turf accountant for a while, but that's not quite the same thing. Even if I was, I would still keep it under my hat this side of the pond. Not that I'm ashamed of it, mind. I think it very creative to help folks look after their money, especially when you are creative enough to look after it for them by helping yourself to some of it. Still, I am more than aware that most people of my generation find the idea a little dull to say the least, so I am going to have to use my imagination a little. A writer is good for some of the time, but not all of it. There will be some places, here for example, and almost certainly LA, where everybody is going to be pretending they're a writer. There again, if it's anything like the provinces back home, there will be places where no one would believe it, and some places where they will throw rocks at you for it, so that has to be nothing other than an occasional option. An up and coming business executive who has dusted down his old blue jeans for a well-deserved sabbatical is another possibility. When I do eventually hit the road, and get a ride off some guy wearing a tie and with jackets on hangers in the back as I surely will, I'll pick up my identity from the Iroquois and run with it. For hippies I've decided to be a market trader. That's right, just like dear old Dad.

There's a lot to be said for being a market trader so long as you don't mind getting up early. You don't have a boss, and you're outside the system as well, so the hippies should relate to that, and I can still affect a certain air of superiority over them because it implies that I don't mind a bit of hard graft. Which I don't, as it happens, which might surprise you a little. There's lots of things that I don't mind doing in the work line. Sitting behind a desk dropping biros and looking up the girls kilts was all right for a while. Shifting trays of ring doughnuts from oven to conveyor belt all night was another. Well, I only did that for a week, but it was the hours that were a trifle inconvenient at the time, the job itself wasn't so bad. I've never been too keen on ring doughnuts since, mind. What I don't like is being exploited, and even when I'm not I don't like repetition, and I resent too many demands on my time. That's when I have to get away.

So New York, since you bothered to ask you can have a combination of the market trader and the writer. I do the occasional piece for this rock paper called NME. I'll file the odd story while I'm here, already sent back a review of Al, bullshit, bullshit. Robyn has heard of the NME, which surprises me. She's full of them today.

"I know Al has got Dylan's number. Why don't you call him, see if you can get an interview?"

"I'm not on the staff. There's a real hierarchy for this kind of stuff. Senior reporters fly over and stay in the best hotels to interview the big stars. They would be seriously pissed off if I trod on their toes."

This seems to be a pretty good answer seeing as how I'm thinking on my feet, although if I were a budding rock journalist, I would surely do anything to get Bob Dylan's phone number. Truth is, I see Al as an extremely streetwise dude who would see through me in a second. Never mind Dylan.

Now David thinks I'm an antiques dealer. I tell him I've knocked out some dodgy old gear on occasion, but nothing that really qualifies as antique. He immediately loses interest. Patti, on the other hand is interested. It's on account of me being a bloke I guess. Patti works for a law firm in downtown Brooklyn and lives with her Mum and Dad. She doesn't mind the job, but wants to study more and get a better job in the city. Compared with Robyn and Shannon she's an open book. It's fascinating that Patti is Shannon's friend, of all people. All the studied cool and glacial indifference that reflects from Shannon's gorgeous but vacant eyes is notably lacking in her pal. It is to Shannon's credit that she is still her friend, I guess.

We stroll the boardwalk. I've forgotten to bring any cigarettes so I stop at a kiosk and buy a pack of Winstons. I feel like an American. The sun is high, and half the city appears to be here. I even think I could make a fair stab at identifying who comes from Brooklyn and who comes from Manhattan. Couples in their forties out in their Sunday best looking like your Mum and Dad at Margate twenty years ago. Groups of black teenagers that look as if they could be menacing if they weren't on their day off. White kids in t-shirts and cut off Levis looking like they're adrift on the wrong ocean. Coming towards us is a tall lithe black man, wearing nothing but powder blue swimming trunks that appear to be made from no more material than it takes to make a woman's handkerchief, and which scarcely contain his bulging manhood. He saunters past us proudly and defiantly, as if challenging anyone to make an issue of his freedom. Nobody does, but there are plenty of gay men around on whom his presence does not go unnoticed. Gay. This year's word for it. Not people you grow up having much tolerance for if you come from where I come from, but I'm not where I'm from right now, and I don't have any problem with it. Besides, three of them are right here with me. Robyn is speaking.

"You gonna ride on the Wonder Wheel, Frank? You can't come to Coney and not go on the Wonder Wheel."

"Depends if you're coming with me."

"Oh no, I've been on it a million times. Patti will go on it with you."

A set up. It occurs to me that if Robyn has been on this thing a million times, then Patti must have been two million times seeing as how she lives here, but I say nothing, and smile and nod at Patti. There is zero chance of bumping in to anyone I know, I'm not going to see her after today, and I think I can tell she has a good heart. Today I shall be charm on a stick. It will be good practice.

The Wonder Wheel is a ferris wheel. The Everly Brothers had a hit song in the sixties about a ferris wheel. At the time I didn't know what it was, but now I know that it's one of those big wheels that go round very slowly, the slower the better as far as I'm concerned. When it comes to funfairs and amusement parks I stand firmly on the yellow side of chicken. I tried the Big Dipper once, and that was enough. I've got too much imagination for my own good sometimes, and anyway it's common knowledge that these things come off the rails on occasion. The Big Wheel is not the most thrilling experience the fairground has to offer, that would be slipping my hand inside Susan Hopkins' knickers on the Ghost Train at Chessington Zoo in 1966, but I reckon it's safe enough for me to keep my hot dog down and my cool intact.

Waiting in line for the Wonder Wheel Patti tells me that it dates back to the nineteen twenties.

"Should be good for one more ride then. So how do you know Shannon?"

"We were at school." She hesitates for a moment and then continues. "Shannon wasn't always like she is now. By the time she was seventeen she'd had enough already of guys hitting on her." She changes the subject before I can respond. "I'd sure like to come to England one day. You blokes, huh?"

Maybe you will Patti, but as things stand at the moment, I'd be surprised to find you ever leave Brooklyn. I can't imagine your cool friends taking you round the Village too often.

The Wheel is just about within my safety zone, but still a little too high and too fast for my liking. Patti puts her arm in mine, and the nearness of her great soft warm body is immediately and strangely comforting. When we get to the end of the ride I whisper in her ear how much I enjoyed it, and then lightly press my lips against her cheek like a TV personality kissing a sick child on Christmas morning.

We buy Dr Peppers, and join the others on the beach in the shade of the boardwalk. David seems to have overcome his sand problem by sitting on a copy of Village Voice covered by an expensive looking sweater. None of us is dressed for the beach. David is holding court with tales of Broadway. No one seems all that interested, least of all me, but David seems oblivious, as he is to his surroundings. David is one of those people who doesn't really need to be anywhere, he is always where David is, at the centre of his own universe. His anecdotes would no doubt seem delightfully bitchy if you knew who all these people were, but I have never really got the theatre. The silver screen is its own world, wide screen, Technicolor and magical, but the theatre? To me it's always just people pretending

It half crosses my mind to disappear somewhere with Patti, as it couldn't be any less interesting and would surely make her day, but as if by some prearranged signal, at five o'clock Robyn, Shannon and David all get up, dust themselves down, and start to make their way back to the station, with me and Patti bringing up the rear. At the station she scribbles her number on the inside of a Hershey bar wrapper, and hands it to me.

"Why don't you call me sometime?"

"Maybe I will."

If I was on my own turf I'd say the odds against that eventuality would be extremely high, but I'm in a different world now and there's nobody around I feel any great need to impress, so maybe I will indeed. I'm half inclined to give her another kiss on the cheek, but I'm suddenly self-conscious in front of the others, so I smile and give an awkward wave as if I'm a junior member of the Royal Family, and then watch her arse make its ponderous progress back towards the street.

The D train is hot and crowded, and no one talks too much on the way back. Emerging out on to West 4th Street I suddenly realise that I could really do with a beer.

"Anyone for the White Horse?" I ask brightly.

35

The girls both decline on the grounds that Sunday is a day off, and for a dreadful moment I think I may have talked myself in to going drinking with David, but Neil will be up by now and he has to get back for dinner, so I'm home free and running down Bleeker Street as soon as they are all out of sight. I can feel myself burning up a little as the second cold one hits home, and I remind myself to raid Robyn's bathroom shelf later. A few more beers down the line and I am extremely comfortable, and reflecting on the day and thinking about Patti. Fat Patti. Pat Fatty. I realise I'm drunk now and all the better for it. So supposing Patti lost a few pounds, say about seventy. Supposing I settled down in Brooklyn and never left. Maybe get a job as a longshoreman, like in On The Waterfront, go home every night to my fat wife, eat a big meal, have a bunch of kids, go to Coney Island on summer weekends, eat a lot of hot dogs, eat pizza. Or I could go back to Europe, go to Lisbon, learn the language, get a job, find a fat wife, eat sardines, drink a lot of rose wine. So many lives to live. Yeah, but you have to pick one. Most have it picked for them. Some of us, in time, will do our own picking. When we're ready that is, when we're ready.

On Monday I find out what Robyn really does. I say that as if she's been giving me a line, and I'm a fine one to talk in that area, but she is an artist, only she's a different kind of artist from what I first thought. She illustrates children's books. She works for a publishers uptown, and some days she goes in to the office, but some days she works on ideas in her studio at home. It makes some kind of sense to me. Over the last few days I have come to the conclusion that imagination isn't really her strong point, which would appear to be somewhat limiting for an artist, but for this kind of artist it is more than likely an asset. Author writes about a blue dragon, you draw a blue dragon. It stands to reason, if you employ Andy Warhol, then more than likely you won't get exactly what you had in mind. So this is Monday morning, and my artist friend is about to put her cute little switch hitting butt on the subway with the rest of the milling hordes, albeit an hour or so after most of them.

I take my breakfast at the same diner I stopped by on Saturday, but I am disappointed to find that my smiling blonde isn't on shift. Back on the sidewalk I decide to wander. I've got a full belly, a clear head, and no particular place to go. I walk back through the Village to

Washington Square Park, and head north on 5th Avenue. I liked the feel of the city at the weekend, but now Monday morning has swept away the remaining summer weekend cobwebs. Even the clouds are back after a two day amnesty, and once again the air is grey and humid. The sidewalk is as congested and as manic as the street and walking requires as much attention as driving a yellow cab would. Men in their thirties wearing business suits walk in pairs, apparently holding full blown business meetings while their feet hardly touch the ground, crossing streets and avoiding cars and other pedestrians as if by radar. Winos shuffle along muttering to themselves. Others walk alone, eyes firmly in the direction of the sidewalk, careful not to break the cardinal rule of making eye contact with anyone. At the junction with 14th Street a middle aged black woman is arguing with a Chinese man at least six inches shorter than she is. They appear to be a couple. She pulls an empty bottle from a shopping bag and hits him over the head with it, but she is too drunk to muster enough force to break the bottle, and he remains standing. Like everyone else on the street I pretend I haven't witnessed this, and quicken my pace slightly.

I cross Broadway at 23rd Street, and continue on 5th with the Empire State Building looming large in front of me. I crane my neck unashamedly, looking for the ghost of King Kong. 42nd Street seems sadder and seedier than it did when I was here the other night in the early hours, if that's possible, with all its dirty business open to the daylight. Men are leaving cinemas at eleven a.m. after watching Deep Throat and The Devil in Miss Jones on double feature. I sneak a look down 44th Street towards the Iroquois, and decide it might not be prudent to hang around, just in case I'm a wanted man. It crosses my mind for a second to call Conrad, but I decide it would serve no purpose. I'm still on 5th, and it is getting seriously monied now. Women's clothes are on display with thousand dollar price tags, while just a few blocks away women's bodies are on offer for a hundred. I remind myself that I have already been in New York longer than I intended, and stop into a bookstore and buy a one dollar road atlas. I've got the key to the highway.

I love to walk. Put me out in the country and I can do fifteen, twenty miles, no problem. Sometimes I think that's when I'm most who I really am, out on some country road in rain or shine. It's other people who bring out the worst in me. So I love to walk, but forty eight blocks in Manhattan is a whole different matter, and by the time I reach Central Park I'm ready to cool my heels for an hour or so. If you grow up a Londoner you take many things for granted, and a park is not the least of them, whether it is a local secret like Gunnersbury, the elegant splendour of St James, or the world within a world which is Hyde Park. Dublin has parks because the English built them, and everywhere else I've been has one, if they have any at all. Paris has its gracious boulevards but no parks to speak of, just a scruffy forest on the outskirts of town. Berlin is the same. In Amsterdam the hippies stay under the bridge in the Vondelpark all day in their sleeping bags, so as not to lose their spot. So New York has Central Park, and frankly it doesn't really ring my chimes. A city park should be an oasis where you can leave the rest of your day at the gate. This park is in and of its city, and offers little chance of any exclusion. Maybe it's the buildings rearing up on all sides, but it's more than that. The pulse of this city beats right there on the street, and New Yorkers take it with them everywhere they go, to bars and clubs and restaurants, they take it home with them, and they take it to the park. Automobiles rule the roost inside the gates almost as much as they do out. The men in suits walk in pairs the same as they do on 5th Avenue. Men and women in running shorts pound by with grim resolution, and groups of people playing games of catch on the grass do so with the same steely determination. Nobody appears to be here to relax and watch the world go by. I go with the flow and keep on walking.

To a bar on Broadway. The radio's on, not too loud, but enough so you can hear it. I'm thinking it should be The Drifters, but what's playing is at least as interesting. The song is set in a nameless seaside resort on the fourth of July. It sounds like the singer wants to get away but doesn't know how. He's asking this chick called Sandy to sleep with him because she may never see him again, which is a novel twist in the world of popular song. He gets his shirt caught on a tilter whirl, which makes me think of Patti for a second, and then he sings about hiding under the boardwalk with the boss's daughter, which gets me thinking about Teresa, the boss's niece, and I lose the gist of the story, but it's enough to hear the world weary hipster rasp of the singer accompanied by an accordion which sounds exactly like the one I never heard, but imagined I did, on Mulberry Street the other day, and which captures perfectly the feel of this energy sapping American summer.

"Ninety one degrees in New York City, and that was the sound of Bruce Springsteen and the E Street Band with 4th of July Asbury Park."

Bruce Springsteen. I recognise the name as the one my cool friends were mocking the other night, and I'm seized by a brief but sharp irritation that I didn't take Neil up on his offer. Safe in the knowledge there will be other opportunities for that and much else besides, I down a couple more glasses of watery beer and take the subway back to the Village.

Monday rolls around to Wednesday. I'm comfortable now, I've spent very little money other than on beers and pizza and ninety nine cent breakfasts, and I could imagine myself hanging around for weeks, but the road is calling me, and I've decided I don't need another weekend with David and Shannon. I've spent a lot of time with my road map. I love a map, and even if I didn't, I think I would have absorbed a reasonable geography of the United States purely from musical and celluloid osmosis. My plan, if you can call it a plan, was simple. New York, New Orleans, Los Angeles, San Francisco, and have some adventures in between. Flicking through the pages from Alabama to Wyoming names jump out at me like ghosts of the past and the future. Mobile, where Chuck Berry worked on the railroad with a steel driving hammer and Elvis Presley played guitar in a night club. El Paso, where Marty Robbins died in the saddle. Atlanta, where Little Richard washed dishes at the Greyhound bus station. Memphis Tennessee, Laramie, Cheyenne. You could spend three months travelling around this country every year for the next twenty years and not see the half of it.

Got to start somewhere. I'm still going to make for New Orleans. Experience tells me that hitchhiking out of New York probably isn't the best of ideas. Better to catch an overnight bus somewhere in the right direction, save on a hotel or motel, get an early start the next morning and start thumbing it. So, Wednesday morning, after my usual eggs, bacon and hash browns, I ride the subway to the Port Authority. It's busy, but to a man who once spent the best part of a day trying to buy a ticket out of Marrakesh, it is remarkably ordered. There are windows for suburban destinations, and windows for the Jersey Shore, including Asbury Park. One of these days I will surely get my fortune read and ride on that tilter whirl, but now I'm dusting down my highway shoes. Long distance. I check a timetable. Raleigh, North Carolina. It fits the bill. About five hundred miles, takes all night, gets there at eleven the next morning. Then I've got two options. I can hitch down to Louisiana, either through the Carolinas, or head west towards Nashville and Memphis. Twenty two dollars gets me a ticket for the Thursday night bus. I mooch around town for a while, and look in the windows of some music stores on 52nd Street before heading back to the Village.

I feel like I should spend some time in the White Horse while I've got the opportunity, but I also feel that I should tell Robyn my plans as soon as I can, so I decide to drop by the apartment and see if she's there. She's working in her studio. I tell her what's occurring.

"Well I guess there's more to the country than New York, but I'm sorry you're leaving."

"Do you ever get out of New York?"

"My friends are here."

"How do you know these people?"

"Well I've known David forever. He's been really kind to me."

"How do you know Al?"

"We share a building with some music publishers. Al was always coming in when I first started. He's a sweetheart. I don't know too many people really. I go uptown to work, go to Coney Island sometimes. Mostly stay around the Village. I feel at home here."

"I got the impression you knew everyone."

"No." She sucks on her Kool. "I know Shannon."

"Can I ask you something?"

I pause a second too long, just enough for Robyn's antenna to pick up signals.

"What?" Defensive now, sucking harder on her Kool. "About me and Shannon? You want to know what we do? You want to watch? Well you can't."

This wasn't what I was going to ask, but now I would like to watch very much, since you mention it. She is smiling, though. I'm smiling too because I'm genuinely curious and I'm about to speak the truth, and I'm always a little embarrassed to speak the truth. I hesitate again.

"Why do you like me? I mean you've been so nice to me. I just wondered why that was. You always taking people in off the streets?"

"No I don't take people in off the street. You're a nice guy. Why shouldn't I like you? Don't you like you?"

Good question.

She relaxes a little. "I really don't trust guys. Maybe" and now it's her turn to hesitate, "maybe it's because you remind me of my brother a little. I kind of think of you a little differently I guess."

I used to get that a lot when I was seventeen and eighteen and chasing older sorts. I made a conscious decision to be less soft around women, and I have to say it has worked, in fact it has worked too damned well, and I haven't heard that one for a few years now. So I'm not exactly crushed by this, more amused, but I must register some disappointment, as Robyn moves closer, her eyes full of kindness and sympathy. She puts one arm round my neck and kisses me full on the lips.

"Do you kiss your brother like that?"

She smiles and shakes her head. Now I put my hand on the back of her head and kiss her purposefully. When she draws back I think that's it, but then I get another surprise.

"I won't go the whole hog, but we can do other things"

She leads me to the bedroom, which is pink, feminine. What was I expecting? Robyn takes off her jeans and her top, and indicates for me do the same. Her breasts are small but firm. I take her nipples in my mouth one by one, and find that they are already hard. She pushes me on to the bed and does the other thing, slowly, exquisitely. I reciprocate tenderly and attentively, taking pleasure in her pleasure, until I can't help myself and start moving up her body, but she whispers no, joyfully but firmly, and pushes my head back down until she softly tugs my hair to let me know we're done here.

Robyn goes to the bathroom. She doesn't close the door, and I can hear her toothbrush at work. She comes back in to the bedroom and puts on her clothes. I do the same.

"I told you I liked you. But I'm with Shannon, OK? This is our secret."

"Sure." I kiss her on the cheek and go back out to the living room and put the television on like nothing had happened.

Later we go to the White Horse, me, Robyn and Shannon. Shannon doesn't seem that pleased to be there, or not that pleased for me to be there to be more precise, and I'm wondering if she has any suspicions. There again, Shannon never appears to be happy to be anywhere, so how are you supposed to tell, especially if you don't give a shit, which I don't. Robyn is like she was that first afternoon I met her, relaxed, bubbly, a little flirtatious. Too flirtatious. I'm wondering what promises she has made to Shannon, promises which in her own way she has probably just about kept. Shannon speaks to me, which hasn't happened more than about twice since I've met her.

41

"So did you call Patti?"

Thinks: Listen bitch, your girlfriend gave me the best blow job I've ever had in my life this afternoon. Whaddayou think of that?

Says, studiedly ignoring the sarcasm laced with downright hatred, "Not yet I didn't. Tell her I'll be coming back to New York, and I would love to see her again. I really enjoyed our day out."

How sincere is that? As sincere as fuck, to be honest.

"Sure you would."

The words are squeezed out as if accompanied by vomit. Some guy must really have pissed this chick off somewhere along the line. Robyn looks inscrutable, and more than likely I'm looking a little too much like the cat that's got the cream. The evening is salvaged, for me anyway, by Seamus being on the evening shift and keeping the ale flowing along with sagacious words of wisdom and repartee, none of which I can remember in the morning, though I can remember the ale, as my head is throbbing and I can't face breakfast.

Robyn takes the morning off to get my laundry done for me. By the time she gets back I'm feeling better, and tentatively suggest that we replay yesterday's activity. She declines, politely but with no room for negotiation. She's got to get uptown. She'll be back later, and she's coming to the bus station with me, if it's OK, that is. My brain is still not functioning fully yet, and for a few seconds I'm thinking that Robyn is intending on hitting the road with me, before I understand she's coming to wave me goodbye, like I'm her boyfriend or something.

I get in to my snug put up bed, which I'm going to miss, and imagine Robyn being tucked up with me, but not for very long because I soon drift in to a deep delicious sleep which lasts for three hours, and would have lasted longer if she hadn't woken me at six with a cup of English tea. She's bought it especially, to see me on my way. The tea is sweet, and so is she. It occurs to me that this is probably the first cup of tea I've had since Ma died. More of a coffee person these days. I explain to Robyn that tea isn't English tea, it's just tea. The tea doesn't come from England. She looks a little blank, but not as much as she would have done a few days ago. There's no doubt that the girl has potential in more ways than one. Shame I won't be here to reap any more rewards, but I feel I have made a definite contribution to Robyn's development. There's no sign of Shannon, which is fine by me.

I feel a little pang as we turn out of Jones Street. Perhaps I will come back. I can't afford to think of that now, I've only just started. Nine days. I expected to be half way across the country by now. I really feel like taking Robyn by the hand, but I sense she doesn't want me to, not in the Village anyway. Night has a thousand eyes, and all that stuff. On the subway she is more tactile, grabbing my arm like she did when we first met, all those days ago.

It's one of those nights that feels hotter than the day. The bus station is crowded and sweaty, with people acting like they do in bus stations all over the world and making the act of finding the right bus a hundred times more difficult than it really is. I find my bay straight away, which impresses Robyn. I smile down at her.

"I'm a travelling man, babe. A hitch hiking, Greyhound bus riding, travelling man."

I hold her to me, and whisper in her ear in a more serious tone.

"I want to come back to New York and do more things to you."

She presents me with some bagels and apple juice for the journey, and smiles like the Mona Lisa.

"Maybe."

Then she gives me a real girlfriend kiss, and I'm standing in this bus station with her arms round my neck, and she's telling me in serious fashion to take care of myself, as if I'm off to Vietnam instead of the South. The teenage baggage boy throws my bag in the hold. I give him a dollar and board the bus, show my ticket to the driver and find a window seat. Robyn waits until the bus pulls out and waves me goodbye, and for a moment I see her waving goodbye on behalf of every girl I've ever known, and it occurs to me that I may never see any of them ever again. Then she's gone, and almost immediately we enter a tunnel, and when we emerge New York has gone too, and we're in New Jersey already.

Soon the bus pulls on to the Turnpike and heads south. In the seat in front of me is a nun, and next to her is a guy who is already relentlessly unfolding his life story. Vietnam vet, drug problem, found Jesus. I say a silent thank you Jesus that he isn't sitting next to me. I like hearing people's stories up to a point, but at least in a bar you can drink up and politely say goodnight. An overnight bus is a captive audience if ever there was one. The seat next to me is taken by a young black man reading a book on psychology, and who thankfully doesn't acknowledge my presence. I've bought Time magazine but I haven't opened it. I look out at the New Jersey night and think about Robyn for a while. Could be twenty could be thirty two. I still don't know, I never asked her, although I would guess now that she was my age or maybe a year older. Did she grow up in the Village? Was she Jewish? Where were her parents? I know she has a good looking brother out there somewhere, but that's about it. She didn't give much away but then I hardly asked her anything. That way I didn't have to tell her anything. One more week and I think I would have got to know her really well. She was already starting to open up. Another week and I would have straightened her out. One more week and she would have come to her senses, and Shannon would have been summarily despatched back to Brooklyn. Just a phase, that's all, just a phase.

My thoughts turn to Julie, who gave me everything and asked for very little in return, but still more than I was prepared to give. Then I think of Teresa, my sweet signorina with a little life kicking inside her at this very moment. But mostly I think of Chuck Berry on the New Jersey Turnpike in the wee wee hours, rolling slowly because of drizzling showers.

Bye bye New Jersey.

So long New York.

Good morning America.

Chapter Three: Don't Think Twice

Nineteen sixty three and sixty four, they were big years. Formative you might say. The changes weren't immediately obvious. At thirteen and fourteen I was still shy and spotty and more likely to be found climbing trees than chatting up girls. Summer evenings we would play football or cricket until it got dark. In the winter I would stay home and read and play board games by myself. I always won. Beneath the surface things were changing though, and it was books and then music which opened my mind most as to how big was that great world outside my window.

When you're seven or eight years old you think the world is as it is and as it always was, unless you're some genius kid, and I've never been under any illusions that I was one of those. Bright, yes, but no more so than many others. I was born in nineteen fifty. Five years earlier there was still a war going on. Our side won, as you may have heard, but the country was a ruin. I was born in to a world of rationing and powdered egg. Seven years later things were looking up. Most people had a job. The reward for most was a couple of fivers in an envelope every Friday, but at least it was a job. They didn't have to go twenty miles to get there either, every part of London had an industrial estate just up the road. So people had jobs and if they saved they could even buy a few things.

Most houses had television, though not ours. I always felt out of it when the other kids played games pretending they were in Wagon Train, but looking back now I reckon it was a blessing. We could stretch to a radio, and there were great plays for kids on then, real full length stories that got my imagination racing. The mobile library came round every Wednesday. Children's historical novels got me started, and then one day I brought home a whole new world in Tom Sawyer. I would get it out of the library time and time again and immerse myself in Tom's world. I used to walk the towpath from Chiswick to Kew and imagine I was by the banks of the old Missouri, though of course I had

45

no idea where that was then.

Dad used to work the markets. In the war he was a desert rat. I think he missed out on the serious action, but you would have thought he was Monty's right hand man the way he told it. When he got back he decided he had done his bit, and the country owed him a living. Thinking about it, he may well have been right. He decided he should go into the business of buying and selling things that weren't readily available unless you were a G.I. or knew one. A provider of services. Spivs they were called. The thing Dad either never realised, or did realise but didn't fancy doing it, was that being a successful spiv involved a certain amount of graft. Those who were really good at it became local legends and made a lot of dosh. Dad got nowhere. I wasn't around to witness this first hand, but that's what Ma told me, and nothing I have seen since has ever given me any cause to doubt her.

Ten years on and he had a market stall. He would dutifully get up early every morning, I'll give him that, but all he ever sold was a load of old tat. Crockery, birthday cards, bed sheets that felt like they were made out of paper, towels that took the skin off your face. Even when I was eight years old I was embarrassed to be there. The sad thing is that he wasn't, he thought it was all right. Christmas was a busy time for him, decorations, wrapping paper, even some skinny little trees. Thing was, he had to knock the gear out so cheaply that he still never made any money. So we didn't have television. He didn't want to pay for a new one, and he would hardly ever have been home to watch it if he had, as his usual routine was to pack up about three and adjourn to the boozer, and besides, he was always waiting for a mate of his to get one for next to nothing from the back of a lorry. We finally got TV in nineteen sixty three, and it was Ma who paid for it when she had a rare win at the bingo. This unexpected windfall allowed us to discover America in our front room courtesy of the Telstar satellite. We watched live broadcasts of astronauts in their spacecraft. Secretly I always preferred the Russians. Their missions were cloaked in mystery, and everyone knew they stayed up longer and went higher.

Ma worked as well then, part time in a sweet factory in Park Royal. She had been there since she crossed the water in forty six. When I was small they used to allow her to take me in some days when she was stuck for anyone to look after me. One of my earliest memories was being perched on a big stool next to her while the sweets came down the big belt, and her and her workmates sorted them in to jars. The other women always tried to give me some, but Ma wouldn't have it, frightened she would get the sack. Unlikely, because she was very popular, but she didn't want to take any chances. She liked the camaraderie of the line, and more importantly, the money wasn't great but it was handy. Sometimes it was a lifesaver.

So most of the time she had enough to keep herself looking good and me clothed and fed, and then there was her one luxury item. A Dansette record player she bought when I was around six. Once a month or so, when she had a few spare shillings, we would go to Ewins Electrical Stores in Acton Vale and buy her current favourite record. Rock Island Line was the first I can remember. I didn't have too much idea what pig iron was and I still don't, but the record sounded mysterious and exotic, and I had no idea that the singer was a Londoner like me. Singing the Blues by Tommy Steele was another, and we knew that he was a Londoner because he was born around the corner from where Granny Downes lived, over by London Bridge. Elvis was her number one, and Buddy Holly and Eddie Cochran also found their way into our growing collection. I didn't realise at the time that she must have been pretty hip to be in to this stuff then, as she was already well in to her thirties. Then came the British Elvis, Cliff Richard, and then Adam Faith. Adam, real name Terry Nelhams, was our local boy. He moved away as soon as he got a hit, as you would expect him to, but he bought his Mum and Dad a semi in the nice part of Acton and used to come back and visit once in a while. I remember seeing him driving down the High Street one Saturday afternoon in a big American car, the first time I had ever seen one. He looked like the King of the world, there for all to see.

The Rock Island Line had me fooled, but I worked out early on what was the genuine stuff and what wasn't, in other words what was American and what was English. When I reached eleven, after much nagging cajoling and negotiation, I got my own pocket money and was finally able to buy my own records. Del Shannon was my favourite for a while, a run, run, run, run, runaway, the first record I ever bought, London American, black and silver label. At the same age I moved on to grammar school. For some reason I can't remember I didn't get sent to the local one. Instead I rode the underground to Chelsea every day. The kids all seemed a bit more clued in there. A lot of them had older brothers who were mods before anyone knew what mods were. A few of the teachers were cool as well. I was delighted to find there was a set book called Huckleberry Finn, a sequel to Tom Sawyer aimed at slightly older readers. I lapped it up, which meant I got off to a flying start with the English teacher. One day close to the end of spring term he called me over at the end of a lesson.

"Downes, this is really suited more to fifth year boys, but I have a feeling that you might get something from it." Then he gave me his own dog eared copy of 'The Grapes of Wrath.'

I got something from 'The Grapes of Wrath', but I didn't get all of it. I didn't get any of the politics, or understand why the land was so clapped out, or think too much about what a share cropper might be. Years later when I first heard Woody Guthrie I read it again. That's when I really got it. What I loved most the first time was the adventure of being on the move. Even encountering death on the journey didn't make it seem any less exciting. I hadn't crossed paths with death in any shape or form back then. Once you do you're changed for ever.

So by nineteen sixty four I already knew a lot of stuff, but I hadn't started joining up the dots yet. Somewhere along the line I got my own record player. The Beatles and the Stones were on the scene by now. I still clung to my belief in American superiority when it came to music, but found no contradiction in being a fan of both groups. I quickly realised that they knew what I knew. We discovered things backwards. We found Tamla Motown through the cover versions on those early albums, and fair play to them, the praise they lavished on them in the sleeve notes and in interviews led us to hunt down the originals. Then there was Chuck Berry.

I'll always treasure those years when I was still in short trousers and me and Ma were getting in to the rock and roll together, but by now I was leaving her behind. Shame in a way, but it would have been a bit embarrassing if I hadn't. Buddy died, Eddie died, Elvis went in the army and was never the same when he came out, and she lost interest. Probably slightly more significant was the birth of my little brother Joey in nineteen fifty nine. By the time he had reached the toddling stage she had settled down to being a middle aged mum. In her forties now, she hated the Rolling Stones, tolerated the Beatles, and her current favourite was Frank Ifield, an Australian crooner with a tendency to yodel. I was a million miles from that by now, but Del Shannon was partial to a yodel, and he was still one of my heroes, always searchin', searchin', following the sun, forever haunted and running from the stranger in town.

When Ma was in to it she had great taste, but she never bought any records by black singers, not until Ray Charles went country. She wasn't prejudiced, well maybe a little, though nowhere near as much as the old man, but you never really heard any on the BBC. Most of Little Richard's songs got covered by Pat Boone, and even as an eight year old I instantly dismissed them as fake. Chuck Berry was another one we missed. The thing was, Chuck wasn't labelled as rock and roll in England, which was daft, because he was as rock and roll as you could get. He was labelled rhythm and blues. A racial thing, I guess. Maybe him being outside the mainstream was what turned the Beatles and Stones on to his music. That and playing guitar like ringing a bell, and being one of the best damned poets of the twentieth century. First I ever bought by the man was the rockingest Christmas record I ever heard, Run Rudolph Run. Red and yellow halved Pye R & B label.

Run Rudolph Run had been recorded a few years earlier and re-released. A few months later Chuck came out with something brand new called The Promised Land.

'I left my home in Norfolk, Virginia, California on my mind.'

As soon as I heard that I was gone, gone, gone. I always liked geography at school, but this was the best lesson I ever had, a fantastic odyssey from east coast to west by bus, train and plane. I wrote down the names of all the places in the song as best I could, and pulled out the atlas in the school library to follow his progress. That old school book, years out of date, seemed almost to come alive and invite me in to the wonderful adventures concealed within its pages. I didn't realise it at the time, but this was more or less a mirror image of how Chuck wrote the song. Thing was, he was banged up at the time. He had fallen foul of something called the Mann Act, transporting a minor across a state line for immoral purposes. A racial thing, I guess. He served his time respectfully, longing to get back on the road. He too went to the library, the penitentiary library, to check out his imaginary route. We were both in places where we didn't want to be. We both knew it was strictly temporary.

I myself once took Susan Hopkins on a sixty five bus from Middlesex to Surrey for purposes which were most definitely immoral, but I managed to get away with it. But then I've always been lucky like that.

It must have been a Saturday morning. Dad would have been out on the stall, and I think Ma must have taken little Joey to the park. I clearly remember being alone in the house, doing my homework on the living room table with the radio on as always. Then, out of the old speaker came something the like of which I had never heard before. Simple but eloquent finger picked guitar. Mouth organ. A mouth organ was looked on as little more than a toy. The Beatles used one occasionally, but this mouth organ was different. It blew with all the loneliness of a freight train two thousand miles from home. Then there was the voice of the singer. At first listening it was impossible to put an age to it. Could have been twenty, could have been seventy five, although the world weariness, experience and resignation it expressed seemed to suggest the latter. Then the words of the song. 'Well it ain't no use in sitting wondering why babe, iff'n you don't know by now.' The singer has the wisdom of the ages, but he can't tell you all he knows. You're going to have to find out for yourself. If you're interested, that is. Most people on the planet never will be. I closed my books and resolved to finish my work the next day.

'When your rooster crows at the break of dawn, look out your window and I'll be gone.'

Looking back, I think that was the line that really did it for me, my own personal Book of Revelation. When I heard Chuck Berry singing about the Promised Land, I knew there and then I was going to be a traveller. When I heard Bob Dylan singing Don't Think Twice, that was a little different. Even though I probably couldn't have told you so at the time, I think I realised something deep down. I wasn't only going to be a travelling man. I would be the man who would always leave things behind.

Chapter Four: Southern Man

A squeal of brakes, and a red pickup pulls up about three inches from my foot. The driver is about twenty five, and he's wearing dungarees and an old straw hat. Dungarees. The last person I ever saw wearing dungarees was my brother Joey, when he was six years old.

"Well get in fella! You goin' to Greenville? If you are, you got yerself a good ride, boy!"

Greenville being about a hundred miles further down the road, I gratefully climb in. Taking a closer look, I realise that he's wearing what they call overalls, like I've seen in a thousand films or TV programmes. More than that, he looks like he's stepped straight out of one of them. When I was a kid we used to watch the Beverly Hillbillies. Backwoods family called the Clampetts hit oil, become millionaires, move to Beverley Hills, cause great amusement with their quaint country ways. Not a bad programme in its day, although they repeated what was essentially one joke for about two hundred episodes. The Clampetts had two grown up children. One was Ellie Mae, who provided bad thoughts for teenage boys on both sides of the pond, and the other one was Jethro, who though not exactly the sharpest pencil in the box was an extremely affable young man, as would be expected given his dramatic change in circumstances.

"Say, where you from, boy?"

Said with a smile and genuine curiosity, so I don't take exception to being called boy by someone who is no more than a year or two older than me at the most.

"You from England? Hot dawg!"

He turns to look at me as if I'm a lab specimen, taking his eyes off the road for an uncomfortably long time.

"I ain't never met no one from England before! God damn!"

He shakes his head at the wonder of it all, and slowly turns his gaze back to the highway. Feeling like I'm some kind of ambassador, I respond as enthusiastically as I can.

"Thanks for picking me up. I'm Frank, from London."

Still sounds pretty tame compared with this fellow.

"London, oh man! You know I swear I'm gonna take myself to London one of these days and get me some of that English pussy! I see it in a magazine once. All them miniskirts. Lawd have mercy! Hot dawg!"

He doesn't return my introduction, and this and his rather straightforward attitude to life settles it. I don't need to know this guy's name, in fact I don't want to. He is, and shall remain forever, Jethro.

Jethro goes quiet for a minute or two, give or take the occasional goddamn, as if he's mulling something over.

"Say Frank, if I came over to London, do you think you could fix me up good with some of that ol' English pussy?"

Jethro asks his question really seriously, as if he was a kid asking something of a teacher.

"Well sure I could!" Now is where I should ask him his name, but I don't want to. "I know plenty of girls that would love you, man."

"Hot dawg!" says Jethro, and puts his foot on the accelerator. His driving is erratic to say the least. I grew up thinking that America was the land of big cars and big open roads, and everyone drove at ninety miles an hour with their arm round their best girl and the radio blasting rock and roll. Not any more, it appears. Last year's oil crisis has put the wind up the whole nation. Fifty five miles an hour speed limit, and they take it seriously. Every vehicle I've seen since I got here has rolled along like they're in a funeral procession. Except for Jethro, that is. Jethro doesn't give a flying fuck.

"You don't worry about the speed limit?" I ask, and I regret doing so as soon as the words leave my mouth, as they come with a tone of reproval and downright fear which I didn't intend at all. Jethro looks at me as if I'm mad.

"Speed limit?" Bullshit!"

The last word spreads over several seconds and uses at least six syllables.

"This oil crisis is nothing but bullshit, man. There's more oil in Texas than you can shake a stick at. There ain't no oil crisis."

He accelerates again to prove the point.

I feel like telling him that there are a lot more cars than you can shake a stick at too, but decide against it. Jethro falls silent again for a while, except for the occasional muttered "bullshit."

I finally got my thumb out in the open air about twenty four hours later than I intended. Best laid plans of mice and men, and all that. The bus was fine until we got to Richmond, Virginia. We rolled through four states, and I got to see some of the nation's capital, if you count the bus station in the wee small hours, and a view of the capitol building down a distant avenue. The bus arrived in Richmond in the early morning just as it was supposed to, but the relief driver didn't. We hung around for nearly two hours until he did. Made me feel right at home. By the time the hound finally made it into Raleigh it was already afternoon, and Robyn's bagels were long gone. More to the point, I wasn't just hungry, I was very, very thirsty, so I pitched up on Main Street and had my fill of cold beer. Three hours later it became apparent that I was going nowhere on that particular day. I wandered around the old town, which seemed to consist mainly of tobacco warehouses, and bought as many red packs of cigarettes as I could carry, seeing as how they were more or less giving them away. I checked in to an old hotel where the bathroom was down the corridor and there didn't appear to be any other guests. It cost nine dollars. I checked a few more bars, enough to learn that Seamus was right. New York is a separate country. By the time I got back to the old hotel I was past noticing that the mattress wasn't the best, and I slept sound and long. I breakfasted on eggs and country ham, which was good but didn't taste too different to city ham, and enough coffee refills to put me back in the human race.

My first ride in the United States took me one hundred and fifty miles almost to Charlotte, still in North Carolina. I would dearly love to share some detail of the gentleman who performed this historic deed, but other than the fact that he drove a white pickup truck and wore a red and white check shirt, there's not much to tell. He spoke about ten words all the way, while I looked out at the Carolina woods. That's always fine with me, too. On the other hand, Jethro has got me across the state line into South Carolina before I know it, and he is also a lot more entertaining.

"Say Frank, are you a religious man? People religious over in England?"

I inform Jethro that England isn't a very religious country these days. For the sake of conversation I also tell him I think there's something out there, but I don't know what.

"You think there's something out there, but you don't know what?" Jethro shakes his head and smiles.

"Man, oh man. You ever run into my grandaddy you better not tell him that. He'll kick your ass, for sure. Man, oh man. There's something out there, but you don't know what!"
I say nothing, as I'm fairly sure that Jethro will have some more to say on the subject. He does.

"Now don't get me wrong Frank, I'm a God fearin' man for sure, but I've never been into it like my daddy, and my grandaddy is something else. You know something, he talks in tongues. Yes sir, I ain't lying to you Frank, Grandaddy talks in tongues. Not all the time, but when the spirit is on him he'll talk in tongues, yes sir. There's some believe he's talking the language of the Israelites, you know, telling it like Moses did. I don't know myself, but that's what some folks say. My grandaddy sure don't know what he's talking about, that's for sure."

I feel like I should keep this going.

"Did you know that King Solomon had fifty wives and two hundred porcupines?"

I think I might have heard that on the Benny Hill show. Jethro looks suitably impressed.

"Well you know your scriptures Frank, I'll say that."

He thinks for a second or two, and then a broad smile creases across his big open face.

"I'll tell you something boy. The only time I talk in tongues is when I eat pussy. Yes sir. Man, I just love pussy pie! Hot dawg!"

And with that he howls, Jethro, he opens his throat and howls like a wolf trapped in a forest fire. I'm laughing so much I hardly notice when he pulls out to overtake at ninety five mph and we miss a head on collision by the skin of our teeth.

"Say, Frank. You had any of this ol' here American pussy since you got here?"

He doesn't wait for the reply.

"I can tell you have man, just by looking at you. I bet them girls hear your accent man, and their breeches just fall right off."

Looking a little envious now. Envious of his own imagination.

"I wish."

"Bullshit."

Even more syllables now, if that's possible. He thinks for another second. I know this, because you can see Jethro think, you really can.

"Say Frank, why don't you stay over and party with us tonight? You'll have somewhere to stay, and we'll get you some pussy pie, that's for sure."

Well you don't get an offer like that every day.

"Why not?" I reply.

Because anything may happen in the company of this guy is why not, but that's a good reason why, also. This is an adventure Frank, and the alternative Saturday night is a lone drink in a dark corner, and a soulless roadside motel.

Now that we're official party on down buddies, I find out a little more about Jethro. Like does he come from Greenville, or Charlotte maybe?

"No Frank, I come from a little bitty town, in fact it ain't a town at all, you won't have heard of it. Six o'clock there ain't nobody on the street, eight o'clock the street rolls up and disappears. My girl lives in Greenville. Yes sir, I'm going down to see my girl. You're going to meet her Frank, yes sir, I'll bet you fall in love with her before you drink your first beer."

He looks concerned for a second.

"Y'all drink beer over in England?"

I nod in confirmation. Jethro whoops.

"Man are we going to have a time. I'm going to lay it on you. You and me are going to drink Coors until the sun comes up, yes sir."

"You're not a married man, I take it?"

He looks serious for a second.

"Yes I am, Frank. It didn't work out, man. She's back at her mom's, and she's got my son and my little baby girl. Maybe we'll get back together, I don't know."

The serious expression stays in place for a minute or two. I could tell him that the chances of that happening might possibly improve if he wasn't hightailing it down to the next state to see another woman, but I don't want to put a dampener on things, and anyway I would be a fine one to talk. Not that I've ever been married, or even close to it. Besides, Jethro is a God fearin' man. For sure.

Jethro's mood lightens as quickly as it had darkened.

"Shit, man. We're nearly there, and it's almost Saturday night. Hot dawg!"

We enter the city limits, and it becomes immediately more built up, the highway lined with wooden houses, and looking just like the South should. All that's missing are some good old boys out on the front porch playing banjos. What most of them have got on their porches is the Stars and Stripes, flying proudly, just in case any of the good citizens of Greenville come out of their house in the morning and think they're in Switzerland. Many of the cars on the road make a point of displaying the Confederate flag on their bumpers, but the rebel stand would appear to stop at the front door. Or porch, even. We turn off the highway, and I come within an inch of knocking myself out on the windscreen when Jethro pulls up by a phone box. Jethro isn't a seat belt type of guy. He makes the call, and gets back behind the wheel, his grin even wider.

"That was my girl!" he announces proudly, like I thought it was anyone else.

"She's gonna meet us down at the Strip in a half hour. I told her all about you Frank, she's looking forward to meeting you. Goddamn it, I'm as horny as a dog on a chain with two dicks. Hot dawg."

Greenville is a bigger town that I expected, but still not that big, and it only takes a couple of minutes to reach the main drag. I step out of the pickup into a furnace. There's a bank across the street with an electric sign which shows the time and the temperature. 3.05pm and ninety seven degrees. I follow Jethro into a big rambling bar that looks like it's probably a dance hall in the evenings. At the moment there are just three people sitting up at the bar. One of them is a denim clad guy of about our age with long hair and a beard, the first longhair I've seen since I left New York. Jethro throws his arms around him like a long lost brother.

"Frank, this is my buddy Mike. I'm staying at his trailer tonight, and I'm sure Mike's gonna say it's cool for you to stay too. Mike, this is my buddy Frank from England. Where the Beatles come from."

"Hell, I've never met anyone from England before. Pleased to meet you Frank! Any friend of Owen is a friend of mine."

Owen? Jethro is an Owen? I have to say that he is the most unlikely looking Owen I have ever seen in my life, not that I've seen many. I expect an Owen to look like a milkman. He thrusts a bottle into my hand which is so cold it almost burns my fingers.

"Good to know you, Frank!"

"It's good to know you too, Owen" I say, slowly.

Three beers later and I get to meet Jethro's girl. In a plain white vest and denim hot pants, and with straight blonde hair, she looks about fourteen. Jethro, sorry Owen, runs over and throws his arms around her like he's just got back from a three year tour of duty.

"Anita, this is Frank", he says, in a way which leaves me a little unsure of who he's the most proud of, her or me. I get a hug too, on account of coming from England.

"Do you really know the Beatles?" Anita asks breathlessly.

Three hours later we are still sat there sinking Coors, and Anita is holding her own with the guys. She isn't fourteen. She's eighteen. She's bubbly and she's bright too, a lot brighter than Jethro, sorry, Owen, though admittedly that wouldn't be too difficult. She's also cuter than a squirrel's nut. The bar has gradually filled up during the course of the afternoon, and my fame has spread, so that by now they are almost queuing up to shake my hand, and I'm beginning to feel like a combination of Cary Grant, Mick Jagger and the Duke of Kent. Suddenly Owen gets decisive.

"OK, I tell you what we're gonna do Frank. Me and Anita are gonna go back to the trailer, I'm gonna get changed, and we'll back in half an hour. I'll drop off your stuff at Mike's."

Mike nods in agreement.

I have to think about this for a moment. Rule one is never to get separated from your stuff unless you've got a hotel, in which case rule two comes into play, which is if you've got a hotel room, use it. There's always less risk of losing things there than there is on the streets. Sorry, these are rules two and three. Rule one is to keep passport and folding cash about your person at all times, preferably in the form of a money belt, which I have. On the other hand every little thing I have ever learned in my entire life tells me that Jethro, sorry Owen, is not a guy who is going to rip me off. The bag contains nothing that I couldn't replace over here more cheaply at the drugstore. I nod in agreement. Jethro lets Anita lead the way, and when she's out the door he turns back towards the table.

"Listen Frank, old buddy, I might be a little longer than a half hour, know what I'm saying" and he waggles his tongue before disappearing.

Yes, Owen old pal, I know what you're saying and I have to admit to feeling ever so slightly jealous. Mike goes into the other bar to play pool, and I politely decline the invitation to join him, one because I don't want the pressure of feeling like I'm representing the old country, and two because they've started serving food. I order a bowl of chilli which is so good I promptly order another. The chilli is made with real chopped steak, when anything I've ever had before that was called chilli was made with mince. Two bowls and I'm ready for a long night.

It goes without saying that Jethro is longer than half an hour, and it's gone eight before they get back. He has changed into a blood red shirt with a black silhouette of Elvis Presley incorporated into the design. Anita is wearing the same skimpy outfit she had on earlier. By the look on both their faces it is fairly obvious that Jethro has already had his pussy pie.

"Sorry we took a little while there, Frank" says Owen, while smiling the smile which says he's not sorry at all and why should he be.

"Fact is me and this little girl nearly didn't come back at all. We were just about to head down to Mexico to get married when I said hang on a second there girl, what about old Frank? We've got all his stuff."

Right now I couldn't care less about my bag, but it is good to see them. I've got a bellyful of cold beer and hot chilli, and I feel like all is well with the world. The place is Saturday night full now. There's another longhair setting up drums and amps on a makeshift stage, and at nine a five piece band shuffles on stage. Their dress is altogether outrageous for the South. They look like the New York Dolls, although they draw the line at the make up. At home I think we've just about passed the excesses of the glam rock phase, but these boys have embraced it completely. Further inspection reveals that with the exception of the singer, who is extremely skinny, these boys are a little too beefy to carry off the junkie cool of the Dolls. The Sweet would be a more accurate comparison.

"How y'all doin' folks, we're The Rebels, we're from Knoxville, Tennessee and we're gonna rock you tonight."

Crash, straight into Jumpin' Jack Flash. I've seen a few bands in my time called The Rebels, most of them originating from the stockbroker as opposed to the bible belt, and I have to say these boys are pretty good. All covers, a mixture of English classics, Stones, All Right Now, Black Magic Woman, and southern boogie, Allman Brothers and the like. They do a Lynyrd Skynyrd song, Freebird, and it brings the house down. Seems like Skynyrd are big news down South. After an hour they take a break, and the singer soon comes to seek out the famous

English visitor. I tell him they should come over to England some time as they would go down a storm. I don't really think we need any bands doing covers of Freebird, thank you, but it's not as if they are ever likely to find out. He asks me if I want to sing a number with them in the second half, an offer which I politely decline. We grew up assuming all black people could sing. Looks like it's now the English who have inherited the mantle of natural rhythm. Best not shatter their illusions.

Just before the band get back on stage for their second set, Anita gets up to leave. Her daddy don't like her staying out too late. Well he wouldn't, would he? A kiss on the cheek for me, a tongue sandwich for Jethro, sorry Owen, and she's gone. I ask Jethro how she's getting back, and he tells me she came down in her own Ford Pinto. Old enough to drive then, and old enough for much else besides. She must have had at least a dozen beers, and who knows what else up at the trailer.

Thinking of the trailer reminds me that's where I'm sleeping tonight, something I am not looking forward to a whole lot. Owen hasn't said much to me since they got back, which is fair enough as it is very noisy, and the boy has got other things on his mind. His promise of female company for me would appear to have been idle, and this doesn't worry me too much. I prefer to find my own, and work on them in my own individual manner. My instinct for self -preservation also tells me that I need to be careful in this place. These people are friendly but volatile, and I feel like things could kick off with the least provocation. Owen shouts something in my ear about making a phone call, and gives me a wink. I have quickly grown to be suspicious when Owen winks. He comes back with that familiar grin on his face.

"We're in luck Frank. I just spoke to this girl I know, Janet. Her and her sister are gonna be here in a half hour. Hot dawg."

I feel like I can read the boy's expressions pretty well by now. The phrase, an open book, could have been invented for this guy, bless him, and this particular "hot dawg" is a little less enthusiastic than I've come to expect. Two sisters at home on Saturday night in Greenville doesn't sound too encouraging for a start. I think about asking my man for a little detail, but I decide I'll find out soon enough, and I do twenty minutes later when Janet and her sister make their not so grand entrance. Janet looks about twenty five, and is average at best, but even so, she appears to have copped all the looks in the family. Her sister, who goes by the name of Yvette, is two years older. Yvette. If

Owen doesn't look like an Owen, Yvette sure doesn't......well you get the picture. Late twenties, straight hair, at least a stone overweight, and pebble thick glasses just for that extra touch. If they ever make an American version of 'On The Buses', she'll be a shoe in for Olive. My guess is that her parents realised by the time she was two that she was never going to grow into her name, and gave her sister something a little more apt to go through life with. Fortunately there is little opportunity for small talk as the band is really getting into it by now, or they are until half a dozen cops burst through the door, night sticks rapping threateningly against black gloves, and holsters bulging.

"Turn that shit off."

The music stops abruptly in the middle of Bad Company. Looks like we got it.

"We got a report some people smoking marijuana in here. Some of you are gonna leave right now, some of you are coming downtown."

The whole joint falls silent, and Jethro whispers to me

"Just don't look at them cross eyed, Frank. Just don't look at them cross eyed."

Then the skinny singer makes a move which could be considered rather foolish.

"Motherfuckin' pigs! Bunch a motherfuckin' pigs!"

I watch in fascination and horror as he picks up the mike stand Rod Stewart style, and then, in decidedly un-Rod like fashion swings it at the cop's head. One of the other cops is ready for him. If the billy club had hit him solidly on top of the head I think it would probably have killed him, but instead it crashes into his nose and cheek bone, sending a spray of blood and snot all over the drums. The whole thing is a set up. All the long haired guys are rounded up, including Mike. I'm slightly paranoid for a second, but my Hard Day's Night length barnet is considered O.K, as is Owen's rockabilly quiff. I feel sorry for the bespectacled guitarist, who looks like the kid with no friends who stayed in practising every night. He gets a beating as well, although not as savage as the one administered to the singer, who is still screaming about the motherfuckin' pigs as they drag him away. Everyone else has to leave immediately. Like, right now. In under a minute we're back in the pick up truck and heading for the hills, the pantomime dames following behind doggedly in a beat up Ford saloon.

"Does that happen often?" I ask.

"Sure does" replies Jethro cheerfully.

"Cops feel like they ain't real cops if they cain't go out and bust a few heads on Saturday night. You were all right though Frank, you were with me."

"What about Mike?"

"Oh he'll be OK. They might rough him up a little, but they'll let him out tomorrow."

"Have you got the key to his trailer?"

Jethro looks at me pityingly.

"Keys? This is the South, Frank. We don't need keys. We're all friendly down here man, what's Mike's is mine, what's mine is yours."

Sure. Real friendly.

Jethro remembers who's trailing us.

"Here's the deal, Frank. Me and Janet go way back. Yvette's a nice girl man, I don't know her so well, but if she's like Janet, you're gonna be just fine".

I plead tiredness.

"Bullshit! Ain't never too tired for pussy, Frank" a reply I would have put money on.

Mike's trailer isn't bad at all. I've spent plenty of time in flats which were a lot worse. Bedroom at each end, living space and kitchen in the middle. Couch, table, TV. I'm relieved to see my bag in the corner. Jethro pulls out a bottle of Jim Beam, and the four of us sit on the couch. Real cosy. After at least thirty seconds he and Janet adjourn to one of the bedrooms. Yvette looks at me though a milk bottle lens.

"I never met no one from England before."

You surprise me.

"You're cute, do you know that?"

Well I do actually, Yvette, and I also know that your speech is decidedly slurred.

"I want you to know Frank, if you want to get in my breeches, that's just fine with me honey."

What I really want is a cigarette, and I want my own brand. I fish out a packet of Disque Bleu from the bottom of the bag and tell her I'm going outside for some fresh air.

It's a beautiful night. It's still quite balmy, but there's a delicious cooling breeze blowing down from the mountains, the air is fresh and clean, and the sky is spectacular. I don't think I have ever seen so many stars. I've put away a table top of beers, but I'm still sober. The bar was hot and sweaty, two bowls of chilli soaked the rest of it up, and the Jim Beam has yet to kick in. The sooner it does the better. There are some trees about fifty yards from the trailer and I'm half tempted to lay my head down there for the night, but I reluctantly finish my cigarette and turn back, resigned to my fate. Back inside the trailer I'm surprised to see Owen, wearing only a pair of red jockeys, bending over Yvette, who is now flat out on the couch.

"Looks like you're out of luck, Frank. This chick's done a lot of ludes."

"She's done what?"

"Quaaludes. You ain't gonna get no action outa her tonight, that's for sure."

Quaaludes. Their equivalent of Mandrax, I believe. Yvette has dropped a few mandies before drinking beer. As far as I'm concerned this is a right result.

"You think she's going to be alright?"

It's not as if I give a fuck, but I don't want to be around if she isn't.

"Sure she is, Frank. When she wakes up in the morning she's gonna be ready to fuck your brains out, man. Then I'm gonna lay some bacon and biscuits on you, and then we're gonna party all day. Hot dawg."

None of that appeals to me, but what is important is that we can leave Yvette comatose on the couch for now, and I can sleep in Mike's bed. The man who should be there is currently in a police cell, possibly with his brains decorating the wall, but there's nothing I can do about that. The Jim Beam is just starting to make its mark as I crawl between the sheets. I'm thinking about how I'm going to block out the grunting and the groaning and the laughter coming from the other end of the trailer, but then I go out like a light as if someone has slipped me a mandy too.

I wake up sharp and refreshed and with no trace of a hangover. There's a window open letting in the good fresh air and the pale grey light of dawn. I check my watch. 6.05am. I know instantly what I want to do. Whether I will be able to is another matter. I gently push the door open to find Yvette still in the same position on the couch. I know she's alive because I can hear her breathing. In fact I wouldn't be surprised if they can hear her breathing in Tennessee. From the other bedroom I can hear Jethro snoring. Of Janet there is no sound.

Perfect. Put on my money belt and the t-shirt I wrapped it in, then jeans, socks and boots. I would like to brush my teeth, but that's not an option. I pick up my bag and move gently towards the door of the trailer, instantly wishing that I had waited till I got outside before putting my boots on. I turn the door handle as gently as I can, and step out into the dawn. The grass is soaked with dew, and the air tastes so good I feel I could almost drink it. Picking up pace all the way, I head down to the road, and head off in the direction we came from last night.

I guess walking away from someone without telling them follows more or less the same pattern whatever the circumstances. There's no real difference between skipping off from someone you just met the day before and who has let you sleep in someone else's trailer with a fat, ugly, drugged up woman, than there is from walking out of what we might call a more long term relationship.

Sometimes you just got to go.

When your rooster crows at the break of dawn, look out your window and I'll be gone. It's more than ten years since I first heard that line, and I've heard it many more times since. Sometimes it might be on in the background and wash right over me, but other times I remember the impression it made on me that Saturday morning in Ma's house. The times when that song really hits home are the times when it's playing in my head. This morning it's coming through loud and clear, almost as loud as the real life roosters calling to each other across the valley. A strange looking creature comes out of the half-light and crosses the road, and I recognise it as a possum, even though it's a creature I've only ever seen before in cartoons. It's light within half an hour. The sun is already warm, and the air is clear as the mountain dew. It's one of those rare magical moments that only ever really come to me when I'm on my own, when I feel like the whole world is my own personal secret garden. I don't know in which direction I'm heading, and I haven't seen any kind of motor vehicle, but that doesn't worry me. It's a beautiful day, and I've got eighteen or nineteen hours of it stretched out ahead of me before I lay my head down again. Freedom and adventure, the two things I craved when I first heard young Bobby Dylan singing that song.

Moments can only be moments, and are all the more powerful for it. I cross the brow of a small hill and see a highway stretched out before me. At almost exactly the same time I hear a familiar sounding engine coming down the road behind me. For a second I think that Jethro has

63

sent out a search party, so I am relieved when another pick up, white this time, pulls up beside me. A man in his sixties wearing a baseball cap pushes open the door, and without speaking waits for me to get in. We drive the half mile or so to the highway before he speaks, or grunts to be more exact, at the same time chewing tobacco.

"Where you goin' boy?"

"Atlanta" I say hopefully.

"I'll take you down to Westminster. You know Westminster?"

Well yes I do, but I think it might be a different one somehow.

"Westminster is just this side of the state line. You'll get a ride from there down into Georgia." He pronounces it Joe-Jah.

He looks at me suspiciously. "You from up North, boy"?

"England."

"England?" He thinks for a second. "Uncle Sam sure got a fine army, boy."

I nod in as noncommittal fashion as I can.

He thinks a little more.

"You got any communists over in England? Do the communists run things over there?"

"No communists" I say confidently and truthfully. "No communists in parliament."

He looks at me even more suspiciously.

"Well we got a whole lot of them in this country, boy. All them communists in Washington and the Jews in New York run this country, boy."

I say nothing. Baseball cap falls silent for a few minutes.

"England's a good country, boy. This here is a great country, least it would be if it wasn't for the Jews and the commies and the niggers. I'll tell you something about niggers, boy, a nigger can do three things. You want to know what they are, boy? He can lie, he can stink, and he can steal your woman."

I've been expecting this somewhere along the line, so the blind prejudice doesn't surprise me so much as the sheer stupidity. If we were on more neutral territory I might be tempted to inquire as to why this man has so little self regard that he believes that someone who he considers subhuman could steal his woman. We're not, so I don't. A lifetime of bigotry and hatred is hardly likely to be challenged by a scruffy kid like me before we reach the state line.

"Hey, who were those kids, bunch a longhairs came over from England, made a lot of money? Yeah that's it, The Beatles. They said

64

they were more popular than Jesus Christ. The Beatles more popular than Jesus Christ in England, boy?"

I try and look as nonplussed as if he's asking me about the theory of relativity.

"What you heading down to Atlanta for anyway, boy?"

Thinks: To burn it to the fucking ground if they're all like you. I tell him I'm heading for New Orleans.

"I have to tell you I don't like New Orleans myself. Don't care for it at all."

He pauses to allow me to ask why, which I don't. I hardly need to. He carries on regardless.

"Too many mixtures down there for my liking, too many different races. I tell you boy, America and England don't need no other colours. We would be just fine on our own."

He's talking to himself by now. We pass through a couple of small towns which seem to be nothing more than a collection of churches and gas stations by the highway before he drops me off.

"This is Westminster, boy. You should get a good ride here. Watch out for them niggers down in New Orleans, they'll kill you soon as look at you, boy."

He nods to emphasise that he's not kidding, and drives off.

Thank you and goodbye.

I go in to a gas station and buy a big wide bottle of Gatorade. I woke up feeling good this morning, but my tongue is coated with yesterday's beer and cigarettes, and I'm as dry as dust. It's not just that; I really feel like I need to wash my mouth out. It's not so much what the evil old bastard said to me, it's what I didn't say to him. I spit lemon and lime over the forecourt, before I visit the men's room for a wash and brush up and to rinse out my shirt.

Westminster, Georgia looks like something out of a Capra film. No houses and no bar, but an assortment of stores and an old mill. Everything's closed, it being Sunday morning. No cars around, no people either. It is only just past eight am. This little town looks like it might have a story to tell, but whether I get to hear it depends on who picks me up next. It takes five minutes to walk the length of Main Street, which then joins up with another road and turns back into the highway. By eight thirty there is a steady stream of cars passing. Long sleek Cadillacs and old jalopies, each and every one of them full of people, church bound families in their Sunday best. I wonder how many of them talk in tongues.

I wait over an hour, which is a first for this trip. When you've paid your hitch hiking dues you know not to worry. It's early in the day, and it's just a couple of hours drive to Atlanta. If it's getting late and you're stuck in the middle of nowhere, then that's a different story. That's happened to me a few times, but some good Samaritan has always appeared at the right time. I think for a second of poor Robert Johnson standing at the crossroads, terrified of being caught by the dark, like any black man would have been in the deep south of the nineteen thirties. Baseball cap would have been in his twenties then. It occurs to me that I should have played along with him, won his confidence, asked him if he had ever been in on any lynchings. Then again no, these people have an inbuilt suspicion and asking too many questions is not a good idea. There were college kids came down south from New York in the early sixties who asked too many questions and were never seen again. I remember some black power guy saying a few years back that he never left home without two things, his gun and his paranoia. Sounded like a good quote at the time, but it's only now that I really understand what he meant. I don't have a gun and I most certainly don't want one, but it's reassuring to know I strapped on my paranoia with my money belt this morning.

So I'm thinking on this kind of stuff, when I get a sudden flashback to Europe as a bright orange Volkswagen pulls up.

France. You get rides in beetles in France. The French don't care too much for the Germans, which is understandable all things considered, but they are not averse to buying their motor vehicles. Teachers mainly, French teachers drive VWs if they don't drive those Renaults which only have enough room for them and their books, so they never pick anyone up. In Germany it's the bigger models that are more likely to stop, your Mercs and BMWs, so they can show off what they've got. You see plenty of beetles there, as you would expect, but they are more likely to scuttle along the autobahn avoiding eye contact. The French teachers correct your grammar like they never take time off from work. Ratio of women to men picking up lone male hitchers in Europe is about one in ten. Ratio of blonde women in their twenties? About one in a hundred. This ain't France, though. It is, however, a teacher.

She introduces herself. Debbie. Mid-twenties, short blonde hair, cute without making a big deal of it. Teaches third grade, which is eight and nine year olds to you and me. It's the school holidays now, and she's been up to DC to spend some time with a friend. The friend

66

works for the government in some capacity. The friend's gender isn't specified and I'm not about to ask, but I have to admit to being curious. What I'm even more curious about, and what I can't stop myself asking, is why she's all dressed up like she's going to a party. Yellow polka dot dress that looks like the kind of thing a girl might wear for Kentucky Derby day. Definitely not church attire. She smiles, and informs me it's her Mum's birthday, and she is going straight to her parents' house for a family lunch. Ain't that nice? What's even nicer for me is that their house happens to be in Atlanta. Lucky Frankie does it again.

Cat Stevens is on the tape player. For some reason, and I've no idea why, I tell her I know him, which is complete bollocks of course. I did see him once in a pub garden in Fulham, with a girlfriend straight off the cover of Vogue. They drank white wine, and he wore a Breton fisherman's jersey and smoked Disque Bleu, which looked extremely cool, and led me to switch my brand from Piccadilly the very next day. Debbie is suitably impressed, which suggests she may be a little gullible, but then she's not from New York. I think of Shannon for a second, and decide I am very happy to be where I am, thank you.

Debbie wants to know about London. I would rather drink in the here and now, but fair's fair, so I tell her what she wants to know. Something, anything. I'm first inclined to give her the business exec story, but make a swerve at the last minute to the music writer. More interesting for her, and that's how I know the Cat. I'm checking out the scene in New York and New Orleans. Debbie went there ten years ago when she was fourteen. That makes her the same age as me. I ask her sign.

"Aries. You into all that?"

"Not really. Just seeing if you're older than me"

She is. This is good. We're getting on. Tea for the Tillerman reaches its resounding final chord, and she asks me if I could put the eight track away for her. I check out the dash and find she's got good taste. Sweet Baby James, After the Goldrush, Tapestry, There goes Rhymin' Simon. I pull out Glen Campbell's Greatest Hits. She seems a little embarrassed as if I'm going to mock her.

"Oh that's my Mom's" she protests. "Let's leave the music a while and talk."

Let's, but I don't want to talk about me because I don't want to think about me. I would much rather find out more about Debbie herself, and possibly let the teacher give me a little lesson in current affairs.

She's got friends in Washington, so perhaps she can give me the lowdown on this Watergate thing, for a start.

"So what's that all about? Do you tell the kids in your class all about it?"

She laughs. "A lot of them ask me. I tell them to ask their parents."

"Well you're the teacher."

"I know I'm the teacher, but I'm not paid to teach them about that, and I have to be very careful. There's plenty of old school republicans in this state."

I realise we've crossed into Georgia.

"If I tell those kids what I really think, the next thing I know I'll be branded a communist."

I tell her about my last ride, and she shakes her head sadly.

"Those people are never going to change."

"Well I'm not going to get too much information out of my parents, so you can tell me."

"Doesn't make the news in England, no?"

"Not as much as here." I don't tell her that I've had too much on my mind to watch the news lately.

"I only know what's been on the news like everyone else, but I've been following it. You want it from the top?"

"Sure."

I sit back like a kid at bed time.

Debbie knows her stuff. So what has happened here is that about two years ago a bunch of men were caught red handed breaking into the Democratic Party Committee office in the middle of the night. The office is located in a building in Washington called the Watergate building. That's why it's called the Watergate affair, which was my first question. A day or so later it turns out that the burglars are all either government or CIA officials, and they were as intent on leaving stuff there, like listening devices, as they were on taking stuff out, documents and the like. The Democrats are currently the party in opposition by the way. Nixon is a Republican. Even I know that. So now the newspapers are on the case, and it turns out that all this is just the tip of an iceberg that's been lurking below the surface for a couple of years at least. Government agents breaking into offices, breaking into hotels, money from nowhere turning up in burglar's bank accounts. All part of a government sponsored campaign of political sabotage and espionage against anyone they considered might be a threat to their interests. All of this is beyond denial now, the only question being how high up in the government was the whole thing masterminded.

None of this stops Nixon getting re-elected in seventy two, far from it. He got back in with one of the biggest landslides ever. The Democrats were in disarray, quite possibly due in no small measure to the dirty tricks team. Still, the damage has been done, and during the next year it turned into a big snowball rolling downhill picking up more and more dirt as it did so. Slowly and surely the fingers are pointed up and up, first to the President's aides and advisors and then inevitably to Nixon himself.

Round about here I start losing concentration. I'm looking at the scenery, and some of the time I find I'm listening to Debbie's sweet southern voice more than to what she's actually saying. She's throwing names at me like I should know who these people are. Dean, Erlichman, Mitchell. I may be the only person in the country who doesn't know them. No matter, I think I've got the picture. Now, I'm not a great one for the news. The way I see it news is here today and gone tomorrow. Next day's fish and chip paper. History, now that's another matter. I've always loved history. The way I see it, if things are important enough then they'll become history soon enough, and then you can read about it. The way Debbie tells it, it seems like this is history that's happening right now. Looks like Tricky Dicky's on the way out, destroyed by his own paranoia. He got in to the habit of taping every conversation he had at the White House, every phone call. At the same time he's got the dirty tricks crew out putting the boot in on every Democrat in Washington. The thing is, every conversation, every phone call... Yep, all on tape. My Dad has knocked around with a few villains in his time, all strictly minor league, but one golden rule even those at the bottom of the totem pole know is never to write anything down. Let alone record anything. When the dirty stuff hits the fan, first thing the enquiry commission wants is the tapes. Then, and get this, they don't surrender the tapes but they write out edited versions of the transcripts. Dick's days are numbered, but he's still refusing to give up the tapes. So that's where we stand at the moment.

Debbie's been talking nine to the dozen, so I feel I should contribute something. "Well two things strike me. One, at least it proves you live in a democracy. I mean the guy's been rumbled, right? If something like this happened where I come from, MI5 would get hold of it, and we might find out about it in fifty years time, if we're lucky. The other is this. How many of you are there? Two hundred million? How come you elect a president who is so stupid?"

"People in this country don't like their politicians to be too smart. They want them to be just plain folks. I remember when I was a kid everybody down here hated Kennedy. Too darn slick for their liking. A lot of people were out partying like it was the best thing that ever happened when he got shot. A lot more pretended to be sorry and weren't one bit. You should have asked your guy this morning about JFK, see what he would have said."

Flashback to November sixty three. I was thirteen years old sitting watching the Harry Worth show when the news was announced.

Debbie continues. "Our state governor is talking about running for President next time out. He's a democrat, but people like him. He's already made his fortune, he's got a peanut farm down in Plains, Georgia, but all the crackers down here think he's one of them."

It feels like that we are moving from history in the making to day to day politics, something which is guaranteed to send me to sleep. I move on to the other current issue of the day.

"So what's with this Patty Hearst chick? What's that all about?"

She laughs. "Oh, the poor little rich girl? Let me ask you something, have you ever seen her boyfriend? Not the one in the gang, the one who got shot, but her old boyfriend."

"Can't say that I have."

"Well he looks like the original guy that gets sand kicked in his face. I figure when Patty realised that she was worth a lot more to these people alive than she would be dead, she got a taste for something she never had before, if you get my meaning."

Yes I get your meaning Debbie, and she blushes slightly as if suddenly aware that she's alone in her car with a man she doesn't know, and she has made what could be construed as a suggestive remark. I attempt to broaden the conversation.

"So this Symbionese Liberation Army or whatever they're called, are there many of them around the country?"

She laughs out loud. "No there ain't none of them around the country. They're just a bunch of asshole kids. There's probably only about three of them left. Most of them got shot in Los Angeles two months back."

I don't know what surprises me more, the bad language or the bad grammar that's coming out of her pretty schoolteacher's mouth.
Debbie looks at me sideways. "Say, do you know The Beatles?"

70

There's something about being alone in a car with an attractive woman. It's like being sat on a sofa with one when no one else is home. That feeling that no matter how innocent a situation may be there's always a possibility that something may happen. You know it, and she knows it too. I know full well what is going to happen here, she is going to drop me off in some suburb of Atlanta, I will thank her for the lift and the history lesson, and we will say our goodbyes, never to meet again. What I can't deny though, is that she is the best looking girl I've seen since I've been in the country. A regular Georgia peach, you might say. Her dress has ridden up slightly to reveal her bare suntanned legs. I let my gaze linger just long enough for her to notice. She motions towards a packet of Kools by the gear stick. They seem to be a popular choice with the ladies. She asks me to light one for her, and I feel like there is an easy intimacy between us as I pass the white filter from my lips to hers. Then she asks me to put some more music on, so I slot After the Goldrush into the eight track machine, not without some difficulty. I light up a Marlboro and lay back in the seat as far as you can in a beetle, and listen to Neil Young sing about the Southern Man, while we close in on Atlanta all too quickly, when what I would really like is for Debbie to say she's just remembered that she has to go to California.

We pass a sign saying Center ten miles. Looks like they can't spell any better in the south than in the north. The beetle slows down.

"I would really like to take you downtown and drop you off on Peachtree, but I'll be late if I do that."

She sounds like she feels bad about it too. "If I leave you at this crossroads you should get a ride easy enough. Is that OK?"

"Of course it is. Where I come from Sunday lunch with Mum is sacred. Especially on her birthday."

Debbie laughs, relieved that I understand, and pulls over by the roadside. I hesitate for a second. I really want to tell her that I like her, and I want to get it right. I muster some of the old charm and try and give it a little Southern twist.

"Well Miss Debbie, If I was going to be spending any time in this city I would be asking you your phone number and inviting you out to the best restaurant in the whole town, because I think you are a real Southern belle. As it is I'm just going to say goodbye and thanks for the history lesson."

She smiles. "If I was going to be spending any time in this city I'd come, believe me I would."

Then she giggles with genuine delight and leans over and kisses me full on the lips, which is so unexpected that it makes me tingle all over. Then she's back on her own side with one hand on the wheel and the other on the gear stick like she's ready to go but she's still smiling.

"You are really nice, do you know that?"

"You are. I know that."

No sooner have I got both feet on the Georgia tar than she's gone. I watch the little orange car slowly disappear into the distance like the sun going down.

I've been in this country for almost two weeks now, and I've spent the grand total of nine dollars on resting my bones. I reckon a little luxury wouldn't go amiss, so I check into one of Atlanta's impressive looking hotels, one with uniformed bellboys, and more importantly a big pool, where I spend the rest of the day.

Travelling plays games with time. It seems days since I crept out of that trailer into the dawn, and over a week since I said goodbye to Robyn, when it's only been seventy two hours. Hitch hiking has its ups and downs, but mostly it reminds you how good people can be when there are no strings attached. Back in the real world it seems that people who give always get asked to give more. I remember my friend Keith said that to me once, and it wasn't until a good while later that I realised he was talking about Julie.

I decide to give the bright lights a miss for once, and catch up with some sleep. Slipping between the cool, clean sheets my head is filled with thoughts of Debbie. Her kiss was so unexpected that it thrilled me to the marrow. She may have been game for it, and now I'll never know. There was a time when I would never have got out of that car without trying my luck, but if I had it might have spoiled everything, like what she thought of me for instance. There was a time when that wouldn't have worried me either. Still, I can't help imagining my hand sliding up her sun kissed thigh while she was driving, and then inside her crisp white panties. Her words are still echoing in my head. You are really nice, do you know that?

I'm not really, Debbie. I've done bad things. If I was nice I wouldn't be here, I would be where I'm supposed to be, doing what I'm supposed to be doing. I'm not really nice at all. But I'm trying.

I really am.

Chapter Five: Still On The Line

1968

I was still a kid when I started work but I grew up soon enough, in some ways if not in others. I got my first start in a news agency, which was a pretty cool place to work, although I can't say I was particularly appreciative at the time, having nothing to compare it with. The agency specialised in news film, and based itself in our neighbourhood because it was on the right side of town for the airport. My job was to take care of the paperwork, before hairy arsed despatch riders would zip off to the freight terminal with the canisters that spread the gospel, back in those heady days when London was the centre of the world.

The money wasn't great, but it stretched a fair way back then. Threads were important, although I never went as overboard as some. The mod scene was fading, and something else was happening, not that many of us knew what it was, except that there were mysterious goings on in Ladbroke Grove and South Kensington. I made sure I had a good pair of shoes, two good shirts and a well pressed pair of strides, but I was always happiest in my one pair of Levi's. I reckoned they would never go out of style, and I've seen no evidence since to prove me wrong. Most of my spare cash went on music. It was an unbelievably rich period. Beatles, Stones, Dylan, Stax, Motown. Buying obscure singles on the Sue label down the Bush market on a Saturday morning, then the next week I might catch the tube up to the Folk and Blues record shop in New Oxford Street and listen to them play records by Sonny and Brownie and Rambling Jack Elliot. Getting in to stuff backwards, like Muddy Waters and Howlin' Wolf through the Stones, and old blues and Woody Guthrie through Dylan. I learned the rudiments of political thought from Woody, and the romantic notion of being a lonesome traveller from everyone.

Tom Paxton was a favourite. He had a fantastic album out called Rambling Boy, which was packed with great songs; Last Thing On My Mind, I Can't Help But Wonder Where I'm Bound. This last song was written from the point of view of an older man, probably in his thirties, who has lost everything and doesn't know what will become of him, but to my eighteen year old self it seemed to be written just for me. The Paxton record in particular inspired lots of kids to buy an acoustic guitar and learn how to play those simple but still wonderful songs, but I never got round to that myself. I didn't want to play those songs, I wanted to live them.

Looking back it seems like it was an important time, and it surely was, but to me the present often seemed fleeting and mostly irrelevant when compared with the swelling ocean of the past washing up new treasures every day, and the endless, boundless future which lay stretched out ahead. Looking back, sixty eight was one of the most significant years since the end of World War Two. Martin Luther King and RFK got shot. The Russians invaded Prague, and in Paris and Chicago they manned the barricades. I even went on an anti-Vietnam war demo once myself. We got to the US embassy in Grosvenor Square before things got rather seriously out of hand. I had an ulterior motive in the comely form of a very serious minded A Level student, who gave me my sweet reward in a Holland Park Avenue bedsit that same evening.

Oh, and in nineteen sixty eight Wichita Lineman came out.

I have to say that from an early age my musical tastes were impressive if not to say impeccable. By the time I was eighteen I could hold my own in conversation with mods, rockers, folkies and blues cats alike. Some stuff I kept to myself. I never stopped liking Del Shannon, and once I'd had my heart broken a few times his songs made even more sense. Ricky Nelson was dismissed as a lightweight, but he took me around the world when he sang about being a travelling man, and came back strong in the seventies as a singer songwriter. I always had a soft spot for Bobby Vee from Fargo, North Dakota, not that far from the frozen field where Buddy Holly met his sad end, and not too far from where Bob Dylan grew up near the Canadian border. Rumour had it that Dylan may even have played in his band as a teenager. Bobby picked up Buddy's torch and ran with it for a while before fading away with most of the other Bobbies. Then there was Country and Western.

Country records were in the pop charts all the time when I was a kid. Marty Robbins wrote a screenplay for a full length cowboy movie in El Paso, and boiled it down to a three minute song, one of the greatest ever. Every time I heard it I thought the hero might get away yet. Another favourite was I'm Moving On, written by some old guy from way back called Hank Snow, and covered by Ray Charles and by The Rolling Stones. Both of them sang it too fast to be able to understand the lyrics, but it didn't matter. I'm moving on, that's all you needed to know. Someone whose name I don't recall sang about the girl from Wolverton Mountain, which may or may not exist, but seemed real enough to me, complete with birds and bears. Roger Miller made a hobo the King of the Road, and offered up a life anyone would surely aspire to. A life without responsibilities. Third boxcar midnight train, destination Bangor Maine, or Hanger Lane as we so wittily renamed it in year four. I liked those songs then, and I like them still. Johnny Cash, who shot a man in Reno just to see him die, but who you could tell from his voice was as good a man and true as ever walked the earth. Just a week or so before I left home I heard a new record by Doug Sahm, a country singer from Texas last heard of in the sixties when he was pretending to be English. Is anybody going to San Antone or Phoenix Arizona, any place is all right as long as I can forget I've ever known her, as if the big country just possibly might be big enough to swallow up his sadness and his bitter memories, and give him one more chance for a new start.

Then there was Wichita Lineman. I was still living at home when I was eighteen. I may not have been there much, but I wasn't living anywhere else. I first heard the song about the Wichita Lineman on the same radio in Ma's living room as I had heard Don't Think Twice five years earlier. A lot of apples had fallen off the trees in between times, but the record grabbed me in the same way, even though it was as different a song as it was possible to be.

"I am a lineman for the county and I drive the main road."

A simple enough statement, but what did it mean? As the story develops we find that the singer is employed by the state to drive round checking and repairing telegraph lines. Not the whole state, just the local county. It sounds like a solitary job, and while he's driving he thinks about a woman who may or may not be his wife. He feels like he could do with a holiday, but he's going to be busy, and he knows he's not going anywhere. And that's about it. Except that the singer was a guy by the name of Glen Campbell who could sing like James Stewart could act, with a supreme and seemingly effortless artistry that put you right there with him all the way from the start. Glen didn't write the song, though. That was a fellow called Jim Webb, who wasn't much older than me, about twenty one when the record came out. Glen Campbell was a country singer, but Jim Webb wasn't a country writer, he was a musical genius from Los Angeles. The arrangement for Wichita Lineman tells the story as effectively as the words. It's so perfect you don't even know it's there until you've heard the song a few hundred times, and realise that the strings play the part of the wind singing in the wires.

Where the song was different from Don't Think Twice or The Promised Land, or any other song I had ever heard in my life, was that the singer wasn't going anywhere, and wasn't intending to either. He could do with a holiday, but he takes quiet pride in his work, he knows every inch of those county roads, and there's a woman at home he's never going to leave. Never going to leave! Every song worth a damn I had ever heard before was about leaving and never coming back, or wanting to be someplace else. The Mamas and Papas, stuck in New York on a cold winters day and wanting to be three thousand miles away in California, struck a chord with millions of people all over the world who had never been to either place, and were never likely to. This guy would hardly cross the county line, but he had a real life.

That's when it dawned on me. All these lives people are leading all over the world, and who's to say any one of them is any more significant than any other. That's when I knew for sure there was a life out there waiting for me, and it wasn't going to involve working in an office or factory, and definitely not on any market stall. I also knew that if I was going to find it I would have to seek it out. There's nothing in the song says that the Wichita Lineman was born and raised in Kansas.

If I was responsible for a piece of perfection like that record, I think I would sit back and admire my creation for all time, but Glen and Jim had other ideas and followed it up with two more gems, both equally profound if slightly more traditional in story line. Galveston was about a guy on the front line in Vietnam missing his home and missing his girl. Nothing new, but a beautiful record none the less. By The Time I Get To Phoenix is something else entirely. The narrator gets up early in the morning while his girl is still sleeping, and gets in his car to drive to Oklahoma, via Phoenix and Albuquerque. He's not coming back. Except that the further away he gets, the more certain it is that he is coming back. He knows it, and we know it too. She's right there with him, just as much as if they were both still tucked up in bed.

By sixty nine I had moved on from the news agency and I was working in a map printer's office. A mistake, and one that made me even more certain things would have to change and sooner rather than later, but at least there were plenty of maps around to help me improve my geography and plan my getaway. I learned that Wichita is on the lonesome plains of Kansas. I imagined it as being freezing in the winter and hotter than hell in summer. Galveston is a seaport near Houston, Texas. Oklahoma City is more than thirteen hundred miles from Los Angeles. Glen must have got up early to get to Phoenix by the time she wakes up as it's nearly four hundred miles. I realised then that he probably never even went to bed, he waited till she did, and then snuck out of the house before midnight.

He probably did the whole drive in one hit, maybe got to his parents' house and spent the night, before turning around and driving straight back.

If I'm asked what my favourite record is I always say Tracks of my Tears. I've never had a conversation about the Wichita Lineman, because I've never yet met anyone I thought would have any idea what I was talking about. Maybe that's another quest. If there was some way you could not have a car and still carry music around with you, that's what I would carry. The truth is I do carry it with me; I carry it in my head, along with all the others. That's why I didn't need Debbie to play it on her eight track.

Chapter Six: Pepper In My Shoe

Monday.

I know I really should see some of Atlanta, but that crescent city is calling me on. The hotel foyer is full of Gone With The Wind related tourist information, but it's a film I've never seen and a book I've never read, so I take a bus to the city limits and head for the highway.

It takes a while to get a ride, but when it comes it's a hitchhiker's dream. A Corvette Stingray, Florida bound. My driver today is Julian, who's twenty eight and in the Navy. He's a flight trainer, teaches recruits how to fly helicopters. Stationed in Pensacola, Florida, which is where he's heading now. Short hair, naturally, and a moustache, and in his jeans and sweat shirt he looks like an off duty cop. Joined up seven years ago, getting out of the service in three months.

"Well that's going to be some party" I say, partly as conversation, but more because I'm thinking, yes that really would be a party after seven years serving Uncle Sam.

"You betcha. It's gonna be some party, alright."

Julian's a happy man. His educated southern accent is easy on the ear, and he's a good listener, genuinely interested. I tell him about my adventures in Greenville. He laughs affectionately.

"Those hillbillies, man. Most of them are good people. Dangerous, mind, but they've got good hearts. Tell me, did you see many dead animals on the roads around there, possums and the like?"

Come to think of it, I didn't.

"That's because round those parts as soon as they hit anything they scrape it off the road and take it home and eat it."

"Just as well I didn't stay for dinner."

"I'm just kidding. People will tell you that everywhere you go, but it's not really true."

"I'm relieved to hear it." I am too.

"No, it's true. I was kidding just now."

No mistake about it, the kidder's being kidded. I've finally met one with a sense of humour.

"So how come you know so much about it? You a hillbilly yourself?"

"No my friend, my name is Julian William Deacon, and I am of proud British stock. I am one hundred per cent a son of the Pilgrim Fathers, born in Norfolk, Virginia, in the year of our Lord nineteen forty six."

There's a twinkle in Julian's eyes which displays a trace of what might even be irony. Up to this point I'm not aware that irony is listed in the American dictionary.

Mention of Norfolk, Virginia sets me thinking of Old Chuck and his journey. He got the bus, and the hound broke down and left him stranded in downtown Birmingham. We're on a different road heading down through Montgomery, Alabama and on towards Mobile. Pensacola is just across the state line in Florida, and I'm not expecting this Stingray to break down.

"Norfolk is a Navy town, right?"

"Yes it is." He looks surprised and pleased that I know this.

"My family has always lived in Virginia, and as long as there has been a Navy we've been in it. My Dad was in the Pacific in World War Two."

I tell Julian that he's probably more English than me, me being half Irish, which could be a mistake as he asks me questions about the troubles I can't answer. He's sympathetic enough.

"Yeah, I guess it must be weird when you're all the same people really. At least in Vietnam you know your enemy. A gook is a gook."

Vietnam. That place on television. It's a little more than that to Julian.

"You flew helicopters in Vietnam?"

"I sure did. Right now I'm very happy not to be training guys how to fly those things just so they can go over there to get killed. The last troops came home on the twenty ninth of March. In a year or two they'll be some other bullshit going on somewhere else."

I can tell Julian doesn't want to say too much more. He's a patriot and I'm an alien, no matter who has got what blood in their veins, so I change the subject.

"Did you ever meet Gene Vincent?"

Eugene Vincent Craddock, the only other person from Norfolk, Virginia I can claim to have met. A Navy man himself, he saw service in Korea before badly injuring his leg in a motor cycle accident. Wore a leg brace which he hid under his trademark black leather, and for the rest of his life was in constant pain which he numbed the best he could with morphine and Jack Daniel's. John Lennon said he heard Gene Vincent sing Be Bop a Lula in nineteen fifty six and felt half American from that moment on. I knew exactly what John meant. Gene was in the car when Eddie Cochran had his fatal accident in the West of England, and spent much of the latter part of his life in England and France. I bought Gene Vincent a large Johnnie Walker in the Packhorse in Chiswick High Road one night about three years ago. Half an hour later he was thrown out for picking a fight over a girl and told never to come back. Six weeks later he went back to the States to die of a stomach ulcer. He was thirty six.

"Did I meet Gene Vincent? The old rock and roll singer? No, did you ever meet Mick Jagger?"

Nice one Julian.

"By the way, my friends call me JW."

"OK JW."

"You can call me Lieutenant Deacon."

I love this guy.

We talk easily halfway across Alabama. JW is probably the first person I have met so far who I could imagine chewing the fat with in the pub back home. Robyn wouldn't get any of my jokes, Debbie, as far as I'm concerned, will live only in her car and in my mind, and as for Jethro, well the man had a good heart, but let's just say he would be something of a liability. JW, with his openness, his honesty, and his plain decency, makes me feel good about the world, and even a little good about myself for recognising it. And JW, most assuredly, has a good heart. I have a little trouble reconciling this with the eager servant of Uncle Sam who writes off all gooks, even though half the gooks were on his side, officially anyway. I tell him about my Klan man, just to check his reaction. He shakes his head in a concerned fashion.

"How old was he? In his sixties?" He pauses for a few seconds.

"You see the thing is this. People like that, they would have lived through the depression, times were really hard, probably lost what little he had, including his dignity. One thing he had left to hold on to was his belief that he was better than the black man. The blacks have got something to look forward to now, eyes on the prize and all that. Guys like you met yesterday got nothing left, they'll go to their graves with nothing except hatred."

He pauses again.

"Then again, he could be just plain evil. A lot of them are. I'll tell you something for nothing. You spend seven years in the service and you quickly learn to tell the good from the bad, and a man's colour ain't got nothing to do with it."

That still doesn't match up with the gooks, but I'm not going to push it.

JW is playing around with the radio dial. He tries the AM band and finds nothing but three religious stations. One preacher is warning against the sin of shacking up, his words not mine. The other two are asking for money. JW's good humour is momentarily disturbed.

"It's Monday, for Christ's sake. You would think they might take the day off, give everyone a rest."

He suddenly looks like as though he's said something he shouldn't have.

"Are you a religious man, Frank? If you are, I didn't mean to cause offence."

I quickly reassure him that I am not a religious man, and tell him about Jethro's grandaddy talking in tongues, which gives JW a further opportunity to talk some more about hillbillies.

"I used to serve with this guy from West Virginia, and he told me that his father would pick up snakes. As a test of his faith, you understand, he would trust in God not to let the snakes bite him."

"Is he still with us, as far as you know?"

"Nope. One day a snake bit him and he died."

"Are you kidding me again JW?"

"No I'm not. This is the South, Frank. You're not in New York City now. Or London."

"So what happened to the snake?"

It seems as good a question as any. JW laughs.

"I'm glad I picked you up man, I appreciate your company. How about if we give up on this radio until we get near Pensacola, and put some music on?"

He slips in a cassette by a country singer called Jimmy Buffett. There's one song on it I know called Come Monday, and me and JW sing along with it as we bypass Montgomery, where George Wallace's state militia tear gassed black schoolchildren no more than ten years ago.

I find myself talking to JW about stuff I haven't told anyone for a long time. I don't tell him about Gino or Teresa, that's mine and mine alone to deal with, but I tell him about Ma, which appears to genuinely sadden him, I tell him about the old man, although I have to admit to exaggerating his war record, and I even tell him about my brother Joey, who I never think about at all to be honest, unless he's in my face or under my feet, which he often is. This bonds us even more.

"Little brothers drive you crazy don't they? My brother's twenty one."

"Is he a Navy man too?" I venture.

"Oh, sure. He's stationed up at Newport News. That's perfect for me, he's in the country but he's not too close."

Serious again for a second.

"I really hope there's no more stupid wars break out while he's in service. Wouldn't bet on it though."

"So you don't want to stay on yourself, be an admiral some day?"

I don't even know if they have admirals here.

"No Frank, I've done my time. There's other fish to fry."

"Like what?"

"I'm going to fly 747s. I get out in October, I'm going to take a vacation, then I'm going to commercial flying school in January. The Navy is paying for it."

"So they should."

"Damn right they should. Give me a year or two, and I'll be flying TWA to London and I'll be the driver."

"Well you just make sure you look me up."

JW acts like he's honoured, as if I've invited him to my wedding or something. I think it might be a while before he gets his captain's hat, though I bet he's no slouch. Long, long while before my wedding, I know that much.

"Listen, it's getting late. I can drop you at Mobile if you want, but you might do better coming back to the base tonight. I can get you back on the road in the morning. I wouldn't recommend getting in to New Orleans late at night with nowhere to stay. I wouldn't recommend that at all.

"I'm intrigued. "Am I allowed on the base?"

"Well if you turn out to be a spy they'll shoot us both, so I'll take that chance."

We turn off the highway and drive on a back road until we cross the Florida state line and see a sign saying Pensacola thirty miles. There

82

are hardly any cars on the road and the Stingray eats it up. If it was old Jethro driving I'd be looking to change my pants in double quick time, but JW is in control.

"This isn't the Florida you see in the movies Frank, Miami and all those places. This is what they call the panhandle. It's none too interesting, to be honest with you. Hey do you want to get something to eat?"

"Is the Pope a Catholic?"

We've done three hundred miles and breakfast in Atlanta seems a long time ago. Damn, I mentioned religion again.

JW laughs. "I have to tell you Frank, there's a lot of people round these parts who wouldn't know the answer to that question. Does a bear shit in the woods is what they say. Come on man, let's go" and he pushes the Stingray up to a hundred and ten on this old country back road as the Sun starts sinking down over towards New Orleans.

Downtown Pensacola looks like a fun place for the weekend. Bars where you can look at women, bars where you might meet women, bars where you might even take women, and bars where you might just sit and drink, if that's your inclination. It's a Navy town sure enough, but on this Monday night it's dead. We go into a bar where there are a few guys playing pool, some of them in uniform and some of them not. All of them know JW. Before I get a chance to protest I'm at the table, and it's me and JW against a pair of uniforms. I haven't played for months, but to my relief and surprise neither of our opponents are any good at this game, and with my memories of a misspent youth and JW's pilot's eye and steady hand we beat them three out of three. Then they're all buying me beers and calling me a great guy, and then they're calling me a great guy again for knocking them back so fast, and they buy me more beers, and them I buy beers all round which makes me a great guy one more time, and before I know it it's one a.m.

JW looks at me as if he's just remembered something.

"I was going to get you something to eat, wasn't I? Come on, let's go. See you, guys. Nine o'clock, right Jeff?"

Jeff is a young uniformed black guy. Back in the Stingray JW tells me that Jeff is going to drive me to Mobile in the morning where I can get on the road to New Orleans. I'm thinking for a second that JW has given him an order, but it turns out he's going there anyway. JW himself is on duty at seven. It is now one thirty. We go to a diner on the outskirts of town which is busier than any of the bars in town were, and over eggs, sausage, bacon, hash browns, toast and very welcome coffee that keeps on coming, we talk some more. I ask him what he thinks about Watergate.

"To be honest, I don't really care. I've served my country. I'm from a long line who have served the country. Those people aren't the country. The country's going to throw them out. It's a matter of days, Frank. He's going down."

I ask him about draft dodgers and anti-war protesters.

"This is a free country. People want to protest, they should be able to. I don't know if I believe in the draft. If it ever starts with the Russians we're all going to die, don't matter how many we got in uniform. Let me put it this way, I never met anyone in the service who didn't want to be there and was worth a lick. If you're white and you got a decent education you can get out of it anyway. You're travelling around the country, you're going to meet a lot of thirty year old students, I'll tell you that."

"Do they all drive Volkswagens?"

"You've seen 'em buddy."

I suddenly realise that JW is looking at me intently.

"If you don't mind me asking Frank" and he starts to laugh "Why do you eat like that?"

I don't get what he means for a second and then notice that JW is eating with his fork in his right hand while his knife lies redundant and forlorn upon the table. I sneak a look around the diner, which is still almost full at two am on this Tuesday morning, and everybody is eating the same way. They cut up their food, and then they put the knife down and eat with their fork. They only other person I've ever seen eat like that is my brother, and he stopped doing it when he was about seven.

"Come to England JW and I'll take you to the Ritz, and I'll think you will find everybody eating like this."

It would probably be the Ritz cafe in the High Street but the result would be the same. I polish off my plate using my infinitely more efficient method, although in a slightly self-conscious way. JW shakes his head in amusement and goes to pay the check.

Back in the Stingray and JW guns it.

"You don't pay too much attention to the speed limit do you?"

I have to say in his defence that JW probably drank one beer to every three of mine in the bar.

84

"Oh the cops don't bother us around here. It's the Shore Patrol we have to worry about, and I know all those guys."

I have no doubt that he does. He knows the guard on duty at the base as well, and after some banter about his car the barrier is lifted with no questions about who I might be, and I'm on the United States Naval base. I've been in smaller towns. It's got streets, and the streets have got names, and the streets with names are lined with bungalows which are the officers' quarters, and there's me expecting Nissan huts. JW has a fairly spacious one bedroom pad which is kept in immaculate order. Even though he is going to be lucky to get four hours sleep he takes the time to convert his sofa into a bed, and pulls out bedding from a cupboard for me. He's not done yet, and pulls some brochures out of a drawer.

"Me and some of the guys went down to New Orleans a few months back. There's a street map here and some other stuff. My advice is to stay around the French Quarter except for taking a riverboat ride, maybe. I would rather be in Khe Sahn than get lost in the wrong part of New Orleans. I'm giving you my address in Norfolk as well. I'd really appreciate it if you let me know you got back home safe."

"I'll see you in the morning, JW."

"I doubt it. I'm an expert at getting out of places without you knowing it. Something I learned off Charlie. Take care, Frank. You're a great guy."

What I should say is that you're a great guy yourself JW, but I don't. After all, it's not really our way. We exchange the firmest of handshakes and say goodnight.

At nine am precisely there's a no nonsense military style rap on the door. JW is long gone like he said he would be. Jeff is polite almost to the point of being respectful, and gives me as much time as I need to get ready. Ten minutes later and we're driving out of the gates in his Ford Pinto. Jeff wants to talk about baseball and basketball and television programmes that I've never heard of, so I'm forced to feign tiredness even though I'm feeling as sharp as a tack. Drinking beer till the early hours and then having your breakfast before you go to bed seems to be a most sensible idea, and one I'm surprised I have never thought of before. Mind you, it was American beer.

We grew up on American television. Gunsmoke, Rawhide, 77 Sunset Strip, Batman, Perry Mason, Dr Kildare, Just Dennis and Casey

Jones. It's one of the reasons this country has always fascinated me, that and the music. The thing of everything being different but familiar at the same time. When I left school I more or less gave up watching television all together. The only thing I've watched in the past few years is Budgie, which is most assuredly a London programme about a small time criminal, which stars our local boy Adam Faith as the loser with a heart of gold. Somehow I don't think Jeff is likely to be too familiar with that one, so I fall back on music. We find common ground in Al Green and that keeps us going for the hour and quarter it takes to get to Mobile.

Mobile looks the sort of place they had in mind when they built ring roads. Oil refineries give way to factories as we approach the centre. Jeff takes me clear through to the other side of town, and drops me at an on ramp where he tells me I'm assured of a good ride down to New Orleans. Five minutes later a truck pulls up, my first one. Driver about my age, carrying frozen food, and yes he's going straight to New Orleans. Thanks Jeff.

"You wouldn't happen to have any speed on you would you?"

"No I never carry anything when I'm travelling" I coolly reply, as if the rest of the time I'm a regular Doctor Robert.

"Yeah, I can dig that. That's OK, these fuckin' Kools will keep me awake till we get to New Orleans" as he lights up.

Well I fuckin' hope they will. I think that possibly a little conversation may help, but my man gives all his attention to the road and to constantly lighting up menthol cigarettes, which so far I have only observed being smoked by women. I remember once when we were still at school, me and Keith got away with a packet of Consulate on one of our usually futile shoplifting expeditions. Cool as a mountain stream, according to the advert. I've never been able to face one since.

I guess my driver must have been hoping I was a wandering dope dealer on a mission to minister to the sleep deprived truck drivers of this nation. Sorry to disappoint you fella, but thanks for the ride anyway. I light up a Marlboro, and think about JW as we cross the Mississippi state line. I think JW might possibly be one of the finest people I've ever met. I always come back to that old travelling thing. The longer you know people the more chance you give them to let you down. There's so much more I want to ask him. Four years older than me, and done a lot of things I haven't done. No racist, but he showed understanding and compassion towards the old Klansman when I told him the story. Well, no racist until you get round to the gooks. All things considered, I think you should know someone a while before you ask them what they did in the war. Sure, some will tell you without being asked if they corner you in a bar, or even worse on a Greyhound bus. So what did JW do? That line about learning to be quiet from Charlie must surely have been another example of his sense of humour. You can't be too quiet when you're driving a helicopter. Not too impressed with religion either. Yes, me and JW might have a lot to talk about.

Then again, there are plenty of things I've experienced which he hasn't. In 1968 he would have been just out of officer training. 1968 was the year when I first stepped out in to the big bad world. I didn't tell him I had been on that demo, but I would have done, given time.

Maybe we will meet up again somewhere down the line. He'll haul the big bird across the pond as effortlessly as he drove that Stingray and we'll go out on the town with a pair of stewardesses. You never know.

The road takes us past more places that I've heard of in song. Biloxi, which had been serenaded by a homesick draft dodger called Jesse Winchester while he was exiled in Canada, and Gulfport, where Robert Johnson's last fair deal went down. Then we're out of Mississippi and into the Bayou state, and then it's just a few miles before we're crossing a big stretch of water, and twenty minutes after that we hit the industrialised suburbs of New Orleans. My nameless driver stops at a light and points me to the downtown area. About four miles, he tells me. There's a bus stop on the corner, but it's not unpleasantly warm, and I could do with a little exercise. I put my bag on my shoulder and make my way towards the Crescent City with a grin on my face and Fats Domino's Walking To New Orleans on my lips. It's as much as I can do to stop myself cakewalking into town.

I came in to New York City having heard of one bar, one club, one building and one statue and I still felt like it was somewhere that I knew. Like it was the other half of my own city, with just a piece of ocean keeping us apart. New Orleans is different. I felt like I knew a lot, and I suddenly realise I know nothing. I know enough about Mardi Gras to know that it's on Pancake Day, so that's been and gone. I know that they eat jambalaya, and I don't know what that it is. Same goes for crawfish pie and file gumbo. I know about Louis Armstrong, but even though Satchmo only died three years ago, it's more like forty since he left town. I was singing Fats Domino earlier, but I haven't heard of him for a long while. I know Eric Burdon from Newcastle-On-Tyne singing about the house called the Rising Sun, Gary U.S. Bonds, Freddie Cannon, The Allman Brothers and Creedence Clearwater Revival all singing about New Orleans, Arlo Guthrie, the son of Woody, riding the train from Chicago, and not one of them coming from anywhere near the old Crescent city.

A couple of things I do know. One is that there is a mistaken belief that the blues hails from New Orleans. That's on account of the city sitting right at the heart of the Mississippi Delta, and people thinking that's where the delta blues comes from. Easy mistake to make, but the people of Mississippi call the delta area the land caught between the great river and another river, the Yazoo. That's a couple of hundred miles upstream. I read the backs of a lot of LP covers those Saturday mornings when I was hanging round Collett's. Never think I was wasting my time. Not me, mister. No, Memphis and North Mississippi are the blues, New Orleans is jazz. But what jazz?

For a long time I never cared for jazz because I didn't know it. Back when I was eleven and twelve, before the Beatles made it, there was a craze in England for old time jazz, which went under the name of trad. Old geezers in bowler hats and waistcoats gave themselves names like Bill Stickers and his Storyville Stompers, and for a short while monopolised every television variety programme going. The moment the groups crashed the scene they sunk like a stone. So that was jazz for me, and seeing an old black man called Louis Armstrong mugging and clowning on Sunday Night at the Palladium did nothing to change my mind. In sixty eight, that year again, I found myself in an art gallery in Amsterdam. I can't remember what took me there, but you can bet it was wearing a very short skirt. We watched some slide show of trendy pop art images, but I lost interest after the first few minutes because I was entranced by the accompanying music, music that I had never heard before. I had always instinctively liked music that was solid, with a backbeat and an obvious structure. This music was fluid. It flowed like water, shapeless yet perfectly formed, and was as subtle and rich and with the hidden depths of the finest wine. I hung on to the end of the slide show hoping that the music would get a credit. It did. Kind Of Blue, by Miles Davis.

When I got back to London I went out and bought the album the next day. Then I discovered other jazz players, John Coltrane, Charlie Parker and Charles Mingus. I probably know too much about music. Julie certainly thought so. What I like about jazz, the great artists anyway, who are the only ones I know, is that I don't know anything about it at all. I don't listen to it that often, but when I do I lose myself in it completely. It still flows like crystal water, so that Kind Of Blue sounds different every time I listen to it.

What I have learned since is that Satchmo Armstrong was a serious player when he was a young man playing in the joints and brothels of this old city, and then when he made the first jazz records up in New York and Chicago. He more or less invented the music that led to Bird and 'Trane and Miles, as surely as it led to the old English lags I hated when I was a kid. Maybe New Orleans will reveal some of its secrets to me. More than likely it won't, but I intend to have some fun finding out. I check into an old hotel, pull on a clean t-shirt, pull out a fresh pack of Disque Bleu and make my way down to the French Quarter.

On Bourbon Street the narrow pavement is crowded all the way along, but outside one doorway it's even more thronged on account of there's no one moving. This whole street is bars, clubs and restaurants, with tourists making their slow progress cruising the sidewalk in both directions while girls periodically pop out of upstairs windows on swings, like cuckoos out of clocks. Outside this particular club there's a poster of a white guy in a tuxedo.

"Frankie Ford. Sea Cruise."

As far as I know, everyone in the whole world must know that song. Inside the door of the club, about ten feet inside to be precise, sitting at the piano facing out to the street is the man on the poster. Frankie Ford, in the flesh. Mid thirties, which would figure, blondish hair a little like Jerry Lee, and get this, he's actually singing Sea Cruise, he's

89

singing it right now, for anyone passing by or hanging out on this sidewalk to hear. Sneaking a look inside the club I instantly decide that it's too much of a tourist trap to be my kind of place. Frankie finishes Sea Cruise to a ripple of applause and starts another number. It sounds like Sea Cruise without the hook. I decide that this snapshot magic moment will stay with me if not forever then almost that long, and move on down the street.

I go no more than twenty yards down the street before the whole experience is repeated. This time the singer is even nearer to the door, and being a considerably larger man it feels as if he's right there on the street with me. No one hit wonder this guy. Mr Clarence "Frogman" Henry, no less. So called because he could sing like a frog, which is as good a reason as any. He even had out and out pop hits in Britain in the sixties, and appeared on Thank Your Lucky Stars. Now he's playing what sounds like real down home New Orleans R & B, and is looking impossibly young. Frogman Henry's first big record was called 'Ain't Got No Home' and it was recorded so long ago that Buddy Holly even covered it when he was still back in Lubbock. It may be true that Clarence "Frogman" Henry didn't have a home at one time, but I doubt it. He looks as happy as a man could be, and right at home in this city, in this street and in this club, although he's almost more on the sidewalk than in the club. I still don't go in, but this time I linger on the pavement a little longer.

I picked the hotel out of one JW's brochures. The words historic and traditional should have been a warning. In the daytime, when I was still full of the excitement of getting here, I might have said it had seen better days but still had a faded elegance, a certain funky charm. At three am, when I'm tired and more than a little drunk, it feels like a mistake. Cockroaches are running wild, there's a spider in the sink, and I swear I saw a lizard disappear into a crack in the wall when I came in. I doze fitfully till seven before I give up and turn on the TV. There's no picture to speak of, but the tinny little speaker is more than adequate. The Supreme Court has ruled that Nixon must hand over the tape recordings of sixty four White House conversations. Da Prez argued that he didn't have to purely on account of the fact that he is Da Prez, executive privilege being the precise term used, but the Supreme Court didn't wear it. The question appears to be how much longer he can stick around. Not for much longer would appear to be the answer. I stand under the tepid trickle which passes for a shower in this hotel, throw on a clean t-shirt and head up St Charles Avenue in the direction of St Peter St.

You have to queue to get into Preservation Hall, and then you pay five dollars, and then when you do get in you can't get a beer. You sit patiently with a bunch of other tourists, and wait until a group of old gentlemen take the stage to polite applause and begin to play old style New Orleans jazz. What's special about this place is that the musicians are the same guys who played the music back in the twenties. Well not all of them, a lot of them are dead. Satchmo's dead, King Oliver is long dead, and so are many of the countless and nameless others. These are some of the survivors. They all look to be in their seventies, and a couple of them look older than that.

I never even thought of seeing any jazz in New York. Like I said, I look on that music as a place I go to occasionally, and more importantly I didn't have the clothes with me. Live jazz to me is a sharp suit and Saturday night at Ronnie's digging Sonny Rollins or Rahsan Roland Kirk. In New York I was a visitor. In New Orleans I'm a tourist and I would be happy to do what tourists do, if it wasn't for the fact that these tourists here would all prefer to talk about Watergate, and what part of Indiana they're from, and Watergate, and how much you paying for gas in your neck of the woods, and Watergate again. I try and block it out and conjure up a time half a century ago, imaging a room filled with blood, beer, sawdust and raucous laughter, with the girls competing with each other down at the front trying to catch the young bucks eyes. Back then the street girls used to fight for the honour of carrying these guys' horns down the street when it was parade time. In 1974 you can see that there is still some occasional spark there. These old men are playing for themselves and each other. In the right place they could still do it. Sadly this museum isn't it. I give it half an hour before taking my leave.

So I'm in a bar on Royal Street on Thursday night minding my own business, when this girl comes over. She looks vaguely familiar.
"Excuse me. Weren't you on the boat today?"
Bang to rights, I did indeed follow JW's suggestion and take a little cruise on the big river. Once you've mooched around the French Quarter for a while and taken a ride on the streetcar, there doesn't seem to be a whole lot to do in this town during the day other than drink, and I did more than enough of that yesterday. I regretted it instantly. Taking the boat that is, not the drinking. Last time I was on

the water I visited the green lady. That was a tourist trip, but it still seemed as if everyone had a noble purpose for being there. As far as I could see the only reason for taking this particular excursion was to stay out of the sun for a while, wear bad clothes, and talk about Watergate and gas prices. There were two girls on the boat, and they were doing none of those things except staying out of the sun, and now they are in this bar and inviting me to join them at their table. Well, hello.

The girl who came over is Pamela Jo, late twenties, short blonde hair, Scandinavian looking. Not bad at all. Her friend is June, older, darker, not bad, but not as nice as Pamela Jo. They're on vacation from Minneapolis. Pamela Jo is wearing a cream mini-dress with a chain belt, just like the ones the girls in London would wear to the disco or the office five years ago

"So did you come down the river?"

The Mississippi winds practically the length of the whole United States, north to south. They could also have hit Highway Sixty One which does the same. Obviously they did neither.

"No, we took a plane."

Well I rather thought you would. There's a guy with them who has latched on to June, name of Bill, mid-thirties, businessman from Wilmington, Delaware. Bill is wearing his golf gear. He looks out of place in this bar. Come to think of it he would look out of place anywhere, the golf course included. Still, I'm glad he's here, because he makes me look good, comparatively speaking, and I can see that Pamela Jo is pleased that I'm at the table.

"We thought maybe you were from Europe" says Pamela Jo.

"Well so I am." I reply reassuringly.

Cue puzzled frown. "I thought you said you were from England." Cue geography lesson.

"Well, we're really from Europe. My family are from Sweden, and June's came originally from Norway."

I'm tempted to recite a poem I once heard about a young woman from Norway who got her foot caught in a doorway, but rein myself in just in time. Pamela Jo looks like she's in the mood for a little holiday fun, and there's no need to be too much of a smart alec. I think of something else.

"So we're a regular little Abba then. Me and Bill can be Bjorn and Benny."

92

If Benny is the weird looking guy who plays keyboards, which I think he is, then I will be Bjorn. They don't know Abba. Lived their whole lives without ever seeing the Eurovision Song Contest. Pamela Jo continues with her line of questioning.

"No, we thought you were German or something. Like you didn't speak English you know, because you didn't speak. Why didn't you come over and talk to us?"

She's smiling but I can tell that it's a genuine question.

"My dear young lady, where I come from it is considered very bad form to engage in conversation unless one has been formally introduced."

She likes that one. I thought she would.

Bill gets a round in. They're all drinking tequila sunrises so I join them. The girls have been knocking them back ever since they got off the boat, which was five hours ago. By the time Bill gets back from the bar a band has started playing, which makes conversation more of a struggle. Pamela Jo leans forward to heard what I'm saying and rests her hand on my thigh rather longer than she needed to if she needed to at all, which she didn't. I get a round in, and when I get back Bill has an idea. They're all staying at the Holiday Inn. That's where he met the girls. Bill thinks that we should go back and have a drink in the lounge of the Holiday Inn, on account of it being quieter. The kind of place I try and avoid like the plague, but on this occasion I don't need asking twice.

I've never set foot in a Holiday Inn before, but I feel like I've been here a thousand times already. It's that sort of place. No matter. Bill gets another round of sunrises in. Fifteen minutes later I reciprocate, although I'm getting a little worried as to whether Pamela Jo is going to last the course, seeing as how it's as much as she can do to stop falling out of her chair. There's nothing hip about either of these girls, Pamela is a secretary in a patent agents, and June does something equally exciting. Then Bill leans forward conspiratorially, and saves the day in spectacular and most unexpected fashion.

"Why don't we go back to my room? I've got some really good cocaine."

Bill, I didn't know you had it in you, son. I don't say anything, but I have to admit that I am more than a little wary of his kind offer, alcohol always being my particular drug of choice. In London, Coke has always been seen as the property of the rich, rock stars and the like. It is most definitely classified as class A, and I can't say that it has ever been in my vicinity. I heard my dear friends David and Neil talking about it in New York the other week, but I was never offered any. Still, there's a first time for everything.

In New Orleans even the Holiday Inn has a piano player in the lounge. As we get up to leave he's playing a song that was out last year called Such A Night, not the Elvis song. The chorus goes 'If I don't do it somebody else will', repeated ad infinitum. He sings that line while we're walking towards the elevator, and I can see that he's looking straight at me.

The room is on the third floor. Bill and June sit on the bed, Pamela Jo is slumped in what could loosely termed as the armchair, and I've pulled up the desk chair. Bill has placed the bedside table between us. He theatrically pulls a small shaving case from his suitcase and produces a tiny phial of white powder. He puts a sheet of paper on the table, and shakes a good measure of the powder on to the paper. Then he produces an American Express card, the first one I have ever seen, and shapes the cocaine into lines. He then bends down to the table, puts his finger to one nostril and hoovers up one of the lines with the other. The girls follow suit, and it is apparent that this is not a new experience for them. Then it's my turn.

My first impression is that I have inhaled concentrated peppermint but without the taste of the mint. Instantly my senses feel three times as sharp, and my head is clearer than it's ever been. I feel like my eyes are on stalks and they're all over Pamela Jo, who is now looking like the horniest bitch in the world. The impact it has on her is quite profound also. Suddenly she looks like she doesn't need to sleep for a year, which is exactly how I'm feeling. She's looking right back at me with flying eyes. Bill is talking nine to the dozen but we're not listening. Pamela Jo looks away for a second to exchange a secret glance with June. They nod and laugh. Pamela stands up and says to no one in particular,

I'm going back to my room now."

Then she takes me by the hand and wordlessly leads me through the door and down the corridor.

So, in Room 327 of the New Orleans Downtown Holiday Inn I officially sink the sausage for the first time on American soil. It's sex of the very best kind, pure and lustful, untainted by secrets, lies or compromise. After the deed is done Pamela Jo wants to talk. Usually in this situation I want to split as soon as decently possible, and if that's not possible then indecently, but we're both still buzzing and

I'm not going anywhere, not yet anyway. She's twenty eight and worried that she can see thirty, Minneapolis is boring, her job's boring, she was going with a guy for six years but they've split up, she's never done this before, she's fantasised about having an English boyfriend since she saw The Beatles on Ed Sullivan, oh and John is her favourite, and she's never done this before, really. I tell her I always find the girls who like John best are the most interesting. Girls who like Paul lean towards the superficial. Boys with guitars like George, and Mums like Ringo. She talks some more and I listen, and when she's done we make love again. Not a term I use lightly, but that is how it is in this room that I will never be in again with this woman I will never see again, with the drug still coursing through our veins, and thinking about nothing else other than giving each other everything we've got and making it last a long, long time. And then we are both satisfied and physically spent, and the tequila finally catches up with her, and at five am I realise I will never hear her voice again unless I stay in this hotel room until midday at least. I do the only thing I can, which is to get dressed, leave the room as quietly as possible, though I don't know why because nothing will wake her now, take the stairs down to reception and walk out on to Canal St. There are plenty of people about even at this hour as I make my way through the still black night.

Back in the old hotel I stand under the lukewarm shower for the last time. As the water slowly trickles down on me I find myself wanting Pamela Jo again, even though I surely had more than my fill. I know sleep is impossible. I had paid for three nights here with an option to stay on for the weekend, but I know I am done with New Orleans. I feel like a tourist here. I know that more than anywhere New Orleans has a soul. I think that maybe the reason it still does is because it keeps it so well hid. Somewhere in this city there's a heart and a soul hidden beneath all the bullshit which keeps it alive. Three days isn't nearly long enough to find it, but stick around long enough and you surely would. One day I will. You could say the same thing about me, I guess. I wait until the shower gives up the ghost before I dress and pack. I splash my face with cold water which is warmer than the hot, and make my way down to the Greyhound station in good time for the first bus to Baton Rouge.

Listen Pamela, I really would have liked to stayed until you woke up, had a shower together, maybe have gone for a leisurely lunch in the

French Quarter, got your address and promised to write, but it was never meant to be. So please don't think badly of me.

Don't think badly of me, Julie. Don't think badly of me, Teresa. Don't think badly of me, Gino.

Ma.

The bus is three quarters full but silent on this steamy Friday morning. I'm still buzzing from the night's activities, but most of my fellow passengers choose sleep, lulled by the drivers gentle down home banter.

"Smokers at the back of the bus, but make sure what you're smokin's got writing on it."

I accept his invitation. One more packet of Disque Bleu for La Louisiane and then I'll save the rest for L.A. It's the least I can do to smoke French cigs as long as I'm around places with French names. One hour and forty five minutes later we are deposited in Baton Rouge. So much more inviting than Red Stick. It is now ten am. I breakfast on Gatorade and chocolate in the bus station, and without further delay follow the sign for the Mississippi Bridge. Some other time, Baton Rouge. Ten minutes later I'm looking deep down into the Big Muddy.

Heading west means bypassing Memphis and the Mississippi delta. I've already missed Nashville, seen nothing of the nation's capital at some unearthly hour, and cut through a corner of Florida without seeing as much as one beach. I'll catch them all next time. I'm twenty four. Twenty four and there's so much more. Today I feel I could live like this forever. My jeans are faded, but I'm not.

It takes a while to get a ride. There are times on the road when that can get to you, if you're feeling tired, hungry and friendless. Not today. If there is a comedown off that white powder it hasn't caught up with me yet. Everybody's my friend, it's just that some of them don't know it yet.

First friend of the day weighs in at around twenty stone, and sports the biggest black beard I've ever seen. A real old man of the mountains, or he would be if there were any mountains around here. Looks like I've found a bona fide Cajun.

"Well you're in coonass country now. You come all the way from England to coonass country."

He smiles, and shakes his head at the absurdity of it all.

"I'm going to Rayne. From there you can get a ride into Lake Charles easy enough, and then you're almost in Texas."

Sounds good to me.

"You ever heard the French music?"

There are definitely traces of France in his accent, like the way he tends to leave the final consonant off words, so Lake Charles becomes Lake Charle. The only reason I know better is because I know that song by The Band, 'Up on Cripple Creek'.

"Sure."

I have, too. Another part of my musical education. He fiddles with the dial, and the infectious sound of fiddles and accordions, and high lonesome voices singing in unintelligible French comes pouring out of his little speaker. Immediately it feels like we are in a completely different country. We drive in to a small town, and he pulls up on the main street.

"This is Breaux Bridge. I got a little business to take of. I'll be back in ten minute."

He points to the keys in the ignition.

"You know how to shift it if you have to?"

"What?"

"Maybe someone want to unload or something. You know how to shift it?"

Standard pick up, regular gearbox, sure I know how to shift it. Or how to steal it, if I was crazy enough to even think about it.

When my man gets back, which is a lot longer than ten minutes - seems like they have a more continental take on time - he has an idea.

"You like the French music, why don't you let Texas wait for a couple of days? I can drop you in Lafayette. That's where everything happens in coonass country. Plenty of places to stay, plenty places to eat. Maybe tomorrow you get yourself a ride up to Mamou, go to Fred's Lounge. Damn shame to come to coonass country and not hear some French music. Texas is a big heap of nothing, anyway."

"Sounds good."

And so it does.

"I could take you to Rayne, but we ain't got nothing there. All we got there is the frog jumping competition, and that's been and gone."

Well it's too bad I missed it, but that's life. Twenty minutes later he drops me off on Main Street Lafayette, and hops off to Frog Town.

"Oh, country music has always had a big following in England. The big difference is that we don't have nearly as many radio stations as you do, so the music has always been a lot more part of the mainstream. There were always country records in the pop charts when I was growing up, people like Jim Reeves, Don Gibson and Roger Miller. The Beatles recorded a straight cover of a country song called Act Naturally, originally recorded by Buck Owens, I believe. Younger people in England have also become a lot more aware of country music through records by Bob Dylan and The Band, and also The Byrds, who have all been increasingly influenced by country music in recent years. We have a big country and western festival at Wembley Stadium every year, where the real keen fans get to dress the part, and go and see all the top acts. Johnny Cash, Don Williams, George Jones and Tammy Wynette have all played the Wembley festival in the last few years."

To be honest with you, I have no idea who has played that show this year or any other year. Wild horses wouldn't drag me anywhere near the place. Nothing wrong with the music you understand, but the place being packed with bus stop cowboys from Carlisle to Carshalton would take the edge off it for me.

"Well that's fascinating." says Molly Malone.

No, I'm not kidding, that's really her name. Well her radio name, at least. That's what I'm doing this Friday afternoon; I'm on the radio talking about country music like it's the most natural thing in the world for me to do.

I walked along Main Street and saw a small building that I would have never have known was a radio station if it wasn't for the sign in the window. It occurred to me that if this town had a jumping music scene, then someone there would surely be able to tell me the best place to catch it. The door opened to reveal a dark haired young woman wearing a cowgirl shirt, Wranglers, and the obligatory cowboy boots.

"Come in and sit down, I gotta change the music."

She slid behind a desk with a few knobs and levers on it, faded the record and leant in to the single microphone.

"That was Ronnie Milsap with Pure Love. You're listening to Molly Malone bringing you Louisiana country out of Lafayette. Now Tanya Tucker's got a question for you. She wants to know if you would lie with her in a field of stone."

Well, yes I would, since you ask.

So this is the first time I've ever been inside a radio station, and it's not how I imagined it. This is not the BBC. Molly plays records by Conway Twitty, Porter Wagoner and Dolly Parton, Loretta Lynn, Charlie Rich and Merle Haggard, and while they're playing we talk and smoke cigarettes. She doesn't have any records, all the music is on cassettes, and she just fades it in and out and announces who's playing. So we talk, and she sees that I can talk, and she thinks it might be fun to put me on air. I'm game for anything, me, and I'm warming to the task now.

"I myself am half Irish, and Country and Western music has always been massively popular there. This is no surprise as a lot of the content and the form of contemporary country music comes from Appalachian mountain music, which in turns derives directly from old Irish ballads"

I can see from Molly Malone's face that this is getting way too technical for her, and sure enough she cuts me off just as I'm hitting my stride.

"You've been listening to our special guest all the way from England, Frank Towns. Tell me Frank, is Hank Williams Junior big in England?"

"Oh sure" I lie. That'll be news for Hank if he's listening, which is unlikely unless he's within a twenty five mile radius of Lafayette. She puts on a track which sounds more like London pub rock. Making sure the fader's down, she whispers to me.

"Tell you the truth, I don't like any of this country shit."

Turns out that Molly isn't all alone here. There's an engineer called Buddy, who's been in the bar across the street for the last hour. There's not a whole lot of engineering needing doing in this little studio. He comes through the door bearing a smile, and equally welcome beers and cheeseburgers.

"Good to meet you, Frank. You sounded pretty good out there. Man, you know your stuff."

They had the radio on in the bar. I knew I was on the radio, and I knew that it was going out live, but I never really thought in terms of people listening to it. If I had I might have been nervous.

Molly and Buddy are a couple. I feel a slight pang of disappointment, but not too much. At a quarter to five Molly's relief arrives, a slim blonde wearing the same cowgirl uniform. At five o'clock she takes over.

"Good afternoon everybody, and welcome to drivetime with Marie-Carol Fontaine."

Then Buddy says the words that I believe I've heard before somewhere.

"Hey Frank, why don't you come out and party with us tonight?"

Well it would be rude not to.

We adjourn to the bar across the street and trade stories. Neither of them are from Lafayette. Buddy's from Northern Louisiana, a place called Fereday, Jerry Lee Lewis's home town. Nice guy when he's sober, according to Buddy. Molly is from Mobile, the industrial city that I was glad to breeze by just three days ago. Her real name is Mary Malone, but everybody calls her Molly. Her grandfather came from County Clare and jumped ship in Mobile, never to leave. Buddy and Molly both moved around the country radio station circuit before they met each other in Lafayette. Never of them are in a hurry to leave, though Buddy does slightly hanker after a big job in Houston.

After a while we're joined by Marie-Carol Fontaine's boyfriend, Rich. He's a singer and guitarist with his own group, the Rich Henry Band. They've got a gig tonight in Crowley, about twenty five miles down the highway. Tomorrow night they're playing in Lafayette. It is taken as read that I will be there. I believe I will, too. Already I feel more at home than I did in New Orleans. Marie-Carol Fontaine finishes her drivetime stint, and joins us for one, before her and Rich head off to Crowley.

"OK" says Buddy, who is nothing if not an assertive kind of guy. "We got a real treat for you now."

We climb into Buddy's beat up old Plymouth and drive all of four hundred yards to another bar, bigger this time, with an amateurish poster stuck on the door.

TONITE ONLY : CLIFTON CHENIER.

Clifton Chenier. A name I vaguely remember from a record sleeve in a dusty rack in New Oxford Street. The King of the Zydeco Accordion. I never let myself think for one minute that any of those Saturday mornings I spent hanging round that shop were wasted.

The joint is already busy, and is full to the rafters within ten minutes of us getting there. We get special treatment on account of Molly being something of a local celebrity, and get a booth. It appears that Dixie beer doesn't extend the eighty miles from New Orleans to Lafayette, but Buddy orders up pitchers of some nameless brew which does the job well enough. I'm really in the mood by the time Clifton Chenier and his band hit the stage.

At first glance the guy is all pompadour, accordion and teeth. There's another fellow with him who can only be his brother and may possibly be his twin, and he's got this metal washboard kind of contraption strapped to his chest. The rest of the group are a more conventional electric guitar, bass and drums. They kick off with a song I know well, Key to the Highway, recorded by everyone from Broonzy to Clapton, but it's never sounded like this.

These guys can play anything. Tonight they've got a Louisiana Friday night dance hall crowd and their job is to get them moving and get them drinking, not that they need much encouragement. They play a few more blues with the accordion trilling all over the rhythm section's tight twelve bar groove, he sings a few songs in raw French, and they play impossibly infectious dance numbers which get the whole place jumping. We jump out of the booth, and Molly's dancing with Buddy and she's dancing with me, and everyone in the whole joint is dancing with each other and by themselves, and brother Cleveland is rattling his metal washboard like a one man tin can army, and Clifton himself keeps shouting out the words although all you can pick out is the title, "Got a Pepper in my Shoe" over and over again, with beer spilling and feet flying, and me feeling like I've never been more alive and that when music is like this it's a more powerful drug even than the cocaine which had me flying less than twenty four hours ago.

The band's set finishes, and they amble off stage to no great applause while the punters carry on with their Friday night. Just another night for a Zydeco band. We get more pitchers to replace the sweat, and before I know it it's three am and closing time.

Buddy and Molly's apartment is barely furnished, but has a lived in feel to it. Buddy puts on a great compilation Rhythm and Blues album with tracks by Slim Harpo, Lightnin' Slim and Lazy Lester, local boys all, and then he takes out his stash and rolls three joints.

The unlocked door opens, and for a paranoid moment I think it might be the cops, but it's Rich and Marie-Carol bearing a bottle of Jim

Beam. That sees us through to eight am, and I'm thinking sleep might be a good idea, but no, Buddy announces that we're off to Grand Mamou to hear some more music. Grand Mamou, where the old man of the mountains told me I should go. One cup of coffee, and then it's back in the Plymouth.

We drive through flat land and narrow straight roads with little traffic apart from the occasional dilapidated pickup truck going towards Lafayette. The sky is overcast and the cloud cover is low, but it's already sticky at this early hour. Then we pull on to a side road which is little more than a track, and we're outside a big old bar surrounded by a few small wooden houses.

"Welcome to Fred's Lounge" says Buddy.

Then we're drinking redeye for breakfast, beer and tomato juice in the same glass. There's already what looks like a couple of hundred people in, mainly an older crowd but not exclusively so, and at 9am without further ado the music starts.

It's a whole different scene to last night. The musicians are all white, even older than Clifton, and they're playing acoustic instruments, fiddle, accordion, and acoustic guitar. There's even an old boy with a triangle, an instrument which I once wielded with distinction myself in a school concert when I was seven.

"All these guys will have jobs" says Buddy. "Farmers, mechanics, furniture makers. They just play at weekends."

There's something here which reminds me of sessions I've seen in pubs back in Ireland. That lonesome sound which is totally of the players, yet also manages to appear somehow otherworldly, as though it's passing down through the ages and only temporarily inhabiting these musicians. This mysterious music which must have originated somewhere in rural France, and picked up a hell of a lot more on the way via Canada, before the Arcadians were run out of the country by the British and somehow found their way down to the backwaters of Louisiana.

Six redeyes later it's twelve o'clock, and it's back to Lafayette for lunch, and time for me to find out what jambalaya and crawfish pie are all about. It ranks among the best food I've ever eaten in my life, and I'm not even that hungry. Then it's back to the apartment to watch cartoons, and before I know it darkness has fallen and we're out again, this time to see Rich's band.

Rich is playing in a bar on the edge of town, smaller and considerably rougher than the dance hall or Fred's Lounge. The band plays for an hour followed by a twenty minute break. They then play another set, which may or may not be identical to the first one. The band can play, but there's not a whole lot of imagination put into their repertoire, which consists of fast blues in the same key, with the occasional slow blues in the same key thrown in for variety. This routine goes on till three am, when the band stops playing and immediately starts packing up the gear. The bass player and drummer pick up their stuff and leave without ceremony, and Rich joins the rest of us. The club is still half full.

I tell Rich I enjoyed the show, which I did, sort of. What I don't tell him is that I would have enjoyed it a lot more if they had played for twenty minutes instead of getting on for six hours. Then the bar owner buys us all a drink. It's four am before we leave, and then there's breakfast and more cartoons, so it's almost midday before I'm finally allowed to crawl into the bed in Buddy and Molly's spare room.

I wake up to find there's nobody home. I turn on the radio and hear Molly introduce the new record by Olivia Newton-John. If you love me let me know, if you don't let it show. Molly works from two till five in the afternoons. It is quarter past three. I can remember going to the bathroom at some point, but other than that I seem to have slept for the best part of thirty hours. I stand under the shower for a good while, feeling like a dried out old plant that hasn't been watered for six months.

My hosts get home at five thirty.

"Well you slept good!"

Molly is smiling at me, and she looks relieved that I'm in good shape, like a big sister might. I thank them for their hospitality, and tell them I think I should be on my way in the morning. Buddy thinks I should rest up a while.

"The road can eat you up, man. Take it easy for a day or two."

I'm thinking that it's not the road that's likely to eat me up, but the distractions I fall into whenever I get off it. I graciously accept their invitation, and agree to stay another night and press on to Texas on Wednesday.

Tuesday afternoon I walk down to the bar next to the radio station and find Buddy sneaking out for a crafty beer. His job is as easy as it looks. This is a small station without too much equipment to fix. He's talking again about Houston, and the big stations there that will pay a lot more, but Molly likes it here. He talks about Houston as if it's some mythical place, rather than somewhere you can be in four hours, even if you obey the speed limit. He's fascinated when I tell him about the days of the pirate radio stations in England in the sixties, when a few bright sparks put big radio transmitters on ships moored just outside territorial waters and gave Britain a taste of American style pop radio for the first time. They didn't last too long, but it was long enough for the BBC to cotton on to the fact that it was time to get with it. They hired most of the DJs and let them do their thing. I tell him how many of them are now major celebrities back home, host quiz shows, get to open supermarkets, the whole bit. Buddy smiles ruefully at this. A DJ was what he wanted to be, but he never had enough gift of the gab. That's what you need on this side of the pond, unless you're a girl, and they have to develop a whole different style all together. He learned about electronics and became a sound engineer. He reckons there are enough radio stations in Louisiana and Texas. Someone will always be hiring.

In the evening Buddy is a little morose, and gets out a bottle of Wild Turkey. I blame myself for making him think about lost opportunities. Eight years ago he would have been the age I am now. Not too young to have signed up for Radio Caroline with Emperor Rosko and the gang. Buddy finishes off the bottle, with a little help from me. Molly, who would appear to be a completely different person from Monday to Friday, makes clear her disapproval of Buddy drinking hard liquor on a week night. There's a tension between them that I feel wouldn't be there if I wasn't. If I had any doubt that I would be leaving in the morning, it's gone now.

Buddy gives me a ride down to the highway before he goes to work. It's not yet nine. I don't manage to set my eyes on Molly Malone one last time, on account of her still being asleep.

"Good luck, old buddy" says Buddy. "Send me a postcard from Houston."

Not send me a postcard from London, or Hollywood even, but Houston. I realise now that Buddy's never going to make it to Houston. If he was serious he would take the day off and drive me there now. We would be there by lunchtime, he could hit the big radio stations in the afternoon, get hired, drive back to Lafayette and give his notice the next day. Instead Houston will continue to serve as some distant horizon on the edge of his world of small town radio and increasingly desperate weekends with sad eyed Rich, who may have got all his blues licks down, but who knows in his heart of hearts that he hasn't the imagination to write his own music or even to make it out of Lafayette. Still, if you had to spend your whole life in one town you could do a lot worse. Buddy puts the old Plymouth into a U-turn and drives back towards town with a single wave. I've been off the road for four days and it's good to be back.

Chapter Seven: It's Going To Take Some Time

I get a ride almost straight away. Dark blue Cadillac, driver about thirty, moustache, suit and tie. Going to Beaumont, Texas which is more than halfway to Houston. I'm back on track.

"So you're going to be in the country while history is being made. We're gonna impeach our president, the first time ever."

"You think that's going to happen?"

"I know that's gonna happen! Ain't you seen no news lately?"

I tell him I've been following the Watergate business with interest but I haven't seen the news for nearly a week.

"Well that figures if you've been down in this Cajun country. Everywhere in the whole country people ain't talking about nothin' else. Round here's different. These people don't really consider themselves part of the United States. I bet if you'd been here on the Fourth of July you wouldn't know it was any different to any other day. Since you're interested, the House Judiciary Committee have adopted the articles of impeachment. He can either resign or wait for the legal process to take effect. Either way we're going to have a new President this summer, and that's for sure. Sonofabitch been lying through his teeth for years. That's not where he screwed up, though."

"He got found out, right?"

"You got it. Politicians all lie like hell, only the stupid ones get found out, and they ain't got no business being President."

My driver visibly relaxes now, thinking I'm on his wavelength.
"I'm Axel Froehling from Beaumont, Texas. Good to have you on board. I'm in the real estate business. I just tied up a little deal yesterday down in Baton Rouge. I should have been back last night, but I found myself a little poontang down there. Called my wife, told her I had a late meeting, thought it better to stay over. Done it a thousand times before. So this is your first time in Texas? You'll find it different to Louisiana. We haven't got all the mixed up races like they've got."

I try changing the subject. "Any more about Patty Hearst?"

"Not that I know of." He thinks for a second. "People making a lot of fuss about that Patty Hearst because of who her daddy is, but she's just the first of many. Give it a year or so, everybody in this whole country is going to be in one private army or another. She's only doing what she thinks she has to in order to survive. We're all going to have to decide what side we're on soon enough, that's for sure."

That sounds like a line of conversation which is interesting if a little paranoid, but now Axel switches it back, as I knew he surely would

"Like I said, Texas is different to Louisiana. In Texas we got black and we got white. And Texas isn't exactly what you would call a nigger lovin' state." He pauses for effect. "I'm from German stock myself. There's a lot of us in Texas. We're the original Anglo Saxons."

Louisiana is rolling past the window. Rayne, where there were no sign of any frogs, and Lake Charles where I didn't spot one signpost for Cripple Creek. One day I will return to this mysterious country within a country. Whether they'll still be singing songs in seventeenth century French is open to question. Axel is telling me how Germans are good hard working people, which I won't dispute, although it does occur to me that this particular German might have been happier if his grandparents had never left home and he had been born thirty years earlier. Some things you think but don't say. Still, we've got a way to go yet before we reach Texas, and I don't think Axel's likely to shoot me if I disagree with him. I try a little flattery.

"Yeah, but Axel you're an intelligent and clearly a successful man. You must know that one race isn't naturally superior to another."

"Well thanks, but that's exactly what I do know. I'll tell you something else as well, my friend. The white race is going soft in this country. I'm working now so I can make as much money as I can, and in a couple of years I'm getting out of Texas before it goes the same way as Louisiana."

"Where would you go?"

"Idaho. That's good country. You can still put up on a piece of land there and make a claim. Homesteading, they call it. Grow your own food, put a big fence around your land, get a couple of shotguns. No blacks, no Mexicans, just a little piece of heaven on earth. That's what I'm planning for me and my family."

I ponder this for a second. "Well if there's no blacks and no Mexicans, why do you need the fence and the gun?"

Axel's looking at me like I'm much too much the smartarse.

"What are you, a goddam hippy?"

I can't resist this one. "Well you sound like a hippy yourself, Axel! Getting back to nature, growing your own food. It's time for us to get back to the garden, Woodstock generation. You've just got a slightly different take on it, that's all."

I think I might be pushing him too far now. I'm in the man's car, after all.

"I'm just kidding you, man." I say in my best American. "Maybe we can just agree to disagree."

A reluctant smile slowly comes across his face.

"Well we sure do that, my friend. We sure do that."

Then we're crossing the state line, and I'm in the Lone Star state.

"Say goodbye to the South" says Axel. "And say hello to the West."

We drive the twenty miles or so from the state line to Beaumont in silence, agreeing to disagree. I can't have pissed off Axel too much, as he graciously goes out of his way to leave me back on the highway on the other side of town.

"Ain't nothing in Beaumont. You're best off getting straight to Houston."

With that I'm back on the side of the road and Axel's gone, back to tell a story to his long suffering wife. I imagine him being earlier than she expected, and finding a Mexican gardener giving her a seeing to as he walks through the door. Then I realise that he wouldn't have a gardener. Grow your own man is old Axel.

An Oldsmobile glides to a halt, and I've got my next ride. Mid thirties, tan suit, bootlace tie, cowboy boots and a cowboy hat, the crown creasing slightly against the roof. Dionne Warwicke is on the car stereo. I'm tempted to ask if he knows the way to San Jose, but I don't want to risk being left by the side of the road for another hour, so I keep that one to myself.

"Well you're a long way from home son. Sure I'll take you to Houston. I'll drop you right downtown if you want."

Sounds good to me.

"Hi, I'm Jerry Fell. I'm in the insurance business."

He hands me his business card, which tells me that his name is Jerry Fell and he is in the insurance business. Works for a company in

Dallas. My conversation with Axel was starting to get interesting until it hit the wall, so I'm ready to chat.

"You're not about to try and sell me some are you?"

"You're in this business son, and you're always in this business, you know what I'm saying?"

I do know what you're saying Jerry, and I make a mental note to add insurance salesman to the long list of professions of which I never want to have any part. Jerry is dressed like a cowboy, but a bit of a soft one. If he had the glasses he would be the Milky Bar Kid thirty years on.

"You trying to tell me you're a bad driver? Selling me insurance as soon as I get in your car?"

"No. I'm a good driver. I'm very careful."

He sounds hurt. "Sorry Jerry, I was just kidding. I really appreciate you picking me up."

Maybe he should put "No sense of humour" in big bold letters on his card. I've seen enough episodes of Bilko to know that Americans do have a sense of humour, at least some of them do, it's just a little different. He thinks it over for about a minute.

"We got this fifty five speed limit now. People take it very seriously. I click in my cruise control at fifty four and sit back and enjoy the ride."

"You click in your what?"

"Y'all don't have cruise control over in England?"

He tells me what cruise control is. I tell him there are probably only two roads in England where you would ever use it.

"Guess that's two things you need to get used to down here. That and us saying y'all. We thought they would relax the speed limit when those A-rabs lifted that embargo a few months back, but it seems like it suits a lot of people to keep it. Did they lift the embargo in Europe?"

Pronounced Yoorp. I could tell him that I have hardly left London in two years and I haven't got a clue, but I tell him with some kind of authority that yes, things are the same in Yoorp.

Jerry tells me a little about himself. He's from Fort Worth originally and now lives in Dallas. Had an early morning meeting in Beaumont so stayed overnight, now he's on his way to another meeting in Houston.

"Ain't nothing to keep a body in Beaumont longer than he needs to be there."

This appears to be the popular view.

"I like the scene in Dallas. Houston is good too, but you have to know it."

Something about the way he says "scene" strikes me as a little creepy. New York has a scene, London has a scene. Dallas should have bars, steakhouses and men with big hats.

The tape comes to an end, and we ride in silence for a while before he replaces it with The Carpenters. It would be perfect if he were to stop talking now, and let me relax in this comfortable car and listen to Karen all the way to Houston, but that's not going to happen.

"I guess this isn't really your kind of music. I'm sure you prefer the Rolling Stones and all those groups. I like a little more easy style myself."

I tell him I love the Rolling Stones, but I like the Carpenters and Dionne Warwicke as well. I tell him I like the Carpenters so much I went to see them once at The Talk of The Town, which is true. I'm transported back four thousand miles and twelve months before I am pulled sharply back to the present.

"I hope you don't mind me asking you this Frank, but what's the gay scene like in London?"

My easy listening is now disturbed by big red warning lights flashing.

"Er, I don't know really."

"They have their own bars don't they?"

"Er, yeah" I mumble.

"Don't get me wrong, I'm not gay myself, but I've got a lot of gay friends in Dallas and I really enjoy their company."

I flashback to Greenwich Village and I hear the words of my good friend David. *"All those cowboys down in Texas are faggots anyway. They hate themselves for it and they hate everybody else too."*

I make another mental note, this one being to be very careful should I ever find myself in Dallas. Jerry changes the subject, for the moment anyway.

"What car do you drive at home, Frank?"

"A Ford Capri" I reply brightly.

The truth is I have only ever owned one car, and it wasn't a Ford Capri, it was a Mk 1 Cortina, vintage nineteen sixty three. It lasted all of six weeks before I suffered a little mishap. The other Frank drives a Ford Capri, preferably a yellow one. The Frank who hasn't been unveiled yet, the one who may go back home and get a sales rep job some time I don't know when.

"Can't say I've heard of that model. Would you like to drive this car?"

Sure I would, Jerry. I only packed my licence at the last minute as another piece of I.D. Somebody told me that up in the hills they don't know what passports are. I don't tell Jerry that I haven't been behind the wheel for two years, or that I have never driven an automatic. He pulls over to the side of the road, gets out of the car and walks round to the passenger side while I slide across to the driver's seat. The vehicle takes me a little by surprise when it creeps away as soon as I let the brake off, but after that it rides like a dream. Thirty seconds later Jerry tells me I'm doing seventy.

"Bring it down to fifty four and put the cruise control on."

He shows me the button.

"Don't worry, it switches off whenever you touch the pedals."

Within five minutes I feel like I've been cruising these highways for years. The speed limit makes sure that it's not exactly Maybelline, but it's comfortable. Jerry is speaking.

"Like I was saying I'm not gay myself. I've got a lot of friends who are, and I've been to bed with some of them, sure I have. I just laid back and enjoyed it. There ain't nothing wrong with it Frank, really. You're a good looking young fella. You should enjoy yourself with men, women, whatever turns you on. Just enjoy it."

There's not a lot you can say to that, so I concentrate on the road and count down the miles to Houston. Thirty, twenty five, ten. Five miles to go, and I'm listening to Karen singing about how it's going to take some time to get in shape when Jerry's hand is on my thigh, and he says "Frank, I hope you don't mind me saying this, but I would really like to-"

"I think I'll walk the rest of the way, thanks Jerry"

I check the mirror, indicate, and then pull over to the side of the road as carefully as if I'm taking my driving test, except the car doesn't stop as I want it to, so I have to jam on the hand brake. I calmly lean back and open the rear door and push my bag on to the blacktop before taking off the seat belt, opening the door, and getting out of the car. I pick up my bag and set off down the highway without a word, while Karen's still singing about the young trees in the winter time.

Jerry gets out of the car but doesn't attempt to follow.

"Now come on fella, we can talk about this. Just a little misunderstanding here, is all. At least let me give you a ride into the city."

"Thanks for the lift, cowboy" I say without turning my head, and Jerry walks round to the driver's side, gets in and drives off without further word. I watch him go past me, and I am relieved to see that his eyes are fixed firmly on the following traffic in the mirror, and not on me. Careful driver, old Jerry.

Susan Hopkins was my first girlfriend. I left school in sixty six and she left a year later, and as is the way with girls she grew up a lot quicker. There was no doubt that I was still a kid, and even if I wasn't she was always going to think of me as the grubby little boy trying to get his hands in her pants. Still, we survived the transition from back of the bike shed fumblings to all grown up working teenagers surprisingly well for a while, until one Saturday morning when I saw her getting out of a Sunbeam Alpine with some flash Harry. Turned out to be some bloke from her office who was clearly keen on giving her some out of hours dictation. My pride was hurt a little, but I wasn't that bothered, if truth be told. After all, it was bound to happen sooner or later.

Our break up came just a couple of weeks after my success with the sixth former on the day of the demo, something I repeated round her posh house the following weekend while her parents were away, so I wasn't really in a position to say much. If you're going to have double standards then you had better work twice as hard to maintain them. This all took place during my brief spell at the printers, and it was shortly after this that I hit the road for my first European trip. I bought a corduroy cap and the finest pair of boots that R Soles of the Kings Road could provide, and set the heels a-wandering.

I caught the boat train to Amsterdam, which was hippie heaven then, and quite possibly still is. I spent my days in the Vondel Park, my nights in the Club Paradiso, and lived on meatballs in a student cafe. Things were very different when I moved on to Paris, and found a city still reeling from the student riots, and where les flics viewed anyone in jeans as a threat to state security. Bad vibes all round. From there to San Tropez, where a citron presse cost more than my daily budget. I didn't spend too much time in France that year. I spent a lot longer in Spain, which away from the Costas felt like a country frozen in time, held in Franco's iron grip since the civil war. Once I learned not to make eye contact with the flat hatted policemen, I found that the people were as sunny as the weather, a few pesetas went a long way, and the living was easy. I reached the deep south, and spent some time in the wondrous old city of Granada, where I took a room in a hostal for the equivalent of seven shillings a night. I saw out the summer in the fishing village of Estepona, swimming by day, and drinking Bacardi rum at night until the money ran out.

When I got back in October I felt as if I had learned more in three months than I had ever learned at school. For a while I continued to live as if I was still on the road, in my mind if not in the here and now. Every day felt like a potential adventure, though not many of them turned out to be. A main squeeze wasn't really what I was looking for then. I always found the whole routine of having a steady girlfriend made too many demands on my time. Sure, I developed my boy about town skills, but I needed time to myself as well. I was deep into the blues by now, Robert Johnson, John Hurt and Blind Willie McTell, and there were a thousand books to read.

Come Friday evening I would leave my blues behind me and go to a club called Samantha's. Funnily enough, I found out some time later that five or six years previously it had been the home of the Ealing Blues Club, and it was here that Mick and Keith first met Brian Jones. They used to travel up from Kent every Friday by train and tube, which shows how keen they must have been. By my time it was sadly a lot less interesting, being your basic 60's discotheque, although the music was always good. It could hardly not be.

So I never met Brian Jones, God rest his soul, but I did meet Julie Grey. Her name was Grey and her eyes were green, and she had a way about her that I had never really encountered before. It was as though she knew everything. I knew this was scarcely possible, but when those eyes met mine I felt instantly that she knew everything about me at least, which was intriguing, if not more than a little daunting. More than that she liked me, which was not that unusual thank you, but in a way it was, because it was as if she liked the real me, the me that nobody else knew, the me that I didn't even know myself. She would patiently allow me to practice all my lame patter and then politely ask me if I had finished. If I started going on too much about Charley Patton, or some obscure soul B-side, or even worse, my Christmas Humphreys book on Zen Buddhism, she would hold up her thumb and forefinger about a quarter of an inch apart and say "That much interesting, Frank, that much interesting."

She was the same age as me, three months older to be precise. She went to Sam's occasionally with her mates, and had something of a reputation among the blokes down there of being snooty, meaning that none of them had managed to get in her knickers, or anywhere near it. Perfect. I don't claim to be the wisest old owl on the block at twenty four, and I had even less sense when I was nineteen, but I wasn't stupid enough to let this one pass, so we became a couple. She lived with her Mum and Dad a fifteen minute bus ride away from my house, and her work place was even nearer. She was a secretary in a sales company just off the High Street. Her work mates were a lively crowd, and we would meet every Friday evening in the Six Bells. No more Samantha's. Sometimes we would go the cinema, other times to the Chinese restaurant. Regular boyfriend, girlfriend stuff. She made me wait ages before she let me have my way with her, but when she eventually did it made everything that had gone before seem like kid's stuff. Sorry, Susan. So I was more than happy, and Ma loved her as well.

My newly increased social life combined with a little pressure from Julie, exerted in her own quiet and logical way, meant that I needed a more steady income. I knew that my travelling days weren't over. My three month sojourn in sixty eight had only whetted my appetite, so I knew they weren't over, because they had hardly begun. On the other hand, there was no rush. I was not yet twenty and I thought I was going to live forever. I knew deep down that one day I would hit thirty and the game would be up, but that was far enough away to be as good as forever. So I got a job. I didn't fancy another office job, so I got myself a start at Victor Chandler's bookmakers as a trainee cashier. This seemed to amuse a few people, but I enjoyed it. It was a shock to the system having to work Saturdays, especially when we'd had a late one on Friday, which was every Friday, but I used to get Mondays off, so it wasn't so bad.

The one person who objected was my old man. He reckoned it would put me on a slippery slope being around gambling all day, which was a bit rich coming from him. Needless to say, I had long stopped listening to his opinions, if I had ever done so in the first place, and it turned out he was wrong, as he always was, because it had quite the reverse effect. Seeing three windows taking money and one paying out, told me what I knew anyway. It's a mugs game. What always amused me most was when a punter won big and slipped me a quid for a drink, like I had just paid them out of my own pocket. The boss cruised round town visiting his shops in a Roller. There's only one side of the bookie's window to be on, and I was on it. I had always been good at figures, and I picked it up quickly, working out the odds and stuff like that. Six months later and I was assistant manager.

So I'm earning a few bob, me and Julie are set fair, and everything in the garden is rosy. She's happy, I'm happy, her Mum's happy, so's mine, and so's Uncle Tom Cobley. I'm happy for a slightly different reason, which is that I know that none of it's going to last. Still, there were some times when I would forget that, and they were the best times of all.

My pal Keith, who is six months older than me, got married the week after his twenty first birthday. Sounds insane I know, but he was always that sort of bloke. Him and Linda were childhood sweethearts, inseparable since they were fourteen, so it seemed quite the natural thing to happen. Time has proved that it was too, as they've already knocked out two kids and have never been known to have a cross word, at least not in public. They got married on a beautiful summer's day, her dad splashed out on a hotel reception, and a good time was had by all. The old man put down a deposit on a house on a new estate in Langley, way out on the other side of London Airport. Three months later they invited us to dinner. The Scandinavian style furniture was new but it was cheap, and they served us spaghetti bolognese which we washed down with Blue Nun. You could laugh at them if you had a mind to, but we didn't, because there was such a warm atmosphere in the room that it felt like there was nowhere you would rather be, and it wasn't coming from the Belling two bar complete with imitation flickering flames either. I felt it, and Julie, who knew everything, was more than aware that I did. After dinner Linda put on her Carpenters LP.

"Did you know it's the bird who plays the drums?" I said.

"That much interesting, Frank" said Julie, but when the bird sang 'We've Only Just Begun', I looked at Julie, and she looked at me with those eyes, and if she had asked me there and then I would have gladly given up on every dream I had ever had. Since then I've always had a soft spot for the Carpenters. It's like another place I can go, though I wouldn't bother trying to explain that to a Skynyrd fan.

If a way of life like Keith and Linda's was something you could buy the occasional ticket for, like a day at Southend, or a rock festival, then I would be first in the queue. Pick a cosy evening in November, book it about three months in advance so you know you've got something to look forward to when the winter starts digging in. Except it doesn't work like that, does it? You have to live it every day and give stuff up to do it. When you don't start off with much, giving things up doesn't come easy. Julie, you know everything, so how come you didn't know that?

So it's going to take some time this time to get myself in shape. I know how you feel Karen, I know how you feel.

Chapter Eight: Way Out West

Don Hargreaves motions for two beers. "So does a cup of tea still cost a threepenny bit in a Lyons Corner House?"

He's surprised and a little disappointed when I tell him we don't have threepenny bits any more, or tanners, or half crowns, or florins. I think we may still have Lyons Corner Houses, but I'm not sure. I remember Ma would sometimes take us to one as a treat. We would have steak pie and mash followed by apple pie and ice cream. And tea. I think the price might have risen since Don was in London.

Don has got a small ranch, nothing too fancy, or so he says. It probably isn't by Texas standards, but I still wouldn't be surprised if it's the size of Hampshire. Don signed up for Uncle Sam the day after Pearl Harbour. He was nineteen, and had never been out of Texas other than a few miles into Coahuila, across the Mexican border. They sent him up north to undertake his basic training in the depths of a raw New Jersey winter. When the time came he was shipped across the Atlantic on a Liberty ship, bound for deepest Essex. His company were landed in Normandy four days after D-Day and fought their way across Northern France. Nearly three months later they crossed into Belgium, two weeks later into Holland, and on February 3rd nineteen forty five they crossed the Rhine. Three months after VE Day he was on his way back to New Jersey. His company was formally inactivated on November 25th, Nineteen forty five, and Don got a Medal of Honour and a one way ticket back to San Antonio. He was twenty three years old. Younger than I am now. In the last twenty nine years he has been to Oklahoma and New Mexico a few times, and to Mexico lots of times. Other than that he's never left Texas.

Don had picked me up outside the Laughlin Air Force base, six miles from Del Rio. He asked where I was from, and didn't say much until we got into the old frontier town.

"That's a nice friendly bar. Why don't you go and get yourself a beer? Tell them Don said to give you one on the house."

With that he put his truck back in gear, but hesitated before driving off. "Tell you what. If you're still there in an hour I'll buy you one myself."

Three Lone Stars and forty minutes later he's on a barstool beside me in the Rockin' R, and this time he greets me like an old friend.

"I'm really glad you're still here. I had a few things on my mind when I picked you up. Do you know, you're the first person I've met from England since I was there myself."

I didn't tarry in Houston. I took the bus to San Antonio and checked into a motel near the Alamo. The old town was touristy but not tacky, with tall trees and pretty white buildings which made it feel like a whole other country. I could have lingered, but there was a feel of Mexico about San Antonio which aroused my curiosity and pushed me on towards the border.

I headed due west on Highway Ninety, which hits the Mexican border a hundred and fifty miles down the road at Del Rio, and then loosely tracks the border most of the way to El Paso. I said a silent prayer that I wouldn't fall in love with a Mexican girl and end up like Marty Robbins. I soon got a ride almost all the way to Del Rio from a fellow stationed at Laughlin. He didn't have the personality of his Navy counterpart in Pensacola, but he was a nice enough guy, if a little reserved. His old radio tuned in and out of top forty, country, and Mexican stations as the sun got higher and hotter the closer we got to old Mexico. He dropped me at the gates of the base and that's where Don picked me up.

So Don Hargreaves tells me his story. He tells it in a hesitant fashion which suggests that it doesn't get an airing too often. Don is still a young man at fifty two, square jawed, lean, and dressed much the same as I imagine he was when he was eighteen. He would have been cool then and he's cool now, looking how a Texan should look in his jeans, boots and check shirt. His conversation is punctuated by silences, as though I've opened a series of doors for him, and he has to look through each of them very cautiously before he can move on. He ponders on the demise of the threepenny bit, and much else besides. Then he smiles.

"Tell you something else, Frank. I don't mean to cause you any offence, but what I remember about most about London is how many queers there were. I remember going down to Piccadilly, and they would grab us by the arm, tell us how strong we were. Not the thing to do to a young guy fresh out of cow country".

I tell Don that he had best stay away from New York City, and then go on to describe my encounter with the travelling insurance salesman, which causes him great amusement.

"I was going to buy you another beer, but I'm worried now that you might think I'm one too."

Nearly falling off his stool now.

I don't think that's very likely somehow" is my reply. "Back in forty four all the real men were away, like you were. They had a job to do. My old man was at Tobruk."

"We had a job to do, all right" says Don, serious again now.

Don gives me the historical sweep of his adventures without going into too much detail, and I'm not going to press him. I sense that by talking to me he's stepping out of Texas for a short while, back to that part of his life so removed from everything he has known before or since, a time when he must have lived every day wondering if it would be his last. I ask him what seems like an obvious question.

"Did you keep in touch with any of your old buddies?"

He pauses for what seems a long, long, while, gazing into the darkness of the Rockin' R, and when he replies his voice is soft and far away.

"No I didn't. I don't know why, but I never did."

I ask him what he thinks about Watergate, and his voice becomes markedly louder and angry for the first time.

"Goddam lyin' sonofabitch. A disgrace to this country. Lyin' sonofabitch."

Then another guy walks in the bar and sits down at the next barstool, and Don is instantly back in his own world.

"Hey Pancho, say hello to a friend of mine from England. You can get us both a beer while you're at it."

Pancho's real name is Jose Gonzales. American citizen, born and bred. Airforce captain, stationed at Laughlin. He looks about forty, but his dark leathery skin suggests that he could easily be younger, prematurely aged by the Texas sun. Jose is big in the world of supplies. Don reckons he can get you anything you want. Again I think of the old man, this time concerning his immediate post war activities, but I feel that Captain Gonzales may not be someone to mess with, so I shrink from comparing him with a failed post-war spiv.

I realise I'm not going to be travelling on anywhere from Del Rio today, so I ask about a motel. I'm kind of hoping that Don will invite me back to the ranch so we can spend the weekend sitting out on the porch while he relives his youth, but this time it's not going to happen. Instead I'm directed to a motel next door which comes well recommended by all. Three dollars fifty, the cheapest so far. Basic but clean, and with a noisy old air conditioner that just about works. I have a feeling that I won't be noticing such niceties by the time I get to bed. When I get back to the Rockin' R, Don's got an idea.

"Listen Frank. We got an idea. Me and old Pancho here thought it would be a shame for you to come this far and not see a little bit of Mexico. How about us taking you over to Boystown later?"

"Boystown?" I say.

Cuidad Acuna is a small city on the other side of the Rio Grande from Del Rio. I knew this before I went in the Rockin'R. I learned a few more things in there, most pertinently that every Mexican border town is known as Boystown to the good citizens of the American town on the other side. The place where the boys go, where the bars close only when they want to, and the pleasures of the flesh are freely available for a few dollars. Captain Gonzales takes charge of the mission, and the three of us get in his car, me in the back. I raise concern that my immigration card tells the world that I'm staying at the Schumann residence on E68th St. I think for a second of Conrad, who passed across my vision twenty four days and a lifetime ago.

"That won't be a problem" says Pancho. "I know all those guys on the border."

Like Lieutenant Deacon, Captain Gonzales knows everybody, or at least, everybody he needs to.

Then we're on a bridge and we're crossing the Rio Grande, the big river which isn't as big as I thought it would be. Through both border posts with no formalities, and I'm in Mexico. The old part of San Antonio felt to me like a Mexican city with its cantinas, and the sound of accordions coming at you from cars and bars in riotous cacophony. Now I'm seeing the real thing, and if this is Boystown, then San Antone must be Toytown. Early evening and it's getting dark, but the white buildings seem even whiter and even though we're just across the border it seems hotter, if that's possible, as if there is a pure tequila fuelled heat radiating out of every cactus plant from here to Mexico

City. Men in big hats sit motionless in doorways like big cats, while children no older than five or six play in the street unfettered by any sign of parental care. Out of the car, and a boy who looks about nine or ten speaks to us more in hope than in expectation.

"You want to come where are the girls? Very beautiful."

Pancho leans down, and tenderly whispers a few words in his ear before giving him a dollar. At the sight of a greenback more children appear seemingly out of nowhere and we quickly seek sanctuary in the bar. Once inside, it doesn't seem too different from the Rockin' R or any other bar, other than that there's no air conditioning and everybody is speaking Spanish, everybody except me and Don, that is. Pancho knows the owner, as he would. The clientele don't appear to be too different, either. Respectable looking working men, mainly middle aged. No hint of debauchery, although the night is still young.

"Hey Frank, do you know how to drink tequila?"

Now we're south of the border, Pancho's accent sounds less like Captain Gonzales and more like Speedy.

"Yeah" I reply, noncommittally. Like you drink anything, I guess, by mouth.

Pancho gives an almost imperceptible nod to the barman, who brings us a bottle of tequila, three shot glasses, some half lemons and a salt cellar. He can see straight away that I'm at a loss.

"Oh no you don't" he half says, half sings. "You don't know how to drink tequila!"

He fills the three glasses to the brim, and then he and Don both pour some salt on to the back of their left hand between thumb and forefinger. They then thrust their fist into their mouth, at the same time picking up the glass with the right and knocking it back in one hit. They then slam their glasses on the table, and at the same time take a long suck on the lemon. Then it's my turn. I can't taste the tequila. Maybe that's the idea. Pancho slaps me on the back.

"We'll make a Mexican out of you yet, hombre!"

He gets in some bottles of dark Mexican beer, which is by far the best I've drunk since I left London town. Then we drink more tequila. I can sort of see the point of what at first sight seems a bizarre ritual. The salt intake is by no means a bad idea in a hot climate, and the lemon refreshes the palate. And the tequila? Well, it most definitely gets you drunk. After four of them Pancho has an idea that he can smuggle me aboard an Air Force cargo plane bound for Northolt Aerodrome.

"I just left there, Jose! I can go back when I want, I've got a ticket. All above board."

Pancho is one of those guys who wouldn't do anything above board if he could do it the other way. He taps his nose.

"Things happen! Mistakes get made, and things happen."

Don can hold his liquor, as I expected he would. He tells me a little about his family. He got married soon after he got out of the service. Has a daughter my age who got married three years ago, and lives over two hundred miles away in Odessa, Texas. He also has a son four years younger at University in San Antonio studying business. He won't be taking over the ranch.

"I guess I'll just work till I can't do it no more and sell up, get me something smaller. Might find the time for a few vacations while I'm at it, take my wife for a cup of tea in Piccadilly."

Both of us know it's not going to happen.

I realise that neither of these men have any attention of doing anything involving women tonight. I ask Pancho if the kid's offer was genuine. Now it's the Captain who's looking serious.

"There's a lot of poverty down here. I'm lucky, I was born on the right side of the border. I'm Yankee Doodle Dandy through and through, but I'm always going to be Mexican, whatever I do. I like to come down here and help them out by spending a little money, but I don't get involved in nothing like that. I know that kid. His name's Alfredo. He's twelve years old. He looks younger because he don't eat right. You know who the girls are? His mother and his sister. You want some of that?"

He's looking at me very intently. I reply with the truth. I've never felt comfortable with any invitations to go where the girls are. Maybe that's why I'm not big on night clubs, meat markets, or pick up joints of any description. I like chance encounters in a bar, or on a train maybe. A little verbal sparring that may or may not lead somewhere. Never paid for it and I never intend to. Made it through Amsterdam, Hamburg and Marseilles with my money in my pockets and my pants inside my trousers. I reckon I can safely negotiate Acuna.

The Captain likes the reply. He leans over conspiratorially.

"You know, I've known old Don a long time now. I don't believe he's had another woman since he got married. He likes the idea of going down to Boystown, but that's it. He's a good man. And you're a good man too, my friend."

122

I could swear there are tears in Pancho's eyes, and I realise that the beer and tequila has had its way with all three of us. Don, who is a man whose instinct I would trust every time, knows it's time to go.

"Hey Pancho, how about we get Junior here back on the right side of the border while he still knows where he is."

"I'm more worried about you guys knowing where you are, I'm not driving."

No the Captain is, although it feels like he's on autopilot as we breeze across what is supposedly one of the more heavily guarded land borders in the world. It's all of ten minutes before we're back in the Rockin' R for nightcaps of Johnnie Walker Black.

Pancho says goodnight at a quarter to three, after giving me his details and telling me the offer of the free flight to Northolt is there any time I want to take him up on it. Don leaves fifteen minutes later. He too gives me his address.

"If I was thirty years younger I wouldn't mind coming with you to see California for myself, but I don't believe it's any place for an old timer these days. I know you're going to find yourself in a few dangerous places somewhere along the line. I would appreciate it if you let me know you made it back it home safe and sound."

I'm thinking of Don's old buddies who he never kept in touch with, and the ones that he couldn't have if he had wanted to, the ones who died on foreign fields before they had reached my age.

"While you're at it, you can tell people that Texas isn't a bad place."

"I'll do that, Don. You can count on that."

Then after the firmest of handshakes he's gone, and I cross the parking lot to my three dollar motel. Today has been another of those days that you get on the road which feel as though they've lasted a week, when it's been all of eighteen hours since I left San Antonio. I fall asleep almost instantly.

****

"Well I don't care if Lucy Carmichael is a friend of yours or if she ain't, she's still gonna die."

The crazy woman's eyes are fixed on the road ahead. It's about the only thing to stop her hitting ten out of ten on the crazy scale. No, this one just makes the nine. Still, I reckon a nine in Texas is equivalent to breaking the scale anywhere else.

"Can I ask you something?"

So what do you do if I say no?

"Sure."

So you're from England, right? How many cents are there to a dollar in England?"

"We don't have dollars. We have pounds and pence. One hundred pennies make a pound. Used to be two hundred and forty until three years ago."

"But if you don't have dollars, how the hell do you buy anything? Sounds the darndest thing I ever heard."

"It's money, we just call our currency by another name."

A way to explain it. "You know in Mexico they use pesos? Well we have pounds. When you go to Paris France, they have francs."

I don't know if it was too much detail, but I lost her there. We can see Mexico just over there on the left, although it's true that you could hit those border towns and never need a peso. She fell silent for about thirty seconds.

"She called me a bitch and a whore."

There's no answer to that, as someone once said.

"I watched my Momma kill my Daddy with that gun, and I swear to God it's gonna kill again. Ain't that right, Frank?"

How does she know my name? She hasn't asked me my name. Then I get it. She's talking to the dog stretched out on the back seat next to the shotgun. The dog's called Frank.

124

"Frank here's my brother. After Momma killed Daddy and they put her away, Frank swore he'd always look after me. Then he went and got himself killed in the threshing machine. Six months later this fella showed up at the back door. I knew he was Frank straight away, I could tell by his eyes. Hasn't left my side since. Sleeps in my bed, just like when we were kids."

Her brother is a Labrador, and she wants to shoot someone for calling her a bitch. Don't say anything, Frankie. Now is not the time for wit, repartee, or irony.

"You sleep in my bed just like when we were kids, don't you honey?"

I turn around to look at the other Frank and he gives me a long soulful look. His eyes are full of sorrow, and they're saying, get me out of here man, please get me out of here.

I'm getting out of here myself as soon as she slows down, or at least when we get to somewhere which is anywhere, of which there is no sign.

The beat up old Ford had no seat belts and couldn't seem to manage much above fifty miles per hour. Any faster and I would have probably gone through the windscreen when she slammed on the brakes. I could feel the double barrel slam alarmingly against the back of the seat. We sat there for about three seconds.

"Well get out of the goddam car then, asshole!"

The crazy woman was loud before, but now she's screaming, she's completely out of her tree, off her trolley, round the bend and back again.

"Get out of the goddam car, asshole and get your ass back to Paris, France or wherever the hell it is you come from! You think you're so smart with your damn fancy money! Get out of my car before I give you both barrels, you damn sonofabitch!"

Like I needed asking twice.

"Merci beaucoup madame et bon voyage" I said as soon as my feet were on the road, but she was already gone. Through the dust I could see Frank looking out of the back window at me with his sad, sad eyes, and I could have sworn he was shaking his head.

The snake is still following me, and I'm hallucinating now because I can see a white pick up in the distance, and I know that there will be no traffic on this road until Monday morning at the earliest, which is when my burnt and poisoned body will be found at the side of the road. The pick up does appear to be getting closer though, emerging out of the haze, the sun reflecting wildly from the windscreen and the white roof. Nearer still and it slows down. A hand comes out of the open window on the driver's side. An empty bottle emerges, lobbed as if in slow motion. The bottle hits the snake on the side of the head. The snake looks stunned for a fraction of a second before disappearing behind a rock. The pick up comes to a stop beside me, and the passenger door opens to reveal two men in their thirties on the wide bench seat. Plenty of room for one more.

"You look like you could do with a ride, fella" says the driver.

I climb in, and the other passenger moves over to the middle, at the same time dipping into a cool box and handing me an icy bottle of Lone Star. The pick up has stereo speakers in the doors, and out of the one on my side Keith Richards is laying down a lazy, but oh so perfect riff. I try and speak, but I need to drain the whole bottle before any sound will emerge.

"Thanks for saving my life."

A little dramatic, I know. I've never thanked anybody that much for anything.

The driver looks puzzled at first, then amused.

"Oh you're not from these parts are you? You thought that old snake was gonna kill you? That was just an old rat snake. Wouldn't do you no harm. We got plenty of snakes in Texas that'll kill you, but that ain't one of them. Hey Manu! Our friend here thought that was a rattler."

Manu looks at me seriously. "I hope you haven't shit your pants, amigo. If you have, you can start walking."

Then the three of us start laughing, and we're laughing so much that we're ten miles down the road before we can talk. Manu hands me another bottle, and I tell them about my previous ride, which gets us laughing again, in Manu's case almost to the point of hysteria.

"The dog, he is her brother! Woo, hoo, hoo, hoo! The dog, he is her brother!"

Again and again, occasionally controlling himself enough to take a swig. The driver, who is blond and called Jed, is more controlled, but still highly amused.

"The thing that gets me is that the dog had the same name as you. I tell you, that would have spooked me for sure."

He thinks for a second. "Tell me, how long were you out in that sun? Sure it wasn't a mirage or something?"

It wasn't that much more than an hour, but it felt like a week.
"I'm just kidding man, I believe you. You'll find 'em all in Texas, I can tell you that. We're all crazy out here, but some of us crazier than others. You found a peach there, for sure."

Jed and Manu are from Pecos, two hundred miles west. They've been fishing at the Amistad reservoir, just outside Del Rio. Left home at midnight to get there for sun up. Fished till midday, now they want to get back to Pecos in good time because, get this, it's Jed's wedding anniversary. Stopped off at a store by the reservoir to fill up with beer and ice for the drive. These boys have got their priorities right.

"So did you catch anything?" I ask.

"Sure" says Jed. "The fishing was pretty good today."

"So are the fish in the back?"

"No, we throw them all back. They wouldn't be in great shape by the time we get back to Pecos."

"You know what I think?" I say.

"What?"

"I think the two of you are crazier than that woman."

Then we're off laughing again.

"OK" says Manu. "We're crazy but we're smart as well. Thing is, we don't always go fishing. Not good to sometimes bring back fish and sometimes not. You understand?"

Si hombre, comprendo todos. To tell lies successfully you have to be consistent. "Yeah, I get it. That's when you want to make sure you don't catch anything, right?"

"You got it fella" says Jed.

Turns out I was only about five miles from a town. Well a place anyway, name of Comstock. It takes us ten seconds to drive through, but that was enough to see it contained what you might call the bare essentials, those things that will keep you alive, a store and a bar. We don't need a bar. The cool box is well stocked, and my hosts are more than generous. I've got good company, I've got a beer in one hand and a cigarette in the other, we've got music blasting from the surprisingly good Del Rio rock station, and my pulse rate is almost back to normal. Now we're skirting the reservoir again. Jed tells me it's thirty miles long. The recreational area is back down the other side, away from the border.

"We'll be coming up to Langtry soon, I guess you'll be wanting to see that."

"Why, what's there?"

"Why that's where old Judge Roy Bean built his own town back in the last century. You never see that movie, 'Judge Roy Bean and the Hanging Tree?' Paul Newman was in it."

"Was that the one where he had to eat the eggs?"

I like a lot of his work, particularly the one where he wielded a mean pool cue, but I wouldn't pretend to be an expert. Couldn't tell you whether he was Butch or Sundance, for instance.

"No, that was 'Cool Hand Luke'. Anyways, Judge Roy Bean was a real Texas character back in the days of the Wild West. Built his own little town just up the road about twenty miles from here. I'm surprised if you've never heard of it, on account of the town being named after your famous English actress. You telling me you've never heard of Lily Langtry?"

Something is stirring at the back of my mind that tells me that I have somewhere. The Jersey Lily. Music hall star of the Victorian and Edwardian age. Rumour had it that she was the sometime mistress of King Edward VII, although it could be the one that came before, and I may have imagined that bit anyway.

"Sure" I say brightly. "I've heard of Lily Langtry. She's still a famous name in England." Famous may be stretching a point, but Jed has clearly got a story for me and I don't want to spoil it.

"Well Judge Roy Bean was a big fan of Lily Langtry. As far as anybody knows he never met her, never saw her perform, like as not he never even got to hear her. I don't believe they had phonographs back then. But old Judge Roy saw a picture of Lily Langtry one time, and he was in love with that woman for the rest of his life. Now Lily Langtry did come to the United States several times, and she was a big success back East in Washington and Philadelphia and those places."

Jed is telling the story now like he was there at the time.

"So the Judge figured that maybe if he built his own town and named it after her, then maybe its fame would spread back east, 'cos Judge

Roy Bean had something of a reputation by then himself, and Lily Langtry would get to hear of it and pay a visit."

Jed pauses, waiting for the question.

"Did she?"

"One day she did."

He pauses again for dramatic effect.

"Thing was, old Judge Roy Bean drunk himself to death three weeks before she got there. Can you believe that?"

Seems to me like one of those stories that has grown in the telling, but a good one nonetheless.

"Life is full of little ironies" I say, like I'm an authority on the subject.

"Sure is" says Jed, "better have another beer is what I think."

We drive through Langtry without stopping. It makes Del Rio look like Houston. Still, Judge Roy Bean lives on, if only on celluloid, and the name of Lily Langtry lives on also, if a little tenuously. Fifty miles further on the road forks into two. Jed gives me a choice.

"Go left and you're on Highway Ninety for El Paso. You still got two hundred miles to go. If you get any rides they're gonna be short ones from one small town to another. I really don't think you want to be caught out on the road anymore today. I strongly suggest you come with us to Pecos. There's motels and diners, and it's right on the main highway going west. You'll get a ride to El Paso tomorrow, no problem. You could stay on that road all the way to California if you've got a mind to."

I've got a map. I know the road I want to take into California and that's not it. On the other hand, Saturday night in Pecos, Texas makes a lot of sense. Jed laughs.

"You never get out of Texas as quickly as you think you will, son. That's the first thing you learn."

We're heading north now, away from the Rio Grande and the immediate landscape is even more barren, although I can see mountains peaking through the heat haze miles away to the West. We're so far from anywhere that we're losing the radio signal, Creedence Clearwater Revival fading slowly in to the ether. Jed doesn't bother to change the dial, allowing an occasional blast of static to punctuate the conversation.

"I don't think I've ever met anyone from England before" he remarks in a manner which is observational rather than hot dog Jethro style. "I know that's what kids do these days, roll up a few bucks and take off. I sometimes think I was born about ten years too early. All those chicks waiting out there for me in the sixties and I got drafted. Soon as I got out I met the little lady, and that's all she wrote."

He doesn't sound as if he regrets it that much, he's just saying that's the way it is. Apart from that they don't talk a great deal about themselves, and they don't ask many questions about me either. They've probably made this trip a hundred times, but they're living in the present as much as I am. I feel like there is nothing I would rather do than sit in this truck and drive to California with these guys, but the town of Pecos is almost upon us. Signs of irrigation, and then we're crossing a large lake, and the radio is picking up a country station. The Texas equivalent of Molly Malone is playing George Jones.

"You know what Pecos is famous for?"

Sure Jed, I really know what Pecos is famous for.

"Cantaloupes. Texas melons. That's what keeps the town alive now. Send them all over the country. You go to the best hotels and restaurants in New York City, they'll all have Pecos cantaloupes for dessert."

Maybe they do. All I know is that there were none in Robyn's fridge.

"Course we need a lot of wetbacks like Manu here to pick 'em."

Manu is off and laughing again. Across the lake and we're driving through fields of melon, and then we cross the Interstate Highway and we're in the town of Pecos, which at first glance is about the same size as Del Rio. Jed pulls up outside an old motel.

"Listen Frank, I'd love to have you stay at our house tonight, but being our anniversary and all it ain't really convenient. I wouldn't send my worst enemy to stay where this fella lives, so I'd stay here if I were you. I know the people, it's clean and it's four dollars."

Almost fifteen per cent up on Del Rio.

"Thanks for the lift guys, and thanks for the beers. Oh, and Jed, happy anniversary, man."

We shake hands and they're gone, and I check in at the Pecos Motor Inn. The desk clerk is ninety if she's a day, the building is possibly older. The last place I was in was made of tin, this place seems like it's made out of plastic. Plastic windows, plastic curtains and a plastic refrigerator, inside of which is a surprise. A small melon, what I take to be a Pecos cantaloupe. There's even a little plastic knife to cut it with.

I hit the hay before Saturday night in Pecos really gets going. I grabbed a beer in a deserted bar, and a steak and fried potatoes in the adjoining diner. Back in my room I had the melon for dessert. It tasted like melon. I was asleep before it was even dark.

In my dreams Frank the dog is waiting for me. He's talking to me like a human, but it's as if he's talking in a foreign language, one that I don't understand. He's still sad. Then I'm in Paris, on the left bank of the Seine. I'm strolling down to a pavement cafe on the Boulevard St Michel, where I've got a rendezvous with Francoise Hardy. When I get to the cafe there's no sign of her, but sitting at a table with a big smile on her face, who should I see but big Patti. I'm a little disappointed at first about Francoise, but I'm still pleased to see Patti, and it's a good dream.

"I bet you never expected to see me in Paris, France, huh Frankie?"

At the words "Paris, France" the mad woman emerges from the cafe brandishing her double barrel, and calls Patti a bitch and a whore. I move towards her and try and grab the gun. She pulls the trigger, and then I'm awake, covered in sweat, looking through an open plastic window at the starry Texas night.

Chapter Nine: The Promised Land

Sunday morning in Pecos, Texas is overcast and cool, and it looks like it's been raining. Compared to the alien planet I traversed yesterday it almost feels like home. I'm up early and make my way towards the highway. El Paso is only two hundred miles down the pike, and I should be there by lunchtime.

Rain is not really what you want when you're standing by the side of the road, but there are times when it can be the hitchhiker's friend. Some people never pick up anybody ever, and that's fair enough. Consistency has its place in the world. Some may or may not, depending on how they're feeling or where they're going. Generally these folks will pick you up when it's raining. The rain starts as soon as I put out my thumb. I know rain. I've been all points north, south, east and west through England, Scotland and Ireland, so I consider myself something of an authority on the subject. Nonetheless, I can't say I've ever seen rain like this before, or indeed felt rain like this, because with no warning or preceding drizzle, great big gobs of water are falling out of the sky like liquid hailstones that I'm sure will leave me bruised later, if not drowned. Thirty seconds is enough to get me soaked through, and enough for a battered station wagon to pull up on the hard shoulder and for the rear door to open.

"Lucky I saw you, man. Raining so hard I can hardly see anything."

The driver looks about thirty, shoulder length hair, moustache, black leather hat. His companion looks younger, although his ginger hair is slightly balding. The driver smiles, and turns his head while pulling out onto the rain drenched highway.

"Hi man, I'm Phil. I'm heading for Phoenix, Arizona. If this old wagon plays along, that is."

I introduce myself, and ask if that means he's going to El Paso, though I'm pretty sure that it does.

"Sure thing, straight through the middle of it."

The companion seems a little peeved.

"I would really like to step out of the car for a while and relate to the rain."

"You can step out any time you want man, but you ain't stepping back."

"I've given you gas money now, so I'll ride on to El Paso. I just think we should open ourselves up to nature more than we do, that's all."

"You want to open yourself up to nature, get yourself a ride in a convertible."

Phil laughs at the idea of it, and turns his head in my direction.

"Hey, you couldn't spare a couple of dollars for gas money, could you? Things are a little tight."

So Phil has adopted a certain rock and roll outlaw look, but he's too hard edged to be a hippy. His companion, who is also a hitcher, is the hippy. I've told him my name so I ask him his.

"You can call me Hodi. Or you can call me friend. I don't like all these labels we give each other. Oh hello, this is so and so, and my name's this, and his name's that. It's all bullshit."

I think on this for a second and suddenly get a flash of inspiration of what will surely irritate him even more.

"So where are you from, Hodi? I mean friend."

"See that's another one. I mean, does it really matter, man? I'm from everywhere."

I'm still wet, but I'm pleased with myself now. I knew that would rattle his chain.

"Well that must be very convenient for you, friend."

Phil guffaws into his moustache. I can feel we're bonding here. I pass him a five for the gas money.

Hodi Friend continues. "I just think where you're at is more important than where you've been. So is where you're going."

"So where are you going?"

"Costa Rica."

Our friend intends to cross the border at El Paso, travel the whole length of Mexico, then he'll have to get through Guatemala, then let me see, Honduras probably, Nicaragua maybe. A long and possibly hazardous expedition whichever way you look at it.

"You speak Spanish?"

"The world is so hung up on language. You don't need it. Really, you don't."

"Got friends in Costa Rica?"

"I'm surprised you're asking me that, after what I've told you," shaking his head now, disappointed.

Phil is chortling away, loving it. "You're crazy man, do you know that?"

I suspect he may have already had this particular conversation. The rain is easing now to what you might call just a regular torrential downpour, so Phil can relax and give me some of his own story.

He's no hippy, he's a working man. A railroad man. A track man, to be precise. He's got a new job starting tomorrow in Phoenix with the Southern Pacific. He's driven down from Chicago, stopping off on the way in Little Rock to visit his ex-wife.

"I owed her a little money and I wanted to get her out of my hair, at least for a while. Like she always did, she ended up taking me for more cash than I'd planned, that's why I'm hustling you guys for gas money. Six hundred miles to go, maybe a little more."

Six hundred miles to Phoenix. Phil is planning on getting there before nightfall.

"Is a track man similar to a lineman?"

"No, a lineman, in the railroad business anyway, works on electrified railroads. They got some back east. The lineman looks after the electricity cables and the pylons."

Like old Glen back in Wichita, apart from there being no railway involved there.

"A track man looks after the track. I'm the best damned track man in the business. I can look at a railroad iron anywhere, and I can tell you how long it's going to last, and how to fix it. Southern Pacific got a lot of track. They need me, for sure."

"Which company did you work for in Chicago?"

I'm genuinely interested now.

"The Chicago, Rock Island and Pacific Railroad."

"Is that the Rock Island Line?"

Phil smiles. "Yeah. They changed the name some years ago when they amalgamated, but it's the Rock Island Line, sure enough. Oh you know the song, right? Johnny Cash. Was that a big record in England?"

"It was, but not by Johnny Cash."

For a moment I'm back in Ewin's Electricals. Ma is handing over her five shillings, and in exchange the man behind the counter is handing over the big seventy eight rpm disc. I can still see the blue Decca label. Chris Barber and his Jazz Band. Then in small letters 'Vocal Refrain: Lonnie Donegan.' I think old Lonnie got about three quid for the session.

I tell Phil about Lonnie Donegan, and I tell him about Leadbelly, who I found out years later, wrote the song. He's heard of Leadbelly somewhere, but not Lonnie. I've never heard Cash sing the song, though I would very much like to.

"Hey Phil. Do you know what pig iron is?"

"Pig iron? Sure. It's what you would call iron ore, I guess. They would transport it on the Rock Island Line up to Chicago for smelting. The railroad put a toll on iron ore, but you could transport livestock toll free. So that's the song."

In the normal way of things I'm shy about sticking my neck over what you might call the performing parapet, but at this present moment there is nothing else I can do other than to start clapping my hands and launch into a chorus of the old Rock Island Line.

"Well the Rock Island Line is a mighty good road
The Rock Island Line is the road to ride
The Rock Island Line is a mighty good road
If you want to ride it got to ride it when you find it
Get your ticket at the station for the Rock Island Line"

Phil is quick to join in, and then almost magically, Hodi Friend produces a harmonica from his Levi jacket and starts blowing along in amateurish but enthusiastic fashion. It's almost enough for me to be able to overlook him being a pillock. Almost.

Phil loves being a railroad man. I can't say I blame him. It sounds like the most romantic thing I've ever heard. I suppose you could get a job in the signal box at Clapham Junction easily enough and say you were a railroad man, but it wouldn't be the same really. A million miles of track opened up the big country in the last century, and if it wasn't a million miles it must have been damned close to it. God knows how many men died to make it happen. Now Railroad Phil travels the country keeping the wheels turning, and the dream alive. He lives in the moment, but rejoices in his history. The future is a different pan of beans. The future, as it often is, is cloudy.

"The Rock Island has got big problems. Probably won't exist much longer. Railroads are dying all over the country. There's very few passenger trains left now, people like their cars, and air travel gets cheaper all the time, and these interstate highways are taking care of most of the freight. The Southern Pacific is good for a few years yet. I would guess I'll be looking for another job by the time I'm forty."

He shakes his head in resignation. "All things must pass, I guess. Hey, how come you don't talk like The Beatles?"

Now it's my turn to give a little geography lesson.

"I love The Beatles, man" says Phil, and opens the glove compartment to reveal cassettes of most of the Beatles albums plus Imagine, a couple of Paul's solo efforts, and All Things Must Pass.

I'm thinking that there is no little irony here. My dreams have been fuelled by the songs of the great blue yonder. I meet someone who appears to be living that dream, and find him in thrall to the lads from the Pool. Think about it a little more and there is certain logic to it, with the big ocean seeming more like a stream that we can cup our hands and call across, passing language and culture from one side to the other as a matter of course. Lightning flashes away to the north, and I realise that one of the reasons for my fascination with this old new world, is that the language of Shakespeare is the language of Mark Twain, is the language of Keats, is the language of Steinbeck and Chuck Berry, and it's as much the familiarity as the search for adventure which brings me here. Twenty miles across the English Channel and it's a different world again, although a wonderful one too, enticing and inviting, and in many ways impenetrable. I'm all for going European, but we can never really share with them the golden treasury of George Formby and Hank Williams. While I'm pondering on this, the car breaks down.

It had stopped raining a few miles back, and the Sun was once again his old imperious self. This is the Sun's domain and you can't expect to keep him hidden for too long. There are still a few clouds to be seen back in the direction we've come from, but where we are now it looks as if it hasn't rained for a hundred years or so. We've got mountains on either side of us. Spectacular red and sand coloured mountains split by passes, from which it's easy to imagine a marauding bunch of Apaches emerging. Or the cavalry, depending on your point of view or state of mind. At this precise moment either one of them would be welcome if they knew how to fix this car. There's an ominous trail of oil spread out behind us.

"I don't suppose you know anything about cars, do you?" Phil asks me, more in hope than expectation.

No, I don't know anything about cars. "Well, you know trains. Don't you know cars?"

He shakes his head. "I know track. I'm a railroad man. Cars are strictly to get me from one railroad to another. I know enough about cars to know this one is a crock."

We both look at Hodi Friend and wordlessly agree that the question isn't worth asking. Hodi, meanwhile, crosses the barrier and stretches on the ground, his head resting against a rock. The proximity of the rock reminds me uncomfortably of my near death rat snake experience yesterday. Hodi opens up his shirt, exposing his milky white chest. It must be at least a hundred and ten degrees. With his pink scalp and wispy ginger beard he looks like he could fry faster than an egg.

"Oh man, I just want to relate to the sun."

Phil shakes his head sadly. Looking at the rock gives him an idea. He goes back to the car and extracts a phial from his pocket.

"Speed" he explains while placing it behind the rock next to Hodi.

"The track man's friend. If a state trooper stops, I don't want him searching us. You're not carrying anything, are you?"

I shake my head briskly, and Phil calls to Hodi Friend.

"Hey bozo! You carrying any dope?"

"I've got a little marijuana to see me through Mexico."

Phil starts to laugh, a laugh that soon turns from a trickle into a raging torrent of uncontrollable mirth. He's on the ground, rolling in the dust. It takes him several minutes before he can speak, and it requires more than one attempt before he can finish a sentence.

"Let me get this straight. You are actually planning on smuggling marijuana INTO Mexico! I've met some dumb assholes in my time, but you take the fuckin' biscuit, man."

Then he's off and laughing again while Hodi Friend looks on serenely. I'm laughing too, but I'd be laughing a lot more easily if I knew where my next drink of water was coming from. We're on a main highway, so we're not exactly in the middle of nowhere, but for all that, there's not a great deal of traffic about on this Sunday morning, and none of what there is seem inclined to do the Christian thing and stop to give us a hand.

After about an hour our good Samaritans duly appear in the guise of two Mexicans in an old truck, which looks as though it needs almost as much immediate attention as Phil's wagon.

"We help you, no problem." One of them opens up the bonnet, while the other stands there grinning. His pal soon gives us his diagnosis.

"We can patch your car up enough for you to get to Van Horn. Is ten mile. Is a repair shop there. You pay me twenty dollar."

"I don't have twenty dollars." replies Phil instinctively. Equally instinctively I pull a twenty out of my pocket and hand it over. The Mexican winks at me and says something in Spanish to his companion, who retrieves a small tool box from the truck. It takes him two minutes to fix the leak, temporarily anyway.

"You take first exit into Van Horn, and repair shop is on your right. Don't try and go any further. Vaya con Dios, amigos."

Sure enough the wagon starts O.K. and Phil keeps to the slow lane, not daring to take it over forty. Should be fifteen minutes to Van Horn, though it seems longer. As well as the oil we're running dangerously low on gas.

"That's one way to earn a living" muses Phil. "Cars overheat, tyres blow, why not? I'll bet it's a relative who owns the repair shop, if there is one, that is. I'll tell you, I thought I was finished with that woman, but she still brings me nothing but trouble. If I hadn't stopped off there I'd be in Phoenix by now. By the way, thanks for the twenty. I appreciate it, man."

The repair shop is where it's supposed to be and it's open for business. The verdict isn't good. Just about every valve, pump or tube or whatever moves any kind of liquid around the old heap needs replacing. It will take four hours and cost a hundred dollars. Phil suggests that me and friend get another ride. We're about a hundred and twenty miles from El Paso. Friend is reluctant to do this on the basis that he has paid gas money and he knows that Phil won't be handing it back now. It seems a slightly twisted logic to me. If he gets a ride now he won't be any worse off, and he'll be in Mexico four hours earlier. Still logic and Hodi Friend don't exactly spend much time in each other's company. His nose and head are peeling alarmingly from his Sun relating. As for me, I really want to see Phil make his job on time, or at least see him on his way. It's got to be five, probably more like six hundred miles to Phoenix. It's going to be touch and go.

The three of us adjourn to a diner, wondering how we are going to make a burger and coke last four hours. The diner is the only place open on Main Street, and we are the only customers. Phil is suggesting that I ride on with him to Phoenix.

"I can understand you wanting to see El Paso, you liking that old song and all, but it's not really like you think it's going to be. The places you've heard of are the places that will disappoint you. I mean, I've been everywhere in the country, I've been to Laramie and

138

Cheyenne and Dodge City and all those old frontier towns, and they've grown in the last hundred years. They were there first, that's why everybody knows them, and El Paso is a lot bigger than any of them. It's the little towns that nobody has ever heard of that still have some of that old Wild West feel to them. For instance this town here, which is hardly a town at all, is probably more like the El Paso of your imagination than the city down the road there."

I think Phil is probably trying to tap me for some more gas money, but I get his point. Hodi, meanwhile, suggests that I go south of the border with him. Says we could make a good team. I don't think so somehow. I'm going west, not south, and even if I wasn't I would be now. Hodi asks the waitress if they have any locally produced fruit juice. He doesn't care for sodas, and he doesn't like contributing to the profits of big corporations like Coke and Pepsi. She thinks he's crazy. Me and Phil nod conspiratorially to her behind his back. He tries to find some common ground with me.

"Do you think Paul McCartney is dead?"

"That was just a rumour put round by someone who had nothing better to do."

One noticeable difference between Americans and English people, Londoners anyway, is that they do tend to be a little, shall we say, gullible.

"What about all those clues on the album covers?"

"You can find clues for anything if you look hard enough."

"I tell you who I think is really dead."

"Who?"

"Dylan."

"Bob Dylan?"

"Yeah, man. Dylan died in that motor cycle crash in the sixties. That guy they got now man, he don't even look the same, never mind sound like him."

"You didn't like Knocking on Heavens Door?"

"I wouldn't listen to anything with the guy's name on it. It's a fake."

Phil is enjoying this. "I wait till I hear it on the news or read it in the newspaper before I say anyone is dead. Mama Cass is dead, I know that."

"Since when?"

"Since last week. It was on the news. Died in London, choked to death on a ham sandwich."

Now I was never a fan particularly, but neither did I have anything against the lady, so I don't know why it is that I'm now the one who's laughing. We're still the only customers in the place, and our waitress looks like she's just about ready to throw us out. Time flies when you're having fun, and four hours have rolled around in reasonable fashion. On the way back Phil speaks of weightier matters. Well probably not weightier than poor old Mama Cass, but of slightly more relevance to our immediate, and Phil's long term, future.

"The thing is, I don't have a hundred dollars. I don't have anything like it. The bitch cleaned me right out."

He looks remarkably unconcerned.

Back at the car repair shop and our man appears to have done a good job. He's even washed it.

"You'll be needing gas."

"Sure man, fill her up."

And he'll be needing paying, Phil.

"That'll be a hundred and five dollars and sixty cents including the gas."

Phil explains his predicament. He has the sum total of twenty six dollars. He offers to give the pink slip, which I assume is the equivalent of the registration document, as collateral. Our man is not impressed. Neither would I be. Then Phil pulls an old brown leather flying jacket out of the back.

"This is worth a hundred and fifty dollars at least. Take it."

The mechanic, who is indeed of Mexican stock, though clearly higher up the gringo ladder than his compadres, is beginning to lose patience.

"Look pal, I'm stuck out in this hundred degree heat all fucking day. Do I look like I need a fucking leather jacket?"

Then he has an idea. He's looking at Phil's head.

"That's not a bad hat, mister. I tell you what, you give me twenty five dollars and the hat and we're even. Keep a dollar for Coca Cola."

Phil is visibly crestfallen. The hat looks like it may have seen slightly better days, but it still looks great on Phil, the leather aged like a favourite old armchair. He thinks for a second and realises that he is really in no position to bargain.

"OK man, you got it."

Now it's my turn to speak. "Can I use the rest room?"

The toilet is evil smelling, fly blown and hotter than hell. Thankfully, I don't need to use it. I unfasten the top of my jeans, and unzip my money belt. Passport and return ticket safely wrapped in one plastic wallet, dosh in the other. Ten thousand dollars I started out with. Ten thousand greenbacks, in fifties, hundreds and Bank of America cheques, and it's been weighing me down ever since I got off the plane. I got off to a flyer in New York, thanks to Conrad and his freeman's hotel, and what with peoples hospitality, and cigarettes and cheeseburgers being so cheap they practically give them away, I've managed to get through no more than three hundred dollars since I got here. That's everything you need to know about life, right there. When you've got nothing no one will give you fuck all, whether they know you've got nothing or not. I pull out two fifties and transfer them to my pocket. I can afford to be generous. After all, it's not exactly mine.

Ninety seconds in that hole and I'm sweating like I'm about to melt. Maybe that's why they call it the can, 'cos that's what it feels like, one made for sardines. Back in the dry but clean air, the mechanic is examining the hat. I press the cash into his palm and remove the hat with the other.

"Sorry pal, but it isn't really you."

He looks for a second as if he would have preferred to have the hat and then shrugs, pockets the hundred, and moves off without a word. Hodi is in the back of the car. Looks like I've been promoted to shotgun. I give Phil back his hat, and he looks at me like I've saved his life.

"I don't like to see a man separated from his hat" I say. "Come on, we've got some driving to do."

Phil eases the wagon through the little town, and we're back on the highway in less than a minute.

"This is handling good now. We're gonna make it. Listen Frank, I don't know how I can thank you, really I don't."

"Just get me to Phoenix and we're even."

Hodi is acting like he's never seen that much money before. It works out to about forty two pounds. "You gave him a hundred dollars?" He says it slowly, repeating himself several times. "If you've got so much money, why are you hitchhiking?"

Straight back at him. "I don't have a great deal. I've got people in LA that I'll be staying with, and I'm getting some money wired over when I get there."

Rule one of travelling, never be separated from the essentials, rule two, whatever else you got doesn't matter, rule three, never ever let on if you've got a reasonable stash about your person.

"I still can't believe you got him his hat back. I mean, what's it to you? You could have got a ride in to El Paso and caught the bus all the way to California for less than half that."

Phil speaks. "You're an asshole and he's an English gentleman. That's the difference. I appreciate it man, I really do."

I couldn't explain to Phil, much less Hodi Friend, that although I've done some shameful things in my time, and most of them in the last six months, to allow a man who has worked for the Rock Island Line to be deprived of his hat when I had the power to intervene would have put me on the lowest rung ever. Stack O'Lee killed Billy Lyons for a hat, and I bet it wasn't as good as this one, not anywhere close. The hat is part of Phil. For him to show up at the Southern Pacific without it would be like him turning up with a broken arm. I could explain to Hodi Friend about accepting graciously from some and then giving to others, I could even couch it in his own language and start talking about karma, but it would be a waste of time. Hodi is one of those hippies who give the rest a bad name, big on the take, not so big on the give. Too many of them are like that, that's why they haven't exactly achieved much since they started throwing their flowers and ringing their bells.

"Time for a little Beatles" says Phil and puts on Abbey Road. It's side two, and I'm soon singing along, scousing it up for all I'm worth to Mean Mr Mustard and Polythene Pam.

"Hey, now you sound English" he says approvingly, and asks me what a ten bob note might be.

"Hey, maybe it was Mean Mr Mustard who did for Mama Cass, what do you think?" and then we're off and laughing again, the old car is cruising the highway like a dream, there's a breeze coming through the open windows, and all is right with the world.

Phil leaves the engine running, but delays driving off while we watch Hodi make his way to the pedestrians' border point. Now I'm white, me, Anglo Saxon Celtic white, but at least I tan. Hodi is like peaches and cream without the peaches. You just know that as soon as he gets south of the border people are going to point at him and say, hey look Rosita, there goes the whitest gringo I've ever seen. Don't bother relating to the Sun down there Hodi Friend, the further south you go the whiter you are going to get, if the Sun doesn't kill you first that is, that or something worse. Maybe his innocence will protect him. Maybe. I look at Phil and we shake our heads like the two men of the world we are, before Phil pulls the car back out into the traffic and makes for the Interstate highway in the direction of New Mexico.

Phil was right about El Paso. With its freeways and factories we could be in Brentford, apart from there still being one connection to the song, which is that there are plenty of Mexican girls on the sidewalks, any number of which I could fall in love with. The Interstate delivers me from temptation, and we're ten miles out of town before I know it. A sign says Tucson, three hundred and ten miles.

"I know for a fact that it's another hundred and twenty from Tucson to Phoenix" says Phil.

It's eight o'clock. Phil's happy now. He knows he's going to make it. What's four hundred and thirty miles to a track man? Ten more minutes and we're saying goodbye to Texas. I turn on the radio and we listen to the Mexican station out of Juarez playing a mixture of mariachi music and the kind of latin lover smarm that your aunt might bring home from the Costa Brava. When this fades away into the night Phil puts on Revolver.

When they sing 'Taxman Mr Wilson, Taxman Mr Heath' it hits me that back in Blighty we're still stuck with the pair of them. They've seen off flower power, skinheads and glam rock, not to mention the break up of The Beatles. On this side back in sixty six they were still going all the way with LBJ. They seem to have seen a hell of a lot since then. That's the thing about England. It always feels like things are going to change, like it must have done after the war, or during the rock and roll years of the fifties and then on into swinging London, but when all is said and done it's still England and you can't get a drink in the afternoon, and you can't get anything at all if the afternoon in question happens to be a Wednesday.

This isn't a Wednesday it's a Sunday, which is ten times worse, or would be if that's where I was, but I'm not and I've got more pressing things to concern myself with. John is singing I'm Only Sleeping, and the man behind the wheel looks as if he soon will be if he doesn't take a break soon.

At ten o'clock Phil sees the neon lights of a diner at an intersection, and pulls the wagon off the highway and into the parking lot. Stepping out of the car the desert air is fresh and cool. We get cheeseburgers and much needed coffee, and Phil buys a quart bottle of drinking water. Back in the car he opens the glove compartment and fishes around with a puzzled expression before burying his face in his hands.

"Oh man" he moans softly.

For a second I'm thinking there is something seriously wrong, and then I realise that he's laughing. Sort of.

"It's my own fault" he says. "Calling that kid an asshole, thinking I'm so smart, I've done the dumbest thing anyone could possibly do. Ever."

"Which is?"

"The track man's friend. My pills. I thought I was being real cute taking them out of the car, only thing is, I left them behind that fucking rock."

Time for Frank to take charge.

"OK Phil, here's what we're going to do. You are going to get in the back and get your head down, and I'm going to drive you to Phoenix. No ifs or buts."

He thinks for a second. "You got a licence?"

"Sure. It's in my bag if you want to see it."

It's not in my bag, it's in my secret belt. Much as I trust Phil, and I do, nobody, but nobody, gets to know about that.

He doesn't have to think for much longer.

"That sounds like a pretty good idea to me."

Phil stretches out on the back seat with his hat over his face. He doesn't bother to remove his hand tooled boots, which comes as some relief to me, as I think it may be some while since he last did. I ease behind the wheel, and move the wagon out of the parking lot and back onto the Interstate. My brief lesson with an automatic, courtesy of old friend Jerry Fell proves handy here, and driving the wagon seems as easy as falling off a bus, especially as it's got a lot less power than Jerry's shiny new Oldsmobile had. Phil's voice sounds slurred.

"You know what Frank, you're a regular English knight in shining armour, do you know that? I didn't know how tired I was, man."

Knight in shining armour. That's rich. I can think of two people that would disagree with that for a start, and a lot more besides.

Phil sounds like he's about to drift off any second.

"Hey Frank, you're out here seeing the country or seeing the world, and I can dig that, but have you got a woman waiting for you at home? More than one, maybe?"

Good question. Julie knows everything apart from one thing, which is that Frank Downes isn't worth waiting for, so she might be. I hope for her sake that she isn't. Teresa? Well she's waiting for something, all right. Four more months to go. So she'll be waiting. So will about twenty of her cousins. I can't be thinking of that now. I've got to keep my mind on this highway.

"Maybe" I reply casually. "One or two, maybe," but Phil doesn't hear me. He's slipped into a deep sleep, leaving me with the highway and the question he left me with, the one thing I don't want to think about. I try and think about where Hodi Friend might be now. Did he press on south in the dark, or did he put up in one of those border town flophouses? I don't know how much money he's carrying, but however much it was he definitely has an aversion to spending it. All he has to offer is his hippy bullshit. Where you're at is more important than where you've been. So is where you're going. Yeah, but you are only where you're at because of where you've been. Obviously. That much we hold self-evident. That starts me thinking about where I'm at, and where I've been, and what put me on this road, and that brings me right around in a circle back to what I was trying to get away from. He did have one good question. Why are you hitchhiking when you've got so much money? I'm sure he would have freaked out something spectacular if he had known how much I did have. I'm hitchhiking because I want to hear peoples' stories, that's why. I don't want to be stuck at the back of a Greyhound bus day after day, or even worse night after night, trapped there with my own story. That's the story I want to leave behind.

I think about Railroad Phil, and I realise that I'm going to say adios without ever knowing too much about him. Being the best damn track man in the country doesn't appear to have brought him much in the way of material rewards. A beat up old car on its last legs, a hat and a pair of boots, a travelling bag no bigger than mine, an ex-wife bleeding him dry, maybe more than one. In Phoenix there will soon be another woman, and the wagon will get sold for next to nothing, and there will be another second hand model with not quite as many miles on the clock as this one. One day it will all seem stale, and it will be time to move on again to the Santa Fe, or some other name of legend. Then one morning Railroad Phil will wake up and he will be forty, and all of the railroads will be gone, and he will be forced to take up some other line of work, and you know what, he will look forward to it, because Phil is one of life's optimists. And so am I.

On the border of New Mexico and Arizona there's a checkpoint. All vehicles must stop, there are men in uniform with guns, it's for all the world like a regular border crossing. Roll down the window, heart beating faster, try and act cool.

"Are you carrying any cacti, fruit or vegetables?"

I hear what he's saying but it seems such a strange question that I can't help but ask him to repeat it.

Markedly more impatient now. "Are you carrying any cacti, fruit or vegetables? We got cacti in Arizona that take a hundred years to get to be ten inches tall, and we don't want them mixed up with any other kinds."

"No sir, we've got nothing like that."

"You wouldn't mind me taking a look then, would you?"

"Of course not."

He looks in the back and takes a perfunctory look in both our bags. Phil's isn't locked, which is just as well, as he is sleeping innocently through the whole scene. Then the guard, or whatever he is, opens the glove compartment, just in case we got a miniature cactus growing in there. He pulls out a couple of Beatles tapes, looks at me sadly like I'm a Communist, shakes his head and puts them back, and then we're on our way again and we're in Arizona. If Phil hadn't left his pills behind that rock we would have been on our way to jail. Life is funny like that sometimes.

I drive through Tucson at three am. Tucson, where JoJo left his home looking for California grass. That's about the one tape Phil doesn't have, but I wouldn't play it anyway. My mission is to deliver him to Phoenix rested and ready to go. The sign says a hundred and eighteen. I watch the headlights bearing down from the eastbound lane, and think of all the other stories on the road at this three am hour. Three am, when B B King got the blues, and Frank Sinatra drained his last double bourbon while Joe the bartender waited patiently to close up the joint. One for my baby and one for the road. I stop at a gas station and fill the tank. I'm taking it nice and easy, but we should still be in Phoenix before five. Phoenix. Silence on the airwaves allows Glen Campbell to come through to the antenna of my imagination loud and clear. We're coming from different directions, but our destination is the same. My take on the song was always that Glen would spend one night in Phoenix, turn around and head back to the girl in LA. I'll be there myself in a couple of days. Maybe LA will prove to be my Phoenix, and I'll turn around, go home and face the music. Maybe I will, but not for a while. Not till I'm good and ready.

It's four forty five when I pull into a truck stop five miles outside Phoenix. The first rays of the morning Sun are trickling into the rear view mirror, and my night's work is done. I give Phil a shake.

146

"Are we here?" He springs to life instantly, alert and refreshed.

"Man, I feel good!"

He looks like he does too, and keen, like a school leaver ready to start his first job. "Could use a little coffee, though."

He takes his rightful place behind the wheel, and drives us to a diner for coffee and doughnuts. I pay. Phil spent his last dollar on cheeseburgers and water. I consider slipping him a ten, but decide against it. I don't want to appear too much the Mr Bountiful. He can get a sub when he starts work.

"So you're heading west to L.A.?"

"I'm going to head up north for a bit. I'm planning on hitting sixty six into Los Angeles."

I instantly feel a phoney, talking about hitting sixty six and all that crap, but Phil lives his dream every day, and now I'm living mine.

He smiles. "Hitting that old sixty six, eh? You see, I'm a railroad man, Frank, and you're a man of the road, ain't you? You love it. Just don't stay on that road too long though, will you. One of these days you might find it's all you got."

Phil's got more than two hours before he reports to the Southern Pacific, so he drives me out to the road heading north and leaves me by another truck stop.

"You'll get a ride here, no problem. Hey, thanks for everything."

He fumbles with his hat. "You should have this."

He's trying, but he can't summon too much enthusiasm.

"It wouldn't fit me. It's your hat, Phil. Yours, and no one else's."

Then he gives me a hug, which is a first for me, and I don't really know how to react, but he doesn't appear to notice.

"Remember what I said about staying on that road."

"Don't run out of track, track man," I reply, but I don't say it until the old wagon is a hundred yards or so away, and disappearing in the direction of the railroad yards.

Tuesday

I awake to the sound of a train in the distance. It gets gradually louder until it thunders past the back of the motel. It takes all of five minutes to pass, the big locomotive hauling a mile of freight cars to who knows where. Railroad Phil would know, but he's not here. He's in Phoenix. I'm in Flagstaff. Still in Arizona, but one hundred and forty miles to the north. Flagstaff is cool, green and friendly, and I would be tempted to stick around for a few days if it wasn't for the road outside calling me on.

I'd swear that it was already ninety degrees in Phoenix at six am. At seven it must have been nudging a hundred. I got picked up at ten past by a trucker starting fresh out of Phoenix on his way back to Utah, the home of the Mormons. The driver's name was Joseph, which led me to suspect he might well be one himself. Any other state and he would be plain Joe, surely? He had all mod cons in his cab including a miniature fridge stocked with sandwiches and Dr Pepper and Mountain Dew, which he shared with me all the way. No cigarettes, no polite enquiries as to the availability of amphetamines. Yes, he must have been a Mormon, all things considered, but he never tried to convert me, and I didn't egg him on by asking how many wives he had, either.

We drove North, with the desert slowly giving way to the mountains, and with Joseph almost counting the miles to the state line and telling me that if I thought this was pretty, I hadn't seen nothing till I saw Utah. I didn't want to hurt his feelings, so I told him I would make sure I saw Utah on the way back from California.

I'm beginning to believe this hitchhiking caper is making me soft, what with buying people hats, and being sensitive about their feelings, and all.

Joseph took it nice and easy on the winding road, and we stopped off for coffee once, so it was past midday when he dropped me in Flagstaff. Sixty six was right there calling me west, but I quickly decided to pamper myself a little. The road man was a little road weary. With luck I could still make California in one big hit the next day. I ate country ham and eggs, with fresh orange juice and good coffee, and checked into a swanky Motor Lodge. I bought suntan lotion, and spent the afternoon swimming in the pool, and soaking up the Sun shining down through the mountains at a very reasonable seventy five degrees. In the evening I found a quiet bar on Main Street, and had my fill of beer before walking back to the lodge through the delicious night air at ten o'clock ready for an early start in the morning. I thought of nothing and no one. All in all, a damn near perfect day.

The train couldn't have woken me. It was too far away when I first heard it. No, I wake slowly, naturally, as befits a man who has had ten hours of best dreamless. Eight thirty, and time to get up. I've got to be taking the highway that's the best.

The first stage of Route 66 opened in Nineteen twenty six in Chicago. A few years later the route was open all the way to California, although much of it was still a dirt highway. In the thirties, when soil erosion ravaged Oklahoma and turned it into a dust bowl, the Joad family and thousands of others took to the highway going west, their jalopies loaded with children, cardboard suitcases, and little else beside a prayer. Some made it. Some didn't. Woody Guthrie slung his guitar over his shoulder and set off for some Hard Travelin', heading for the old peach bowl, as he called it. Cali-for-ni-a. I first heard of it myself from the Rolling Stones, who at the time had ventured no further west than the Ealing Blues Club. Mick Jagger garbled some of the place names on account of not knowing them, but I soon printed them onto my memory from the school atlas. St Louis, Joplin Missouri, Oklahoma City, Amarillo, Gallup New Mexico, Flagstaff Arizona. This is where I get on. Kingman, Barstow and San Bernadino lie ahead.

I say goodbye to the lodge with some regret, and resolve to come back another day. Flagstaff looks like my kind of place. Must be a busy time for the trains, as no more than ten minutes after the last one a big Santa Fe engine hauls some more freight cars in the direction of New Mexico. At the crossroads the sign points north to the Grand Canyon, and I know I should, I really should, but I quickly reason that the Grand Canyon has been there for a couple of million years or so, and it can wait for another time. Yesterday I was a tourist, today I'm a traveller again. I walk out of town for about ten minutes until I see the magic sign "66 West". I wrap my left arm around the sign, like it's an old friend I've been waiting all my life to meet, and stick my right thumb out.

The big truck went past me before it started to slow down, gradually changing through however many gears before coming to a halt about a hundred yards away. A moment's hesitation wondering if it's stopping for me or for some other reason, and then I'm running for all I'm

149

worth, and if I'm made to look foolish, so be it. Wouldn't be the first time.

"I was beginning to wonder whether you wanted a ride or not."

I clamber up into the cabin to find the driver looking a little pained that I've kept him waiting but bearing a friendly expression. Friendly and black. I try and hide my immediate surprise, but probably not too well. He looks as if he's used to it.

"These babies take a while to slow down" he explains. "Anyway I could hardly see you, hiding behind that highway sign. Where you going, fella?"

"Los Angeles." I savour the words as they slowly roll off my tongue.

"Well you're in luck. I doubt very much if I'm going to the part of Los Angeles that you'll be wanting to go to, but you won't be far away."

This is all getting too easy. He pulls the giant truck back on to the old road, and it picks up speed with the enthusiasm of a mule that has just been roused from a deep sleep.

"I don't always pick people up, but you look like a gentleman, and I enjoy a little company occasionally."

Seems you don't need to be too well dressed to pass for a gentleman round these parts, but I am well scrubbed and rested after my sojourn at the Motor Lodge. Someone says they enjoy the company, and you then feel obliged to make the conversation. Not that I wouldn't anyway, but I'm just a little more conscious of doing so. We exchange the essential details. His name is Ernie, he lives in South LA., he's bringing a load back from Albuquerque. Spent last night in a truck stop in Flagstaff. I would hazard a guess he's in his late thirties. I ask him if he went into town last night.

"Nope. The only time I go out for a beer is when I get back to South Central. I never know what I might find in these Western towns."

The way he says the word "western" he could just as easily be saying southern.

"So is the west your patch?"

"My patch? I guess so. New Mexico, Arizona. Bakersfield. Sometimes get up to San Francisco and Oakland, that's a good run."

"So what do you carry?"

"What do I carry? Man, you ask a lot of questions, do you know that? Matter of fact I don't always know what I'm carrying myself. The man says take this load somewhere and they'll give you something to bring back, and I do it. If I get pulled at a checkpoint I

150

got the paperwork right here. That's all I need to know. Let me tell you something. Never ask a trucker what he's hauling. If he's got a big rig with "Pepsi Cola" painted all over the side then you don't need to ask, otherwise he's gonna wonder why you're asking."

"Sorry Ernie. Just making a little conversation."

He softens. "That's OK. I'll tell you something. I'll be glad to see my kids. Been away three nights. That's the part of this job I don't like."

Kids. You live in a world without children when you live this travelling life. It's rare for people with children in their car to pick anyone up, and you can't blame them for that, and evenings are generally spent in the company of men, or looking for women. What do I know of kids, anyway? The only kid I know is my brother Joey, and he stopped being a kid when he was twelve.

"So how many kids have you got then, Ernie?"

"Six."

I let out an involuntary whistle. Ernie laughs.

"How old are you Frank? You're twenty four? When I was your age I had two kids already. I couldn't be doing what you're doing, running wild without a care in the world. So I know you ain't got no kids, unless you got some you don't know about, which might well be the case, with you being a travelling man."

Ernie, you're four months this side of being right. I wonder if his kids ever ask him what's in the back of his truck?

Ernie likes the company, he likes to talk, but he wants to talk about what he wants to talk about. Right now he wants to talk about race. He wants to know how things are in England, how it compares, what life can a black man have there. Appreciating that he is genuinely interested, I take time with my reply. I tell him about the old guy who picked me up in South Carolina and how you wouldn't find that at home, and no sooner are the words out of my mouth than I realise that I'm not being honest with him, there's plenty like that at home, they're just more careful who they share their opinions with. I tell him one thing I have observed though, in New York and New Orleans.

"Back home you wouldn't see any black cops."

I could also tell him that I've never seen a black lorry driver, but I don't. Driving buses is allowed on both sides of the pond. In New Orleans I saw an old white man refuse to get on one because he didn't want no black driver. The driver cheerfully told him he had a long wait ahead of him, and closed the door in his face.

151

"Being a cop's a good job. Good pension and everything. What, they're not allowed on the job because they're not British?"

"No, they wouldn't want to do it. They'd be looked on as traitors."

Ernie's a little puzzled now. "Well if I'm going to be stopped and searched on the corner, I'd rather it was by one of my own."

That makes sense. I tell him that in Britain blacks and Asians possibly have more sense of their own history, even those who are born there, whereas in the U.S. there doesn't seem to be much of an alternative to mainstream society. I realise as I say it that I am almost certainly talking out of my arse and could well be putting myself on dodgy ground, but to my surprise Ernie agrees enthusiastically.

"You got it. Black people in America, none of us know our own real names, none of us, and we get shown the American Dream, then we're told it's not for us unless we can sing, or play basketball or football, and that's it. I can't do none of those things, that's why I'm hauling my ass out of bed at five most mornings driving a damn truck."

This time I stay silent. Ernie is on a roll, and I don't want to push my luck and say the wrong thing.

"There's some things I like about driving truck. You know what I like best? I ain't got the man in my face all day. I know what I'm supposed to be doing, and I get on and do it. I don't even bother with this damn fool CB radio most of the time. All those redneck truckers think they're cowboys, that's just a bunch of foolishness."

Ernie is warming to his subject now. "You know, if you work you can have a good life in this country, whatever colour you are. A lot of the brothers don't get that. Live off women, get strung out on dope, they don't do the rest of us no favours, that's for sure. You know who the folks back in South Central hate the most now? Not cops, not white people. Koreans. You know why? 'Cos they make black folk look bad, that's why. They open up a store, work all day and most of the night, and make a living. Black folks won't do that. Most of them won't, anyway. I ain't got no beef with Koreans. I say good luck to them."

He pauses for a few seconds to concentrate on the road as a Thunderbird overtakes the long vehicle, and it's only then that I notice that we've left the green of Flagstaff far behind and are back in the desert. The T-bird disappears off ahead, and Ernie continues.

"Thing is, when you talk about race, sometimes you need to forget about racism and think about tribalism. You know what tribalism is?"

Tribalism. Flashback to getting beaten up once as a teenager when I wandered out of my territory up to Harlesden. Seeking shelter in the

152

Underground while England and Scotland football fans went at it full tilt at Kings Cross. Mods and rockers. Skinheads and greatcoats. Yes, I know what tribalism is.

"What I'm saying is, it's like you can have a college football team, and they can be half white and half black, and the coach tells them all the other teams hate their guts, and then they become a tribe. You get what I'm saying?"

"Sure." I nod agreement.

"You see, back in the days of the cavemen, you had to stick with the tribe, 'cos if you saw someone coming over the hill who wasn't in the tribe, you knew he was planning on killing you, having your woman and taking your cattle. So tribalism goes deep, you know what I'm saying? It's a natural thing for all of us. What do you call it, ingrained. What I'm saying is, the tribe can change. One thing for sure, if the little green men ever come down from Mars, then we're all going to be on the same side. Black and white ain't gonna mean shit. It's all about who you see as a threat. Take me and you. We can have a good conversation, and I can go home and tell my wife I picked up a nice kid from England, because we ain't no threat to each other. You get yourself a job as a trucker and start taking all my best jobs because the boss likes your white ass, then that's a different matter."

"No chance of that Ernie. I might come and move next door to you though."

Laughs long and loud. "You see South Central, which you probably won't, then you won't say that."

We pass Kingman without me noticing it, and then I see the sign welcoming me to California. The Golden State. I took a different route to old Chuck, but I've finally made it to the Promised Land.

I wonder whether Ernie, born and bred in Los Angeles, ever thought of it so. The land is still parched. We got a lot of desert to get through before we hit the peach bowl. We stop at a diner, seemingly in the middle of nowhere. There's a dozen trucks parked outside. I tell Ernie I reckon this must be the top place in the neighbourhood, and he gets the joke. Inside he exchanges nods with a couple of guys without entering into conversation. Ernie is the only black person in the place. Nearly all of them have big hats which they don't bother to remove while they're eating. I think of what Ernie said back down the road. Foolishness indeed. The blowsy waitress is asking one of them if he would like mayonnaise on his French fries.

"Nope. The only time I use that stuff is when I put it on my dick."

153

She shrugs like she's heard it a million times. I smile involuntarily while Ernie remains impassive. We make the same order, cheeseburger, fries, coke, coffee. Ernie eats without talking. When we're done he gets the check, and counts out his half before passing it to me. He gets up in the morning to feed his family, not itinerants from the other side of the world. I consider paying for both us, but quickly decide that it could be seen as patronising. He exchanges more wordless nods on the way out without disturbing the flow of the conversation. Gas prices and Nixon.

Back on the road he looks at me a little reproachfully.

"So you thought that guy was funny?"

I have to admit that I did think it was quite funny. I might even use that line myself some time.

"Well two things, Frank. One, that cracker uses that same damn line every single day. Two, I couldn't say it. Know what I'm saying?"

I look suitably contrite, like somebody who has been caught laughing at a cripple.

"Hey Frank, what do you think of our President?"

I wait a second and turn and smile. "I think he's a son of a bitch."

That laugh again. "Well you've learned something since you've been here, I'll give you that."

I'm expecting Ernie to preach on the evils of Nixon and Watergate till we get to LA, but he leaves it at that, and we fall silent for a while. No CB radio and no other kind of radio. It occurs to me that Ernie has asked me nothing about myself. Not that I welcome that line of conversation, far from it, but I realise that Ernie is a man who is happiest with his own thoughts when he's not with his family. Kingman to Barstow takes nearly three hours. San Bernadino is another hundred miles. His eyes are fixed on the road and his mind on South Central. He'll be home tonight. I'm not sure if I want to arrive in Los Angeles after dark. Ernie's not so wrapped up in his own thoughts that he can't read my mind.

"You know the best thing for you to do. Stay in San Bernadino tonight. I can fix you up in the overnight truck stop. Seven fifty a room with a TV. I'm not supposed to, but I will. Get the bus to Los Angeles in the morning. I don't want to be thinking of you on the wrong side of town late at night."

"Sounds good to me, Ernie."

It's dark by the time we pull into the truck stop. Ernie gives me strict instructions to wait in the cab while he takes care of business. He returns a couple of minutes later with a key, a bag of doughnuts, and coffee in a plastic cup.

"You got seven fifty? The coffee and doughnuts are on me."

The night is hot and the neon is shining, and I feel the same buzz as I did when I walked out to the cab rank at JFK one long month ago. Ernie tells me I should go into the room and stay there. In the morning I'm to leave the key in the door and walk downtown without looking back. This motel and others like them are supported by the trucker's association, and are strictly for drivers only. Ernie is doing me a big favour here. What he doesn't know is that I would rather stay in a regular motel and creep out for a few beers, but I have no intention of throwing his kindness back in his face. There's plenty of beer in LA, and more besides.

"Thanks Ernie. It's been nice talking to you. Good luck."

What I should have said was "nice listening to you."

"You're alright, Frank. Take care, man."

I watch him drive off into the night, next stop some industrial suburb where he will drop off his mysterious load before going home to his wife, six kids, and the ghetto. I never thought of it as that while Ernie was talking, but that must be what it is, I guess.

The room is clean, the television works, the coffee is good, and the doughnuts are fresh. I watch the news. Nixon is not expected to last the week. I sleep better than I reckon he does.

It takes more than two hours to get to Los Angeles. I'm up and out early, and the bus is full of commuters and stops at every dormitory town on the way. It's after ten when I walk out of the bus station and into the middle of downtown Los Angeles. A lot of tall buildings, but no apparent centre. I buy a map on the corner, find that I'm not far from Sunset Boulevard and start walking. If I had bothered to check the scale of the map then maybe I wouldn't have walked along Sunset for two and a half hours while buses cruised by fairly regularly. By the time I realise I am on a serious hike I decide that it is somehow appropriate to finish this part of my journey on foot. I won't be here forever, but I have no real plans either. No particular place to go, as the man once said. I know I'm in Hollywood when the signs start saying Hollywood this and Hollywood that, Hollywood Real Estate, Hollywood Pizza.

Near the corner of Sunset and Vine, an address which seems to come straight out of rock and roll history, I check out a motel with an inviting pool. Ponytail and moustache on the desk quotes me twenty two a night, seventeen fifty per night for a week, and fifteen a night if I take it for the month and pay upfront. I ask to see the room first. I don't as a rule, but it makes sense if I am to be there a while. Ponytail and moustache shows me one in a courtyard, out of the sun but just around the corner from the pool, and with a drinks machine right outside. Spacious, and with a great bathroom, tub as well as shower. I'm inclined to take it for the month straight away, but that would mean revealing my stash, so we return to the desk and I pay him the hundred and twenty two fifty for the week.

I empty out my bag completely for the first time in twenty nine days, and put everything in drawers and on hangers. The Riviera Motel is going to be home for a while, unless I meet a West Coast Robyn, which is not beyond the bounds of possibility. Then I don my swimming trunks and grab a towel, get a can of Mountain Dew from the machine, and take the few steps to the pool. Finding I've got it all to myself, I stretch out on a sun lounger next to a palm tree and light up a French cigarette.

California. Top of the world, Ma.

Chapter Ten: All The Young Dudes

Thursday August 8th 1974. Hollywood, California.

"So a modern town?"

A skinny girl has materialised on the barstool next to me. It's ten pm, and I'm nursing the first one of the evening a little later than I usually would, so I'm not altogether sure if I welcome the distraction.

"Excuse me?"

"So a modern town?"

"Sorry, I'm not with you."

Hardly up to the usual standard of Frank Downes repartee, but I'm temporarily lost for an answer, a position I seldom, if ever, find myself in. It's either that, or say yes, this is so a modern town.

"You're with Mott the Hoople, right?"

Speaking a lot faster this time, and a little peeved, but this time I get her drift. She thinks I am a member of Mott the Hoople.

"No, I'm not in Mott the Hoople," I reply, as casually as if it is the kind of thing I get asked every day.

Now she's getting angry and speaking even faster. The angrier she gets, the faster she speaks, and the easier I find it to understand her.

"I know you're not IN Mott the Hoople," and the way she forces the word IN from the back of her throat makes it perfectly clear that I have no more chance of being IN Mott the Hoople than I have of being Steve McQueen.

"You look a lot like a guy who works for them. Used to come in here last year. Obviously my mistake. Excuse me."

Great. She thinks I'm a roadie for a band, who if I remember rightly, hail from Herefordshire. I glance down to check that I don't have a big bunch of keys jangling from my belt, before politely confirming that, yes, she is mistaken on this particular occasion. I pull out a Disque Bleu and light it without speaking. Curiosity gets the better of her, as I knew it would.

"Can I have one of your cigarettes?"

I pass the packet and she frowns, confused by the white filter. I light it for her, again without speaking, and take a closer look. Nothing special, to be honest. Her hair is straight light brown and the lack of meat on her bones is exaggerated even further by her spray on jeans and glitter vest. Lot of make up around the eyes, pale lipstick. I would guess her to be about eighteen, but there again, she could be several years younger than that if she started this night life when she was thirteen or so, which is quite possible. Need to be careful Frank, they've got laws about that sort of thing over here. I quickly decide that she doesn't have enough going for her to be worth the risk. She though, wants to talk.

"So what do you do?"

I take another drag before replying. "I'm on vacation."

That's one American word I like. It seems so much more grown up than saying you are on holiday. It has more of a sense of purpose to it somehow. But then I am on neither.

"I'm Leah."

"Like the Roy Orbison song?"

Now it's her turn to look blank. She knows Mott the Hoople, but she doesn't know the Big O. She tells me again. "I'm Leah."

"Hi, Leah."

She gets up from her stool, and I can see now that she's little more than five foot tall and seven stone, if that.

"Fuck you" she says, although with the emphasis on the first word, which I always think makes it not quite so bad. "The British have got no fucking manners, do you know that?"

Then she's heading off towards a table.

"I'll have you know we invented fucking manners. Anyway, I'm half Irish."

I think briefly of a man in another bar three thousand miles and three time zones away. He'll be Irish when it suits him like most of them, that's what he said.

Leah turns and throws her Disque Bleu at me. "And your cigarettes taste like shit."

I casually stub it, and put it back in the packet. I've got to make these last.

Nixon resigned today. I watched it live on television before I came out. I spent the morning on the tourist trail, walking on the names of the stars on Hollywood Boulevard, then back down to Sunset, where I checked out both sides of the Strip before returning to the Riviera for a little more pool time. I clocked a few people coming and going from their rooms, but it would appear that business is slow. Why I don't know, as it seems like a perfectly suitable establishment as far as I am concerned. For the second day running I had the pool to myself. At eight o' clock I was getting dressed when the news came on. The old fellow reading it looked very serious, and announced that the President would be addressing the nation at nine. The game is up. I had expected to be doing the rounds by nine, but I can be flexible when history is taking place in front of my eyes, so I crossed the street to buy Mexican food and brought it back to the room. Then I settled down to watch Tricky Dick.

Nixon looks small and insignificant, a man in need of a personality transplant. The type of man who was born with a five o'clock shadow, he's clearly had some make up applied to his heavy jowls, which give him a ghostly appearance on the mostly green and red motel TV. He looks like some sad person's even sadder uncle, the kind you only see at weddings and funerals and politely nod to, steering well clear of for the rest of the day. His suit must be expensive, he's still the President, though not for much longer, but on him it looks cheap. You can almost see the sweat working its way through the seams, and smell the body odour and the fear and the lies coming at you down the tube.

History in the making this may well be, but once he starts droning I find it difficult to concentrate for more than thirty seconds. He makes a half-hearted attempt to justify himself. The basic gist is that if he had time he could prove his innocence, but it would damage the nation to do so. Best go now and allow the new president to deal with more important issues. Nobody is going to buy that, and you can tell that he doesn't either. Even Nixon isn't that stupid. I think of the teacher with the orange car and the yellow dress back in Georgia, and the question I asked her.

"How many of you are there? Two hundred million? How come you elect a President who is so stupid?"

I imagine her watching right now, three thousand miles away, shaking her head and smiling sadly. It takes him five minutes to get to the chase. He's officially standing down at noon tomorrow. Vice President Ford will take over. Then he starts talking about all the good things he's done in the last six years, and I imagine people all across the country turning off in disgust and do the same. Then I think of Don Hargreaves who must surely be watching also. He'll be shaking his head too, but he will be nursing a bottle of Lone Star and muttering "sonofabitch" over and over again. Don, who fought for his country in a war that was justified, the equally admirable JW and all the others who fought in one that wasn't, Ernie the trucker, fighting his way out of the ghetto, and how they've been betrayed, just as Washington, Lincoln, FDR and JFK have been betrayed, each and every one of them.

Then I think of Patti. I'm sure that Robyn and the Village crowd could care less, but I can picture Patti in her clapboard house in suburban Brooklyn watching television with her Mum and Dad. I realise that I'm seeing her slimmer than how I remember her from Coney Island, her jeans better cut, her hair styled. Just my imagination running away with me. I have no idea what her neighbourhood is like, nor her house. I turn off the TV, and for a few seconds at least, the image is replaced by one of me and Patti on the ferris wheel, her warm body as welcoming as the Statue of Liberty.

In Stanley's Bar nobody gives a fuck about Nixon or Watergate. Nobody seems to give a fuck much about anything except who's wearing what, who's got what drugs, what's on the charts, and whether Mott are in town. Well in all fairness most of them aren't too bothered about that, only Leah, who is now sitting at a table with some other girls of her own age, whatever age that may be, and occasionally throwing me poison glances via the mirror. Most of the men in this joint are older than me, and all the girls would appear to be younger, which makes me wonder exactly what kind of place it is. On the surface it is a shrine to the English music scene. On the wall is a large picture of David Bowie, made up to the nines. It suits him better than Nixon. On closer examination the photo appears to be of him sitting at a table in this very establishment with a guy who looks like a rock star himself, but who I don't recognise.

I remember my reaction when I saw Bowie on Top of the Pops in seventy two. He had a hit with Space Oddity in sixty nine and then seemed to fade from the scene, only to come back three years later with a new image. New and very different to the folky strummer of his previous incarnation. Earrings, make up, limp wrist round his lead guitarist's shoulder, eyeing him up like he was about to stick his tongue down his throat. It was one of the great TV moments, like

160

seeing Hendrix playing the guitar with his teeth on Ready Steady Go, or James Brown fooling half the nation's youth into thinking he had suffered a heart attack, the Stones showing their contempt for the sacred cow which was Sunday Night at the London Palladium, and Elvis Presley's rampant comeback in nineteen sixty eight.

Bowie's new song was called Star Man, and he had invented a whole new character for himself called Ziggy Stardust. There was no doubt that it was very good, but in some ways I found it a little disturbing. Not sexually you understand, but it was just that at twenty two I suddenly felt a bit old for the first time. I was a couple of years younger than Bowie, but I realised then that the Stones, Dylan and the solo Beatles were all heading for the wrong side of thirty, if they weren't there already. He had his own teenage fans who didn't give a monkey's about Crosby Stills and Nash, or The Beatles come to that. Something was happening here, and I knew very well what it was, thank you Mr Jones, but I knew that it wasn't aimed at me. That was when the seventies really started. Ziggy, Roxy, Bolan. Suddenly we had a whole new order. Decades never begin and end as tidily as they sound. The fifties didn't get going until Rock Around the Clock, and hung around until at least sixty two. The sixties didn't really exist until the Cuban missile crisis had been resolved, and the Beatles first album and The Freewheelin' Bob Dylan were in the shops and on the turntables.

I got to like Bowie's stuff well enough. I think back to just a few weeks ago, sitting in Robyn's apartment listening to Diamond Dogs. Rebel, rebel, put on your dress. Then I remember how my brother idolised David Bowie when he was fourteen, and then it clicks how he loved Mott too, most of all the line about your brother still being at home with his Beatles and his Stones. All the Young Dudes, a Bowie song. God knows Joey needed something to hang on to during the dark days of seventy two, and they provided it for him.

Set back from the bar there are a row of alcoves with tables, and I notice that there are two at the end which are roped off in red velvet. The far one would appear to be where Bowie is sitting in the photo. I'll admit to being mildly impressed. I seem to have stumbled on to the English rock scene's Hollywood hangout. Bowie, all the way from Bromley, Mott, all the way from Memphis. Or Herefordshire. So whose company are we likely to have the pleasure of tonight? That's what all the girlies are waiting to find out. The guys are probably

161

hanging around waiting to sell them stuff, and to chance their arm with the little girls if they don't show up. Yes, I get it.

Tonight it appears that they are out of luck. There's no one in that I recognise. The music is how I would imagine a school disco to be back home. Slade, Sweet, Suzi Quatro, Elton John. Oh and I've come six thousand miles or whatever it is to discover that Paper Lace are number three stateside. Some American bands, Alice Cooper, Iggy, but they are in the minority here.

In the men's room two young girls are standing by a stall in conversation with an older man. As I enter, they adjourn to one of the cubicles, quite unconcerned. For the rest of the evening I notice that the doors to both of the johns are swinging a lot more than they really should be. It's not as if there is anyone seriously sinking pints, although I'm finding the Mexican beer more than agreeable.

On another night I may well have said thanks but no thanks and made tracks for somewhere a little more authentic, but I'm comfortable at the bar and I've struck up some kind of conversation with the bartender. Marcel, black, about my age, well spoken. I suspect he might well be gay, but I'm already more easy going about that then when I left home. He too thinks I might be in the music business and is fishing to find out, although in a slightly more subtle manner than Leah. I can't imagine that he could possibly like much of this music. I ask him if he does, and he is strangely reticent in his reply. Maybe he thinks I have some connection with one of these groups, or he could be just reluctant to speak out against company policy.

Leah and her pals leave about one am, after she makes yet another trip to the bathroom and fires daggers at me from her stoned and heavily lined eyes on the way back. We're deep in the summer holidays, but even if we weren't I still couldn't imagine her going to school tomorrow. One of the biggest cultural differences I've noticed is that where I come from you have to be a real swot to make it past sixteen, but over here some people seem to still be going to school when they're thirty. Not Leah though. School's out forever. That's one thing we've got in common, I guess.

I order a Jack Daniel's, which goes down so well I promptly order another one before making my way back down Sunset at a quarter to two, wondering if I will wake up tomorrow to a new America. Meet the new boss. Same as the old boss.

Malibu beach looks much like any other beach. I'm sure it's a picture at sundown, looking out to the west, the Pacific stretching out to Honolulu and beyond, but I'm not going to stick around that long. Not today, anyway. I played on better stretches of sand when I was a kid. Dymchurch, Cromer, the Isle of Wight. Then when I started travelling I discovered the Atlantic beaches of Brittany, Portugal and Morocco, all of which blow this away. The Atlantic, which I've now seen from both sides, and which I last looked out on from the Coney Island boardwalk.

So now I've crossed this country from sea to shining sea. I can't help but think that the final frontier has been conquered more than the first one. Looking back to the old world from Brooklyn, the Atlantic was gun metal grey even under a blue sky. People were swimming off the beach but nobody was venturing too far out, as if old Neptune was stretching his icy fingers all the way down from Greenland and making it very clear that he would give up a hundred yards or so, but the rest was his and his alone. Here the Pacific is calm. Surf's not up today. Further along to the north the shore is lined with beach houses, some with their own private path down to the sea. Film stars residences maybe, rock stars even. Set in the cliffs they look fragile, as if they could crumble any minute. Buy a dog that looks like you. Buy a house that resembles your career. Back east the sea is still the master. When the winter winds blow you had best sit in your wooden home and hope for the best like the captain of some old whaling ship. Out here it's the land which is untamed. There are no earthquakes in New York.

I had no intention of hitching to the ocean. Contrary to rumour the greater Los Angeles area has a perfectly serviceable bus service if you stick to the major routes. Once again I had foolishly underestimated the sheer size of this town, if indeed it's a town at all, and set out to walk. What my brief explorations around the Strip area had not thus far revealed to me was that Sunset Boulevard is only a main artery for a mile or so further west. The traffic then joins up with Santa Monica Boulevard which leads directly to the Ocean. It's still another ten miles, maybe more. Sunset then takes its own winding course around the southern reaches of Beverley Hills before hitting the beach several miles north of Santa Monica.

So I take the Sunset option, and it takes me about twenty minutes before I realise that it's the wrong one. There's a midday sun blazing, no breeze and no bus. No pedestrians either. I suddenly feel as vulnerable as I did standing by the road down in Texas. Nobody walks around here. I feel that any time the LAPD could swoop down on me for the unamerican activity of strolling. More in hope than anticipation I stick my thumb in the air, which is probably an even more heinous crime. A sleek black Lincoln rolls by. I can feel the driver's eyes looking through me like I'm a dog turd smeared on his shiny new tyres, even though I can't see through the tinted windows. This doesn't feel like fun. Still, unlike Texas, I know that if I retrace my steps I'm little more than a mile from a bus stop. Then a jeep pulls up. No mirage either.

No tinted windscreen on this baby. No windscreen of any description. I don't notice this until the jeep starts moving and I feel the California air in my face like a warm flannel.

"Malibu beach, huh?"

One of those old hippie types who could be fifty, or could be twenty eight and had a hard life. Long straggly hair parted in the middle, black with touches of grey. Thick beard. Aviator shades to keep out the wind and retain his inscrutability. Reminds me of someone, but I can't think who.

"I live in the desert. I only come here when I have to."

Have to what, I wonder.

"I don't care for the beach myself. California is where all the crazy people come. The beach is where the crazies out of the crazy end up. Any further and you're in the Ocean."

Well the last part has some logic to it. Nodding his shaggy head as if he has just revealed to me some great wisdom.

"The desert has its fair share of crazies too. There's a whole lot more Charlie Mansons out there biding their time and waiting for their fifteen minutes."

And that is who you remind me of, my friend. I've got it now. At least there are plenty of potential escape routes on this glass free, General Purpose vehicle.

As it was I exited the car by more conventional means soon enough. I would have loved to have shared a meaningful conversation with my host and made myself familiar with his own particular take on world affairs, but in no more than ten minutes we were at the Pacific Coast Highway. He wished me an enigmatic good luck, and turned around back towards the Hollywood Hills. Could be looking for some luckless film star, might even be one himself. Didn't catch his name. Thanks for the lift fella, but I think I'll get the bus back.

The bus that runs from downtown LA to Santa Monica carries on up the coast highway to Malibu at weekends. Makes me think of catching the seventy one to Chessington when I was a kid. Extended on summer Sundays, the legend had it. That in turn makes me wonder why suddenly everything is reminding me of something else. I'm twenty four, for Christ's sakes. Maybe it's an LA thing. Like the man just said, what do you do when you can't go any further? If you can't look forward you can either live in an eternal present where the days run into each other, and it's always summertime and the living is easy, or you can gaze out over the Ocean and reflect on what you've left behind.

Sat at the back of the bus are two blond dudes with a cassette player. Both about twenty, t-shirts, cut offs. One of them switches on the tape as the bus moves off down the coast, the Sun just beginning to swing over to the west. I recognise the riff as the one I heard back in Texas in the pick up truck that saved my life, or so I thought at the time. I know it's only rock and roll but I like it, goes the chorus. Must be a new one. For a second I'm tempted to ask one of the dudes, but instantly kill the impulse. The song ends and he presses the rewind button.

"The greatest rock and roll band in the world, The Rolling Stones" he announces solemnly and then hits replay. He does this over and over. Nobody pays him any attention, including his buddy. In Santa Monica a middle aged woman gets on and takes the seat opposite. She looks as though she lives on the streets. Leather shopping bag and tennis shoes. I can't help but notice her bright blue eyes, and think she must have been a looker years ago. She catches me looking, and before I can avoid it eye contact is made.

"I like your hair." She has an actress's voice which fills the bus, even temporarily drowning out Mick J. "Is that your natural colour?"

I have Ma's blue eyes, but my hair has always been a fairly nondescript shade of brown, except for when I'm exposed to the Sun for any duration. Living on the beach in Morocco turned it a rather winsome burnished gold colour, if I may be so vain. A few weeks standing by the highway, topped off with the pool time I've been putting in are having the same affect.

"More or less" I reply in as offhand a manner as I can muster, but I'm forgotten now and she's looking out the window.

"I had the best hair in this whole town once."

The sad thing is not that she's mad, but that she quite possibly did have the best hair in Hollywood some time around nineteen forty two. Came to town with her bright blue eyes, and her raven hair and an hourglass figure, and a pocketful of hopes and dreams and trust. Took a tumble on the casting couch a few times, maybe. Ended up one more hard luck story, beaten up and faded as the Hollywood Sign. Like the Shangri-Las, she could never, ever go home again.

She may have retreated to her own private hell, but half the bus are now shooting sidelong looks at my barnet. As soon as we reach the part of Santa Monica Boulevard I recognise I take my leave of the cracked starlet and the would be disc jockey and walk back to the Riviera.

This is where the crazies end up. I liked the Stones track though. Every time I heard it I could feel that Lone Star beer hitting the back of my parched throat.

In LA the time passes slowly, yet the days are gone before you know it. I quickly fall into some kind of a routine. Wake up around ten, though this gets later by the day. Then I generally take a walk. I soon discovered that the Riviera is the bargain that it is because of its location, which is just a little further away from the action than it would like to be. That part of Sunset Boulevard which is forever known as The Strip is a fair walk further west. That sits fine with me. A fair walk has always sounded like a welcome idea to me, which immediately sets me apart from the good citizens of this fair city. Little happens on the Strip in the daytime. Of Efrem Zimbalist Jnr and Kookie there was sadly no sign. At first my morning promenade would take me up to Hollywood Boulevard and back down on Sunset in a circle, but as the days go by I find that my compass is getting wider, and I'm taking long walks up in to the hills, looking out on the smog which seems more like benign hazy cloud cover from street level.

Back at the Riviera for a swim, and an hour or so by the pool. I still nearly always have it to myself. There are always plenty of cars rolling down Sunset in the late afternoon, but there's also a feeling that nothing much is happening. On days when the sky is overcast it could almost be an English Sunday afternoon, circa nineteen sixty.

There's a young gay guy who sits out there sometimes, drinking Dr Pepper and talking about his mysterious lover, who is supposed to be staying there with him, but who I never see. Once he asks me to go back to his room to do some drug that I have never heard of. I decline the invitation as dismissively as if he was offering me a cream cracker, but he doesn't seem to take offence.

Before the first week was up I took the room for the month. I seriously love the room. I love the way it's hidden from the sun and allows me to sleep as late I want, I love the spacious bathroom, I like the closet with more than enough space for my few things. I like being tucked away in this courtyard so I don't hear any traffic. I like the fact that no one talks to me here, no one apart from gay friend that is, and he doesn't go so far as to ask me any questions, he only tells me about his lover who I am seriously beginning to doubt the existence of. This is where the crazy people end up.

Early evening is the time for a beer. Maybe even a little conversation. I still want to hear people's stories, but I want to hear them on the move or in a bar, sitting no more than an excuse away from the door, not by the pool. In the pool, even less so. A favourite happy hour venue is a small place on the Strip that doesn't appear to have a name but which is known to all and sundry as Pete's place. This pisses off the real owner, a taciturn fellow by the name of Doug, as Pete is no more than barman, chief cook and bottle washer, but until the day that Doug acquires either a sign or a personality, I suspect it is always going to be Pete's place, even when Pete isn't around.

Pete is from the Elephant and Castle, no more than a stone's throw from where I used to go and visit Granny Downes. Served his apprenticeship as an electrician and lived your regular South London existence up to the age of thirty, wife and two kids and a few pints on a Friday night. Then his life changed dramatically when one of his mates wangled him a job as a roadie for Blodwyn Pig. Six months of club and college gigs around the UK, and then he hit the big time. North American tour with Humble Pie. Word got around that Pete was a hard worker, stood no nonsense, and more importantly was a geezer, and he was in demand. Next up was a World tour with Led Zep, and all the excess and craziness that went with it. Everything has its price. Pete's price was losing his kids. Being a roadie is no job for a married man. Pete gave up the road but it was too late. Missus took up with an estate agent and moved out to Surrey.

The reason I know all this is that when Pete has had four or five drinks he gets a little confessional. Lachrymose, even, on a bad day. He's usually reached that level by about six o'clock. That's about the time I get there. Pete has lost his taste for the road but found a liking for Los Angeles. He's got his green card, so he's legit, which is unusual in itself. Been working here for two years now. Fell in love with a twenty year old redhead, and lives with her in a long term rental low budget motel. Every now and then the redhead takes off with her ex boyfriend, who's a bass player in an unsigned band who play the west coast from San Diego to Seattle. This is one of those times. I know that she's a looker as he shows me her picture more than once. On a bad day he digs out snaps of his kids.

I don't tell Pete my story. Well I do to a point, but I leave it a couple of years back, so I've just left the betting shop. I've got the world at my feet, and I'll return when I'm ready to take up another lucrative line of employment. Americans will believe anything, but I'm a little more self-conscious with my own. I'm sure that not so long ago things were very different, but in nineteen seventy four to be an Englishman in LA who is not in a band, or isn't a roadie or a fucking publicist, or at least something in the music business, is a bit like being a Frenchman who doesn't drink wine or a West Indian who doesn't like cricket. All in all, you're a bit of a sore thumb.

There's a mate of Pete's called Stu who I hit it off with right from the start. Stu's in town with Leo Sayer. He's in a different part of town, as Leo is holed up in the Beverley Wilshire, but he's on the team. Also on the team is Leo's manager, one Terry Nelhams, otherwise known as Adam Faith, the former local hero. He's up in the big hotel as well. Where else would he be?

"So what do you do then?" Asks Stu, obviously one of those blokes who gets straight to the point.

"I'm an accountant."

"Really? Chartered or certified?"

"Turf."

He likes that one. Loves a laugh, does our Stu. He's from Ponders End. Never been there myself. Neither has anyone, else according to Stu. Pete's is at its best around this time. Later on Pete turns up the music, and the place fills up with a local crowd, mostly male and hairy. If Stu is in he will generally move on to Barney's Beanery for a game of pool. My appetite fuelled by a few beers, I'm more inclined to

168

make a beeline for the Mexican takeaway and go back to the Riviera to eat.

John Sebastian may well have written the best song ever about rock and roll in Do You Believe In Magic, but he surely wrote the best song ever about a city summer's night. "And babe, don't you wish that the day could be like the night in the summer in the city."

The Spoonful were a New York band, Greenwich Village to be precise, but in LA I like night and day both just fine. In London a warm summer's night is a rare occurrence, a thing of beauty to be treasured. Here it's like it all the time. At ten pm I step out into the balmy evening air, fresh from the shower. I've found a local laundry, so my shirts are always clean on each night. I even bought a couple of new ones in the slightly cowboy style which seems to be in vogue around these parts. I feel good. Like I knew that I would.

Sometimes I make for Barney's Beanery, but only if I think Stu is going to be there. Barney's is a seriously crowded hangout popular with bands, roadies, general music business types, and punters alike. They've got every kind of whisky you can think of behind the bar and a lot more besides, and you can even get a Guinness if you want, although I pass on the offer. We play pool with a couple of roadies called Jeff and Graham. I surprised myself with my form on the pool table down in Pensacola, and I'm even more surprised to find that it's stuck with me. I've hardly played since I was a teenager. Here I'm shooting good, probably because I'm so relaxed. I don't play for anything more costly than a beer and I really don't care if I win or lose, which is not the way things are done down Shepherds Bush way.

Jeff's been a regular here since the days when Jim Morrison was the king of the Strip. Jeff tells a tale of how he went for a hot dog with the lizard king one time, and he spilt ketchup down the front of his white dress shirt. He saw him again ten days later and he was wearing the same shirt, still adorned with condiment. Very rock and roll. I understand why Pete was in such demand as a roadie. He was very discreet. I was hoping for tales of satanic orgies with Zeppelin, but Pete kept mum. No, Pete had other favoured topics for conversation. Mind you, nothing much is likely to get back to poor old Jim.

There doesn't appear to be too much live music around. There's The Troubadour down the road, which is traditionally the showcase gig for new artists getting the big push, and is said to be cliquey even by LA standards. A couple of small folk places down in Santa Monica, the usual bar bands working the clubs, and not a lot else. Graham tells me that he went to see Aretha Franklin at the Hollywood Bowl a few weeks back, and a man in the audience got shot. I tell Graham it must have been his own fault. Obviously wasn't showing someone enough R-E-S-P-E-C-T.

Music, music, music. For the first time in my life I feel like I'm getting a little bored with it. I know this is a music business town, but I also know that it's a movie business town. The movie business town. Somewhere not far from here people are making movies, making lots of them, but you don't see them. Well you might see the films eventually, but there must be as many people in Hollywood either living for or feeding off the film industry as they're are doing the same for rock and roll. There's a whole alternative world out there somewhere. Somewhere up in the hills, maybe. Ten miles south, maybe even less than that, is what most of us would call the real world. My pal Ernie hauling his ass out of bed at five am to go to work, when most of the residents of Tinsel town are just about ready to haul theirs in. Ernie's world, which is not a lot different to the one I grew up in, is less real than Planet of The Apes to the midnight cowboys and cowgirls who cruise these boulevards.

I don't think I'm going to be staying in Los Angeles too long.

Chapter Eleven: LA Woman

For some reason I can't quite put my finger on, I seem to be drawn to Stanley's more than anywhere else. I finally got to meet Stanley himself after I had been in a few times. He is indeed the character in the picture with Bowie. Scrawny little fellow of about thirty, who at first glance looks about five feet eight, until I clock that about seven of the eight are supplied by platforms that could quite easily be a pair of Elton's cast offs. The hair style is Rod Stewart, the satin jacket is Bolan, as is his height, and the look is completed with a pair of Lennon specs. It looks like Stanley is the type of guy who would die if he ever had an original thought, but he seems to have got this place together. Maybe he's just a front man.

So Stanley may be togged out like a composite all-purpose English pop star, but when he speaks it sounds like Peter Lorre, only more camp. "Well hello, I'm Stanley."

No kidding.

"I've seen you around. So who are you with?"

Well if you've seen me around Stanley, you will know that I'm not with anyone in the conventional sense, but that isn't what you mean, is it now? As Leah and Marcel both did in their own different ways, you are enquiring as to which famous pop person or people I may be connected with.

"I'm here on my own, actually."

My enunciation has become markedly more English again since I've been here, and I hear myself saying actually as if I were Leslie Phillips. Stanley scarcely bothers to conceal his disappointment.

"Well I hope you enjoy your stay in LA" he whines before turning with some difficulty on his quite frankly ridiculous heels, and going in search of someone who is worth talking to. Sorry to disappoint you, Stanley. Well not really. I take it as a fucking compliment.

I think that's when I decided that I felt at home in Stanley's. I've even got to know some of the regulars, although there are a whole lot more I stay out of the way of. There's an older girl called Michelle who I've got time for. Michelle has a boyfriend who DJ s at Stanley's sometimes, and she's not interested in getting off with any division two pop stars, or me, come to that. She doesn't take the scene too seriously, which in itself puts her apart from most of the others. She also appears to be friendly purely for the sake of it, which puts her even further apart. Leah and myself have arrived at an uneasy truce, but there's another chick called Stone, or who calls herself that anyway, who doesn't look a day over fourteen, and is pilled up to the eyeballs whenever I see her. Stone is one of those I give a seriously wide berth to. Considering that the legal drinking age in the state of California is twenty one, I'm surprised that some rival concern hasn't tipped off the heat about what goes on at Stanley's, not to mention the teenage runaways and the goings on in the rest rooms (American euphemism for toilet and a singularly inappropriate description of the ones in Stanley's). I'm making sure I'm as clean as a whistle in case I'm around when they do get busted. I'm drug free and I got ID. Sounds like an Alice Cooper song.

There's one girl that I would like to know better. Zaria is not unlike Michelle in that she doesn't appear to take this place at anything other than face value. What is different is that I could be interested should the opportunity arise. Dark curly hair falling on to her shoulders, skin that looks as though it may see the Sun sometimes, and healthy looking curves that suggest that she may even eat. I don't want to blow my cover by making myself look stupid in front of Leah and the others, but I'm hoping we can have a chat sometime.

Not tonight we won't. Zaria is in, but she leaves before midnight. I stay till closing time, then I go for breakfast at Denny's. Having my breakfast before I go to bed is now firmly part of my routine, and seems such an obviously brilliant idea that I am amazed that I never thought of it before. Probably because such an option is not generally available in London unless you cook it yourself, which isn't really part of the plan. Denny's is a nationwide twenty four hour diner chain, and I feel safe there no matter what time it is because it's where the cops eat. You can get a steak or an omelette, but I always have the same thing. Two fried eggs, bacon, sausage, hash browns and a glass of milk. Guaranteed to make me sleep late and wake with no hangover. Stop off at the all night gas station for milk and orange juice for the morning, and hit the hay some time before four.

So that's the Frank Downes guide to your average day and night down Hollywood California way, in this long hot summer of nineteen seventy four. Pretty damn interesting, huh? Well maybe something interesting will happen tomorrow. You never know.

172

Down at Stanley's the roped off booth is occupied for the first time since I've been there. John Lennon, Ringo Starr and Keith Moon are holding court with a large bearded blond chap, and a woman who looks like Yoko Ono's younger and prettier sister. Stanley is all over them, fawning sickeningly. Lennon is loud, seemingly contemptuous of Stanley's obsequiousness, but accepting it as his due all the same. The blond fellow, who I now recognise as Harry Nilsson, is barely conscious. I think of that Midnight Cowboy song, and how much it meant to me when I was planning one of my getaways. Maybe I should go and tell him. Yeah, right. I'm not about to look directly, but I can't help myself from sneaking glances in the mirror. John is wearing a red shirt, is clean shaven, and looks in surprisingly good fettle. Squint your eyes a little and he could have stepped off the set of Help. The woman is wearing a business suit, and is hanging on his arm and his every word. If there is something going on they want to keep a secret, they are not exactly making much of an effort. Ringo, with neatly trimmed hair and beard, is wearing a dark jacket, dark shirt and dark sunglasses, despite the fact that he is indoors and it is night time. Unusual behaviour in the Dingle possibly, but not in Stanley's. Nilsson is wearing a thick tweed suit that would be more suitable for grouse shooting than for hitting the town on a hot California night. Keith Moon has a full length dark brown leather coat which he hasn't bothered to remove. He looks like Keith Moon.

Seeing Moonie makes me think of my pal Keith and his brother Paul, who was three years older than us. Still is, I suppose. Paul caught a lot of the sixties that we were just too young for. He used to go and see The Who down at the Goldhawk Social Club around sixty four. They might not even have been called The Who then, I think they were the High Numbers for a while. Paul idolised Keith Moon, and slavishly copied his hairstyle and his wardrobe, which at that time consisted mainly of striped t-shirts, tight white Levi's and elastic sided boots. I think Paul identified with him because he was the same age. Moonie was no more than eighteen when The Who first made it. Paul loved The Who and the Stones, and black rhythm and blues. He used to track down the most obscure singles and pin them on to his bedroom wall. Paul was a mod. We thought Paul was the acest of the faces. I last saw him at his brother's wedding. He was a chartered surveyor, living in

Dorking with wife and child.

Keith Moon. Three years older and twenty feet away from me. I flashback to seeing him on Ready, Steady Go, fuelled by pills and teenage arrogance, being interviewed by Cathy MacGowan.

"Welcome to the programme Keith, it's very nice having you."

"Fank you Caffy, it's very nice 'avin' you."

Cue ribald laughter from the mods in the audience. That was considered bold in sixty six. Had us in stitches for months.

I temporarily wish Paul was here, and it also occurs to me what a kick old Railroad Phil would get out of it, but my most pressing concern is trying to get a bloody drink, as the bar staff all have both eyes fixed on Stanley in case he should click his fingers and instantly require refills for his esteemed guests. Then he's back at the bar demanding a round of Brandy Alexanders, like, right now. He is the only one who is allowed to wait on the royal visitors. He's excited like a kid who has just got his biggest ever Christmas present.

"They're working on Ringo's new album" he splutters, barely unable to get the words out. "This is just the greatest thing ever."

I'm not about to look down at his green velvet crutch, but I wouldn't be in the least surprised if he's got a bone on.

Most of the regulars are posing as normal, doing what they spend every waking moment doing, trying to look cool. I catch Michelle's eye and she gives me a wink. Michelle and Marcel are the only people here who genuinely couldn't give a shit. I can't help but be impressed, but I'm determined not to show it. Zaria smiles at me from across the room as if she's reading my mind, and for a moment she reminds me of Julie, even though she looks nothing like her.

Five minutes later and the royals are leaving, Stanley running around in front of them like the White Rabbit, Beatles moving swiftly and silently, well practised, eyes moving neither to the left or the right, as if this is Shea Stadium and the helicopter's waiting outside. Moonie and the woman each have the comatose Nilsson by an arm, and are more or less carrying him.

"Come along old chap, the night is still young!"

The boy from the Wembley council estate is now speaking like Laurence Olivier. He is the only one to acknowledge that there are other people in the place.

"Everybody's talking at him!" He proclaims, each vowel fruitier than the last, "but he can't hear a word they're saying!"

On a whim I turn on my stool and catch his eye as he passes me.

174

"All right, Keith mate! Might see you down the Goldhawk Road some time."

He pauses for the briefest of moments, and then a smile crosses his still youthful but slightly ravaged features.

"You may indeed, dear boy. But not tonight, I would wager."

And then they're gone and Stanley is back at the bar, slightly deflated but still excited. "They're probably going to the Rainbow Room now" voice wracked with envy. "One of these days they won't want to go there. This will be number one."

"Dream on Stanley" says Michelle.

I like Michelle. I like Zaria too, but for different reasons.

Later I ask Marcel what a Brandy Alexander is.

"Well, it's brandy." Yes I might have worked that part out myself Marcel, "and you put it in a mixer with creme de cacao, cream and ice, then you lose the ice, sprinkle a little nutmeg on top and that's your Brandy Alexander. Comes out like a brandy milkshake"

"Hmm" I reply. "A few of those and a lamb madras would certainly help you to redecorate the bathroom, would they not?"

For some reason unbeknown to myself I hear myself talking like Moon. I could be the Man in the Moon for all it means to Marcel.

I mess with my routine, and pay for it by not sleeping well. Stanley was unbearable after the royal visit so I left early. I looked in on Barney's Beanery, but there was no one there I knew and it was uncomfortably crowded, so I gave it a miss. I stopped off for a Jack Daniel's in a regular bar where the thirty something waitress started to tell me her life story. For once I wasn't in the mood and made my excuse and left. Not having had enough to drink to work up an appetite, I skipped breakfast and returned to the Riviera intent on an early night. Mistake.

When I do finally get to sleep I have a variation of a dream I used to have a lot when I first started going to parties. I would come home and go to bed, and then dream that the party was still going on around me, never quite sure if I was awake or asleep. This time my bed is in the middle of the floor at Stanley's. I'm surrounded by a room of figures that I recognise one by one as The Beatles, all of them, Bowie, Elton John, Marc Bolan, and many more who I know to be famous but whose faces I can't see. At the other end of the room stand The Beach Boys, marginalised in their own town. Keith Richards is leaning against the bar, mean and moody, and nursing a tumbler full of Jack

Danny. Cat Stevens is standing smiling in a familiar Breton jersey, clutching a glass of white wine. None of them pay any attention to me, although I am clearly in the way. They're either too polite to disturb me in my bed, or more likely too cool to acknowledge the presence of a mere mortal. I'm looking around in vain for someone I know.

Sitting at a table are Francoise Hardy, Joni Mitchell and the Queen. Not the queen of soul, not even the queen of folk, but The Queen, Elizabeth Windsor H.M. I get up and approach the table. Francoise Hardy, who stood me up in Paris, or was it Pecos, and is now here when I don't want her to be, ignores me completely, as does the Lady of the Canyon. The Queen doesn't ignore me, in fact she's looking straight at me. It's then I realise that I'm naked.

Drink less than usual, go to bed three hours earlier, and wake up feeling rougher than I have for a long while. Let that be a lesson to me. I fumble with the television trying to get the news, and discover that I can get the radio as well. It's only taken me two weeks. I lie in bed for the rest of the morning alternately dozing and listening. The rock station DJs all have the same laid back style which makes me feel I'm in Los Angeles even more than physically being in Los Angeles does. They favour English music of the less adventurous kind, Elton, Eric Clapton in his present incarnation, Ten Years After. Gordon Lightfoot from Canada, who I remember from years ago singing one of the great folky road songs, Early Morning Rain, is big of all a sudden, although his arrangements now make him more or less indistinguishable to everyone else. The California jocks all seem more impressed by record sales than by quality or soul or real meaning, the truth that comes shining out of genuinely great music for all to see.

"This album went platinum in seven days."

"Tickets for three shows at the Coliseum sold out in ten minute flat. That's how much LA loves Elton John."

They love him because you're telling them to, Mr DJ, and you're playing these records because they're buying them, and the circle goes on and on, as it will until the day comes as it surely will, when it falls apart and takes everyone by surprise, because even though that's what always happens, no one is ever expecting it when it does.

I did hear that song Sandy again, the one that got through to me in that bar in New York. I find it even more intriguing on a second hearing. It seems out of place here, even though it is a song for a summer day. More out of the place than the English music does. I can see the seaside town in New Jersey and the characters in the song, the waitress, tired of the singer and probably tired of life itself, the fortune teller who got busted by the cops for telling fortunes better than they do, the singer himself seemingly bored with the town and the beach, but still able to describe it in a tender fashion that he wouldn't be able to unless he really loved it as well. New York City is just up the turnpike, but he doesn't seem too impressed with that either, judging by his dismissal of the silly girls who come visiting.

I finally get myself moving a little after noon, and compensate for missing breakfast by hitting the nearby pancake house for lunch. Pancakes with sausage and hash browns bear little resemblance to how I remember things being on a Shrove Tuesday in West London, but the carbohydrates followed by the sugar from the blueberry waffle dessert go a long way to reintroducing me to the human race. An afternoon swim completes the job. There's no haze today. It's a beautiful LA day.

Sunbathing by the pool, I ponder on my brush with rock's aristocracy. The new lords. I'm still a little taken aback at how casually I found myself sharing licensed premises with half of the most famous musical combo of all time, and it dawns on me that for all its pretensions, this town is like London, only ten years behind. In the mid-sixties all the groups used to hang out at places like the Scene club and the Scotch of St James, and anybody could go there if they were in the know, and if they were old enough, which I wasn't. In the seventies it's not like that. I've never really been one for club scenes, cliques, whatever you want to call them. The idea of there being one club in one street where you were of no account if your trousers weren't exactly the correct width always struck me as fairly ludicrous, even when I was a teen and paying a certain amount of lip service to it. So although I never doubted that I had the street smarts to blag my way in to El Sombrero in Kensington and rub padded shoulders with Bryan Ferry, I never had any desire to do so.

On the Strip I have a certain place on the totem pole by virtue of nationality, though not like in Greenville, South Carolina where I was a celebrity myself, purely because I was English. Here that gives me a certain kudos, but I am still essentially anonymous, mysterious even, if anyone is interested enough to wonder. So what, apart from being good at their job, has elevated these men not much older than me to the status of Greek gods? The initial fame and wealth comes in a heady rush, and can't help but be as much fun as you've ever dreamt of if you've got anything about you at all. These people were all

177

famous when they were younger than I am now. After that, I imagine, it becomes much more insidious. Special treatment in restaurants, fashion designers giving you free gear, surrounded by toadies and sycophants, the simpering Stanleys of this world. If you're famous at twenty one it means that you don't know what it's like to be a normal grown up. At best you may have had a couple of years as a regular adolescent, a couple of years soon forgotten as a life of limos, cocaine, and Brandy Alexanders becomes the norm.

I'm trying to be as fair as possible. I'm a fan, after all. Even so, it feels like we've got lost somewhere along the line. I wonder what Del Shannon is doing now, and then my thoughts turn to poor Gene Vincent in the Packhorse and Talbot, unloved, uncared for, and not long for this world. Fifteen years earlier he had been touched by real greatness. He could still sometimes display glimpses of it on stage on the rare occasions he was given a band that could play at all, but mostly it was gone, gone, gone. I know that John Lennon had idolised Gene, but like everyone else, he wasn't there when he could have helped him. How could he have been?

Moonie wasn't in my dream, not that I remember, but I can see his face before me now. I see his eyes in that brief moment when they were locked with mine. Was that fear I saw? If it was, what was he frightened of? Did he see himself in me for that fleeting moment? The boy from West London on the loose, free and unfettered by fame. No, that's surely fanciful. It's dark in Stanley's, and he was gone in a flash, poor old Nilsson's feet barely touching the ground. Even so, I could sense that he was well on the way to forgetting who he was and where he came from, and in his sober moments he knew there wasn't a single thing he could do about it. What do you do when you are confronted with that? Make damned sure that you don't have too many sober moments, I guess.

I remember reading an article in a Sunday magazine once which said that dreaming of being naked before the Queen was one of the more commonplace dreams of the English middle classes. Your classic anxiety dream, reflecting fear of embarrassment, loss of status, and public exposure, those demons which stalk the corridors of the middle class psyche like Dracula. At the time I thought it was laughable, with an air of the self-fulfilling prophecy about it. Float the idea into the ether and people will pick up on it. Then when I'm far from home and least expecting it, who should appear in the middle of the night but the old bird herself, staring sternly down at my shrinking member. I'm not middle class. I'm not anxious. What the fuck?

I'm inclined to blow out Stanley's tonight, but once again I find myself walking through the door at ten pm. Anyway, I need to exorcise my dream. Stanley wants to talk to me. Tells me it's good to see me. Gets me a drink on the house. Asks me how I'm doing. Invites me over to a table. Not on the other side of the cordon, but the one next to it. This is a strange turn of events, and no mistake.

"So how long are you figuring on being in LA, Frank?"

Thinks. What's it to you, Stanley? I'm not in the music business. I don't exist. Says. "I'm not sure exactly. I've got a few offers back home. I'm just taking a little r and r while I think them over."

Then I flash him one of those two second smiles that is really no more than a twitch. A real Hollywood smile. Maybe I do have a future in this town.

"Have you thought about staying longer? Maybe taking a job?"

I have to admit to being ever so slightly intrigued as to where Stanley is going with this. He sounds more like Peter Lorre than ever.

"Marcel's going back to school in September."

School? I thought Marcel was my age. That's how it works here.

"You get on well with people Frank, and you know a lot of people. I think you could be a great bar manager. Where are you staying?"

I tell Stanley where I'm staying.

"No problem. I'll take care of the rent and give you a hundred a week on top. You get Sunday and Monday off."

Thinks. That's about forty quid a week. Stick it up your arse, Stanley. Says. "Well it's tempting. Like I said, I've got some offers at home. I'll let you know."

"I would appreciate it if you let me know as soon as possible, Frank." Stanley's into a full on whine now.

"Sure, Stanley. I'll let you know Monday. Thanks for the offer. I appreciate it." Listen to yourself, you insincere fucker.

"So tell me, how long have you known Keith?"

Keith. You know a lot of people. Now I get it. Stanley is offering me a job because he thinks I know Keith Moon. I knew he was shallow, but fuck me.

"Oh I know The Who from way back. You know Tommy, the deaf, dumb and blind boy? That was inspired by my brother."

Stanley is peering at me uncertainly through his rimless specs, which I would wager he doesn't actually need.

"No, I'm just kidding you. I don't know Keith that well. I know Roger better." Keith Moon is the only member of The Who who wasn't brought up in my part of London. Roger Daltrey I know as well as I know Adam Faith. A full head of curls behind the wheel of a Lamborghini disappearing up East Acton Lane one time.

"You see, that's what we need Frank. That English sense of humour. I think you would be really great."

I don't think Stanley would know humour if he had some rammed firmly up his jacksie. I thank him again for his offer, and tell him again that I'll think about it but now I've got to go, like I've got a business meeting or something. I move on to Barney's Beanery and play pool for the rest of the night with Stu and Jeff and anyone who wants to take us on. This time we play for money. We make, coincidentally, a hundred dollars, although that goes three ways and most of it straight back behind the bar. Stanley's job offer causes no little hilarity, more so as the beer and the sunrises go down.

Venice Beach is about a mile down the boardwalk from Santa Monica pier. Once again I am reminded of how Los Angeles and New York are worlds apart. Coney Island was host to people from all five boroughs taking a day off from their labours, like East Enders on a beano down to Southend. In Venice it would be easy to believe that none of the people here ever leave. The jugglers and the men on stilts look as though they belong in no circus that I can imagine, and the strung out hippies thumping conga drums with no sense of purpose or rhythm don't belong anywhere on the planet except here. Make that including here. An old black man singing country songs passably well to the accompaniment of a beat up acoustic guitar is upstaged by a blond longhair who has no discernible talent other than to be able to sing and play after a fashion while roller skating. A man on a unicycle parades up and down repeatedly along a hundred yard stretch of boardwalk, with no sign of stopping or of showing any pleasure in his activity. Why does he do it? For the same reason that a dog licks his own balls, I suppose. Because he can.

A bunch of freaks are sitting in the shade, talking and smoking. They appear underfed and overdressed in thick denim shirts buttoned at the wrists. Their hair is lank and their beards are scruffy, and their pale, grubby complexions suggest they are rarely exposed to sun or water even though they are on the beach. I think back to those heady days of ninety sixty seven. All you had to do was wear some flowers in your hair and you could change the world. None of these blokes look as though they have the wherewithal to change their pants. I leave hurriedly before I turn into my Dad.

I walk back up to Santa Monica and watch the sun go down from the pier. The ocean, so calm when I was at Malibu the other week, is fresh, vibrant and inky blue. The pier is crowded. Sunset is still the most popular show in town. It's free for one thing, and it has been running for a long, long while with no sign of the closing notices going up. I'm surrounded by people, but I feel alone. I know I'm not going to be staying in LA. I've been here little more than two weeks and it seems like longer. Where to next? Mexico? No, that's for another time. San Francisco? Sure, why not. When? I've paid for two more weeks at the Riviera. That will be about right.

On the bus I see the homeless woman again. She's wearing an old gabardine raincoat. Then I realise it's not the same woman. She is a still handsome woman, but her eyes are brown. Thankfully she doesn't speak. I ponder a moment how many failed rock stars are going to be riding around Los Angeles on buses holding shopping bags in twenty or thirty years' time.

I get off the bus at Clark, walk up to the Strip and make straight for Stanley's. I could do with seeing a familiar face even it belongs to Marcel. I know Stanley is unlikely to be here this early. In four days time I'm going to have to tell him that I don't want his job. The bar is quiet at this hour. I take my regular stool and to my surprise and delight I am immediately joined by Zaria.

"You don't happen to have seen Michelle, have you?"

Not really. The only place I happen to see any of this crowd is in here. Zaria is bright enough to know this. This can only mean one thing. She's interested. My melancholy mood is lifted in a heartbeat. Zaria asks if I want a sunrise. I decline and join her in a beer. Sunrises are strictly for after sunset.

"I wanted to talk to Michelle about Susanna's party."

Then a pause. "Are you coming?"

I can answer this one truthfully. "I don't know who Susanna is, and I haven't been invited, so I would think probably not."

"Susanna doesn't get out too often. Her parents are kind of strict."

"So where's the party?"

"Her parents' house. They're going on vacation Friday."

"I get it. I've been to parties like that before."

That's true also.

"Why don't you come as my date?"

I don't need asking twice. Zaria has drug free brown eyes, and colouring which suggests she might have some latin origins. Could even be Italian somewhere down the line. She scorns glitter for washed Levi's, and a fresh white t-shirt which she manages to fill nicely, but not in a cartoon Jayne Mansfield kind of way. She could fit in anywhere. Anywhere except here, probably. She's already made my day, but now she is being reproachful.

"You hurt Leah's feelings, did you know that?"

Once again I give an honest answer. Three in a row, must be a record. "I wasn't rude to her. I just didn't want to cop off with her." I could have added that neither did I wish to tell her my life story, but I don't. I continue. "Anyway, she might have hurt my feelings. She swore at me."

Zaria's eyes are twinkling now. They really are rather lovely.

"Cop off? She might have hurt your feelings if you had any, right?"

You're sharp, Zaria. What's more, you have caught me when I'm vulnerable and I feel like I'm falling in love here. Well I exaggerate, but not by much.

"So what do you do?"

I like her to the point of being intrigued, but do I wish to tell her my life story also? Not yet I don't. I edge closer and lower my voice to a whisper. "Can you keep a secret?"

Her beautiful eyes open a little wider.

"Well, the truth is, I'm a private eye. What do you call it, a private dick? I've been tailing someone for over a year and I've got a hot tip that he might show up in this neighbourhood." I nod conspiratorially.

"You're full of shit, do you know that", but said with a smile and laughing eyes which display that she is in on the joke in a way that I don't think Leah would have been somehow.

"Are you going to work for Stanley?"

Word gets around. Sadly I don't completely extend my honesty to four in a row.

"I don't know yet. I've got used to this side of the bar."

"Maybe you'll know by Saturday?"

"Maybe."

"Anyway, I've got to run. If you see Michelle tell her to call me. Oh and I'll see you here on Saturday at nine thirty."

Then she's finished her beer, and she's gone before I can buy her one back. I think about getting myself another one, but don't. Stanley's suddenly feels empty without Zaria's presence, empty and fake, which it always has been of course. My weariness from the beach has evaporated, and I almost skip down Sunset. I seek out Stu, who is going home on Tuesday, and a most rip-roaring time is had by all for the rest of the evening.

On Saturday morning I mooch down to a trendy emporium in West Hollywood and buy myself a new shirt for the party. It's a rather fetching pink and green check affair which shows off my tan to good effect, even if I say so myself. A steal at fifty bucks. I resist the temptation to buy a new pair of strides. This is after all the Egalitarian States of America. Anywhere old Levi Strauss is not welcome is somewhere I don't want to be.

Jeans are another commodity, which like petrol, ciggies and hamburgers, are ridiculously cheap in America the beautiful. I haven't bought any yet, on account of I'm mindful of how much I have to carry, my luggage already three shirts heavier, and also because I have a sentimental attachment to the two pairs I brought with me, one pair for the road and one for evening wear. I plan to buy a suitcase and stock up before I go home.

Go home? My mood has changed in the day and a half since I watched the Sun go down from Santa Monica pier. Now I'm even thinking of staying on in LA. If things go well with Zaria tonight then I might even take Stanley's job. Why not? What have I got to lose?

The rest of the day I spend by the pool. I line my stomach with an early supper of tacos and burritos, and I'm freshly scrubbed and shaved, and sitting at the bar at Stanley's with a cold one in front of me at nine o'clock. I've never been a great one for parties, but I'm up for this one. It suddenly occurs to me that I don't know the location of this bash. I'm assuming it's not too far from this area but Los Angeles is a big place. No, Zaria and Michelle wouldn't stray too far from their world. Everything is going to be great. Groovy, in fact.

I was hoping Stanley wouldn't be in tonight, although he is every Saturday, but no, he's here, he's seen me and he's making a beeline in my direction.

"Hey Frank, you're looking great man! Have you considered my offer?"

Then I am more than slightly surprised to hear myself reply, "Yes I would love to work here Stanley. I can't stick around right now, can we discuss it on Monday?"

I wouldn't say Stanley looks quite as ecstatic as he was when Johnny L and his mates were in, but he looks pretty damned happy.

"That's wonderful, Frank. Come and see me on Monday at six o'clock. You can start on Tuesday."

Then he's calling people over that I don't know, telling them I'm going to be the new bar manager and how I know everybody, and how great it is, and how Stanley's bar is going to be the best bar on the whole Strip, and then these people are buying me drinks, hoping no doubt I'll slip them cocktails on the house when I'm the other side of the bar, and the next thing I know it's ten fifteen and there's still no Zaria.

It's ten thirty when Michelle appears on the scene. She's with Rory, her DJ boyfriend whom I have already bonded with slightly, him being Irish and all, although it is my contention that he is a lot less Irish than I am.

"Hey, Frankie. There's a little change in the plan here. Zaria is going to meet us there. Me and Rory came to give you a ride."

My good mood deflates more than slightly. It doesn't seem to matter whether they're in Hollywood or High Barnet, parties never seem to go to plan, not the ones I go to. I'm reminded once again that I don't know the venue.

"That's O.K. So where are we going?" Trying not to show any hesitancy in my voice and none too successfully.

"Coldwater Canyon. It's a fifteen minute drive. Twenty at the most."

I shrug and finish my beer.

"Ready when you are folks."

The pick up truck appears to be something of a fashionable accessory for the beautiful people of West LA., so it comes as no surprise to find that Rory has one parked outside. We roar off down Sunset with Bad Company assailing us from four speakers, take a right on to Laurel Canyon Boulevard, and soon we're in the hills. There are a lot of big trees, interspersed with a number of impressive looking residences, though not so many of them as I expected. Coming from where I come from, I'm always impressed by houses where there is no chance of you being disturbed by the neighbours pulling the chain. I'm clocking the time and the direction in case Michelle was being less than truthful with her e.t.a., but a couple more turns and we're in the driveway of a most well-appointed gaff which you couldn't quite describe as a mansion, but is not far from it. The driving time was seventeen minutes.

Michelle takes me inside and introduces me to Susanna, our hostess. I don't know her, although I've seen several thousand like her since I arrived in this town, blonde, blue eyed, you know the rest. Susanna has got a brother called Scott who has very long hair and looks about twelve, although Michelle tells me he is seventeen, and has some kind of muscle wasting disease and an I.Q. of a hundred and fifty. Mother nature obviously hadn't been too kind to him in the first place, but I can't help thinking that it must have been a particularly cruel twist of fate which decreed he be born here rather than in, say Oxford, or Tunbridge Wells.

The music is Creedence, which is fine with me, but it's on so low that it is difficult to decipher which song is playing. Most of these kids in this music town aren't interested that much in music itself, but the stuff that comes with it, the famous people they occasionally get to rub shoulders with on the Strip, the drugs and the sex and more drugs. There are two large posters pinned up in the living room, both clearly there on a temporary basis. From one wall the Rolling Stones leer down at the parade of jail bait on offer. Stray Cat Blues could have been written for any one of these nymphets if it wasn't for the song being six years old now, which would have made most of them about eight when it came out. I see straight away that with the exception of Michelle, who is around my age, and Rory who is probably a little older, everyone here is younger than me.

Pinned on the opposite wall is a ceiling high, black and white poster. The picture is blurred because it is a blow up of a newspaper. Patty Hearst is holding a sub-machine gun while acting as look out on of her captors' bank robberies. Above her head, crudely scrawled in thick black capitals is the legend TANIA.

The boys, with the exception of Scott, are all surfers and high school jocks in their late teens, drinking beer and looking to score, like teenage boys anywhere. There are people here from Stanley's who I have spoken to but never got to know the names of, there are a lot of kids I've never seen before, and there are a few people that I know. Like for instance Stone and Leah. Still no Zaria. Great. Still, there's a massive tub of Mexican beers on ice, so I help myself to one and it's as good a companion as any, as is the next one and the one after that. Fuck Zaria. I'm having a good time.

Then I hear a shrill voice somewhere around the region of my ribs. I look down to see Scott.

"Hey, are you the guy with the weird cigarettes?"

That must have come from Leah. He probably wanted to ask me if I was the fucking rude guy with the cigarettes that taste like shit, but was worried I might blow a smoke ring and send him flying to the next county. As I do indeed have a Disque Bleu on the go as he speaks, I cannot really deny that I am the man who smokes what might be termed unusual cigarettes in these parts, but a brand which acts very much as a conversation piece. Breaks the ice at parties you could say.

"Do you think I could try one of your cigarettes. Please?"

He sounds like Oliver Twist asking for more. I almost ask him if his parents know he smokes, but thankfully stop myself just in time, mindful of how hurtful that might be. I flip one and give him a light, and he takes a long drag like Humphrey Bogart drawing on his first Lucky Strike of the day.

"That smokes pretty good."

The boy knows how to smoke a cigarette.

"Do you mind if I look at the packet?"

I hand him the packet.

"French. All right! Hey you must like wine, right?"

I nod.

"Hey, you want to drink some French wine with me?"

Sounds good to me. Scott leads me to the kitchen, and asks me to open a top cupboard. I do so, and pull out the single bottle. I don't kid myself that I'm any kind of connoisseur, but I recognise the label on this one, Chateauneuf du Pape. I remember me and Julie chasing a steak down with a bottle of this once, and very agreeable it was too. A little outside our normal price range, but I seem to recall that it was her birthday. Things are looking up, as is Scott, who then instructs me to open the adjoining cupboard, where I find a pair of rather elegant crystal wine glasses. Scott manages to find a corkscrew in the drawer himself. He then removes the cork as if to the manner born, and pours me a glass. I take a hefty swig and savour. It is as enjoyable as I remember it, and a real bonus to find around these parts. Also goes very well with a Disque Bleu.

You are never alone in the kitchen for long at parties, and this one is no exception. We're about three quarters of the way through the bottle when a gaggle of girls, one of whom is Leah, come in and commandeer the table. I thought it would be just a matter of time before the old white powder put in an appearance, and sure enough, in a couple of minutes there's enough cocaine lined up to fill one of those giant sized tins of Johnson's baby powder I remember being around

186

the house when Joey was a kid. Then Susanna joins the merry throng. She's entitled to after all, she lives here. She takes one look at the kitchen table and looks as if she is about to seriously freak. I can't say I blame her. The cops come calling now they're going to have this place down as a class A drug warehouse. Then I realise that isn't her problem. Her eyes are firmly focused on the now empty bottle. Then she starts screaming.

"Ohmigod, ohmigod, how could you? What gave you the right? Ohmigod they'll kill me."

She's looking at Scott, but I get the feeling that she is talking to me just as much. A few more ohmigods before she bursts into tears and runs out of the kitchen towards the stairs, no doubt heading for her room, where she will throw herself face down on her bed in time honoured fashion.

I'm still in a mellow mood, but I can't help be concerned, not to mention curious. Apart from Leah, who appears surprisingly sympathetic, the girls are all looking at me as if I've just pissed all over their nose candy. Scott is looking like the naughty schoolboy he is, a smirk across his angelic features.

"Scott" I say slowly. "What the fuck?"

"Well my grandparents always wanted to go to Paris, France and last year they finally did. They brought back a bottle of wine, and they decided to give it to my folks to drink on their twentieth wedding anniversary, which just so happens to be next month."

"They went all the way to France and came home with one bottle of wine?"

"That's right."

"So why did you do it, Scott?"

"Because my folks wouldn't appreciate it. You smoke these cigarettes, you're from England, it's the next country to France, I thought you would."

Well thanks for the kind thought and go straight to the top of the geography class. I know a woman in Texas who you should meet. Now I don't kid myself that I'm any kind of wine expert, although I'm pretty damn sure I know more than anyone in this house. The thing is, when me and Jools shared that bottle of Chateauneuf du Pape, we were definitely pushing the boat out a bit, but it didn't exactly break the bank. I know there are different vintages and all that, so some are going to be pricier than others, but the bottle which my diminutive friend and I have just shared didn't taste noticeably any different. An extremely nice bottle of wine and no mistake, but one which shouldn't be too difficult to replace. For a start I would bet that my shirt cost more than that bottle did. What puts the situation even more into perspective is that three quarters of the gross national product of Bolivia is currently lined up on the kitchen table. You could buy your own vineyard with what's on that table, and more than likely have enough left for a chateau to go with it. Still, I'm hardly likely to be invited to Scott's parent's anniversary dinner, so I quickly decide that all in fucking all, I don't give a shit. Scott looks at me lamely.

"Do you want something to eat?"

"Why, did your grandparents go to Russia while they were at it and bring back some finest caviar? Saving it for your sister's wedding perhaps?"

"Hey that's funny, man. Let's go get some fondue."

Fondue is the sole item available on this particular party menu. No sausage rolls or vol-au-vents here, no sir. Instead there is an enormous metal pot in the corner of the living room balanced on a matching portable stove. The pot is full of gooey white cheese, to which one of the girls is adding some white wine. Swimming in the cheese are some meatballs smothered in sauce. All I can say is I'm glad I ate before I came out. Scott and myself are joint recipients of looks which range from the reproachful to the downright dirty.

"You really upset your sister, Scott" says one of the girls, but she's looking at me while she says it. Her friend ignores Scott and addresses me directly.

"He's just a kid" she hisses. "What are you, thirty? You should know better."

The ultimate insult.

"Not yet I'm not" I reply, "You can still trust me" but it goes over her head as I knew it would.

Scott meanwhile, decides to go the offensive. "I think we need more cheese" he announces, while standing over the pot. Then I watch in disbelief as our junior Einstein undoes his jeans, and then pulls out his puny pecker and pretends to masturbate into the fondue, to a chorus of "Jesus Christ" from the boys and "ohmigod that's disgusting" from the girls. I say nothing. I'm dumbstruck.

I'm rescued by Leah, who pulls me into the kitchen. Leah looks different tonight, softer. Most of the cocaine has gone now but there is still more than enough for a good time.

"You want to do a line with me Frankie?"

Then it hits me that this is all a set up. Zaria was never coming.

"How old are you Leah?"

"Eighteen."

Pound to a penny she's lying, but so what. Good wine always goes to my loins. I'm surely not going to be staying in LA., not now; Stanley can stick his job where the Sun don't shine. I haven't seen any action since a one night stand in New Orleans, so why shouldn't I fill my boots with some free drugs and with this skinny girl who is almost certainly underage? Anyone comes looking for me I'll be long gone. Leah smiles sweetly at me while cutting us both a line, and I smile back, almost lovingly. When I look up Zaria is standing at the kitchen door. If she set this up she sure doesn't look pleased. Her eyes meet mine, I lip read "asshole", then a shake of the head and she's gone. Before I can go after her or decide whether I want to, another nameless blonde bursts into the kitchen.

"Leah! Stone's OD'd."

"Ohmigod"

Then she's gone too, and I'm alone in the kitchen. The coke is neatly lined up on the table. I think about it for ten seconds. Then I hear screaming and crying from the other room.

"Ohmigod, she's not breathing! Someone call an ambulance! For Christ's sake call an ambulance!"

Ambulance. Where there's an ambulance cops usually follow. When they get here the last place I want to be is in this kitchen. Make that this house. I walk through the kitchen door and pass down the hallway unnoticed while everyone is freaking out in the living room. I gently open the front door and make my way down the expansive driveway into the California night.

Two hours later I'm tucking into eggs, bacon, hash browns, the full Monty. Nothing like an eight mile walk to help you work up an appetite. I kept a keen eye on the route going there in case of just such an eventuality, although if I had any idea of how it was going to turn out I wouldn't have gone anywhere near the place in the first place. I enjoyed the walk. It gets cool out there in the small hours, and I heard some strange animal noises, but it cleared my head. More importantly, it reminded me that it's time to get back on the road.

Up at the counter two cops are drinking coffee. One is black, one Hispanic. Apart from Marcel and some dope dealers down on Venice Beach, the only black people I have seen have been driving buses, the only Mexicans the maids at the motel and the staff at the taco place. I haven't met a single person who does a real job except bartenders and waitresses. I don't know Los Angeles. Not many people do. It's a whole bunch of self-contained worlds with nothing in common other than being joined up by a freeway system.

I pick up some supplies from the gas station and head back towards the Riviera. It is nearly time to leave, and I'm going to miss my room and the little routines I have fallen into. I wonder how Stone is. I head distant sirens blaring not long after I left the house, and wondered if they were for her. I never wanted anything to do with the kid, but I hope she's going to be all right. Probably not the first time it's happened to her. Let's hope it's not the last.

I'm about an hour ahead of the dawn when I get back. I make sure the shades are drawn tight, before climbing between the sheets for a long and dreamless sleep.

Monday afternoon and I'm back in Pete's place. More and more I'm looking on Pete's as some kind of sanctuary, if only for these few hours in the afternoon. I think I can safely say that I won't be setting foot in Stanley's again. Shame about Zaria, but I have fucked things up in a very similar fashion before, and I have no reason to believe that I won't do so again in the future. That's how it goes.

Pete and myself are having a farewell drink with Stu, who is flying back to London tomorrow. Pete is smiling, happy, though I know he won't be for long. The realisation that Stu will soon be within a few miles of Pete's kids and Pete won't, be will press the morose button soon enough. From the evidence I've seen Stu is always happy. Happy in London, happy in Los Angeles, happy when he's on tour. Seeing as how he has never shown any indication that he ever does anything else, there is no reason for Stu not to be a happy camper. I take down phone numbers for Stu for both sides of the pond, which is something I rarely do with members of my own sex.

Then a fellow floats through the door as if he owns the place. Five foot four if you're being kind, mid-thirties, old jeans and plimsolls, blond hair carefully coiffured to get that scruffy look just so. Nothing unusual about that in Hollywood, but there is when it comes wrapped in a three quarter length fur coat.

Stu looks over. "'Ere Tel, say hello to a mate of mine. He's from your old manor."

Adam Faith fixes his blue eyes on me in a quizzical but not unkind fashion. No fear or uncertainty there. Instead there is a cocksure confidence which would border on arrogance if it wasn't tempered by a humility which is immediately apparent to me, even if it may not be to others. He is, after all, our local boy made good.

There are a thousand things I could say to him, but what emerges is this. "I wish my Mum was here."

Tel turns from Adam to Budgie before my eyes, and flashes that familiar cheeky grin. "Well I hope she's better looking than you. If she's on the right side of fifty she might stand a chance."

The top of his head comes no further than my shoulders. I'm looking past him and through the open door at the big convertibles cruising down Sunset Boulevard, but all I can see is Acton High Street, circa nineteen sixty.

Chapter Twelve: The Last Thing On My Mind

Every now and then I have to change things. Sometimes I have no choice in the matter, and other times, even when things appear to be going well, I have to change them anyway. I got bored with turf accountancy. It was fine at first, I was getting on, and I felt good about myself compared with the walking wounded who passed their wages over the counter in such a docile fashion, but eventually I wanted out. It was like seeing my Dad walk through the door five hundred times every day. It was nearly three years since my European adventure, and it was now two years me and Julie had been together. She was doing well in her job, and what with me pulling in a decent wage, we were never short of spending cash. Still I wasn't satisfied. I was twenty one, and you're not supposed to be satisfied when you're twenty one. Julie wanted us to go on holiday together to Majorca. I suggested she went with her mates. I knew what I wanted to do. I packed in my job and promised Julie faithfully that I would be back in a few weeks. I would get a better job, something more respectable, something with prospects. I just wanted a little break first to get my head together, three or four weeks. Except I said weeks when I meant months.

I set my compass a little wider this time. I took the night ferry from Harwich, which steamed up the Elbe and dropped me in the flesh pots of Hamburg. I walked the Reeperbahn, searching for the ghost of Stu Sutcliffe, and fearful of catching a dose. Neither of them was to trouble me. I took the train to Berlin, feeling like a spy when the train crossed the forbidden corridor of the GDR. In Berlin I got a day visa to visit the east, where many of the buildings were still raddled with Russian bullets from World War Two, and Checkpoint Charlie was a meeting point of two worlds and three decades. I caught a train back to the west and hitched down through Germany and then in to France, where I spent a week padding the roads of Provence, tracing the footsteps of Vincent Van Gogh. France was more relaxed this time round and so was I. I took the midnight train from Marseilles to Barcelona, where I stayed in a room with cardboard walls in a hotel in the Chinese quarter which doubled up as a brothel, before moving on to Madrid, which was hot like an oven, and almost empty in midsummer for that very reason.

From there to mysterious Lisbon, where I could have lingered indefinitely in the bars and cafes of the Alfama, but moved south to soothe my soul and eat sardines on the empty beaches of the Algarve. Sitting at a pavement cafe in the Spanish port of Algeciras I met a pair of longhairs from San Francisco. On the spur of the moment I accepted the invitation to hitch my star to their wagon, and bought a boat ticket to Tangier. We took the train to Casablanca, where there was no sign of Humphrey Bogart or anyone who looked remotely like him, and then rode the Marrakesh Express as though we were Crosby Stills and Nash, the two Californian hippies and the solid product of the English working class. We bought djellebas, and moved on to the coastal town of Essouira, where we smoked kif every day and watched the Atlantic roll in. We stayed in a commune where Jimi Hendrix had visited a couple of years earlier. My old pal Cat Stevens as well, or so I was told.

My new friends stayed on, and may be there still for all I know, but my funds were running low. I caught the bus back to Tangier and spent one night in a fleapit in the Medina, before running the gauntlet down to the port in the morning after a street hustler put the word round that I had insulted the King. Safely back in Algeciras, I bought a bus ticket to Victoria Coach Station, which left me with exactly enough pesetas for a bottle of water and a packet of cream crackers to last the three day journey.

I arrived home on a Saturday lunchtime craving sausage, egg, bacon, chips and beans. I could manage it myself, but I wanted Ma to cook it for me. Her fry ups were the best, and I knew the pleasure she would get from doing it for me, happy to have her wandering boy home for a while.

"You fucking bastard."

Not really the greeting you expect from your thirteen year old brother when you've been away for four months. Then he breaks down in front of me. I hadn't seen him cry since he was six. Ma's dead Frankie, you fucking bastard Frankie, why did you go, why did you fucking go, she's dead, why have you come back now, why have you come back now that she's dead?

The sad tale of Uncle George.

I used to have an Uncle George. He was my Dad's brother. Compared to my Dad he was a fine upstanding pillar of society, but looking back in the cold light of day, he was still something of a feckless fellow. He had no kids of his own, and he was the kind of uncle who would turn up unannounced and persuade Ma to let me leave my homework so that he could take me to a football match or to speedway. Naturally, I never needed too much persuading. I remember one Christmas he slipped me my first ever light ale while no one was looking. That kind of uncle. Every boy should have one.

One Friday in nineteen sixty one, an unidentified secretary in a certain solicitor's office in the City of London was having a busy day. Either that or she was daydreaming about Elvis or Tony Curtis, or trying to decide what to wear at the Ilford Palais that evening. Either way, she made an error, which unbeknown to her was to have grave consequences. One of the partners dictated a letter, which she took down in shorthand at the regulation hundred and twenty words per minute. The letter was a routine affair of no great importance, but it was her practice to get all correspondence in the post before the weekend, leaving nothing hanging over for Monday morning. The letter was for the attention of a client who lived out in Ealing. Windmill Road, London W5 to be precise. However, our secretary's precision, something which she always took great pride in, temporarily deserted her on this fateful occasion. Her touch typing skills, which were usually as accurate as her shorthand, somehow rendered the address as Windmill Road, London W4. She read back the letter as she always did, but didn't bother to check the address. The letter was franked and posted within twenty minutes of being dictated. If she had erred on the other side of the keyboard, in the direction of W6, then the chances are the mistake would have been picked up at the main West London sorting office. There is no Windmill Road in W6. There is however, a Windmill Road in London W4. That's where Uncle George lived.

The post was more reliable in those days. Two, sometimes three deliveries a day, and usually two deliveries even on a Saturday. The letter came first thing on Saturday morning. Thick, expensive looking cream window envelope, typed, and with the senders name incorporated into the frank mark. It was the sort of official looking letter which would automatically put the wind up the working classes back in those forelock tugging pre-Beatles days, when the sixties had arrived on the calendar, but nowhere else. Uncle George picked up the letter with some trepidation, which then turned to relief when he saw that it was addressed to someone he had never heard of. Uncle George had lived in the house since the war, and he knew everybody in the street, so this was clearly a mistake. If the letter hadn't looked so important he would probably have binned it and thought no more about it. As it was, anxious to avoid seeing any more scary looking epistles on his mat, he sat down, took out his fountain pen, and carefully wrote on the envelope "Not Known at this Address. Return to Sender", drawing an arrow to the name of the firm in the top right hand corner. He then put the envelope in his jacket pocket, intending to put it back in a post box when he made his usual Saturday lunchtime stroll down to King Street Hammersmith for a light ale and a bet.

The smash and grab raid was a criminal practice which had its heyday in Britain during the immediate post-war years, and possibly for another ten years after that. Motor cars were available, but not so readily that there would be enough traffic to impede the getaway. There was no shortage of Bobbies on the beat, but if they weren't on foot they were on bicycles. Perfect. Smash and grab belonged to the days of spivs, rationing and food coupons, when flash Harrys in black cars with moody plates would put a leather gloved hand through jeweller's windows as easy as winking, and have it away with as much as they could carry. Any number of fences would be waiting with cash in hand, and the gear would be melted down by the next morning if it was quality or end up on a market stall if it wasn't. By the end of the fifties security measures had become slightly more sophisticated, though not that much, and smash and grab raids had more or less gone the way of the Ealing comedies they so resembled.

Uncle George put a bet on, as he always did on a Saturday, and then adjourned for a light ale. As was his habit, he then had a couple more before setting off home in good time to catch the 3.15 at Sandown Park on Grandstand. He hadn't gone far when he felt a rustling in his inside pocket, and realised that he hadn't posted the wrongly addressed envelope on the way down to King Street as he intended. It was his regular custom to walk along the north side of Chiswick High Road to Hammersmith and make his return along the south side, crossing the road at Turnham Green Terrace. On this occasion, however, he saw the post box on the corner of Dalling Road, and eager to remove the mysterious letter from his person he started to cross. He never made it.

My guess is that it was the car which gave them the idea. Nineteen thirties Citroen, long and black, and ridiculously low slung with a great wide running board. They were surprisingly common in England, well in London anyway, around that time. Some Herbert whose previous amounted to little more than once nicking a jar of bullseyes from a sweet shop, scraped together forty quid for a twenty five year old French motor, and suddenly got ideas above his station. All he needed, or so he thought, was a willing accomplice and a hammer. Both duly acquired, he set off in broad daylight with mischief in mind. He parked outside the big jewellers in King Street with the engine running, while his partner, hammer in hand, crouched on the ample running board until the pavement was clear of passers-by. When the coast was clear he leapt forward, swinging the hammer with all his might. So much so, that the hammer bounced off the recently installed reinforced glass window and gave him a glancing blow on the temple, drawing blood and knocking him to the ground. I'm sure it was a truly priceless moment for all who witnessed it, only lacking the presence of Peter Sellers, Wilfred Hyde White and a film crew.

Our driver may have been stupid, but he did have enough sense to leave his companion to his fate, and set off down King Street like Stirling Moss. Seeing a red light ahead he swung the Citroen hard right into Dalling Road without any warning. Uncle George never saw it coming. The Citroen hit him full on, sending him flying up in the air and on to the low roof. The driver then lost control, and crashed in to the back of a 266 bus, fortunately inflicting no injuries other than a ricked neck for the conductor, something which he milked for all its worth and got three months on the sick for. Uncle George wasn't so lucky. He was dead before he hit the ground.

The reason I know the details of this case so well is that I made most of them up for an essay I wrote for an English homework assignment entitled "Something That Happened in My Family." Much of the rest has been embellished over the years in the telling of the tale. The bare bones of it are essentially true. George had lost his wife to a V2 rocket in nineteen forty five, just weeks before the war ended. Fate had laid some nasty tricks for him, that's for sure. My Dad was his next of kin. At the time of the accident he had about his person his house keys, a fiver and some loose change, a betting slip, and clutched in his right hand still, the rogue letter. The horse came fifth.

The driver of the Citroen was found not guilty of attempted robbery, claiming he didn't know what his mate's intentions were when he got out of the car. He was, however, found guilty of causing death by dangerous driving, and served two years in Wormwood Scrubs. He was released in nineteen sixty three, just as the sixties were really getting underway. George never even got to hear Please Please Me.

When Ma saw the envelope and worked out what had happened, her first reaction was to ring the solicitor's office and tell them exactly what they had done. She had always liked George because he was basically a nicer, kinder version of my Dad, which is why she never minded him taking me to football and stuff. Ma didn't have a vengeful bone in her body, and so by Monday she had decided against that course of action, and returned the letter without further word. She didn't want some pour soul to have that on their conscience.

That was my first encounter with the old grim reaper at first hand. In the selfish, artless way of all children, my first concern was who would ever take me to Wembley speedway again. He was from the English side of the family, but I'd say it was the Irish in me, and growing up with the tradition of celebrating life leaving the world in much the same way as life entering it, that allowed me to adjust to his passing fairly quickly. Still, I missed old George and in many ways I still do. I never did go to speedway again.

So I learned that fortune is random and life is inherently unfair. Ma said that what happened to George was just one of those terrible things that happen sometimes. I knew she was right, but I also knew that most of those terrible things that happen sometimes happen because somebody somewhere has done something that they shouldn't have. Or not done something which they should have, which when you think about it amounts to the same thing.

Ma knew she was ill. She knew before I went. She didn't know how little time she had left, but she knew she was ill. She had never been a drinker but she enjoyed her Embassy tipped, and that's what did for her in the end. She thought she had a fighting chance of beating it, but by the time I had been gone a few weeks it had spread to her liver, and then it was downhill very quickly. No one knew where I was, why should they? I sent one postcard from Portimao when I'd been gone two months. My Dad wouldn't have the nous to contact the Foreign Office to see if they could track me down, but even if he had I would have been on the other side of the Straits of Gibraltar by the time the card arrived.

I don't blame Joey for being bitter, it was him who got lumbered with most of the bedside duty, poor little bastard. My Dad couldn't handle it and spent most of the time in the pub. Joey told me that during the last few weeks when she was morphined up to the eyeballs, she would often think he was me. At first I thought he was making it up to make me feel guilty, but he's not clever enough to do that. She told him things that she would never have knowingly told her youngest, things she had never told me. She told him she had never really loved Dad. The love of her life was a merchant seaman from Liverpool who jumped ship in Canada not long after the war started, and was never seen or heard of again. Even though I was born ten years down the line she always thought I was more like him than I was the old man. Well she was proved right there wasn't she, when I went AWOL when she needed me. Then she met my Dad and felt that if nothing else, at least he'd done his duty. Did his bit for King and Country and gave her two sons. If you look at it that way, then it's a lot more than some.

My aunt, who I used to go and stay with in Ireland when I was a kid, had moved to Coventry during the nineteen sixties. It goes without saying that I never went to see her up there. When it was clear that the final days were at hand, she came down and took care of things. Ma was buried within three days as is the Catholic way. Auntie Phil wanted to take her back to Tipperary, but my Dad put his foot down for once. If I had been there I think I would have been in favour of her being laid to rest in the old country, but I wasn't, so that was that.

The day Ma died I was in Essouira. It was a day no different to all the other days I spent there, which were twenty one in number. Swam, smoked kif, drank wine, ate fish, and slept under the stars, untroubled by any thoughts of past or future. If I had known what was happening I would have been where I should have been, but I didn't know, did I? If I had known what was going to happen to Uncle George ten years earlier I would have gone with him and held his hand across the road.

I quickly learned to live with it, because at the end of the day, that's about all you can do. Another one of those terrible things that happen sometimes, only this time there was no one to blame. Learning to live with things can work the other way as well, though. Sometimes when you start believing that whatever is going to happen will happen, que sera sera and all that, well then sometimes you're just a whisper away from thinking that nothing really matters. And who's to say it does.

Chapter Thirteen: Song To The Siren

San Luis Obispo is a five hour bus ride up the California coast from Los Angeles. It's a small town about twenty miles inland from the Ocean on Highway One, the coast highway which sometimes has to give up the fight and deviate from the shoreline for the odd few miles. Five hours, about two hundred miles, but it seems more than that. It is noticeably cooler and it got darker earlier. I'm heading north now, and we're in the last few days of August.

If it appears to be further away from Tinsel town than the Rand McNally says it is, it also feels at least twenty years away from what's on the calendar. Old fashioned main street, old fashioned hotel with wooden furniture, people tip their hat to you as they pass by. Well not quite, but you wouldn't be too surprised if they did. I eat fried chicken in a diner, and spend the rest of the evening in a bar drinking beautiful nut coloured ale from San Francisco. My companions are a mixed crowd of regular working guys and academics from the local college, with nary a rock star or would be starlet among their number. Everybody is in a good mood. Tomorrow is Friday and it's a holiday weekend, Labour Day. The juke box plays Steve Miller and Skynyrd, as well as Buck Owens and a lot of golden oldies. I am welcomed in to the friendly conversation, precious little of which I can recall the next day, but which seemed to be of great import at the time, which is how conversations in bars with strangers should be.

Walk back down the old street under the star spangled sky, and I feel like thanking each and every one of them that I've escaped the clutches of LA.

I didn't see the month out. I managed twenty three days. The vague possibility that I might take up Stanley's offer, and it was always the slimmest of possibilities that I might, went out the window with Zaria and the wine and the fondue. It was meeting Tel which galvanised me into action. It's not as if we sat and chewed the fat. He showed polite interest in his old manor, but with the air of a man to whom the future is more important than the past, as it should be to all of us. Tel had a

199

nasty car crash about a year ago, and it was headline news every day for a week or so whether he would pull through or not. He looked none the worse, apart from a slight limp. Wiry little geezer, tougher than he looks. Something like that happens, it must quickly sort your priorities out for you. They didn't stick around Pete's for too long. Stu gave me a hug, which did nothing other than embarrass me and suggest that he had been in California too long, and Tel shook my hand firmly and said good luck as if he meant it. Then they were gone, leaving me with Pete, and a couple of punters who had no idea who had just been amongst their midst. I gave it fifteen minutes before going back to the Riviera to plan my next move. The next day I bought a one way ticket for Thursday morning. As soon as I had I wished I had made it for Wednesday.

Friday morning I find the junction where Highway One parts company again with 101 and makes its way back to the Ocean at Morro Bay. It seems like every college kid in America has the same idea. Holiday weekend, one last trip before school starts again, the kind of scenario that an experienced hitcher like myself would normally steer well clear of. I had been so wrapped up in my own thoughts these past few days that I hadn't considered what anyone else might be doing. There is a fair amount of traffic on the road, although a lot of it is families, which doesn't bode well. I told myself I might walk all the way to Big Sur, and even though it looks for the moment like I might end up doing that, it feels good to be back on the road. Sometimes when you're travelling and you stay in one place for a while, you get that feeling telling you to move on and you have no choice but to obey, just like every country song you ever heard. Makes up for all those times in London when I've wanted to hit the road but couldn't. I reach the end of the straggly line of thumbsters and keep on walking. You sometimes get rides like that. Some people feel intimidated by a whole bunch of kids running towards them if they look likely to stop, and keep their foot to the floor. See somebody walking on their own a mile or two down the road, think well at least this one's not lazy, why not give pick him up.

Another rule of the road is that new cars rarely, if ever, stop. They've got rich owners who have probably got stuff they're worried might get stolen, and even if they haven't they don't want some road guy's dirty old jeans messing up their pristine upholstery. So when I see a shiny blue Oldsmobile that looks like it left the showroom this morning pass me, I think nothing of it until it slows down and stops about a hundred yards ahead. I'm about to start running, when it starts reversing back and meets me half way. The near side window winds down and a familiar face emerges.

"Hello Frankie."

It's a cool cloudy morning which allows no possibility of a mirage. I look again, although I knew well enough who it was the first time.

"Hello Zaria."

I climb in back and the car moves silently away. The driver is a slim blonde woman in her late thirties, wearing an immaculate pair of jeans, and a blue silk blouse which looks as though it came from one of Beverley Hills' more expensive boutiques.

"Mom, this is Frankie" says Zaria. "Frankie is a friend of Michelle and Rory's."

I note how Zaria distances herself from me in front of Mom, and also how she must surely take after her Dad, as she and Mom share no physical characteristics, none that are visible anyway.

"Hi Frankie" says Mom. "I'm Lucille."

Lucille? Nobody's Mom is called Lucille. Well, Desi Arnaz Jnr's, maybe. "Well this is a happy coincidence. I must tell you I don't usually stop for anyone, but it's good for Zaria to have some company other than her ancient old mother. So where are you going to, Frankie?"

I read something in a magazine once by a scientist, who said that the strangest thing about coincidences was that there weren't more of them. Think about it and it's not that weird for Zaria and her mother to be getting out of LA for the holiday weekend, though they must have started out several hours ahead of what I would imagine to be Zaria's usual wake up call. Nevertheless it feels strange to be in this car. It's like one of those dreams where you think you are getting away from somewhere, and you turn a corner and you are right back where you started, as if we're going to make the next right and end up on the Strip, or even worse, Susanna's house. Ah, Susanna's house. Maybe we'll get the chance to talk about that, though not in the company of the anything but ancient Lucille. Still, Zaria must still be reasonably well disposed towards me, or else she wouldn't have asked Mom to stop. She could have just pressed the button of her electric window and flipped me the bird while Mom drove on unawares.

"Big Sur" I reply evenly, resisting the temptation to give any compliment to a woman who looks as though she gets more than her fair share of them.

Then it's Zaria's turn to speak, and though her face remains impassive, her voice cannot help but reveal that she is pleased that I'm here. "Well you're in luck this time. We're going to spend a little time at our house in Santa Cruz. We usually take 101, but this time we thought we would take the coast road, stop off at Hearst Castle and Big Sur. So there you go."

So indeed there I go. Lucky Frankie is back.

We're quickly past Morrow Bay, and then we're back on the edge of the continent, the Ocean revealing itself dark and magnificent behind the trees. I find the small talk harder to make than I would do with total strangers, and I get the feeling that Zaria is counting on there being an opportunity for us to be alone somewhere on this ride. In the meantime I make do with allowing my eyes to reacquaint themselves with her silky skin and shiny hair that is so perfect that it is as much as I can do to stop myself stroking it from the back seat. It's the first time I've seen her in natural light. With the sea and the sky and the forest, not to mention the car and its driver, it is one big beauty overload for a Friday morning.

Traffic is steady, but no more than that until we slow to a crawl and Lucille informs us that we are approaching the gates of Hearst Castle.

"Have you heard of Hearst Castle, Frank?"

"Yes I have. I saw a thing on the news about it the other week."

Hearst Castle was built at San Simeon by Patty's grandfather, William Randolph Hearst, newspaper magnate and thinly veiled inspiration for Charles Foster Kane, the doomed megalomaniac of Orson Welles' Citizen Kane. Hearst is Kane, and San Simeon is Xanadu. Needless to say, old man Hearst did not approve of the film and did everything in his not inconsiderable power to suppress it, but the young Orson stuck to his guns, and it regularly gets voted the best film ever. I might even get round to seeing it one of these days. The last time I saw Orson Welles he looked like Henry the Eighth, and was reduced to advertising sherry on television in order to maintain his own opulent lifestyle. So it goes.

The last time I queued up for a ticket to look round a castle was at the Alhambra in Granada, the seat of the Moorish kings when they ruled Andalucía. Built over six hundred years ago it is a wonder of design and perspective, which used light and water in such a brilliantly scientific fashion that it brought home even to someone who knows as little as I do, that all we have really learned over the centuries since are more efficient ways to kill each other. Much as I feel at home in the United States, it's times like this when I feel European. If I was on my own the last thing I would want to do would be to join the tourist trail around a monument to greed and bad taste when we are in the midst of some of the most natural beauty the planet has to offer. I am not on my own though am I, I am in the presence of Zaria, who turns and smiles at me.

"What are you thinking about Frankie?"

"Oh, nothing. I haven't really woken up yet."

If this is a dream then I don't want to.

I'm spared the tour of the castle. Everything is pre-booked. Lucille is disappointed, and I find that in spite of it all I am a little bit myself, purely because I thought there might be a chance of getting lost with Zaria, who couldn't appear to care less. So we get out of the car and we look at Hearst Castle through the trees. It's like looking at Buckingham Palace from the other end of the Mall. It's times like these when I realise how young our cousins are, and how easily impressed. I come from a country where we have more castles than you can shake a stick at, and this isn't a castle at all, it's no more than a faintly ludicrous gothic styled Mediterranean mansion no doubt filled with all manner of junk, and I have to admit now that I would have liked to have gone inside just so I could feel sophisticated and European. Superior, in other words. So why do they come in their masses and shuffle in line with the price of admission in their hands? To admire, or to laugh, or as a moral reminder of what unfettered greed and power will do? None of these, probably. Most of them come only because it's here.

So we stand around for about five minutes not saying much before Lucille shrugs and says OK kids, and we get back in the car, and a few minutes later we're on Highway One going north with it all to ourselves, and I realise that most of the traffic on the way up was for San Simeon.

"Maybe another time" says Lucille. "I guess the day before a holiday wasn't the best time, especially with being in the news and everything. I sure would like to have seen inside. They've got indoor baths like the

Romans had, and big banqueting rooms that look like they were built by Michelangelo."

"Did Patty Hearst ever live in the castle?" I ask.

"She may have done when she was a kid" replies Zaria. "None of the family live there now."

If she did live there it explains a lot. Now I understand how easy it must have been to turn poor Patty, to convince her that anything was the real world compared with the shrine to indulgence and phoniness that was her reality as a child.

Zaria puts on a Grateful Dead tape, and we fall silent as we pass through a long avenue of trees which temporarily hides the Ocean from view. I stretch out on the leather and think about what I'm going to say when we reach Big Sur.

The Oldsmobile continues north at a stately fifty five under rolling clouds with mountains to our right and the ocean to our left, the automatic taking in its stride the climbs and descents which take us from dark forests to cliff top Pacific views which are guaranteed to halt conversation in mid-sentence. We round a curve, and for no more than a few seconds I catch a glimpse of white rollers breaking onto a deserted beach, and I picture me and Zaria running through the breakers hand in hand. We continue on for over an hour, each view more spectacular than the last, until we see the sign for the Big Sur campground, and Lucille pulls into a car park which is mainly populated with mobile homes and beat up old station wagons similar to the one I drove through the Texas night less than a month ago. The concept of the Big Sur site is that it is a gateway to the wild blue yonder, so by definition there isn't much here other than some signs pointing towards designated hiking trails, a few picnic tables and some primitive rest rooms. Lucille announces that she is going to do nothing more than sit down with a cigarette for the next half hour, so why don't we kids take a little walk. This kid is fifteen years younger than her, tops. I could kiss her. Her daughter and I start up a steep incline towards the trail, and even though we are soon out of earshot we don't speak until we are in the trees and out of sight.

"Well here we are" I say.

"We sure are," and she's looking at me the same way that Julie used to, like I'm a naughty little boy. I think of saying something along the lines of this must be fate, but I'm getting the feeling that Zaria can read what I'm thinking anyway, so I skip it.

"So what happened with Stone?"

As much to break the silence as anything else.

"Oh, like you care."

"I don't know anything about overdoses. There was nothing I could do. I'm an alien, I was in a house with half a ton of coke, I couldn't think of anything to do except split. So what happened with her?"

"The ambulance got her to the hospital in time, they pumped her stomach and kept her in for observation. They found her home address in her jacket pocket, they called her parents, and two days later her Dad came and took her home."

"Home where?"

"Boston."

The kid was nearly as far away from home as I am.

"So was Stone her real name?"

"Yes. Bernadette Mary Stone."

"It's the catholic girls you have to watch."

Zaria puts a hand to the chain around her neck, and pulls a crucifix from under her t-shirt.

"So what were you doing with Leah?"

"I wasn't doing anything with Leah. I was hanging out with that little guy Scott, and he kept getting me into trouble. Leah did something useful for once, and came and rescued me. That was supposed to be your job."

Moving a little on to the offensive now.

"I didn't mean to be late. I was with my Dad all day."

"I didn't think you were coming. I thought you had set me up with Leah."

"I don't do stuff like that Frank. Life's too short. So why didn't you come down to Stanley's later in the week?"

"I just thought everything was screwed up."

"Well it was. Sometimes things can be screwed up and you can unscrew them if you put your mind to it. So what do you do Frank, do you just walk away when things don't work out?"

"No."

The evidence says very much that I do, and again Zaria gives me that Julie look that says she knows everything. She waves her arm in the direction of the trees.

"Well, this is Big Sur. You gonna walk off into the woods?"

My eyes fix on a sign which tells you what to do in the event of meeting a mountain lion. "I don't think so somehow. So what's at Santa Cruz?"

"It's a funky little town. Got a boardwalk and some good beaches, bars with live music. It's cool."

"I wouldn't mind staying in a motel there for a few days. Maybe we could meet up sometime" I say hopefully.

"That sounds good" and she gives me a smile untainted by suspicion. I'm going to see Zaria again, and we are going to talk long into the Santa Cruz night, and maybe do more than that. Fortune has handed me a second chance. For now we sit under a tree and smoke a cigarette before making our way back down the trail. We ventured two hundred yards into the interior of Big Sur, if that. Back at the car park Zaria and her Mom make a rest room pit stop before we get back in the Olds. Lucille makes no comment about why I'm not staying at Big Sur, so I take it Zaria has squared it with her for the ride up to Santa Cruz.

We start the winding climb back up from sea level, and Lucille announces that it's just about time for lunch while Zaria gives me that smile again, and then exchanges a quick secret grin with her Mom which suggests to me that they know something that I don't.

Carmel, California has to have the cleanest streets on the whole planet. You could probably eat your dinner off the sidewalk if you needed to, although nobody who lives around here is ever likely to be in that position. Strolling amongst the pastel buildings and primary flowers of the main shopping street, the only smell mixing in with the tangy sea air is that of money, money and the fresh odour of newly laundered fifty dollar jeans. Most of the women on the street are dressed in similar fashion to Lucille, and the men don't look too different either, other than swapping golf or yachting tops for the silk blouses. Lucille leads us purposefully to a restaurant called The Seafood House, where a pouffy little waiter in a sailor suit greets her like a long lost friend, and leads us to a table by the window. I'm wishing that I was wearing my good shirt, the one that Zaria has seen for all of ten seconds, but at least I'm feeling clean. It's a coolish California day, and even if it wasn't I've been chauffeured up the coast in air con luxury. Lucille notes my temporary discomfort, and misinterprets the reason.

"Lunch is on me" she smiles.

I'm not about to argue. Another one of the boys flounces over with some menus. ""Hello" stretching the O into three syllables. "My name is Michael and I am your captain for today. The specials for today are"

"Skip it Michael" Lucille interrupts briskly but not unpleasantly. "We'll order from the menu." She looks up at me. "We usually have

206

the same thing when we come here. Listen to those guys when they get started, you won't know what day it is."

"I'll go with the flow" I reply. I don't want to let on, but I don't know a great deal about seafood, other than prawns and whelks, and cockles and mussels most definitely not alive alive-o. I'm not comfortable with anything that has shells or claws. So we start with prawns which are about ten times more delicious than any of the sorry looking specimens I've had in prawn cocktails at home. So far so good, until they serve the crab. It looks great, but I haven't got a clue where to start. Nothing for it other than to play the innocent abroad.

"I have to tell you that where I come from the only seafood we eat comes served in newspaper" I say cheerfully.

"They do a very good fish and chips here" Lucille tells me, but Zaria takes the cue and shows me how to crack the claw open and what to eat and what not to, and though I get the hang of it fairly easily, I exaggerate my helplessness while this beautiful girl helps me to eat my lunch. The crab is succulent. We wash it down with white wine from just up the road in Monterey, and it's as crisp and clear as anything I've ever drunk in my life. So here I am thinking how life is sweet and how it couldn't really get any better, when it does.

"Listen Frank" says Lucille. "We've got something to ask you."

I'm cradling my wine glass while listening intently.

"So you didn't want to stay at Big Sur after all?"

"It was the mountain lions that put me off. Besides, you've seen one tree and you've seen 'em all, right?"

I'm only on my second glass but I feel slightly drunk already. Intoxicated by the company and surroundings I guess. Mind you, they're both still less than halfway through their first.

"Well I know Zaria told you we are going to our house in Santa Cruz for two weeks. Why don't you stay with us for a while, Frank? We've got plenty of room, and it would be company for Zaria."

My glass is to my mouth, and I hold it there for a few seconds until I realise it must look as though I'm thinking it over. Like I'm thinking it over. "Er, yeah. I'd love to. That would be great. I don't know what to say. Thank you." Then, seized by the magic of the moment. "Only if you let me pay for this lunch" and I wave my hand confidently at our waiter and indicate for another bottle of wine.

"Oh that's not necessary" says Lucille, but it is. I'm taking charge now. If I'm going to be staying with these two well-heeled ladies I'm going to do it as a boy about town rather than as a bum. Lucille looks impressed, and I can see most, if not all, of the doubts she had about asking me to stay fly out the window. So Zaria asked her if I could stay back at Big Sur. I look across the table at her, and our eyes meet for a little longer than they should. I'm going to have to be so careful with this, so very, very careful if I'm not going to fuck this up. I put a hundred dollars in my jeans this morning and I don't have much left after I've settled the bill, generous tip included, but it is well worth it, well worth it indeed.

Back on the highway and we are leaving the coast now. I've loved the drive but now I just want to get there.

"So tell me Frank" asks Lucille. "What do you do? And why are you hitchhiking?"

Saturday afternoon by the pool, and the only way I can keep my eyes off of Lucille's perfectly honed golden flesh is by keeping them on her daughter, gorgeous in a yellow bikini. Either that or keeping them firmly shut, so I lie back on a lounger and point my face at the sky. I'm still on my best behaviour. Last night Zaria took me to a bar in the town, and I was good to the point of being boring, although we had a good enough time. A local band played rocked up covers of Hank Williams to a packed house of local hippies and out of town weekenders. Way too noisy for any meaningful conversation. That is yet to come. Got back to the house around three, where I said goodnight and headed for my room in an almost indecent haste. It was cool, though. Zaria picked up on the reason for it. It is already apparent that she has a wise head on her inviting young shoulders when it comes to stuff like that.

I'm sleeping in what is referred to as her brother's room, although he has left nothing of his possessions or personality behind. He is five years older than his sister and lives in New York. The house is big by my standards, though small by what I would imagine to be theirs. Three bedrooms, expansive through lounge joining up with a kitchen which looks like tonight's star prize complete with a bar for sitting and eating breakfast at. The kitchen opens out to some wooden flooring which they call a deck, and the back yard is dominated by a pool. Lucille pays somebody to clean it out every two weeks, even though she may not come here for months. She has her own bathroom attached to her bedroom, and me and Zaria have to share the other one. Cosy.

In Santa Cruz at this time of year the clouds which roll in every night hold sway until midday at the earliest, before clearing to reveal another beautiful California day. There is little reason to rise before noon, so none of us do. We stay by the pool for the whole afternoon without saying much. Lucille flips idly through a pile of fashion magazines, while Zaria works on her tan and I help myself to a few beers from the well stocked refrigerator. I feel like I've got credit after yesterday's lunch. In the evening we sit out on the deck, drink more California wine, red this time, and eat pizza. We don't leave the house. Zaria dials a number, and twenty minutes later a kid delivers it on a motor bike. What was it Chuck Berry said, anything you want you can get it in the U.S.A? I was never too sure if that song wasn't intended to be ironic. Maybe not. When the Sun goes down we move back inside, and Lucille puts on a Sinatra album that Zaria's dad had left behind. It's only a year or so old, so it's not classic Frank, but it sounds pretty damn fine to me, the man doing love lost as an older man even more affectingly than he did as a young one. Watertown. I make a note of the title.

Then we go to bed. Separately. Something is going to happen. Sometime. I know it, and you know it too Zaria.

Sunday afternoon we go to the Santa Cruz boardwalk. I protest that it will be too crowded, but Zaria says that's the best time to go, and of course she's right. The funfair brings out the best in everyone, or the child in everyone, which may or may not be the same thing. Cares and woe are temporarily suspended like the cars at the top of the ferris wheel while people get on and off at the bottom. Bye, bye blackbird. It's a fairly small concern with a relaxed feel to it, much more than say, Coney Island. Well that's in Brooklyn, people there have an edge to them even when they're eating ice cream. We're three hundred and fifty miles from LA. but we are most definitely still in California. The main attraction of the Santa Cruz boardwalk is the Giant Dipper, a scary looking wooden contraption which Zaria tells me is fifty years old. I say a silent prayer that she's not going to want to ride it.

"You know what, Frank, I don't like the Dipper. It spooks me."

I may be pushing my luck, but I try the double bluff, just in case.

"You don't want to ride it with me?"

Trying not to sound too relieved.

"I really don't want to Frank. I rode it once and hated it. The thing has been there fifty years without an accident, so I always think today is going to be the day. I feel like I have no control over my life if I'm up on one of those things. You can ride it, I'll watch."

I so want to tell Zaria how wonderful it is that she shares my views about fairground rides that go more than twelve feet up in the air, but instead I shrug and smile, and tell her it wouldn't be the same without her.

We get some candy floss and stroll along the boardwalk holding hands, the boardwalk being a holding hands kind of location, but we're both a little self-conscious and separate when we get back on the street. Walking up the hill to the house she informs me of the plan for the next day. That's another thing I like about her, she's decisive.

"You want to come for a walk tomorrow? See a different side to California?" It's not an invitation, it's an instruction.

"Mom won't mind driving us up to the forest in the morning. There's a trail we can follow which leads us all the way down to the Ocean."

"Sounds great. How far is it?"

"About twelve miles. Don't worry" she says cheerfully, "it's all down hill."

I don't know which surprises me more, Lucille calling me at seven thirty, or going downstairs to find Zaria cooking us breakfast.

"You need to get some carbs inside you" she says gaily.

When the carbs are inside me and the fresh coffee has woken me up, I'm told I need a jacket or a sweater, so I dig out my old green jumper from the bottom of my bag. It's the first time it has seen service on the trip. Zaria gives me a spare back pack, and then we're in the car. Lucille drives us about twenty minutes out of town, uphill all the way along a winding road enveloped by trees which reach up to the clouds, until we are in the Big Basin woods. This is where the trail starts.

"I'll call you when we get to the bottom, Mom." says Zaria.

"There's a bar and a diner on the coast road" she explains to me, and then we follow on behind at least fifty fellow hikers and set off into the cloud, which is thick but not so that you can't see the trail pointers. Even if you couldn't and Zaria hadn't done this walk before, there would be very little chance of getting lost here. I wonder if it's always this busy and then I remember that today is a holiday. Labour Day, the public holiday dedicated to the workers. This particular Labour Day it feels like a good percentage of the workers have decided to spend it on this trail. The first half mile is like a pedestrianised version of Interstate Five.

"I forgot it was a holiday today" says Zaria, and flashes a silly me grin. So she doesn't know everything. It's cool up here, and I am more than grateful to have my sweater. It feels like autumn, a carpet of dead leaves underfoot already. It's the second of September. My aunt in Tip used to say autumn started on the first day of August, but then she also maintained that the first day of spring was February the first, which is quite clearly ridiculous. Right now I'm wishing that today was the first of May, and I'm thinking of that old folk song about them chilly winds that will soon be blowing and I'll be on my way, which is the last thing I want to do.

Not long after nine the clouds have thinned out, and so have most of the crowd as walkers find their own pace. The temperature has gone from about fifty to seventy in half an hour, and the sweater is in the back pack where it will stay. We hit a long easy stretch where we don't have to concentrate on the trail so much, and Zaria tells me about herself. Her father is second generation Italian, and Lucille is of German Irish stock. One brother, six years older. We discuss the remote possibility that we may be distant cousins on her mother's side.

"Well it's like Elvis says" I venture, "we're all cousins 'cos we're children of Adam and Eve." She doesn't know that one.

"So what does your Dad do?"

It's a pertinent question, as they obviously don't lack for the necessities in life.

"He's a cinematographer."

"So what is that exactly, sort of like a cameraman?"

She flashes me a come now look.

"Sort of like a cameraman? You're lucky he's not here to hear you say that. The cinematographer works with the director deciding on the lighting on the set and how the scene is going to be shot. He then tells the cameramen exactly what they have to do. It's a big job. It has a real influence on how the movie ends up looking. My dad started at the bottom and worked his way up the way you're supposed to, and Vincent D'Amato is quite a big name in the business now."

Well that's me told. For the first time I get a glimpse of Zaria as being serious minded when she's talking about her dad's job, as if it's of some consequence. Still, what do I know, I've never been out with a cinematographer's daughter before.

"And that's what I'm going to do. I start at the studio two weeks today. I'll give it a year, and if it doesn't work I'll go to college, but I'm not planning on it not working. Things are gonna change."

"What else is going to change?"

"Well I'm going to get up every morning and go to work. Take it seriously. Maybe just hit Stanley's on a Friday night. Find a party on Saturday night, go to the beach on Sunday. Most important of all, I'm going to quit smoking dope. I'll smoke some with Mom while we're here, and that will be it. It's boring after a while, and holds you back from doing stuff."

"You smoke dope with your Mum?"

"Sure. I feel really close to her when we do that."

She thinks for a moment. "Maybe I still will when we come here on vacation, but that's it."

I'm quiet for a minute, trying and failing to imagine me and Ma passing a joint back and forth between us. It's warm now, much hotter than it gets in the town, the sunlight broken up by the leaves and falling into irregular patterns on and around us, Zaria's hair shining like ravens wings.

"Does your Mum work?"

"She was in movies when she was a kid. They still show up on daytime television occasionally. She had enough of it by the time she was seventeen, married my Dad, had my brother, and gave it all up. She gets a little bored now. My brother Stefano moved to New York to work in the music business, and her and my Dad don't get along so well now because he's always working. That's one of the reasons I'm not going to leave LA., not for a while anyway."

I'm doing the calculations in my head and I'm working out that Lucille must be at least six years older than I thought she was. Fair play to you, girl. I tell Zaria about the women on the buses in Santa Monica. She smiles cutely.

"I never ride the bus in LA. Mom was way too smart to ever end up like that, whether she had kids or not."

"Tell you what Zaria, if you get to be a film director I'll come and be your best boy."

She laughs, a beautiful sound pealing around the trees with no hikers in sight to share it with. "If you knew what a best boy does on a picture you wouldn't want the job, believe me" but her shining eyes tell me she knows exactly what I mean, and they're saying yes, but not yet. Then we hit a steep narrow path that demands our attention, and then at long last we emerge from the shadow of the giant trees and Zaria leads me on to a single file path on the edge of the mountain, and we're looking down into the forest and out across the blue Pacific. She stops and turns.

"Isn't it beautiful?"

"Yes, and so are you" I reply, and lean down and put my hand on the back of her neck before kissing her on the lips. She only responds partly, opening her eyes after a few seconds. Yes, but not yet. Then she turns and moves forward purposefully, with me following on like a faithful old retriever. I can see the highway now, and it looks as though we should be there in no more than half an hour, but I haven't taken into account the way the path has to zigzag so as not to be a sheer drop, and it takes three times longer. We awkwardly pass some hikers going in the other direction, brave souls that they are, and finally we reach the bottom, and then it's just a short distance to the highway where there's an old fashioned diner where we get a coke and a cheeseburger when what I really want is a beer. Zaria calls Lucille on the pay phone, and twenty minutes later the Olds pulls up outside. Lucille joins us for coffee and then we stop off at a liquor store to buy some of that San Francisco beer before going back to the house to soothe our aching feet in the pool.

"How about a lazy day at the beach tomorrow?" asks Zaria.

"Sounds good to me" I reply, and swiftly return the bottle to my lips. One of those old seaside postcards that one of my Dad's mates sent once comes to mind. It lived on the mantelpiece for about a year.

It's a great life if you don't weaken.

I had already noticed two bicycles in the garage, but I didn't realise they were going to be our means of transportation for the day. Zaria explains that there are much better beaches a few miles up the coast, so she leads the way again, and I wobble on behind where I am free to admire her tanned legs and perfectly filled shorts with impunity. The holiday season officially ends with Labour Day, and now the workers are back at work and the beach is deserted aside from us and the gulls and the sound of the waves.

The first thing you learn about the Pacific is that it is a lot colder than you think it's going to be. Zaria runs straight in without flinching and I get a nasty shock when I attempt to follow. Zaria breaks into an effortless freestyle and is soon a hundred yards from the shore, gliding like a dolphin, while I splash around in the shallows.

"I was off school the day they did swimming" I tell her shamefacedly when she emerges from the water like a young goddess, Ursula Andress in Doctor No, only better.

"It gets warmer, if that's what you're worried about. It will be O.K. when the Sun's been on it for a couple of hours."

So we stretch out on our towels and chat about this and that. Zaria wants to talk about me, which is nice, but not really what I want at the moment. I told Lucille I'd been working in the fashion business, which if you were being kind you could say contained half a grain of truth, considering I helped my old man knock out some moody gear once or twice. I also told her someone had died and left me some money, which is horribly true, and that's why I'm taking the opportunity to see some of the world. I would love to tell Zaria the truth about myself, really talk to her, but I'm not stupid enough to think about doing so yet. I rub oil on to her silken back, and I am so tempted to move down to her thighs and from there to the forbidden places where the Sun doesn't go, but I know that it's not quite time. Yet.

Then she does my back and it's a while before I can safely roll on to my front. No clouds now, and we lay silently for a long time before she suddenly gets to her feet and pulls me up, and then we're running towards the water. It's still cold, but she's right, it's a lot warmer than it was, and we're laughing and skipping through the foam, and then I'm up to my chest and she's almost up to her neck, and she has still got my hand, and then Zaria starts singing, do you wanna dance and hold my hand tell me baby you're my lover man, and we're jiving in the water, and I don't want to let go of her hand in case it breaks the spell, and then we're so deep into the spell that I've forgotten there even is one so it doesn't matter, and the sea isn't cold any more, it's just perfect, and the Sun is perfect and so is the sky, and myself and Zaria are as one and we're both at one with the beauty surrounding us. Then I know the moment is right, it could never be more right if I live forever, and our lips meet and I taste her mouth mingled with the salt spray, and I'm holding her so tightly with her arms around my neck for a long time until I start to slowly manoeuvre her back to the water's edge, and I want to take her bikini bottom off and have her here and now, but she nods her head towards a couple no more than fifty yards away who weren't there before.

"That from here to eternity moment, huh?" she says softly. "We've got tonight" and I know she means it this time.

"What about your Mum?"

"She trusts me."

I'm still in the moment, but I'm standing outside of it now as well, slightly puzzled.

"She's bound to find out."

"No, I mean she trusts me to make my own decisions. I don't do this easily, you know. I'm not one of those chicks who hang around Stanley's waiting to be picked off like an apple from a tree"

Zaria pauses for a moment, and I'm thinking that perhaps I can see doubt in her eyes and maybe she's thinking of me and Leah in the kitchen, but she carries on

"I want to sleep with you Frank. I'll tell Mom and she'll be cool. You'll see."

Then she kisses me long and slow, and when we look around the unwanted visitors have disappeared as silently as they arrived as if they had been nothing more than a mirage, but the moment has passed now, and it's all about tonight. We pack up our stuff and get back on the bikes, and I have difficulty finding the right gear going up the hill to the house in the afternoon sun so I'm a little more breathless when we get back than I would like to be. I take a beer from the fridge and take it out on the deck. Zaria and Lucille disappear upstairs for what seems like a long time. When they eventually come down I pretend to be engrossed in Rolling Stone when Lucille asks me if I had a good day at the beach, and reply with a grunt and a nod. I studiously avoid eye contact with the good lady, but catch Zaria's and she gives me a wink. Everything's cool.

Lucille may be German Irish, but she has clearly learned what Mr D'Amato likes to see on the table. For dinner we have homemade lasagne and salad accompanied by another good red and fresh French bread which Lucille bought at a bakers in town. I haven't seen a bakers since I was in Little Italy. I didn't know they had them anywhere else in America, which only goes to show how little you get to know about a country living a road, motel and bar existence. Another thing I learn is that they call French bread Italian bread, so we talk about that for a while, and then we have the tomahto, tomayto conversation and Lucille opens another bottle of wine and we are all relaxed and having a good time, which is good because there was a definite tension in the air when we sat down, although all three of us would have denied it.

We listen to Teaser and the Firecat, and this time I don't claim to be a personal friend of Cat Stevens or anyone else. Lucille makes her excuses and bids us a tactful early goodnight. We move to the middle of the sofa we had been propping up like bookends and kiss slowly, almost chastely, before Zaria indicates that it is time and leads me barefoot up the stairs. Inside her room we strip to our underwear and kiss tenderly for a long time before she guides my hand down her flat stomach and through the rich hair to show me she is ready, and then we are naked and I'm inside Zaria with no fumbles or false starts. I'm not always at my best when the spontaneity is removed as it is now, and the presence of her mother down the hallway should make me nervous to the point of disaster, but no, everything is as good as it could be, and we move together in natural rhythm, slow at first, then a little faster, but never too fast, until her moans increase, and then she gives a long sigh and I've brought her to climax a split second before my own sweet release. We share a Disque Bleu, and then we do it again in the same position, no need to think about experimenting yet, and it lasts even longer like it's supposed to the second time, and then we're done, and Zaria drapes her arm around me and goes to sleep. I lay awake for a while thinking that if I could I would never leave this bed, never leave this house, never leave this state.

"If you could have one thing in the world what would it be?"
We're out on the deck and we're both a little stoned. We dined on spaghetti and wine followed by more wine, and then hip old Lucille brought out her stash of Acapulco Gold.
    "It's a mellow high" she explained helpfully. Zaria may be willing to swear off the weed when she starts work, but she isn't about to yet, and the three of us get fine and mellow underneath the stars before Lucille takes her leave. This time it's more about the effects of the wine and the weed than a desire to be tactful, although that she most certainly is. Vince the cinematographer called today, and Lucille exchanged a few terse words before passing the phone to Zaria. I couldn't help noticing that my name wasn't mentioned. I didn't think it would be somehow. I imagine Vince as being a little more old school than Lucille. Still, if that's what prompted Lucille to think she needed something a little extra to relax, then all I can say is, it's an ill wind.
    "So what would you have?" Zaria repeats the question. I stall on my answer, thanking the stars that I still had enough of my wits about me to bite on my first reply, which was you and your mother in the same bed.
    "Ummm, world peace, maybe."

216

"World peace, bullshit" she smiles, and the way she says it makes me think for a moment of my old pal Jethro back in Greenville. "Well, to be honest with you", and again she gives me that same look Julie used to when I said that, knowing that I was going to be anything but.

"Seriously, less than a week ago I was standing by the road with a pair of boots and a couple of clean shirts and nothing else. I wouldn't ask for anything more than I've got tonight."

I mean it too. If this lasts no more than a few days and a handful of blissful nights then I'll treasure the memory and be truly grateful that they came my way. I'm falling in love with Zaria. No, I'm not falling, who am I kidding, I'm already gone, gone, gone. I haven't said the words yet, but I know it's just a matter of time. Julie, who knew everything, never seemed to like me telling her that I loved her. "One of these days you'll find out what those words mean" is what she would say. Zaria doesn't know everything yet, in many ways she's wise beyond her years, and in others she's still a child, but when I'm with her I feel that what she doesn't know couldn't possibly be worth knowing.

"So what would you have, Zaria?"

"I would really like to get somewhere in the movie business."

"That's getting somewhere. Getting somewhere and having something are not the same thing."

She brushes aside the technicality. "I would like to have the feeling that I have achieved something in my chosen field."

In my chosen field? She is more than slightly stoned but I can tell that she's deadly serious.

"You think that life is just like films?"

"No. That's just it. I want to be some part of making movies that are like life."

"Like from Here to Eternity?"

"Well everybody only remembers one scene from that movie, but they still remember it. I think movies should be like a mirror."

"What about music?"

"A million people can buy the same record and they'll all hear different music. A great movie reflects right back at you."

I think about that for a minute. She's right in one sense; a great film can take you outside of yourself, and at the same time reflect how things were, or how they are, how they should be or how they might be. At the same time, Wichita Lineman does all of that for me in two minutes fifty. I change the subject slightly. I am aware that I am very stoned now.

"You know a lot, Zaria."

She shoots me a who do you think you're patronising look.

"No, what I mean is, why do you hang round Stanley's? Most of those people aren't aware there's a big world outside, or that life was going on before the last Bowie record came out. You do."

"Well Michelle is a good friend of mine and it's fun on one level. But like I say, things are gonna change. The thing is, when you grow up like I grew up you get anything you want, in the material sense anyway. By the time you hit seventeen you can either embrace all the crap that comes with it, the pool parties, and the fashion, and the drugs, which is what most of them do, or you can decide what's more important. I worked out a long time ago that none of that shit matters."

We put on a cassette of Deja Vu and listen silently to Carry On and Teach Your Children and Almost Cut My Hair, and then I hold Zaria close to me and we gaze up at the stars as Neil sings about blue, blue windows behind them leaving us helpless, helpless, and then I take the tape off as it goes into Woodstock, and lead her ever so quietly up the stairs to bed.

It's hard to decide what I love best at the house in Santa Cruz. The delicious nights that extend into long mornings in bed while we're waiting on the Sun, the afternoons at the beach or by the pool, or the long evenings on the deck drinking California's fine wine and listening to Jackson Browne and Tim Buckley. So when Zaria brightly tells me that she's taking me to San Francisco for a couple of days, I'm not quite as excited as I should be. It sounds idyllic, visiting the fabled city with a beautiful girl I'm in love with, but I'm wary of breaking the spell. One of Lucille's cronies is coming to stay. She invites her every time, and she called last night to take her up on it for the first time ever. Seems like Murphy's law is universal. Time for us kids to get out of the way. Lucille is still very nice to me, and resolutely inscrutable about what she thinks of the situation concerning me and her daughter. She's done my laundry as well. Truly a wonderful woman.

Zaria might not ride the buses in LA, but she's happy enough to sit with me at the back of the Greyhound for the two and a half hour ride. I'm surprised when she tells me that she has only been to San Francisco once before, with her parents when she was fourteen. If anything she knows the east coast better, although not that much. Her

218

dad's hometown is Trenton, New Jersey, about seventy five miles from New York City. Been there on a couple of family visits and made day trips to Philadelphia and New York, been on vacation to Puerto Vallerta and to Hawaii, and that's the extent of Zaria's travels. I guess if you're born with a silver spoon in the golden state then there's no real reason to want to ramble. I know that I would, but that's the card I've been dealt.

The ride would be boring if I was on my own. The clouds are in for the day, and there is even a touch of rain in the air as we make our way north. The bus clings to the main highway, stopping off at a few nondescript towns with nary a glimpse of the ocean or the forest. I give Zaria an edited version of my adventures so far, and discover that she has never met anyone whose grandaddy talks in tongues, nor whose brother has been reincarnated as a dog. She's laughing so much I'm worried we might get thrown off the bus. I tell her that if she gets to be a movie director I'll write her a script, and she reminds me that I might be getting a little ahead of myself considering that it was only the other day I put myself forward for the job as best boy. A tedious trip for a lone rider it would surely be, but with Zaria I'd be happy to bypass the Golden Gate city and ride all the way up to Canada if we could. We've got one small bag between us, and I'm imagining what it would be like if we were running off to get married. I'm deep under her spell.

Then we're at the bus station, and the first thing to do is buy a street map. This is not Manhattan where you couldn't get lost if you tried, or even Los Angeles with its parallel boulevards sweeping down to the sea. I love it immediately. It's not England, but it feels like home, and the clouds make it even more so. I get our bearings, and we make for Union Square, where I lead a protesting Zaria up the steps of a swanky old hotel and past the man on the door who is all dressed up like the King of Ruritania. Zaria is saying we don't need this Frankie, and the toffee nosed tosser on the desk concurs that they don't need us either, looking up from his big leather bound book for all of a second to inform us there are no vacancies. We're clean and our money is even cleaner, but I guess we're just not their type, and I would be worried if we were. I smile at the King on the way out and he stares straight ahead unblinking like he's on duty at Horse Guards Parade.

Back on the street we head away from the square for a few blocks and find ourselves on Jones Street, where Zaria decides she likes the look of a place that would appear from the outside to be unchanged since the gold rush. Eight dollars a night for the pair of us, no questions asked. I realise this is all part of the adventure for Zaria, she can never have stayed in a cheap hotel before. Turns out to be not a bad choice. It's old but it is clean and has a solid feel to it which reminds me of similar establishments in Paris and Amsterdam, though Zaria has a reality check when she discovers that the bathroom is shared and way down the hall, and she's going to have to find a phone box to call Lucille. No radio or TV, but they're the last things we're going to need. We leave our few worldly goods, and minutes later are back on the street.

We find Columbus Avenue and drink mimosas at Specs bar, and then we walk down the hill to the quays at Fisherman's Wharf. It's unmistakably a tourist area around here although it doesn't appear too tacky, and I get my first view of the Golden Gate Bridge. I put my arm around my girl and start to sing to her.

"I've been wanderin' early and late from the New York City to the Golden Gate, and I don't know when I'll ever stop my wanderin'"

That's me, sure enough. I surely would have sung it just the same if I had been on my own. Across the bay stands Alcatraz, which at first sight seems closer to the shore than it really should be. Zaria may have only been here once, but she knows her stuff. Six or seven men managed to escape over the years but none of them made it ashore due to the treacherous currents in the bay. The last prisoners left the island more than ten years ago. Five years ago a group of Indians landed on the deserted rock and claimed it for the Native American people, which only goes to show how desperate they must have been. They stayed there for two years before the government tired of them and threw them off.

We go to an Irish bar and I drink Guinness for the first time since I left home, playing the old country card with Zaria for all I'm worth as it slides down. She gamely manages a pint before switching to wine. Like every single teenager in California, possibly in America, Zaria has a fake ID, but no one seems to need to see it in old Frisco. We ride the cable car back just like you're supposed to, hanging on as it scales the gradient. Already I feel like Frisco, and I admit that I don't know it well enough yet to be so familiar, is our town. It is everything Los Angeles is not. Surprising, disordered, eccentric and egalitarian. And, for good measure, the bars look like they're for drinking in, not posing.

We get off the cable car in Chinatown and Zaria takes charge, pulling me through the crowded narrow streets in search of a restaurant on Grant Street where her Dad took her before. The story goes that this place is famous for the rudeness of its waiters. People come from far and wide just to be insulted. It takes a while, but we find it and walk through the kitchen and up a narrow flight of stairs to the small dining area, where we are brusquely squeezed on to a small wooden table with two Jewish girls from Philadelphia. I make the mistake of thinking egg fried rice is a side dish, only to be corrected by our charming server in no uncertain terms.

"That a plenty lot a food mister. You jus get out Alcatraz?"

We scale down our order and find that the food is simple, fresh, and abundant as promised, and we are surprised to find that we manage to clear the plates. Just as well we have walked a few hills since we got here and haven't eaten all day. The Jewish girls, who are good company even though they are most assuredly not needed, ask us if we want to go to a discotheque with them. It takes us about three seconds to decide that no, we don't, and all of fifteen to politely decline the invitation. Back on the street we make our way back hand in hand, shivering in what can only be described as a downright cold September night. In our little room we hold each other close underneath the rough blankets for a long time before moving on to the inevitable night time activity.

I hadn't felt noticeably intimidated by her mother's presence in the house at Santa Cruz, but in this cheap hotel our lovemaking is altogether ruder. Zaria is louder, giggling and open to experimentation. The walls are thin, and we can hear the couple in the next room talking in what sounds like Swedish or something similar, which encourages us to shed our inhibitions even more. She's experienced enough to be confident and assertive, but there is still a girlish naiveté to her. She has made no mention of boyfriends past or present and I am not about to ask her. Don't break the spell, whatever you do Frank.

In the morning we explore Haight Ashbury and find it haunted, grey, feeling like it's waking from the middle of a dream leaving it still tired and unfulfilled. A few forlorn head shops selling incense, drug paraphernalia and books on Hare Krishna would appear to be all that's left of the Summer of Love. Zaria is something of a deadhead, but she doesn't know that the band lived right here on Haight Street with the Jefferson Airplane back in sixty seven. This is where that whole thing got started. I have to remind myself that she would have been eleven at the time.

We continue down to Golden Gate Park, and suddenly the Sun bursts through and everything is all too beautiful once more. People playing guitars, throwing frisbees, even some Spanish speaking kids playing football. We walk a mile in the park before taking an exit heading north towards the bridge. I buy a newspaper, though I couldn't say why, the only news that interests me today is the good news about me and my girl. The new president has granted Nixon a full pardon. Well he would, wouldn't he? That's no news at all on the face of it. We stop off in another Irish pub, but this time I pass on the Guinness in favour of that nut brown Anchor Steam. We have fish and chips for lunch, and I tell Zaria I'll take her to Leo Burdock's in Dublin for the real thing one day.

We emerge after an hour or so to a still bright afternoon and make for the bridge, standing magnificent and proud under the clear blue sky, a rare day in this city which is fogbound more often than not.

"You know" says Zaria. "This is one of the few times when it might be cool to have a camera."

"Why don't we walk across it?" I ask.

"It would be romantic if the fog was in," holding my arm tighter, "but there's no point today, we can see right across. There's nothing on the other side, all you can do is walk back."

I would like to be able to say I'd walked the bridge, but we've done a few miles today already and I don't want to tire her out for later on.

"So how come you don't have a camera?" I don't have one myself, I never have so I hadn't noticed, but I thought Zaria would probably get all those kinds of toys straight from the top of the shop.

"I've got a cine camera my Dad gave me so I can make my own little movies, but I don't use it for tourist stuff. You know the Indians used to think that their soul was being stolen if they had their picture taken, and I kind of know what they mean, but I look at it more the other way. I mean, we're here, we're in this moment and it's beautiful, perfect even, and to my way of thinking you just step outside yourself when you start taking pictures, like you're removing yourself from the place you've come to be at. All those tourists you see snapping away, they're not there while they're doing it, they come thousands of miles and then they don't experience it. Then what do they end up with? A flat piece of shiny paper. So that's why I don't own a camera, Frank."

She turns and gives me a dazzling smile that I know is going to be etched on my brain for as long as I live. I've never really thought about why I never owned a camera, it's just something that never interested me, but as of now, as we stand in this perfect moment, I'm adopting that as my reason.

On the Greyhound back to Santa Cruz I feel like I did when I was a kid on the way home from a day trip to Brighton. Sorry to be leaving, but safe in the knowledge that life is sweet and ever more will be so. I'm a little hung over, but nothing can spoil my mood. Neither of us wanted to eat last night, and we ended up on a bar crawl of North Beach. Zaria is asleep, her head on my shoulder. When we did finally get back to the hotel I wasn't about to allow her too much time for sleeping. I'm thinking about how random circumstance put me here, and how if I'd got up five minutes earlier or later the other Friday I would never have seen her again, when she wakes up.

"You know it was fate that brought you to me" I whisper as I kiss her gently on the lips.

"That's funny" she yawns "I remember it as a seventy three Oldsmobile."

"A seventy three? I thought it was brand new."

"Mom takes it to the car wash every week."

"You think she could use a full time chauffeur?"

"Sure, you could do that. You would have to get a hat and wear it at all times. Except when you are doubling up as the butler. Every house should have an English butler and chauffeur."

I was joking and she picked up on it, but I'm thinking of what I'm going to do for a job in LA. Not my favourite city in the world, but it is if Zaria's there, and she ain't gonna be no place else while her motion picture dreams are alive and well. Stanley's is out of the question, and even if it wasn't, Zaria, who has promptly gone back to sleep, won't be there more than once a week from now on, so I have no further use for it. Have to be a bar job of some kind. The Beanery is also a non-starter, the staff there are at the top of the bartending tree and they all know about three hundred cocktails. Too professional by half. Pete's place maybe? Nah, I wouldn't fancy being around Pete for more than an hour and a half in any one day. Anyway, I've already said goodbye to all these people, admittedly without telling them. But what am I thinking, I'm forgetting that I've still got all this dosh that I'm finding harder and harder to spend. I could move back in to the Riviera and live comfortably for a year, easy. I'd be an illegal, but hey, who isn't? Maybe I could sign up for a course in something myself, screenwriting possibly. We could come up to Santa Cruz for the holidays and visit Frisco, our city, every year at this time.

My thoughts get more and more outlandish, until I'm waking Zaria up and we're pulling into the little bus station. Lucille is there to meet us.

"Did you kids have a good time?"

I leave it to Zaria to enthuse while I maintain a stiff upper lip. It seems to be the decent thing to do, all things considered. In the evening we order pizza and drink wine and listen to that Sinatra record again. The next day we cycle to the beach, our beach, and all is well with the world, as it is and as it always will be.

Sunday morning I sleep late. I wake to find the bed empty and Zaria already downstairs, which is not part of the normal scheme of things. I find her in the kitchen with a cup of coffee and one of Lucille's cigs.

"Mom's gone into town" she says, in between drags on her Pall Mall. This is unusual also. The only time I've seen her leave the house was to buy groceries, and I don't even know if the stores open in Santa Cruz on a Sunday.

"Your Mum got religion all of a sudden?" I inquire. I'm waiting to see what kind of one liner is fielded back, instead I get something else.

"Listen Frank, there's been a change of plan." Her voice is flat, and she's pulling hard on the kingsize filter.

"Me and Mom are going home today. We were going tomorrow but we decided it makes sense to go today. I've got to get ready for my job and stuff."

Speaking a lot faster than I've heard her before. She puts out her cigarette and immediately lights another in an awkward, jerky fashion.

"Mom says it's OK for you to stay on for a few days if you want. I know it's kind of short notice. You can leave the key at the house next door when you go."

"But I might nick the stereo."

Suddenly I've got a thousand things running round my head. That's not one of them, but it's all I can think of to say.

"Mom trusts you, Frankie." Mom trusts everybody or so it seems.

"WellcanIgetaridetoLA?"

Now it's me talking fast, garbled and involuntary. We were going to talk about this today, or I was anyway. I didn't mention it yesterday at the beach. I know I should have done but everything was too perfect. Was.

"We've had a great vacation. Whaddya call it, a holiday. Let's leave it at that, huh?"

Huh? "So what are you saying, this was just a holiday romance to you?"

"Yeah." She softens now, and smiles sadly. "You left LA, Frank. You were heading north, remember?"

"I want to be with you, Zaria."

I have no mates that I will be seeing down the pub later. I'm not going to be seeing anyone to whom I can shrug and say we decided it was for the best. No one or nothing to live up to or to prevent me from speaking from the heart.

"I love-" but before I can get the words out she's shaking her head and looking a little angry.

"We both need to get on with our lives. I've got to get back now. LA's not your town and you know it. There's things you need to do. Stuff you need to take care of, Frank. You need to go home. You know it." She's looking deep inside me like an X-ray machine.

"I don't think LA's your town either. Let's go to New York."

"Well that just proves you don't know me at all. I don't want to go to New York."

I know she's right, not when she says I don't know her, because I do, but because Zaria would be a fish out of water in New York. I'm not thinking straight, not thinking at all really, but waving around desperately trying to find something to hold on to like a drowning man reaching in vain for a piece of driftwood. Zaria is thinking though, she's thinking hard, she's a world away from the Beverley Hills airhead I thought she might have been at first glance in Stanley's. She lights yet another smoke, and speaks in a low and strangely distant voice.

"Frank, you're looking for something and you don't know what it is. The thing is, even though you're travelling far from home you're still waiting for it to come to you. You know what? I'd say it's right there at home. That's where it's been all along."

"Maybe I was looking for you."

She shakes her head, and then I hear the Oldsmobile in the driveway, and we don't speak further because we know Lucille will shortly be joining us in the kitchen, which she does in a long, long minute, which gives me the excuse to reach for my mask and flash her a cheery smile. I thank her profusely for her hospitality, and ask if it will be all right if I stay one more night. Lot of families on the road on a Sunday and the buses aren't so great. I'm sure the buses are fine, this is America after all, but Lucille wouldn't know that. Then I go out on the deck and light up my first cigarette of the day, the first of many. I pick up the copy of Rolling Stone I read the other day, and look at it blankly while clouds disperse overhead. Then in what seems like no time at all Zaria is out to say goodbye.

"Don't I even get your phone number?"
My voice sounds like the most pathetic thing I've ever heard. She shakes her head.

"It's been great, Frank. I'll remember it. All of it. Good luck. And go home, Frank."

Then I get a kiss on the cheek, and I hate that, if there's one thing I hate it's that kiss on the cheek like I've turned into her brother all of a sudden, and then Zaria's gone and Lucille is shouting through the kitchen door, bye Frank, have a good trip. I hear the car drive off, and wait until they are out of earshot before going to the fridge and pulling out a beer.

I knock back a few beers during the day as might be expected, and I'm entitled to seeing as how they're the ones I bought the other day. I didn't buy the wine, but I'm sure Lucille wouldn't mind me having a bottle with dinner. I phone a pizza. I wouldn't trust myself to go into town feeling like this, I'm not thinking straight, and I could easily end up in a fight or something worse. I don't want to hear any of Zaria's records, so I trawl through the few that old Vince has left. I find another Sinatra album, this one from the classic fifties period. Frank Sinatra sings Only for the Lonely. Is someone taking the piss, or what? I put it on the turntable and open another bottle of red to accompany it. Old blue eyes had the blues when he did this one and no mistake. It's a lonesome town, Willow weep for me; Guess I'll hang my tears out to dry. The last track is the daddy of them all. One for my baby and one for the road. As the needle runs off to the middle I look at the clock. It's two am.

I never saw Lucille drinking spirits and Zaria's no whisky drinker, but on the shelf is a big bottle of Chivas Regal. Must be Vince's. Vince. I'm thinking about him like an old mate, one I've never met and never will. Things not going so well with Lucille, eh Vince? Women, eh Vince! What can you do with them? Can't live with them, can't live..... The bottle of Chivas is calling to me like a siren. DRINK ME. DRINK ME. Well old Vince can surely afford to replace it. I mean, come on, he's a cinematographer, for fucks sake. Here's to you, Vince my old pal. You could have been my daddy in law. What would you reckon on that, Vince? Not a lot, probably.

I find a suitable whisky tumbler and pour myself a sizeable measure. Then I put the album on again from the beginning. Some singers are here today and gone tomorrow, but Frank is for always. Frank knows. Not this Frank. This Frank never learns. The record ends at ten to three, right on cue. My eyes fix on the phone in the corner. I gaze at it for a good ten minutes. Then I pour myself another drink. I look at the phone for another five before pouring myself another drink, and that's the bottle gone. It's only then that I pick up the phone from the stand and bring it over to the sofa. I look at it for another five minutes while I drain the glass. It's then that I pick up the receiver.

Chapter Fourteen: Leavin' Blues

It was January nineteen seventy two, as cold and bleak a month as any I had encountered in my young life so far. Seventy one had begun on a wave of hopes and dreams, dreams that appeared to be fulfilled during the glorious, carefree, self-indulgent summer. Then it all came crashing down around me. Christmas was cancelled that year in the Downes house. Fortunately there was a ray of light that broke through the winter darkness in the form of Julie Grey. She made me serve a suitable period of penance. For one, she had got close to Ma, and for another, I had sent her precisely one postcard from my trip, the same as I had sent everyone. Will be gone a bit longer than expected, hope all is well, love Frank. For all that, Julie still saw in me something that was worth persevering with. She took me out for my birthday at the end of that miserable January, and once she was convinced I was suitably contrite we gradually got back to where we were.

No sooner were we back where we were, than we were a country mile further down love lane than we had ever been. Julie had left home while I was away. She had been happy to stay with her parents when she was going out with me. I liked to kid myself that it was because she was hoping we might do something more permanent one day. I got back to find her flat sharing in Brook Green with one of the girls in her office. Once I had my feet back under her table it was a given thing that I was there a lot more than I ever was at home. Poor little Joey was left to more or less fend for himself, and was acting more and more like one of those children you hear about who had been brought up by wolves. To my sorrow I didn't know how to help him, and to my shame I really didn't want to be around him. Any small vestige of respect I might have had left for my Dad soon disappeared up the Swannee, as he attempted to drown himself in Bell's whisky, Watney's Red Barrel, and self pity.

So by the spring me and Julie were all but living together and everything was rosy, especially the long Sunday mornings in bed before I would eventually allow her to get up and cook my breakfast. Lucky Frankie was back in business, if a year older and wiser, not to mention sadder. There was just one cloud on the horizon. I was boracic lint. Skint. In the run up to Christmas I had done what I had sworn I would never do, and worked with the old man down the market. Naturally he took that as the perfect excuse to do even less than he would have done anyway, which wasn't much, and I ended up doing most of it on my own. Never, ever again. I suggested to Joey that he might like to come and help me one Saturday morning, and he came at me with the bread knife. I gather that means a no then Joe, was my response as I removed it from him, not without some difficulty, but he wasn't ready for any little jokes at that time. I had never had any trouble finding a job, so it had always been easy come easy go for me. Well now I wanted time to think about it. Julie reminded me that was what I was supposed to be doing on my trip, thinking about it, but it doesn't work like that.

One fine day in March I stepped inside an employment agency, mainly because there was a miniskirted dolly bird sat behind the desk and I wanted to cop a closer look. I dutifully filled in the form while she flicked through some cards in a desultory fashion. The first thing she offered me was a clerk's job down at the Walls Meat factory. Not for me darling, thanks all the same. The prospect of getting anywhere in a place that size was about as bright for the young hopefuls who entered there in as it was for the steak and kidney. She had another look.

"Have you heard of Bandini Brothers?"

"Can't say I have, love."

"Mr Bandini is quite a character."

With that my ears pricked up, following the part of my anatomy which had done the same ten minutes earlier. Must be a small place if she's on speaking terms with one of the guvnors. I fancied a small firm; somewhere a likely lad could make his mark.

"Have you done accounts at all?"

"Well I've done a bit, and at the moment I'm studying accountancy at evening classes."

One of the first things I learned is if you are going to lie, lie big. Another thing, and I know it's very much the sort of thing I should keep to myself, is that I had started to find the idea of being an accountant quite intriguing, attractive even. I was good at maths at school, arithmetic anyway. I didn't shine so much when it came round to logarithms and trigonometry, I never saw the point, but figures, yes. A skill that was rekindled when I found myself behind the bookies window. I blame Monty Python, myself. City gents, bowler hats, silly walks, Arthur Putey, the most boring man in the world, all of it hilarious, all of it making even the idea of entering the accountancy profession seem ludicrous in hippy dippy London town. I laughed as much as anybody and more than most, but I didn't buy it in its entirety. You could be a show business accountant, sitting back in a Rolls Royce with a big cigar. You could be a rock and roll accountant. A whole host of sixties groups reached the end of a decade with nothing, reduced to their last plectrum by shady money men in camel coats. Better to be an honest one, get plenty of work and be popular. So if you're looking for a bright spark to do your books, albeit an untrained one, there's no reason why I shouldn't be your man. So where do this Bandini Brothers ply their trade, I asked. Park Royal. Bus from my house, fifteen minutes on the tube if I'm at Julie's. So the girl got on the blower, giving it the same old flannel they give for everyone who walks through the door.

"Can you go and see him now?"

"Well I'm not really dressed for it." As I said I only went in there on a whim and the scent of girlie. She passed the message on.

"Mr Bandini doesn't worry about things like that. He'll see you in half an hour."

She wrote me out a bit of paper, and I promised to buy her a drink if I got the job, an offer which she appeared to respond to with some enthusiasm. Then, resplendent in Ben Sherman and Falmers, I jumped on the Piccadilly line and headed north west to Park Royal, which is neither of those things, but an industrial estate named after a dog track which had been concreted over years ago. It wasn't without greenery, however. Guinness brewery's London outpost was right in the middle of it, the big chimneys puffing out roasted barley smoke, so that if you closed your eyes on a brewing day you could imagine you were standing on the banks of the Liffey. They also kept a dairy herd grazing in the fields surrounding the brewery buildings, for reasons which have always remained a mystery. When I was a kid Uncle George told me that the milk went in the stout, and I believed him until I was well into my teens. Guinness was the place to work round our way, but it was very much a closed shop that you could only get into if your Dad worked there. Needless to say my old man had plenty of experience of drinking the stuff, but none at all of making it. I reckoned I should have got in there on the strength of being half Irish, but it didn't work like that.

So I checked my directions and set off down the road, deep into the heart of the factory estate. It was a sunny day which made it bearable. If it had been raining and revealed itself to me in its true grey awfulness I think I would have probably turned back. As it was I nearly went past the place. I got the number right, and found it was a caff. Then I twigged the name above the door, Bandini's. Not exactly what I had in mind. A rather suspicious Italian woman pointed to a bell outside for the flat upstairs. I rang it purposefully, my curiosity now well and truly up and running. The sound of heavy footsteps on uncarpeted wooden stairs, and then the door opened.

"Yes? Can I help you?" Said in that tone of voice that doesn't mean can I help you at all, it means who the fucking hell are you. A short stocky man with thick black hair and moustache, flecked with grey. He could have been fifty five, or he could have been forty five and overworked. I decided upon the latter.

"Mr Bandini? I've come from the agency. About the job?"

He looked blank. Come on, the bird was on the phone to you only half an hour ago. Or maybe - "I do apologise, perhaps it was the other Mr Bandini."

Now he looked well and truly mystified. "Other Mr Bandini?"

Then he twigged it. "Oh yes, the agency. Sorry son, I've got a lot on my mind at the moment. Come in."

There was something about the way Gino called me son that made me warm to him. I never like anyone calling me that, but the way he said it somehow made me feel he had a good heart. I followed him upstairs and into what I supposed was the office. I thought my brother's bedroom was untidy, but it had nothing on this place, papers all over the place, piles of what looked like bills on the table, and I couldn't help noticing a hefty stack of fivers on a shelf.

"Are you any good with the figures, son? I know how to work, Jesus Christ I know how to work, but I gotta too much of the paperwork, it a-driving me fucking mental."

His accent veered from Bow Bells to Bologna in the same sentence, and no sentence was complete without an f or two, and more often than not a c for good measure. If I quote Gino from now on, which I probably will, I'll leave most of them out to avoid repetition. I was soon to learn them both and a few more in Italian, purely for the sake of variety.

So I told Gino that I had helped my Dad in the market ever since I was a kid working out the prices and taking the money and all that, and I

231

was about to tell him a few more things that I hadn't done, but it wasn't necessary.

"I like a man who helps his family. I like that very much. A man who doesn't help his family is not a man, he is a - " well, you get the picture. "Forty five pound a week is all right for you?"

Well yes it was thank you, as it happens. Forty five notes was a fair old whack. I had been on thirty when I left the bookies, and that wasn't bad.

"Forty five it is then. But don't tell those people, what do you call them, the agency, forty five, eh? We tell them twenty five and the rest we work out man to man. You can start Monday. But listen son, you work for Gino you have to work, you understand? You don't take the piss. Oh, and you have to work Saturday mornings, that's very important. Anyway I have to tell you very politely to fuck off now, I'm very busy as you can see. I see you Monday morning, eight o'clock."

Eight o'clock starts and Saturday mornings weren't really what I had in mind, but I couldn't really turn it down, and I was intrigued by this unusual and larger than life character. I never even asked him anything about the business. It surely had to be more than one caff. I walked back to the Western Avenue and caught the Piccadilly line back to Hammersmith. I bought Julie some flowers and a bottle of wine, and waited for her to get home from her work so I could impart the good news. I belled the agency dolly to tell her I'd got a start at twenty five a week, but I didn't follow up with the drink invitation. It was time to walk the straight and narrow, for a while anyway.

I soon found out that Gino was something of a local legend, if you can be a legend in Park Royal. Three garages and four cafes, and a small fleet of three ton lorries that he hired out to other local firms. Worked from five thirty in the morning every day of the week except Sunday, and sometimes that as well, on through till ten or eleven or even later. He was making money hand over fist, but he didn't allow himself any time to enjoy it. The next thing I found out about Gino was that he was only happy if he was working. When he wasn't working he would worry, worry that he should be working, and more to the point worry about what the people who were working for him were up to. It didn't take me too long to find out that he was bloody right to.

For a man who loved family, and there was no doubt that he did, he certainly didn't trust any of them. There had once been two Bandini brothers, hence the name. Mario was the younger, and Gino had loved him because he was his brother and hated him for everything else. Gino worked round the clock, Mario was the playboy. When Gino was in a rage, which was at least once a day, and that would be on a good day, he would walk round talking to himself, and then he would start talking to Mario.

"Why did God give me a brother like you, Mario? What did I do? Then he took you away. Why do that to me?"

Gino did all the work, but Mario still claimed his share, and for all his bluster Gino had been too soft hearted to deny him it. The playboy lifestyle had caught up with him five years ago when he bought an Alfa Romeo sports, lost control on a bend and drove it into a wall at ninety miles an hour. Gino kept his brother's name going, partly in memorium, and also because he thought it sounded better.

I learned all this and more very quickly. Gino liked to talk. Born nineteen twenty six, the year of the General Strike, in Clerkenwell, which was a proper Little Italy back then. His parents had come from Parma, like the cheese and the ham. Worked seven days a week for other people until they scraped together enough to open their own cafe. Gino swore blind that he started work in the cafe when he was five years old, putting food on the plates and clearing up. When he was fourteen his Dad was interned on the Isle of Man, and Gino became to all intents and purposes the head of the family, running the cafe while the bombs fell around them. The old man may have been considered an alien, but when hostilities ceased he came home and it was Gino's turn to go away, called up by the British Army, which sounds a bit much, all things considered. When the other recruits heard his accent and found out his name, they used to spit in his tea. Gino moved out west in the fifties when property was cheap and the estate was booming, and slowly built up his business.

Gino's parents were dead now, both gone before they reached their seventies, worn down by a life of relentless toil. He lived in a house which I never saw in the posh part of Ealing next to a golf course, not that he ever played. Apart from the house he allowed himself one luxury, a big solid Volvo which he would trade in every year for a new model, always the same colour, bright yellow. He wore a brown overall for the garage and a white one for the cafe, and I hardly ever saw him wear anything else. He had a wife who I never met, although I spoke to her occasionally on the phone. Gino had met her on one of his rare sorties to the old country. The poor woman seldom saw her husband during the hours of daylight, and spoke hardly any English after twenty years. I never got to find out her name. Gino never dignified her with one on the rare occasions he deigned to ring her back. They had no children, which caused Gino much sorrow and for which he put the blame firmly on his wife.

"A marriage without children. What kind of marriage is that? Is like a tree without fruit." Then he would shake his head sadly. "My wife is a good woman. What can I do?"

What he could do was to look after and provide for Mario's children and his widow. He wasn't so fond of the eldest, a boy who according to Gino was too much like his father, but he doted on his niece who was fifteen. It was rumoured among some of the cafe staff that he provided for his sister-in-law's needs in a more basic sense as well, but if he did, I don't know where he found the time. Gino took to me even more when I told him about Ma, and I milked the whole scene of keeping my brother on the right track for all it was worth, even though I was doing nothing of the sort.

Gino didn't get me involved with the money immediately. He hadn't got where he was by being that foolish. He started me off with the ordering, food for the cafes, tyres, oil, spares and then petrol for the garages. It was a nightmare at first, nothing was written down, and he had no idea of what the expenditure was for each location. All he knew was that his income was greater than his outgoings. After a few weeks I worked out a proper bought ledger for him detailing all his costs per item and per unit. I enjoyed it once I got into it. Julie used to laugh at me because I kept all my LPs in alphabetical order. Girls don't do that, it's strictly a male thing. My argument was that it was easier to do than not to do. I applied the same principle to sorting out Gino's excuse for an office.

Gino was suspicious at first, as he was suspicious of most things. It was as though the imposition of some kind of order was a direct threat to the chaos within which he thrived. It was a different story once he got used to it. Gino was proud and ashamed in equal measure that he had received little formal education, and treated the people who worked for him with a degree of contempt that they were so far down the totem pole to be dependent on him for a living. Of course he loved them as well. He was related to most of them. I was different however, and was held up as a shining example of what an education can do, which as you can imagine didn't do a great deal for my popularity. Not that I gave a monkeys. Once you stepped through the door you were in

Gino's world and nobody else's opinion was worth a toss. He soon upped my wages. The first week he gave me an envelope with twenty five and a bone fide wage slip for the same. Then he winked, and slipped me another envelope with a moody twenty. After a few months the twenty went up to twenty five and then thirty.

Gino's high opinion of me didn't mean I was exempt from the treatment. No chance of that. One thing about me, and I know this is a direct result of knowing Gino, is that there's no use in shouting at me. Do that and I'll let it wash over me like an old rock waiting for the tide to turn. Sticks and stones, and all that. There would be plenty of mornings when Gino would rage at me for not knowing something that I couldn't possibly know the answer to until that afternoon. Then he would calm down slightly and hit me his well worn catch phrase.

"I'm very disappointed in you, Frank. Very disappointed." Spoken as if he was carrying the sorrows of the whole world on his shoulders. The important thing was not to react. Logic and a clear head, that's what you need. Logic and a clear head have saved my bacon on several occasions since, so I guess I have Gino to thank for it. Five minutes later and he would be fine, until the next time anyway.

So all things considered, I was happy enough for a while and so was Julie, with me living at her place in all but name, and with plenty of spending dough for the weekends. I remember her coming to meet me one rainy spring evening when I had been working late. I felt a bit embarrassed at how scruffy the place was, but she seemed pleased more than anything else, as if it demonstrated that I was really digging in, doing a proper job and not poncing round in some flash office. We walked arm in arm by the canal towards Harlesden. The rain had cleared, leaving a golden sky behind us and a rainbow ahead. I fancied for a moment that I could see the rainbow reflected in the water, but quickly realised that it was the same rainbow that was on display every day, the prism of toxic chemicals that choke what little life is left out of the oily waters of the Grand Union. It was another of those moments when everything seemed as it should be, one of those Carpenters moments you might say. They were few and far between, which is why I remember them so well.

Julie passed her driving test in June, so we bought a car to celebrate. I had passed mine two years earlier, but I had never got round to getting any wheels. If you live in London and you like a drink, they're a nuisance more than anything else. Still, it appeared that I had myself a ready made chauffeuse, so I made use of some of the readies that were coming my way. Two tone Mark One Cortina, light and dark blue, ninety sixty five, seventy thousand on the clock, mine for a hundred notes. I spent nearly the same again putting in a cassette player and a tasty pair of speakers, and we were ready to go.

Another one of Gino's many quirks was that he didn't like holidays. It wasn't just that he didn't like going on holiday, which he didn't, but it was more that he didn't see the point. I mean why should anyone want to go to Spain or Morocco, when they could be on a poxy industrial estate in the pouring rain, up to their neck in axle grease and chip fat? The fact that he had been on a holiday of sorts twenty years ago visiting family in the old country, and came back with a barren wife may have had something to do with it, but not much. Basically Gino was only happy when he was working, and he never understood that not everybody else might feel the same way. If you took a day off sick, which I very seldom did, he thought you were looking for another job somewhere. Such was the nature of the man. I could see that this was going to be a problem if I was going to be there for any length of time, but seventy two was never going to be a travelling year, so for now it wasn't. He grudgingly agreed to me having a week off in August, and we hit the old A30 down to Cornwall.

Gino turned out to be right on this occasion. I would have been much better off in Park Royal. We found a B&B in St Ives which was cosy enough, but it rained more often than it didn't, and the sight of the car parked outside made it difficult for me to relax. It was if it was whispering to me all the time, here I am, I'm yours, take me for a ride. We spent most of the time touring the county with the windscreen wipers on double time. On the last night we, or rather I, got talking to some hippies in the local pub. They were camping in Zennor, a few miles down the coast. A couple of drinks later and Mr Bigshot went and got the car and offered them a lift back. Julie was having none of it and stomped off to bed. Back at the campsite I was duly invited to share a spliff as a token of appreciation. In the normal way I wouldn't have, but it had been a boring week, and I had a point to prove by not rushing back to the B&B. It was two am before I left, the road empty but winding and treacherous. I got about halfway back before I accelerated into a corner and turned the Cortina over three times, finishing upside down in a field. I gingerly pulled myself out of the rear window and discovered that no damage was done other than a gashed arm and a few minor cuts on the top of my head. Little damage to me, that is. The car was left like an old sardine can. I walked back to St Ives, my arm dripping blood on the road. If they had put the hounds on my trail it would have been one of their easier assignments. I crawled into bed beside my sleeping girlfriend, and had some serious explaining to do when she saw the state of the sheets in the morning. I didn't feel inclined to go back and retrieve the stereo, and we sat in stony silence on the train back to Paddington.

If I had been in any other job I would have got myself signed off for a few weeks, but seeing as how I was working for Gino, I got myself back there at eight o'clock on Monday. He was angry, which I didn't appreciate at first, it wasn't as if it was his car. Then he got upset.

"I must pay you too much for you to buy this fucking car. I already lost a brother because he drove like a cunt. You kill yourself as well it would be like I lose a son. You buy another car and you get the fucking tin tack, understand? I'm very disappointed in you Frank, very disappointed."

I wasn't about to buy another car, although not because of anything Gino had to say about it. Julie's father bought her a Mini, strictly on condition that I wasn't to be included in the insurance, and I wasn't to be allowed behind the wheel under any circumstances. If she had been in the car with me we would have done all sorts of damage to each other bouncing around when it went over. That was Julie, having none of it. Always the sensible one. I was very aware of how lucky I had been and the need to pay more regard to my own self-preservation in future. More than that, I had a strong sense that it wasn't in the tea leaves for me to die in a field at the age of twenty two. There was a big old world out there, and most of it was still a mystery. I knew that Gino would only be part of it for a while. Julie too, even though I loved the girl well enough after a fashion.

I've never been one for deep psychological analysis, especially of my own self. Looking back now, I think it was when Gino told me I was like a son, even though it was in an emotional and very kind manner, that I began to look at things a little differently. I started to look on him as fair game. He liked me, and I had done a lot for him already, but I had only been there for five months so I was hardly part of the family. I had sorted out his ordering and his stock control, and then he started getting me involved with the incomings. One morning he piled a whole bunch of cash on the desk and told me it was the petty cash for the cafes and the garages, money they kept separate from what came through the till. Fourteen hundred quid, two hundred for each unit. Could I check it and put it in seven envelopes. Then he went back downstairs. I counted it out and found there was sixteen hundred. I played it straight, and went down and asked him where the other two hundred should go. Sorry son, that's my mistake. That's the float for my back pocket. One of the few times Gino ever apologised for anything, and certainly the only time he ever admitted a mistake, to me anyway. As tests go it was an extremely crude one, and something of an insult to my intelligence, but I had clearly passed it. From then on he started giving me more and more stuff to do. Soon I was doing the books, such as they were.

I convinced Gino that he would have to start paying more tax. The business was expanding faster than he could keep up with, and the Inland Revenue surely wouldn't wear it if he kept on declaring the same takings year after year. We didn't have to declare all of it. No need to go mad. Just make it look a bit more realistic, more professional you might say. There was more coming in since I had started going round checking on the cash registers. The bastards weren't dipping their hands in quite as freely as they were before. Like I said, they all hated me, a state of affairs which I was never going to lose one moments sleep over. I sorted it out so that we had a nice legitimate looking piece for the taxman, and still a hefty chunk to go under Gino's floorboards or wherever it was he stashed it. Oh, and a piece for Frank as well. Well I couldn't not really, could I?

So by now I was on sixty quid a week plus the hundred I was taking off the top. I didn't tell Julie about the extra. I'm not that stupid. That all went into different accounts in small amounts that wouldn't attract attention, building society, post office. Premium Bonds as well, not that Ernie ever coughed up a winner. There's a thought, I might get back home and find I'm a millionaire. The fact that I didn't actually spend any of it, well not much of it, helped me maintain a belief that all I was really doing was looking after it for him. I was looking after it all right, that much was true.

As the months went by it worked out that I was spending less time with Julie and more back at the house. Joey was running wild, which meant that he was hardly ever at home, which suited me fine. Me and the old man would pass each other on the stairs occasionally, grunting at each other like rusty old tankers on a pitch black night. I managed the odd dalliance on a week night, indulging my growing taste for restaurants and whatever transpired after, but Julie was still my girl.

The time between finishing work on Saturday lunchtime and going back on Monday morning was ours and ours alone.

It was almost a year after the disastrous trip to the West Country before we took another holiday. Once again a week was all I could manage. Mindful of appearing to be too well heeled I told Gino we had booked a last minute cheapie to Torremolinos. Any other job it would have been nobody's business, but I had put myself in a different kind of situation, one that I couldn't help resenting even though it was of my own doing. Probably because it was of my own doing. Instead we went to Marbella, Torre's more upmarket neighbour. Scheduled flights, five star hotel, the works. In one sense it was great. The last thing we were ever going to do was hire a car, so we spent most of the time within the hotel grounds, sipping cocktails by the pool in the day, and dining under the stars by night. While we were lying by the pool my mind would wander down the coast to Algeciras and chance encounters in street cafes, and then on to Portugal and beyond the far Atlantic to pastures new. I didn't share any of this with Julie, but then I didn't need to. Julie knew everything.

Summer turned into autumn, and I had been working for Gino for eighteen months. I knew the day was coming when I would have to bid him a fond arriverderci. Julie too. It was like I could never give her more than half of myself when we were together. The other half was always somewhere else. That was when I was with her. When I wasn't I hardly thought of her at all. She deserved better. Still, autumn then became winter and things were still as you were. It was all too easy for me at Gino's, and the money was rolling in for both of us. I was also aware of the possibility that some bright spark might come in after me and figure out where some of the undeclared income had disappeared to, but they would have had to be bloody good, as I covered my tracks well. Still, I bided my time.

Gino loved his niece. Doted on her. He paid for to go to private school, and he was always going on about how she was never going to peel potatoes for a living. The girl was university bound whether she liked it or not. So I heard about this kid Teresa all the time, but I never met her and I never expected to. I didn't think Gino would ever let her within a mile of the workplace. So it was a surprise when he proudly brought her into the office on the first Monday after Christmas, five feet two, sweet sixteen and never been kissed, and bright as a button.

He wanted her to find out what went on in the real world, so she was going to be helping out during the school holidays.

Sweet as she was, I didn't exactly welcome her with open arms at first. I had all my own systems worked out and I was worried that her presence might cramp my style. I needn't have worried. She wasn't about to go looking into cash registers. Typical bird, she loved being on the phone, and she was good at it too, so she was soon ordering stock and chasing up payments from customers, all the things that I had long become bored with. Once I realised she posed no kind of threat I got to like her. I needed cheering up. Christmas had been noticeably lacking in cheer once again, although at least it was short thanks to Gino. It was also impossible to turn on the radio or television, or even cross the threshold of a shop without being assailed by Slade. So here it is Merry Christmas, everybody's having fun. Fuck off.

Teresa was bubbly and enthusiastic, and she was pretty as well with black curly hair and laughing eyes, and that kind of Mediterranean skin which could soak up a tan in two weeks during the summer and hold on to it for the rest of the year. Gino had put her brother Lou to work in one of the garages. There was no indication that they might be related. Terry had drawn all the smart cards. Two weeks later she was back at school, and I found it even more of a drag having to be back on the phone half the day, and I missed her presence, but I didn't think too much about it.

Apart from the fact that I was financially in the pink, January was in many ways worse than the dreadful one I had endured two years earlier. A three day week was declared due to the miner's strike. Gino's businesses were exempt, food and transport, but that didn't stop him raging at the miners for all he was worth. You didn't have to scratch Gino too hard to find out his views on most things but it all started coming out now. Musso would have sorted them out he reckoned, Musso would have put them all up against the wall. Mussolini, that is. No wonder his fellow squarebashers spat in his tea back in forty seven. His great fear was that Harold Wilson was going to get his feet back under the table at number ten. Wilson, who I had always reckoned a canny politician who had kept Britain out of Vietnam, was Gino's ultimate bogeyman. He was duly re-elected at the end of February, causing Gino to demand that his floorboards quota be increased to compensate for the massive tax hikes which were surely coming.

Barely more than half a year ago all that stuff seemed important.

Now I know it was no more important than a leaf falling off a tree, or the tide coming in.

Or going out.

At half term Teresa was back for a week, and I was surprised at how pleased I was to see her. I know I've never been one not to have a high opinion of myself where the girlies are concerned, but I fancied that she was pleased to see me too. The Friday was her birthday, and she brought in her cards from home as if she was at school. I didn't usually take a lunch break, but on the spur of the moment I took the bus to Ealing, and bought her a copy of Lord of the Rings. She squealed with delight and blushed when I presented it to her, and rewarded me with a kiss on the cheek. I blushed a little myself for the first time in years. At five o'clock she gathered up her things and said goodbye.

"Might see you in the next holidays then?" I asked, with just a little too much eagerness in my voice.

" No, Easter I'll be revising for my exams."

"Oh." Suddenly I felt as if I had just turned seventeen myself. Probably sounded like it too.

"Some other time, though." She smiled sweetly, and then she was gone. But not forgotten.

Four weeks later, and I was doing my Saturday morning stint. I never did much on a Saturday. There was little reason for me to be there at all, other than that Gino didn't like the idea of anyone having too much leisure time on their hands. Still, with what he was paying me or more to the point what I was paying myself, I wasn't about to argue. This particular Saturday I wasn't intending on staying around for long as Gino was taking a rare day off. Taking the wife out somewhere, he had said. I had been there more than two years, and this was a first. I had been there about ten minutes, and I was going through the books when the bell rang.

"Well, this is a surprise" I said. It was, too.

"I was just passing" said Teresa. "I thought I'd stop by and say hello."

You don't just happen to be passing the estate. Not on a Saturday morning, not at any other time either.

"Well you had better come in then."

She negotiated the wooden stairs daintily, if a little noisily, in red stilettos, while I followed behind looking her up from bottom to top. Bare legs still slightly tanned, short black skirt, trendy red jacket. No doubt about it. She knew Gino was off the scene, and she had come to see me. Here was trouble as I lived and breathed.

"I love the book" she said, removing the jacket to reveal a skimpy white blouse with a red bra clearly showing underneath. "I haven't finished it, but I'm nearly halfway."

"Well you don't want to stop when you're nearly halfway" I replied, to which she smiled in a way which suggested she had no intention of doing any such thing.

"It was really sweet of you. I wanted to come and thank you again. Nobody has ever given me anything before, apart from my family."

"Shouldn't you be revising?"

"I can do that as well. I don't do anything else."

That smile again. Nobody has ever given me anything before?

"Haven't you got a boyfriend?" Careful not to ask have you got a boyfriend, which on the surface carries a different meaning, but she knew what I meant. I had never asked anything personal when she had been there before. I knew her Dad had died, everyone did, but I never mentioned it and neither did she. I was always strictly business at Bandini Brothers. Up until then.

"Have you got a girlfriend?"

"I did have, but we broke up."

I did have a girlfriend. We hadn't broken up, but I realised there and then that we would. Even if Teresa had been doing nothing more than playing a kids game and turned tail and ran, and how I wish now that she had done exactly that, I knew instantly that me and Julie had lost that spark.

I pretended to study the ledger, although there was no chance of me taking anything in. Teresa played around with the radio. I had left a small transistor there strictly for Saturday mornings only. If she had put her jacket back on and said goodbye there and then, I know I wouldn't have done anything, as much as I wanted to.

I don't know what the chances are of me ever bumping into Gladys Knight. Slim, probably. If it was a likely occurrence I suppose it would have happened in LA., but I didn't stick around long enough. LA proved too much for the man. If I had of done, I know what I would have said. You didn't half cause me some aggravation, girl.

Time for a golden oldie. A revive forty five. Teresa couldn't have been more than eight when it came out, if that, but she knew all the words and she was singing along, quietly at first, her eyes averted almost demurely. Come on boy the time is right. As the song went on she became emboldened, singing louder, and then she was looking right at me while she was singing. Boy I'm hungry for your love, give me what I'm empty of, here I am, take me in your arms and love me.

I leaned over, put my hand around the back of the neck and kissed her, her tongue eagerly exploring the inside of my mouth as if it had been released from a trap. I pulled her up against the desk, and lifted up her skirt revealing tiny knickers which matched her bra and shoes, and which looked and felt as though they were new on. Not for one second removing my tongue from her mouth, I pushed my hand down through her rough peasant pubic hair. To my delight she was already moist, hungry for my love and more than ready for it. As deftly as I could I removed the red pants and dropped my jeans and jockeys and eased myself into her with less difficulty than I expected. The radio went flying and we lost the station, but it had done its job as I popped Teresa's cherry on her uncle's office table.

Neither of us spoke for at least five minutes, which was considerably longer than the deed had taken us. Wonderful and life altering as it was, our mutual passion was such that we brought each other to the boil in less time than it takes to listen to a golden memory from yesteryear. I don't regret many things in life, although there are some things which I wish I had done differently. Looking back now and knowing that the damage was already done, I regret very much that we didn't wait ten minutes and do it again slowly, but we were spent, emotionally if not physically.

Finally she spoke. "I'm glad it was you. Even if nothing else happens between us I'm still glad you were the first."

I thought for a second. "Well I'm glad it was me too."

Then she laughed and blushed, and was sweet little Terry again. It was time to go. I walked her to the bus stop although I gave her a minute start, mindful that the cafe was still open and the collective eyes behind the counter didn't miss much.

"Can I call you?"

She shook her head.

"No you can't call me. I'll call you."

Then the bus came, and I got a peck on the cheek and she was gone. I had intended going back to Julie's, but instead I caught the next bus back to the house for a bath and a think.

A month later I broke up with Julie, as I knew I surely would. If anything our sex life had got better since Teresa, but there was no fooling Julie.

"There's someone else, isn't there?"

"No" I replied, which on the face of it was a lie, but not that much of one as I didn't know if I would ever see Terry again.

"I wouldn't leave you for anyone else, babe. I'd only leave you for myself."

I thought that was very profound at the time.

"Well I hope you'll be very happy together" said Julie, and that was that.

A month after that I walked into the entrance of Park Royal tube station to find Teresa waiting for me. I was only going that way because I was supposed to be meeting Keith at Earls Court. Since the split with Julie I was more in the habit of getting the bus home. It was the first time I had seen Terry since that morning. She looked a little jaded, but she was undeniably still sweet Teresa, and my desires were immediately rekindled. She said that we had better go for a drink, and I wasn't about to argue. No mate was that important. In the pub next to the station she hit me with it. She was four weeks gone.

It had been eight years since I had begun practising on Susan Hopkins, and since then I hadn't always been as fussy as I might have been about who I got hold of, and there had been many times when I had been less than careful about using anything. Everything was well organised with Julie, that's how she was, but there had been many others where it had all been left in the lap of the procreative gods. As far as I knew, none of my irresponsible actions had ever reaped any consequences, which came as a great relief, but also planted in my mind the possibility that I might be a Jaffa. Then bingo, along comes poor little Terry and I ring the bell first time out. I know it sounds terrible, and I'm ashamed to admit it, but there was a part of me which was secretly pleased. One thing for certain, whatever was going to happen it wasn't going to be my call.

"What do you want to do?"

"I don't know."

Whispering now.

"Well it's up to you. Anything that needs taking care of, the money is no problem."

She shook her head and started to cry, softly so no one else was likely to notice. She looked about fourteen. "You don't understand. I'm a Catholic."

So am I technically, but she was correct in her assumption. I didn't understand. When she had regained her composure she finished her grapefruit juice and said she had to go. She wrote down her phone number on a scrap of paper and passed it to me.

"I thought you said I couldn't call you."

"Well it doesn't bloody matter now, does it?" managing a smile. I offered to get her a cab, I offered to walk her to the bus stop, but she would have none of it.

"Call me, yeah" she said bravely, and then smiled again and made for the door, leaving me nursing a pint of John Courage.

I stayed there for the rest of the evening, drinking slowly and thinking furiously. What were the options? I could marry Teresa, if she'd have me, that is. Work for Gino, maybe become his partner one day. Teresa was beautiful and intelligent, and I wanted to have again what I'd had on that fateful Saturday morning more than I've ever wanted anything.

But I wanted more besides. Anyway, it would still have been wrong. She was supposed to be studying for her A levels, for Christ's sake. Gino's affection for me would turn to hate. There would be a constant bitter burning resentment coming in my direction from him and the rest of her family for as long as they lived. I knew I was going to have to go.

So Teresa found out what went on in the real world. That was the last time I saw her.

Things happened quickly after that. The following Saturday morning I was in the office as usual, when I received a phone call from Gino's wife. This was a first. I had fielded calls before when she was looking for Gino, but now she was ringing me with a message from him. Her English never got any better, but the gist of it was that Gino wouldn't be in as he was working in the house, and he wouldn't be in on Monday either. I had to get the poor woman to repeat it twice until I got it straight. Gino was staying at home until Tuesday.

Working at home? Something was going on, and I felt distinctly uneasy. Ma used to say that if you've done nothing wrong you had nothing to worry about. Now I had wronged Gino twice over and I was worried, me who never worried about anything. If Gino had thought he was being hey diddled he would have taken the books home, and they were still in the drawer. I had a cold feeling in my bones that Teresa might have given her Mum the earth shattering news. She was going to have to sooner or later. Her Mum would have told Gino soon enough. If she had, then for once in his life Gino had overridden his natural instincts and decided to sit on it for a few days. He probably didn't trust himself not to kill me if he saw me. I had more than twenty years on him, but he was a strong man, one that I wouldn't relish taking on. Gino didn't work at home. He slept at home, and then never for very long. I considered ringing Teresa, but I felt it was hardly a good time. I thought seriously about doing a runner there and then, but I wanted a little more time. Twenty grand had flowed effortlessly into my accounts by now, and I had been more than cute about how I did it, but I still needed to tidy up a few things first.

I went in on Monday ready for anything that came my way. Anything other than what I found. There was a hand written sign in the window of the cafe. CLOSED FOR TODAY. The staff were inside, and all of them were in tears. Angela, the manageress, called my name almost tenderly, which was unusual, as she disliked me as much if not more than the rest of them did.

"Frank. Frank. Gino, he died. Gino is dead."

It took a while to piece together what had happened. Gino wasn't working in the house, he was working on the house. Painting the window frames, replacing a few tiles, touching things up on his big old house. On Sunday afternoon he had been painting the guttering, when he had slipped off the ladder and crashed through the garage roof, breaking his neck. Death was instantaneous.

Why Gino, why? There were any number of no brain cousins or their children he could have given that task to. Why did Gino need to do his own decorating on a Sunday afternoon when he would normally have been hard at work preparing for the coming week?

I'll never know for sure unless I speak to Terry again, which is not very likely now, but my belief is that it was Gino's way of thinking things through. Something concerning me. Get up a ladder where no one can disturb you, and think out a course of action. Gino's normal behaviour was that of a bull in a china shop, but he didn't get where he was without using his brain sometimes. I was convinced he knew.

"I'm very disappointed in you Frank. Very disappointed."

Probably his last thoughts, his last words even, as Gino was always one for talking to himself. So disappointed that he didn't look where he was putting his feet. Gino, who had the heart and strength of a lion. Gino, who had been like a Dad to me for more than two years, and whose trust I had betrayed with greed and lust, was gone.

Nobody did anything that Monday apart from weep and wail, so I soon made my excuses and went home. There was nobody for me to answer to, for a start. Tuesday, there was. Lou came into the office. I had seen him around the place, and exchanged a few words on occasion which were enough to tell me he wasn't the sharpest pencil in the box, but nothing more than that. I could tell straight away that he didn't know about me and his sister.

"We had a family meeting and I am going to take over the running of the business. This week I'm busy with my uncle's funeral, but on Monday I want you to show me how to do the accounts. OK?"

OK? If circumstances had been different I would have laughed in his face. Take over the running of the business? I wouldn't have any confidence in the kid to run a hot dog stand, and more to the point neither would Gino, or he would have given him my job in the first place. Gino would have turned in his grave if it wasn't for the fact that he wasn't in it yet. If I had a mind to, it could have been fill your boots time for Frank, and Lou would have been none the wiser, but I'd had enough. Besides, he was going to be my first child's uncle. I knew what I had to do.

I stayed in the office until gone midnight, so late that I had to walk home. On Wednesday I worked solidly from eight until five thirty. The accounts were now in perfect order. I had toyed with the idea of opening up a reserve account for the business and paying most of, if not all my ill-gotten gains into it, but I decided that it might end up opening a can of worms somewhere down the line. Anyway, none of the nearest and dearest were going to be short of a few bob and I didn't give a toss about the others. I wrote out a detailed list of instructions for the weekly and monthly routines for dealing with bills and bank statements, not that Lou was about to understand any of it. Christ knows what was going to happen with the wages, that had been one thing that Gino had always done himself. I then left a note on top, in which I said I was sorry if I was leaving at a bad time, but I found it

247

too distressing to stay on in the circumstances, which was true enough. Then I walked out into the rain and headed for home without a backward glance. I didn't expect to hear from any of them again. They had no record of my address for one thing. Bandini Brothers wasn't the sort of place where you filled in the form.

As usual I had the house to myself. Dad would have been down the pub, where he always was now, and Joey could have been anywhere. I had no desire to see either of them, but I suddenly felt alone.

I hadn't really listened to my old records much in the last few years. Being at Julie's for much of the time meant that I mostly listened to her stuff, mainly Al Green and Marvin. No problem there, but it had been a while since I had played any of my old favourites.

I took the Freewheelin' Bob Dylan down from the shelf and played Don't Think Twice, and then I pulled out Paxton's Rambling Boy and played I Can't Help But Wonder Where I'm Bound. Then I put on my scratchy old single of Wichita Lineman. The next day I went out and got my visa application form.

Chapter Fifteen: Bird On The Wire

"I think we should say a prayer for this train."

She's sitting opposite me, wearing an ankle length dark brown dress you might have seen worn by a high street hippie chick in London three or four years ago. Lennon glasses, straight brown hair tied back. She's with another girl and a boy. They look about twenty one, maybe younger.

"Dear God, we pray for you to bestow your merciful blessings upon this train and all who ride on her on its long journey. Amen."

Then she smiles at me. A nice open smile, with no trace of embarrassment or doubt.

"Hello, I'm Lynnie. This is my best friend Ellen, and this is our friend Ray." Ray has the good grace to look slightly abashed, while Ellen barely acknowledges my presence. She can't take her eyes off Ray.

"Frank" I reply. The rule with Jesus freaks is either to ignore them, or pretend to be Icelandic or something, but her manner is so open and downright disarming that I find myself engaging in banter before I'm even aware of it.

"So are you just praying for the train to be blessed while you're on it? It's alright if it crashes on the way back?"

"Don't be mean to me because I love God," but she's still smiling, she gets the joke, and she's being kind. "When we get to Toronto safe and sound, as I know we surely will, I will thank God for delivering us, and ask Him to bless the train for all of its long journeys in the future. I know God will take care of it, because God will take care of all of us. All we have to do is be thankful to Him."

I think for a second. "What about any short journeys?"

"Don't be mean! I can tell you love God."

She's telling me this, and we haven't left Vancouver yet. I was here early, and one of the first on the train. Bright imitation leather seats in twos facing each other, aisle down the middle, standard layout. I had toyed with the idea of going first class, but after my forty eight hours of madness in San Francisco, I decided coach was the wiser option. A few people had grabbed seats already, but I found an empty four and grabbed a seat by the window, facing the engine. Let fate decide who is going to sit opposite me for the next three days. Looks like fate has decided it's time for the God Squad. Maybe I should have bought that first class ticket. Too late now, anyway there's no guarantee that I'd be immune up there either. All I really want to do is to look out the window for the next three days. Still, who's to say I can't.

"Ellie and I are from Baltimore, Maryland. We've been to California for the first time and we thought we would take the long way home. It's so exciting."

The train starts with an almost imperceptible jolt, and pulls out of the station at little more than a snail's pace. What was it Chairman Mao said, a journey of a thousand miles begins with a single step? This train has got three thousand ahead, or close to it. It gathers speed slowly as we leave the sparse suburbs, and I bid farewell to Vancouver before I really get a chance to say hello. Some other day, maybe. On the short walk from the bus to the train station I passed a bakery selling real bread, good old English bloomers, tins and farmhouses. I kept on walking, which I'm beginning to acknowledge may have been a mistake. Still, as mistakes go that must rate a one out of ten and most of my decisions lately end up as a full blown nine, if not more.

"Ellie met Ray in San Francisco. Ray's from Brockton, Massachusetts. They're so in love."

Lynnie is talking as if the lovers are elsewhere. Ray, who is sitting next to me, nods awkwardly. Ellie is sat next to Lynnie, and looks uncomfortable that she's not next to Ray. It was Lynnie who sat down first. Maybe she thought it would be too forward to sit next to me, either that or it's against her religion.

"Did you go to San Francisco, Frank? It's so beautiful."

"Yes" I reply, while continuing to gaze out the window. "I went to San Francisco."

I'm halfway across the Golden Gate Bridge and it's very different to how it was the last time. Today it's damp and murky, the fog swirling above and below, obscuring the slate grey water three hundred feet below. I'm looking out towards the city, sometimes managing to catch a rare glimpse here and there when the gale force wind blows a gap in the mist. It's cold out here, my new jacket offering little in the way of protection.

I hear footsteps, and turn to see a woman walking past looking at me intently, concerned even. I don't know why. It seems pointless to continue to the other side, so after five minutes or so I turn back. Through the fog I see someone coming towards me, a young man of about my age and my size. I flash the brief smile of recognition you give to someone who has lived through the same times as you have, whether it's on the other side of the world or not. I meet his eyes for a moment. There is no smile, only a scowl of accusation as if to ask, what are you so happy about? Then he is gone, continuing purposefully at the same pace towards the centre of the bridge, dissolving into the fog like some Dickensian signalman. I shrug and walk on, and it dawns on me why the woman was looking at me so oddly. She thought I was a jumper. Not me lady, but that poor soul is a jumper if ever I saw one. I turn and chase after him, calling out, "Hey! Are you alright?" my voice sounding lost and forlorn in the fog. I know he can hear me, but he neither slows down nor speeds up until I am almost at his heel, whereupon he turns and gives me the same dead stare.

"What are you, a freak or a fucking faggot? Get the fuck away from me!"

He turns back, and continues resolutely on his not so merry way.

"Sorry. I just wanted to see if you were alright."

My voice tails off lamely into the fog. If he can hear me he doesn't pay any attention. I head back towards the San Francisco side, briskly now, anxious to get off the bridge before it gets dark. I'm never going to know if the guy was a suicide or just a miserable cunt. What I do know is that I suddenly feel markedly better. Later I go to Sam Wo's, where the waiter insults me for being alone and messing up his table plan, which makes me feel better still.

I'll give you a little advice here, though you may have long decided that I'm hardly the sort of person to be giving advice to anyone. If you go to Canada and you want to see the Rockies by train, go from east to west. The train from Vancouver leaves in the late afternoon. It's past mid-September now, and the Sun goes down behind us just as the scenery starts to get interesting. The train ploughs its way implacably through the majestic peaks in pitch darkness, the window revealing nothing more than the reflection of myself and my travelling companions, all of whom manage to sleep through the whole night. It must be nearly dawn before I finally doze off. I awake an hour or so later to find the train standing in the station in Jasper, Alberta. We've gone clean through the mountains, clean through British Columbia. So much for the scenic route.

I'm beginning to think that my decision not to buy bread was a mistake that rated considerably higher than a one, when two affable Yorkshiremen come to the rescue. They travelled out a week ago, and befriended some of the galley crew in their bluff, no nonsense, northern manner. Now they're going back east to catch their plane home, and have had the good fortune to find the train staffed with the same crew. Our good fortune as well, as they share bacon and, wonder of wonders, real sausages with us. They also share fresh bread they bought in Vancouver, and they've even got real butter. I take back anything I might ever have said about our northern brothers.

Rain is hammering on the window, and the scenery is still pretty for the next hour. We've left the big mountains behind, and the glistening green slopes and swollen streams remind me a little of Scotland. Then the rain stops, the plain levels out, and we're on the prairies. This is it for the next twenty four hours, says a Canadian woman behind me. Canadians appear to be very much in the minority on this train, outnumbered by Americans, Europeans and even Chinese. I turn away from the window, secure in the knowledge that it won't be changing too much for a while, and try and start up a conversation with Ray. I was only half listening when Lynnie introduced her companions yesterday, but I'm reminded of something now.

"Brockton, Massachusetts. Rocky Marciano, right?"

Rocky Marciano. The Rock. Only heavyweight champion of the world ever to retire unbeaten. Forty nine fights, forty nine wins. Had a fighting weight of around thirteen stone, and regularly beat guys three or four stone heavier to a bruised and bloody pulp. I was never a great one for team sports. I guess I'm not what you call a team player.

Boxing was different, boxing always held a fascination for me. As a young boy I would plead to stay up late so that I could listen to the fights on the radio, my bloodthirsty young mind exaggerating every jab and counter punch into ferocious blows of bonecrushing intensity. For a while I even kept a scrapbook of fighters, cutting their pictures out of the newspaper the next day. I can recall most of the names still, some now dead, some still famous, some successful businessmen and some returned to the back street obscurity from which they came. Terry Spinks, Dave Charnley, Chic Calderwood, Wally Swift, Billy Walker. The great Terry Downes, who was the world middleweight champion, and came from just up the road from me in Paddington. When I started secondary school I pretended that he was my uncle, hoping that it might gain me some respect, and possibly even instil some fear into some of my harder peers. He wasn't of course, and it didn't.

Like their rock and roll stars, American fighters were distant, exotic, and generally better. Occasionally one of them with a name like Zora Folley, Willie Pastrano or Old Bones Brown, would come to England and arrogantly sweep aside the best that Britain had to offer. Uncle Terry bucked the trend when he beat Paul Pender of Boston to win the title in sixty one.

I think I was about nine when I saw a fight on television for the first time, round at Uncle George's house. Ingemar Johanneson from Sweden knocked down Floyd Patterson seven times in the third round to win the heavyweight championship. George was sadly long gone by the time I went to watch a fight live for the first time, when the greatest of them all, Muhammad Ali, defended his crown against Henry Cooper. We were at the back of the stand, but you could have been a mile away and still seen the claret gushing from Henry's brow as Ali stopped him in the sixth.

Looking back, I think what attracted me to the fight game and still does, was how alone a fighter is once he gets in the ring. He and he alone is responsible for his fate. When you're on top you're really on top. When you go down you go down alone, with no goalie or dropped catches in the field to cast blame upon. Being a skinny kid, I never for one moment considered taking up the sport myself, although there were plenty of boys boxing clubs around London in the sixties. Not me, boss. I'm a lover, not a fighter.

Rocky Marciano retired before I was six years old, but I read plenty about him later on. Born to Italian immigrants in the tough industrial town of Brockton, Mass, he was a seemingly indestructible product of the grim factories and harsh north eastern winters which turned out men as hard as nails. Ray seems about as hard as a soft boiled egg. It barely registers with him that I'm familiar with his hometown's favourite son, and he has to think for a minute.

"Rocky Marciano, yeah. He died."

Yes I knew that, Ray. It needed a plane crash to put the Rock down for the count, five years ago at the age of forty six. Ray has nothing more to say on the subject, and here's me thinking we were going to talk about fights all the way across Alberta.

I never catch the names of the two lads from Leeds, being English we never get around to it. I wouldn't be surprised if Americans announce their name, city and state to the supermarket cashier. I'm sure Lynnie knows, she's on first name terms with everyone in the carriage by now, but seems to have taken a particular shine to me. She's not bad really, some imagination with her hair and a little make up, and she would be more than not bad, but it's clearly the last thing I need. I can't help encouraging her though, with exaggerated tales of Catholic grannies and aunties. I don't know why I do this, I just do. Like some old fighter, once I get started I have to keep going until I hear the final bell. Lynnie says that she can tell that I have God in my heart. Luckily for me, the lads across the way are too busy discussing rugby league to notice.

In Edmonton the conductor announces that we have a forty five minute stop, so we leave the train and buy bread, ham and beer. I like the fact that everything is written in French as well as English, despite there probably not being a French speaking person within two thousand miles of this city. What I like even more is that there are French cigarettes on sale, Gauloises, Gitanes, tipped, untipped, in every possible variety. I joyfully buy five packs of Disque Bleu, and immediately light one up on the street and smoke it right down to the filter, while taking in as much as I am ever likely to see of Edmonton, Alberta. Back on the train, me and the boys start on the beers, and Lynnie surprises me by accepting one.

"Just because you love God doesn't mean you can't have any fun. God wants you to have fun just so long as you don't hurt anyone."

Oh, but wouldn't it be nice to live on planet Lynnie.

We're deep in the heart of the prairies now, and one of the Canadian women mildly rebukes another passenger for pulling down the blind halfway to block out the Sun.

"Don't you know the best thing about the prairies is the sky?"

She's right as well, the clouds joining and breaking constantly, and changing colour from red to gold to the purest white as they sail across the Sun. Now I know where Joni found her feathered canyons in the air. The land is unchanging all the way to the horizon, which could be any number of miles away. Every five minutes or so we pass an isolated farmhouse, each one with its individual dirt road to some distant highway. The woman continues with her lesson.

"These houses are pretty fancy now, they've all got electricity and central heating and everything, not like in the old days. That can still be just as dangerous. Every winter you can guarantee that someone will come out of their warm house, get into their warm car wearing just a shirt or a blouse, and break down and freeze to death out on the prairie somewhere. Happens at least once every year."

I'm thinking how that wouldn't exactly be the best way to go, but what I'm thinking more is what it would be like to live in one of those houses, to be a kid in the house running out to watch the big train go by twice a day. Growing up a thousand miles from the sea and dreaming of distant shores, how could you grow up to be anything other than a travelling man? I'm sure most of them won't. Most of them will marry someone from the next farm and stay right where they are.

Night falls, and we stop for thirty minutes in Saskatoon, Saskatchewan. We get down from the train and take in the night sky, cold and clear as mountain dew. There must be a million stars above, their brilliance diminished only slightly by the shining yellow moon. Ray and Ellie take a walk, while I smoke a cigarette and Lynnie talks. This is the first time she's ever been on a train. They like to travel on overnight buses. Sometimes they stay in a hotel, which they did in Vancouver. They're planning to stay a night in Toronto, and then catch a bus back across the border to Buffalo, New York, and then another home to Baltimore. Not that it's any of my business, but I'm immediately curious about the sleeping arrangements.

"So what gives with Ellie and Ray then? Does Ray get a single, or do you?"

"Oh we all stay in one room. We sleep with our clothes on, that's the rule."

She's smiling, but I can tell she's serious. Then, out of the blue yonder, with no warning.

255

"Why don't you come to Baltimore with us? You can stay at our house, and I can show you the city. It will be fun to see Toronto with you, as well."

Again, she's serious. I look at Lynnie, and I realise that for all her Father, Son and Holy Ghost, the girl is lonely. Lonely, and maybe even a little jealous of her friend who has copped off chastely with the gormless Ray. You can sprinkle your holy water round as much as you like, but it won't make you any less vulnerable to the seven deadly sins than anybody else. I learned that at an early age.

"I can't see any reason why not."

If you examine that statement I'm not actually saying yes, I will come to Baltimore with you Lynnie, although I'm clearly implying that I will. Nevertheless it is still a whopping lie even by my standards, because there are any number of reasons why not. A sweet girl will end up getting hurt one way or another, and right now, this is something I need like a fucking hole in the head.

So now she's smiling at me like a kid on her birthday.

"I can't wait to tell Ellie."

We get back on the train, and for the first time Lynnie takes the seat next to me, which I'm sure will make Ellie and Ray happy, if no one else.

"It's too bad we didn't meet in San Francisco, Frank. We could have ridden the cable car together."

"Mmm" I murmur, while keeping my eyes firmly in the direction of the endless black night.

Monday morning I made my way unsteadily downstairs to be confronted with the empty bottle of Chivas and the two empty bottles of wine, grateful to be reassured there was a reason why I felt like I did. I thought for a moment when I woke up that I might be ill or something. Lucille had thoughtfully left the fridge well stocked for me, so I got myself some breakfast, although my befuddled state turned the coffee machine into something of a challenge. I wrote Lucille a note suggesting that she kept some instant in the kitchen in future in case she had any more English visitors. A note which was also intended to let Zaria know that my sense of humour was still intact, even if it wasn't. I took a long hot shower, followed by a dip in the pool and then more juice and coffee. I then repeated the process until I felt something close to human, and went and sat out on the deck to consider my next move.

The sensible thing would have been to take Monday nice and easy, rest up and then move on the next day. No it wouldn't, because if I stayed another night I knew I would only end up doing what I did the previous night, and that's bad, under no circumstances did I want to repeat what I did Sunday night. No. I knew I had to be moving. I picked up the phone which was still on the coffee table, called the operator and asked for the number of the big hotel, the fancy one on Union Square. I rang the number and asked for reservations as if I was Lord Snooty. Single for two nights sir, certainly sir, we look forward to seeing you, Mr Downes.

I packed up my stuff, which took longer than usual as I had already all too foolishly claimed ownership of half a wardrobe. I wrote another note for Lucille, thanking her sincerely for her gracious hospitality, and then checked carefully that all the windows and the back door were locked. I said goodbye to Zaria's house out loud, and locked the front door before putting the keys through next door's letterbox. Without a backward glance, I walked down the hill into Santa Cruz and bought a ticket for the next bus to San Francisco. The bus was half empty, and I sat at the front this time and on the left hand side, in a vain attempt to avoid Zaria's shadow, but the journey still seemed as long and lonely as I expected it to.

I made straight for Union Square and strolled into the hotel reception in my travelling jeans, this time raising not so much as a murmur as I laid down the big bucks to pay for the two nights in advance. Thank you sir, we hope you have a pleasant stay Mr Downes. The porter carried my bag to the room, and I gave him a ten. Thank you sir, please let me know if there is anything I can do for you while you are staying with us. Sure I will. You could play football in the corridors, if the bathroom wasn't marble then it was a fair facsimile, and you could sleep a family of four in the bed, no problem. I didn't stay in the room any longer than I needed to. When I was here the week before the fog had always lifted around the middle of the day, but on Monday it was still hanging around in the afternoon. I went in to a men's outfitters and bought a brown suede jacket with leather buttons for two hundred dollars. I don't need a bag thanks, if you can just take the labels off I'll wear it right now. Yes sir, certainly sir. I put the jacket on and headed out towards the bridge.

Lynnie is saying her prayers in a whisper, not because she wants to keep her religion quiet all of a sudden, but because Ellie and Ray are already asleep, though the way they are wrapped around each other means that if one moves the other is bound to wake up. Lynnie ask God to bless Mom and Dad, and then reels off a whole list of people I've never heard of, which is not surprising considering I don't know anything about her really. I wonder how many of them are relations, and how many of them live in the same house in Baltimore. Then I hear her mention Ellie and Ray, then me, and then the train. Then she takes off her glasses, puts them in her bag, and rests her head on my shoulder. After a few minutes she puts both her arms around my left arm and holds my right hand, effectively immobilising me. I'm holding my breath waiting to see what her next move might be, when she falls fast asleep.

Tuesday morning I slept late and stayed in bed longer, making the most of my surroundings. I guess I was looking for a little comfort from life's luxuries in what I thought then was my darkest hour. I ordered scrambled eggs and smoked salmon from room service, and finally made it out of the room around lunchtime. I walked down to the Haight without knowing why, and instantly realised it was a mistake. The weather was grey and the houses were shabby. It reminded me of the back streets of Ladbroke Grove on a bad day. The hippie dream turned sour long ago, most of the idealists either working in advertising agencies or returned from where they came. Those that haven't have long since become cynical and callous, concerned about little else other than scoring or selling. People disappear from the Grove, it happens all the time. Here one day and gone the next. Nobody knows where, and nobody cares much either. I'm sure it happens all the time in fabled Haight Ashbury too. I hailed a passing cab back to Union Square, anxious to spend some more dough.

I had managed to keep most of my cash close to my skin since I had been in the consumer capital of the world, and now I was making up for it. I went into the same shop where I bought the jacket, and bought a pair of black trousers, well cut and slightly flared. I bought yet another shirt, this one flame red. I bought a supply of good quality underwear and socks, and then moved down the street to a shoe shop where I bought a pair of red loafers with tassels on them. Back at the big hotel, I took another shower and put all my funky socks and underwear in the trash can. I put my new clothes on, and spent the rest of the day in the bar, eating olives and peanuts and drinking dry martinis, tipping the bartenders a dollar a drink. In the evening I hit a club, and ordered Jack Daniel's on the rocks. I was looking the business, and a woman asked me to dance, but I brushed her aside less than politely. They were playing that Philly soul, and I should have been up for it seeing as how I had heard nothing like that since I left London, but I knew after five minutes that I didn't want to be there. I went back to the hotel bar and started on brandy Alexanders, the rock stars drink, thinking it might help me sleep. It did, but it needed around a dozen of them.

In the morning I packed my stuff, and put my new shirt and trousers along with the stupid disco shoes in the bag they came in. I settled my room service bill, said goodbye to the big hotel, and walked the short distance to the Tenderloin, near where I stayed with Zaria. I dipped down a side street, and left the bag with the new clothes under a lamp post. Someone would make good use of them soon enough. I kept the jacket. I knew it was likely to be cold where I was going. Then I went straight to the Greyhound station. I knew I needed to get out of the United States, for a while anyway, otherwise I was going to crack up. I wasn't ready to go home, I knew that, but I wanted somewhere that was like home but not. Somewhere like Canada. It had to be a little bit like home, we used to own it after all, and still do I suppose, in a Commonwealth type fashion. Like home, but with wide open spaces. Perfect. I checked the schedule, and found there was a bus for Vancouver in an hours time. Maybe things were looking up again.

Lynnie sleeps till daybreak and beyond in the same position. I manage little more than a doze. I find the closeness of her body strangely relaxing. When I finally get some sleep I dream of the shiny Oldsmobile driving away the house in Santa Cruz, only this time it's dark and cold, and I haven't got a key to the house. I stand and watch the car disappear into the night, and it's only then that I realise all of my stuff is in the boot. I wake to find a soft fully clothed body beside me, and for one moment I think of big Patti, who hasn't crossed my mind for days now. Lynnie opens her eyes, and I give her a safe little peck on the lips and say good morning.

"Well you sure are a fast worker! I think you're dangerous, buster!" Then she goes to brush her teeth and wash up as they call it, and when she returns she has a more serious expression on her face.

"I didn't mean it."

"You didn't mean what?"

"I didn't mean that you're dangerous. I think you're a gentleman."

"I know you didn't mean it" and I squeeze her hand. She didn't either, but she was right sure enough. "You're still coming with us aren't you? To Baltimore?" and I realise she's apologising, she's apologising for who she is, and there's not one single reason in the world why she should do.

"You bet I am."

I feign tiredness and consider what I'm getting myself into here. It's another thirty six hours to Toronto. Then we are going to have to sleep fully clothed in some cheap hotel room with Ellie and Ray, before catching a bus to Buffalo and then down to Maryland. The morning drifts slowly by, with markedly less conversation among our little group than yesterday. It seems as if everyone is suffering a little from train fatigue

Lynnie goes to the bathroom, and she's away for some while. It's nothing unusual, going to the bathroom on the train is an excuse to stretch your legs, explore, and in Lynnie's case spread the word. She's still not back in her seat as the train pulls into Winnipeg and the conductor announces a forty five minute stop.

"I'll go find her" says Ellie. "She's probably found someone to talk to at the other end of the train. You know Lynnie."

"I guess I'll come with you" says the hapless Ray.

As soon as they have left the carriage I know what I have to do, and I know I have to do it now. The Leeds boys are about to go on a food run, and ask if I'm going with them.

"Change of plan, lads. All the best, eh" quickly pulling my bag down from the rack. "All the best" I say again, before they can respond, and then I'm off the train and quickly off the platform, out of the station and on to the windy streets of Winnipeg, Manitoba. I take a room in the first hotel I see, just in case anyone feels inclined to send out a search party. It's the same type of wooden, turn of the century boomtown hotel as in Frisco, the cheap one, not the big one. Remarkably similar in every way in fact, except that where the other one felt slightly dangerous on account of its location, this hotel feels like the safest place in the world. Lonely and cold, but safe. I'm tempted for a moment to climb into the small single bed, but I know that I will appreciate it so much more if I leave it till tonight. Instead I step down the hall for a shower, which I badly need, put on some clean clothes, and once I know the train must be safely on its way east, set off to explore the sights of downtown Winnipeg. It doesn't take too long.

I step into a record shop on Logan Avenue, the window festooned with Bachman Turner Overdrive. It's an old fashioned kind of place that reminds me a little of the shop where Ma used to take me to buy singles when I was a kid. It has a bigger choice of records, but then it would be difficult for it not to. The records are filed by nationality first, and then into musical categories. There's a lot of Canadian cowboys I've never heard of, and the American section is small by comparison. I remember reading once that there used to be a restriction on how many American records could be played on Canadian radio, so that would make sense. Maybe there still is. The British section contains all the usual suspects, and also some surprises. Cliff and The Shadows would appear to be big in Manitoba, as would Petula Clark.

Smaller than the British, but considerably larger than the American, is the French language section. I rifle through the chanteuses, and pull out a sleeve bearing the enigmatic face of Francoise Hardy. Eyes almost shut, weighed down by thick black lashes. Her skin is flawless, her hair a rich chestnut brown. Classically formed lips, which walk the line between sensuous and demure, and a sad expression. You almost expect there to be a tear trickling down her face, but the girl was always too cool and too savvy to go along with anything that corny for the cover. Francoise Hardy, who was rumoured to have attracted the attentions of Mick Jagger as well as Bob Dylan when they played in Paris, and sent them both packing with a flea in their ear. Francoise Hardy, who shared my teenage bedroom wall with Catherine Deneuve. Francoise Hardy, who had one hit song in English, All Over The World. 'All over the world, lovers must meet and part. There's someone like me with a pen in their art.'

A record that I didn't dare listen to if I was alone on an English Sunday afternoon in the months when it got dark early, as I knew it would send me out to run the gauntlet of deserted streets and shuttered shop displays, its melancholy melody running round my head until I cooled down enough to return home. Francoise Hardy, who sometimes still appears in my dreams to walk with me by the banks of the Seine. There's a smaller picture of her on the back of the album, full length this time. She's wearing a short leather jacket and the tightest white jeans. Ooh la la. She is looking more cheerful, and she's clutching a guitar. She can play it too, and writes many of her own songs. I wish I could have found this album in Santa Cruz or San Francisco and presented it as a gift to Zaria. More than that I wish she was here now to listen to it with me.

I take the album sleeve to the counter, and ask the girl behind the counter if I can hear a track, any track. She shakes her head dismissively, and says no, we don't play that here. Whether she means in this shop or in the whole town is not clear. The French records are in the store because they have to be, there's more than likely a law says they do. They probably stay in the rack forever, or until there's no more room and then they're shipped back to Quebec where I'm sure they sell very well. I'm sure the great majority of them are terrible, but not my Francoise. I step back on to the avenue with another of her songs in my head.

'Mais moi-meme, je vais seule par les rues, l'ame en peine. Mais moi-meme, je vais seule, car personne ne m'aime.'

Eight o'clock, and again I feel like making an early night of it, but I don't want to be waking up in this city at some unearthly hour on a Sunday morning. I've had three nights in my clothes. It's a twenty four hour ride from Frisco to Vancouver, with little to look at on the way other than the interstate, and the industrial suburbs and bus stations of Eugene, Salem, Portland and Seattle. Immigration was a lot less friendly than I expected it to be.

"So what do you want to come to Canada for, anyway?"

That's what the man said, no kidding. Well it's a long story chief, so I make do with "Well I heard Vancouver was a beautiful place to visit" which seemed to be the right answer. Beautiful it may be, but I don't allow myself the opportunity to find out, following the signs to the railway station, and seeing enough to get the impression that it's a hybrid of small town England circa nineteen fifty five and Kansas City, not that I've ever been to Kansas City. Once again I struck lucky. The trains east don't go every day, but there was one leaving that afternoon. I got to keep moving, got to keep moving, blues falling down like hail. Two hours later I was watching British Columbia go by my window, and talking to Lynnie. Poor Lynnie. I step out into the cold autumn night in search of Canadian ale.

In Winnipeg on a Saturday night, and every other night I guess, it works like this. The pubs have two bars. There's the bar for couples, men and women type couples that is, and there's a bar for single men. Single women? Don't even think about it. Not that I want to meet any women, single or otherwise. At the moment a Trappist monastery would be more appealing. One of those in Belgium where they brew their own strong beer would be just the ticket. It's more that I don't exactly welcome with open arms the prospect of spending the evening amongst those whose failure to find a Saturday date couldn't be more spectacularly highlighted if they had it branded on their foreheads. The socially inept, the malodorous, the bearded and the lumberjack shirted. The fucking losers. Still, I really could do with a beer, it is now downright cold on the street, and I can't be arsed with walking all over this town in the hope of finding somewhere better, because I suspect somehow that my quest could well prove to be a futile one.

So not only does it work like that, it also works like this. There are no barstools. There are no barstools, because not only do the punters not sit and drink at the bar, they don't get served at the bar. Everybody sits down at a table and waits to be served by the single white coated waiter. Never has a job been more inaccurately titled. In this establishment everybody is waiting, except for the waiter. Fifteen minutes go by, and he still hasn't reached me. Twenty minutes and he's getting closer. I put my jacket on the chair next to me, light two cigarettes and put one in the ashtray, so I can order a drink for myself and one for my pal who has just gone to the bathroom. You see Zaria, you see what you've reduced Frank Downes to? A twenty four year old man with an imaginary friend.

I remember from the back of my mind somewhere, that Neil Young grew up in this town. He may even have been born here, I'm not sure. I imagine Neil one day when he was barely out of his teens, putting his guitar into a beat up old car and not stopping till he reached Topanga Canyon, searching for that heart of gold. I know for a fact that Leonard Cohen doesn't come from Winnipeg, he's from Montreal, which I picture as a very different sort of place altogether, although equally cruel in the winter. Maybe it is more similar than I had thought. If that's the case it does more than enough to explain why old Len is so fucking miserable.

Another five minutes before the waiter finally takes my order, and another ten before wonder of wonders, he returns with the drinks. By the time he makes his next circuit I'm ready for another beer and a large Canadian Club. I'm learning the game. Two hours later, and I've managed to achieve what seemed an impossible task when I walked in. I'm drunk.

I told Zaria about Teresa and the baby. I told her exactly one week ago today. We were on the beach. I was sober. We were talking, and I came right out and told her. Me, who has never come right out and told anybody anything, not like that anyway. I don't know whether I did it because I felt that I should, all part of becoming a better person and all that bullshit, or because subconsciously I felt that it was all too perfect and I needed to screw it up like I always do. Or maybe I did it for no reason other than that I'm a fool. That's it, fool, fool, fool. I didn't tell her about Gino, but I would have done given time. No, I told her about running out on a girl who is even younger than she is and who was carrying my child. Ever so slightly guaranteed to touch a nerve, we can safely say.

Maybe she would have called time anyway. Maybe. One thing's for certain. I broke the spell all right, broke it good and proper.

I walk out on to the street without looking back, and head straight towards the old hotel. I'm full of beer and whisky, and it doesn't even register with me whether it's cold out or not. No sense, no feeling. That's what me old Ma used to say.

I looked at that telephone long enough in the house in Santa Cruz, but when I did pick it up I didn't waste any time. It was three twelve precisely. Nearly quarter past eleven at home.

There's a long pause before it rings, and when it does the ring tone is familiar yet strangely foreign. Then a click, and a vaguely familiar voice answers.

"Hello?"

"Can I speak to Teresa please?"

"Teresa not here."

You're brave if you've gone to mass Terry. A lot of front in more ways than one. Then before I can ask when she might be back

"She gone to Italy. With my mother."

So now I ask. "So when will she back?"

"She no come back. They gone for good."

I can't say anything. There's a silence like thunder for five seconds and then the voice continues.

"My uncle died, my mother very upset, they go to Italy, start a new life."

I know who's speaking now. Lou, Gino's nephew. Teresa's brother. Why can't you speak English properly Lou, you little prick, you were born in fucking Clerkenwell for Christ's sake? He's not that stupid though, 'cos he's recognising me at the same time.

"I know who you are, you bastard. Don't you ever ring this number again, you hear. And if you ever show your face around here again, I fucking kill you, you understand?"

Then his voice cracks with sorrow and pure flaming hatred.

"She lost the baby, you bastard. She is seventeen years old, and she lost the baby. Get off the phone. I'll kill you, you bastard."

When I put the phone down I couldn't think of a single thing to do apart from reaching for the bottle, which I had long emptied. Not that it made any difference. If it had been a giant hogshead full to the brim, it still would never have been enough.

There's no bar in this hotel, and there's no television or radio in the room. It's not that late. Somewhere out west there's bound to be a ball game in progress. I've never watched a game all the way through, but I've seen bits and pieces since I've been stateside. What I would give now to fill this room with the commentator's voice, excitable but knowledgeable, and reassuring me that for the next few hours my worries are insignificant compared with the result of the game. For a team sport baseball is more individual than most. A player can be having a nightmare, and then turn everything upside down in the last minute with a home run. You can make everything right again in one hit. You can make everything all right until tomorrow, and then you get to go out and start all over again. I'm sure I could be a baseball fan given time, although I'd have a problem picking a team. You need to have a home before you can pick a team. Anyway, this is Canada. They do things differently here. They're more than likely showing last year's Coronation Street or its French equivalent. Not in this room though. No television, no radio, no Swedish backpackers getting down to it in the next room. Nothing.

So I'm in this hotel room in a country I hadn't planned on being in, and I'm wondering what I'm doing here. Lynnie will still be on the train, sad and bewildered about why I ran out on her with no reason, but putting a brave face on it, talking to somebody about the Lord. Zaria has had four days already of learning how to make movies. Perhaps she'll direct one someday and I'll recognise myself in it. Tonight she's probably down Stanley's with Michelle. Weekends only, that's what she said.

Teresa knows Italy, but it's not her home. She only speaks the language a little. She still speaks more than her idiot brother, all that Godfather stuff he puts out is strictly for show. Teresa went during the holidays when she was a kid. She told me she liked it there, but she was always glad to get back home. Home. So where's home now Terry?

A miscarriage. If that's the case, then maybe it was for the best. It's a hard world, and sometimes it deals out hard medicine. Or did you and your mother hope that God was looking the other way, and have the little life scraped out of you before you both prayed for forgiveness? So then did they bundle you up like damaged goods, with your broken

266

heart and your catholic guilt, and take you away to the old country where you hardly know the language?

I never cried when Uncle George died. I was too young then to comprehend how final the final act really is. I never even cried when I found out my own mother was gone. I didn't feel as though I had any right to, me with my Morocco tan, and her already in the ground. Now, in this sad room in a forsaken town on a windswept prairie, I start to cry. For George, for Ma, for Gino, for the father I never really had, for Teresa and my lost child, for Zaria and for Lynnie, and for every hung up person in the whole wide universe, but mostly for my own sorry and worthless self, I bury my head in my hands and cry, cry, cry.

And for good measure, even though it's my darkest hour, because I'm in fucking Canada I still find myself thinking about old misery guts Cohen.

"Like a baby stillborn, like a beast with its horn, I have torn everyone who reached out to me."

Chapter Sixteen: Follow That Dream

Oh let me tell you a story about a man named Jed
Who every night tossed off in bed
Then one night sleeping in the nude
Out of his dick came bubbling crude.

 My new pals Rick and Andy collapse in near hysterics as I reel off one of my old party pieces that had them in stitches back in year three. I was telling them about Jethro, Owen that is, and then we got to talking about old programmes, or shows as they call them and I dug that one out of the memory bank.

"I gotta say, Frank" says Rick, "I was really missing not having any dope with us, but I don't think we need it with you around. You're funny, man."

I'm half waiting for him to say I'm a great guy, but these fellows aren't from the South, they're from Detroit. The three of us are having a high old time without any herbal assistance apart from a few bottles of Labatt's beer, so much so that we can almost ignore the cold. Almost. We're one day past the equinox, and it would appear that's when winter kicks in around this corner of the planet. Andy has rigged up his little stove, and it's the nearest we've got to a camp fire. Yep, that's what we're doing. The last time I was around canvas I had a mishap on the way back in a Ford Cortina Mark 1, but there's no chance of that tonight as I'm sleeping right here, camping out for the first time in my twenty four years.

The blues came from the deep south. Everybody knows that, me especially. I know more about the blues than I have a right to. The blues came up the Mississippi and settled in Chicago, and to a slightly lesser extent in Detroit, where I would appear to be heading next. That's where the boogie man himself laid his hat, old John Lee Hooker. For me though, the blues carried on past there, and kept on going till they crossed the border to come knocking at my door on a miserable Saturday night in the far frozen north.

A good night's sleep cures many things, and my blues clearly weren't deep enough not to be among them. Seems I haven't got 'em like Robert Johnson or Blind Willie after all, so I woke up this morning and put on my highway shoes. I knew it was time to get back to basics. No trains, no buses. I had forgotten that it was other people's stories I had wanted to hear, and I had let my own sneak up on me when I wasn't looking, although I knew it always would. No trains, no buses, and no girls, please no girls, at least not for a while.

So I walked out of the sleepy Sunday morning town, silent apart from the distant peal of church bells, and set my bag firmly down by the side of the highway. The highway is the highway, Canada Highway One, one big road from Vancouver right across. A big road in length, but not necessarily in width. On this stretch it's still just a regular old two lane blacktop. I have learned by now that Sunday mornings aren't the best time to catch a ride. Cars full of kids, lots of people going short distances, church, family outings, that kind of stuff. It was more than three weeks since I last hitched a ride, and the last one I got was from Zaria and her mother. That was then. Today is a new day, the first day of the rest of my life, as that corny old poster is so keen to tell us.

You can see cars coming a long way off in this flat land. After about half an hour I made out the unmistakable shape of a VW beetle in the distance making steady progress towards me. Volkswagens are generally good for a ride, and despite myself I thought for a moment about Debbie the Georgia peach, one of those who got away. One of the lucky ones. This beetle wasn't orange it was blue, and sure enough it slowed right down to a stop as the passenger window wound down.

"Where you heading?"

Guys. Two of them. Friendly looking, both maybe three or four years younger than me. Exactly what I needed.

"East."

Obviously.

"Well you better get in. I'll get in the back."

So I climbed into the front seat of the beetle with the low autumn sun shining in my eyes, and once again all was well with the world. The boys are on their way back from a camping trip by Lake Winnipeg, and they've got the mosquito bites to prove it. These are city kids, Detroit City, to be precise. It seems like I'm destined not to meet too many Canadians. Rick and Andy have been friends since they were six, and share the easy camaraderie which comes with that, and into

269

which, bless them, I am immediately invited. They've both just left college with mixed grades, and in their words are goofing around for a while before they decide what to do. They live in Mount Clemens, a well to do suburb north of the city. Both of their fathers have good jobs, Andy's in insurance and Rich's in the motor trade. Neither of them appears to have any doubts that they will effortlessly assume their rightful place in the hierarchy, with the wife and two kids, and the bungalow and the Cadillac that come with it. They're planning on having some fun first, as if they're not expecting to have much after they cut their shiny long hair, as they surely will.

I learn all this before we're fifty miles out of Winnipeg. Neither of the guys has met anyone from England before, and they're interested, really interested, although they don't display quite the same naiveté as the Southern boys did. This is the first time either of them has really been out of the United States. Detroit is a border city, which I have to admit isn't something I was particularly aware of. Windsor, Ontario sits right across the Detroit river from downtown. Both of them have been there, but no further. They find Canada fascinating but strange, both of them baffled by the two dollar bills, and the licensing laws, which reveal themselves again when we find a pizza place in a one street town and stop for lunch.

It being a Sunday you can order beer if you're ordering food, which is not a problem because that is what we're doing, but they won't even bring it out until the food comes, in case you sneakily drink the beer and cancel the food order. I tell the boys how things are north of our border.

"In Scotland you can get a drink in a hotel bar on a Sunday, but only if you are what they call a bona fide traveller, which means you must live more than three miles away. Needless to say it doesn't do a great deal for the drink driving figures."

I'm sure that if they were on their own turf both of them would instantly reject that as palpable nonsense, but now they're in a strange land for the first time they are seeing how strange a strange land can be. To be honest I'm not exactly sure how accurate my story really is. It's something somebody once told me, and I think it may possibly have been the case then but since been repealed for the very reason I gave, but it sounds good in the telling, which is always the main thing. It does occur to me that the Scots have surely left their mark on this part of the new world with their Presbyterianism, Calvinism and every other kind of ism you can think of to stop people enjoying themselves.

Then there's the other side of the coin. If you're going to commit the sin of taking a drink, then it may as well be the biggest bender of all time. Every Saturday night. But then I'm Irish. Who am I to talk?

Rick has some Italian blood, and Andy is third generation Polish. His grandmother lives with them, and still doesn't speak English that well. Where I grew up in West London the Poles were the second largest immigrant group after the Irish. Any school you were in, any job you had, you would mix with Poles. Good, hardworking people who liked a drink was the general perception. Rick guffaws when I tell him this. It turns out they tell the same jokes about Poles that the English tell about the Irish.

When the pizza comes it is surprisingly good and very big. I tell the guys that if I ever visited this establishment again, which on the scale of probability registers a big fat zero, I would eat somewhere beforehand, come in, order beer and pizza and pay for both without eating the pizza. That would show them all right. This leads me on to an old joke.

"Did you hear about the Irishman who went into a restaurant, ordered a meal and sneaked out without eating it?" I'm allowed to tell jokes like that. This sets Rick off.

"Did you hear about the Polack who ordered a pizza, and the waitress asked him if he wanted it cut into eight slices or ten? The Polack thought for a second and said, oh you had better make it eight, I don't think I could eat ten."

I come back with another classic. "Did you hear about the Irish space programme?"

They both shake their heads, already laughing because they can sense this one's going to be good.

The Irish government called a press conference to announce their first space programme. "Where are you going?" they were asked.

"Well," said the spokesman, "we don't want to go the Moon as the Americans have already been there. No, we're going further than that. We're going to the Sun."

"The Sun!" came the incredulous answer. "You realise the Sun is nothing more than a giant ball of molten gas? Your astronauts will be burnt to a cinder before they get within a million miles of it."

"Sure and haven't we thought of that" said the spokesman. "We're going at night."

Much choking on beer and pizza, and it's sealed that now we're official all time best buddies.

"Where exactly east are you making for Frank, if you don't mind me asking?" says Andy.

"Well I've got to be in New York sometime." That's true enough.

"Come back to Detroit with us" Rick talking now. "Hang out with us for a few days. We'll get you high. Find you a girlfriend, even."

Sounds perfect, boys. Apart from the last bit, but I'm hardly likely to say that am I?

Monday morning me and Rick sleep late, Andy less so as he volunteered to give up his sleeping bag to his new buddy and sleep in the car. I slept as snug as a bug in a rug. We didn't make too many miles yesterday, what with lingering over lunch and then finding a campsite, which we did eventually near a place called Kenora, just across the line into Ontario. They gave us drinking water in containers when we booked into the site. All the tap water here comes out bright yellow on account of the minerals in the ground, or something like that. They tell us that it's quite safe, but the fact that it looks like cats piss puts most people off from drinking it.

Andy and Rick had planned on driving to Toronto and from there back to Detroit in time for the weekend, but selling me on the attractions of the Motor City seems to have made them both a little homesick. The new plan is to be home by Wednesday night. I am still invited. There are two ways of getting there from here. We can drive around the northern shore of Lake Superior to Sault Saint Marie and cross back into the States there, or make for International Falls, which is two hours drive away, and take the American shore of the lake. They decide to go Stateside. By the time they've made their decision and packed the stuff it's already midday, and we're well into the afternoon by the time we reach the border. The border guard is a lot more relaxed than his Mountie equivalent who saw me in. A desultory glance at Rick's driving licence, a cheery "welcome home guys," and we're home free. I make a mental note of International Falls, Minnesota as a suitable entry point should I ever need to get in or out in shadier circumstances. Rick and Andy are behaving as though they're home already, despite neither of them either having been in Minnesota before, and we are still close to a thousand miles from the Motor City. I realise I'm leaving Canada without having really been there. A train, a town, and a mind that was firmly elsewhere. I know I'll come back one day and explore the other big country, and maybe even meet some real Canadians. I might even get to see the Rockies by day.

We take a road of a million trees towards Duluth. We're no more than an hour into the States when I see a road going west signposted Hibbing. We're in Dylan country now. Born Robert Zimmerman in Duluth thirty three years ago and raised in Hibbing. If I had been at the start of my journey I'm sure I would have asked the boys to let me out right here so I could get another ride and walk the same streets the young genius did before he made his escape, but now I don't need to. I feel like I've walked with Dylan on every highway and small town main street in America. More signs tell me we're in the Mesabi Iron Range. It's still forest; the iron is under the ground. There's still plenty of iron ore mines around, though not as many as there were in the early part of the century. North Country Blues will tell you all about that. When Bob Dylan first breezed into Greenwich Village with a beat up guitar on his back, and an even more beat up hat on his curls, he came with a ready made history. Travelled with the circus, worked on the rodeo in Santa Fe and Sioux Falls, all of it impossibly romantic, and not a word of truth in any of it. What he was too young to realise was that if he had told them he was from the Iron Range it would have probably impressed them ten times more, back in those hootenanny days of old New York.

Andy and Rick are both Rod Stewart fans, so that makes three of us. Rick slips Every Picture Tells A Story into the deck. The title track is one of my all time favourites, a London jack the lad not a little unlike myself exploring the world in five riotous minutes, making an unexplained leap from Rome to the Peking Ferry for the last verse. I always couldn't help but think that the Hong Kong Ferry would have sounded more authentic, but never mind Rod, we knew what you meant. Rod also sings a Dylan song as good as anyone and better than most, and without even realising I'm doing so, I find myself singing along with Tomorrow Is A Long Time. The song is a sad one. The singer's love is far away. She may be back next week, next month, or not at all. She may be back tomorrow. What he's saying is that tomorrow is such a long time that it may as well be never. For me now though, singing along with the chorus, riding across this big empty state that I may never see again in the company of two men who feel like my best friends, and who I will probably never see again either once this week is past, tomorrow being a long time is something to rejoice in. My own true love isn't with me, whoever she may be, and on this particular Monday it suits me well enough. We're here now, in this moment, and tomorrow is another day somewhere in the far distance. When it comes it will resolve itself as it always does. If we're lucky it may be as wonderful as today is or even more so, but it really doesn't matter. We live today.

Duluth is old, its solid red brick buildings long since turned brown. Tall chimneys like solid stacks of soot are pumping out grime for all their worth, announcing proudly that is a real working town. In the city we find ourselves rolling down a one in five gradient, like San Francisco without the cable cars or the tourists. Rick and Andy are suspicious of old, so we decline the hotels downtown and drive north along the lake for a few miles. I was outvoted, but what else would I expect from children of the city which invented the built in disposable.

We check into a motel no different to any other motel, except it is because it's on Highway 61. I never crossed the old blues highway down south, but now I unexpectedly find that the lake shore road is the self same highway fifteen hundred miles from where it ends down in Louisiana. I make a mental note for a potential road trip some other time. This time I'll have to be satisfied with the short distance back into Duluth in search of a suitable bar. Someone's going to have to drink and drive, and it's not going to be me. If it had been up to me I would have walked up a suitable thirst, but that constitutes certifiable behaviour around these parts.

We choose a bar at random as they all look the same from outside. Pool tables, sports memorabilia on the walls, juke box. It's quiet, but it's still early evening, and a Monday at that. I'm thinking that this is the nearest I've been to a real working town, a Sheffield or a Nottingham. I've seen bohemian New York, tourists in New Orleans, the cocaine cowboys of Los Angeles, and San Francisco - well I don't want to think about Frisco right now. This seaport a thousand miles from the sea is no nonsense and down to earth, blue collar they call it here. I bet it's buzzing on pay day. The bartender speaks as if he's been reading my mind.

"I can tell you boys are from out of state."

No prizes for that one, friend. It's not the first time I've heard that one either, like out of state is as far away as it's possible to be, whether it's up the road in Canada, on the other side of the world in Europe, or across the bridge into Wisconsin. Out of state is out of state.

"It'll be quiet tonight. Gets busier at the weekends. Not as busy as it used to. There's tough times coming to this town. The steel plant closed down three years ago, and things have been going downhill since. Gonna get a lot worse, too."

I shrug noncommittally. "That's too bad."

I'm half inclined to get a conversation going and compare how things are with home and the three day week and all that, but I have no intention of bringing myself down by thinking about any of that stuff. Instead we take a booth in the corner and start on the beers. The boys are both thinking of home now, and Rick goes to the pay phone to call his girlfriend, which brings great derision from Andy, who split with his girl two months ago and hasn't found a replacement yet. I allow myself to think briefly of Pamela Jo, no doubt safely back in Minneapolis by now, a hundred and fifty miles down old Sixty One, but I quickly retrieve my thoughts on this boys night out. Our banter doesn't quite capture the magic of yesterday, but the beer goes down well enough until we leave at ten, stopping of for cheeseburgers to take back to the motel. Just your regular Duluth Monday night experience.

Tuesday morning we cross the bridge into Wisconsin and pick up US Highway Two, which will take us clean across into northern Michigan. A million trees and two hours later, and we're out of Wisconsin and into the boys' home state, and even more trees. They both whoop as we cross the state line, but we're still six hundred miles short of Detroit, and neither of them has ever been before to what they refer disparagingly as the northern peninsular.

We're so far from anywhere that the radio fades in and out like dear old Luxembourg, and Rick is just about to give up on it, when a half familiar song comes on and I ask him to leave it. It's the song I heard half of once before I left home, and which has been running around in the back of my mind ever since. This time I hear it from the start, and the atmospherics rally enough to allow me to hear all the words. It's a telephone song, a tried and tested genre which has produced classic songs like Memphis Tennessee and He'll Have to Go. Chantilly Lace, even. This one is altogether broader with its brushstrokes. The singer is ringing his ex-wife. He left her eight years ago. He's calling from some place out in the middle of nowhere, some place very much like here. He is clearly drunk to call out of the blue like that, but then I would know all about that.

Three rules of drinking, in ascending order of potential damage.

275

Do not drink and shop.
Do not drink and phone.
Do not drink and drive.

Two of those aren't against the law, but they should be.

Our singer is a DJ. He's currently presenting the bright good morning show for station W.O.L.D., but he's seen them all from drive time slots to the graveyard shift. Everything was sweet at first, as it was with the marriage, but he started drinking and drifting, and got fired when his drinking made his voice sound old. He found himself down in Tulsa, Oklahoma where he got himself a late night talk show for a while, and then moved back up north to Boise, Idaho. That's the way this business goes, he sings wearily, and I'm reminded of Buddy and Molly down in Lafayette, and what Buddy told me. There's enough radio stations in Louisiana and Texas that someone will always be hiring. Maybe there are Buddy, but after a while they'll all blur into one, and you'll lose your soul. Our singer's already past that stage.

He tells his ex that maybe he could settle down if only she would take him back again. It's never going to happen, and he knows she is going to tell him she has someone else, which she does. It's been eight years, what does he expect? The only reason he's telling her at all is to hear the sound of his own sadness. Then the killer lines, which have stayed with me all around these United States.

"Sometimes I have this crazy dream when I just take off in my car, but you can travel on ten thousand miles and stay right where you are."

Or you can take off in someone else's car, or lots of cars. It's the same difference. The singer's name is Harry Chapin. I'll be sure to look out for some more of his work.

We're in iron country again, Iron River, Iron Mountain. We pass through little towns whose names come from Native America and Old England. Waucedah, Spalding, Escanaba and Gladstone, and we take in the small town of Norway for good measure. We sight water again, and it's Lake Michigan, wider and saltier than most seas. More trees and we're in the Hiawatha National Forest, which gets us talking about westerns for a couple of hours, and then we're on the toll bridge back to what they call mainland Michigan or civilisation.

It's seven pm and the boys are still almost three hundred miles from home. They toy with the idea of driving straight through, but come to the sensible conclusion that seven hundred miles in a day would be pushing it for both car and drivers, so we check into a motel in Mackinaw City, which doesn't look much like a city to me, but must be one because it has a sign to say so. We spend Tuesday night in Mackinaw, which is like Monday night in Duluth only less so, and I realise I'm getting ever so slightly bored with my very best buddies of two nights ago.

"Let us be lovers, we'll marry our fortunes together. I've got some real estate here in my bag."

Not one of the best chat up lines I've ever heard, but the opening to one of the best songs. I first heard it back in sixty eight when I had just returned from my first European sojourn. I was instantly transported, my breakfast getting cold in front of me. I knew it was just a matter of time before I went even further afield.

Paul and Kathy, the Greyhound bus overnighters, are still in their teens. They meet in Pittsburgh bus station. Paul hasn't had too much luck hitch-hiking. It has taken him four days to get there from Saginaw. They each buy a one way ticket to New York City. Paul charms his new friend with his playfulness and his way with words, for the character is indeed the articulate songwriter we know well. During the wee small hours he has a crisis in confidence. "Kathy, I'm lost" he says, though he knows she is sleeping. When they reach the Port Authority Bus Station, most likely they will never see each other again. Kathy will have friends to stay with in one of the boroughs, Queens perhaps. It is a brilliantly evocative moment, but still we know Paul will be fine. His youth, talent, and the sheer excitement of counting the cars on the New Jersey Turnpike will overcome all fears, for a while at least.

The cars he was counting were all come to look for their own America, whether it was the America of Chuck Berry braggarts with a short wave radio and a phone, or Harry Chapin's lonely alcoholic DJ realising that the sheer size of the country has fooled him into thinking life was something it isn't. I'm looking for an America which isn't even mine, except that it is, because the music reached across the mighty ocean and made it so. As the little car crosses the Saginaw river and I look to the right at the city, no different to any other small to medium sized city - I wouldn't expect there to be anything special about Saginaw, that's why he left - I know that I've found it, and I've found it a thousand times more than I ever thought I could.

"You're quiet, Frank" says Rick. "You tired?"

We've been making good time at the regular fifty five since we left Mackinaw three and a half hours ago. Two hours more, Rick reckons.

"No" I reply. "Just thinking about some old song."

I could try and explain, but I'm reluctant to. It's a lot more personal than talking about the Beverley Hillbillies or Rawhide. Rick puts on a tape by a Detroit singer called Bob Seger, and he keeps us good company as we head towards the town of Flint and the heart of industrial Michigan, the only part I knew there was until yesterday. Soon we're picking up Detroit stations, and it's all hard rock, heavy and in your face like I imagine the city itself to be. Rick and Andy are excited now, talking about people and places they know like they've been away for a year or more. I'm a little apprehensive. Hang out for a few days they said. Well it would be rude not to. A couple of days and no more, mind. My flight leaves on October 7th. That's twelve days away. It wouldn't break me to buy another ticket, but then I'd have some explaining to do. I'd be an illegal. Two weeks ago I was all ready to go and live in LA where half of the population appear to be exactly that.

When I woke up Sunday morning I felt that my load had been lightened by a deal I had made with some undefined entity. My side of the deal was to go home. At this point I'm fairly sure that's what I'm going to do, though things can change in a minute for a travelling man. There's no doubt I've got my taste back for the road, not that I ever lost it. What I would really like is for Rick and Andy to change the plan and just keep going. A week would be enough. Come on boys, take me down to some of those states I haven't seen yet. Ohio is maybe an hours drive south of Detroit. It's a short hop west from there to Indiana, then due south to Kentucky, the old bluegrass state. Cross the big river and we'd be in Missouri where Huck and Tom used to play and where I would pretend to be, back in my own sunny riverside boyhood days.

That's one reality that is not about to materialise, for we're turning off the interstate and making our way through comfortable green suburbs, and then we're at Andy's house. The bags are quickly out of the back and then Rick bids us a quick "later guys", and scoots off in the beetle at an almost unseemly haste.

"Rick only uses the VW for road trips" smiles Andy. "It's kind of unpatriotic to drive it around here. He got that when he was in high school, learned how to take it apart and put it together again. He drives a Pontiac when he's home. You'll see it soon enough."

"What about you?" I ask.

"Ford Pinto" smiling more broadly. "Rick's dad is an exec. We're on the wrong side of the tracks."

Well you better not come to my house Andy, I'm thinking. His house looks like one you would find down some leafy lane in Wimbledon or somewhere.

"Come and meet my Grandma."

We walk up the driveway past the neatly kept lawn, and Andy unlocks the door while pressing the bell at the same time so as not to alarm her.

"I'm home, Grandma."

A silver haired lady about five feet high emerges from the kitchen, and Andy gives her an unabashed hug. If I had ever greeted Granny Downes like that she would have more than likely thought I was trying to tap her for a few bob and told me to clear off.

"It is so good to see you Andrew. You must be hungry."

The voice is warm, with a noticeable accent. She turns to smile at me, and is a little confused for a moment.

"But this isn't Rick."

"This is Frank. He's a good friend of ours from England. He's going to stay with us for a few days, if that's alright."

Said as if there could be no possibility that it wouldn't be alright.

"You are English, I am Polish, we are friends. You must be hungry. You stay as long as you like."

Colonel Sanders is black. Not where I come from he isn't, you understand, but we're on Gratiot Avenue, and the Colonel is most definitely of a dusky hue. Still got a white beard though, smiling down on the ghetto like Uncle Remus. I guess he must also be black in Harlem and Watts and the south side of Chicago, and all those other south sides I haven't seen. It's as if America is one big rock and roll record and I haven't got round to the soulful b-side yet. Me and Andy are cruising the inner city in the Pinto, and I'm feeling distinctly uneasy, not because I think anything bad is going to happen to us, but because I feel like some kind of voyeur. Still, it's not as if we don't have a reason to be here. Andy is looking to score. I can't help thinking for a moment of Lou Reed's hapless rube waiting for the man on the corner of Lexington and 125. Hey white boy, what you doing uptown indeed.

He's not looking for anything heavy duty. Some pot, maybe some uppers. Nothing that I'm sure you couldn't find without too much difficulty in the shiny shopping malls of Mount Clemens. I think Andy just wants to give me the full on Inner City experience, that and show off his street smarts. That's the bit I'm not too sure about. He stops the car, and before he can unclip the seat belt, a dude wearing a white vest with a gold chain around his neck, slowly glides towards the car with what you might call a lithe, panther like grace. He's read the script of how a ghetto drug dealer walks, and he'll be damned if he's going to try it any other way. Andy winds down the window. The dude casually leans down to give us an appraisal. He looks friendly but suspicious. I am aware that either or both of these poses may be a put on, and I can tell Andy is aware of it too.

"Hey, what's happening? Are you guys cops? You sure look like cops."

"We're not cops, man."

Andy smiles at him in come on now fashion. Then the dude fixes his gaze directly on me.

"Where you from, man?"

"London."

"London, Ontario? What, are you one of the Mounties, come to get his man?"

I think he's joking but I'm not completely sure.

280

"I'm from London, England."

He looks serious for a second.

"Hey, England like The Beatles? This is Motown, man. The Beatles stole our music."

I could tell him that the Beatles and the Stones promoted the music of this city around the world more than anyone and helped Smokey make his fortune, but now is most definitely not the time for that conversation. Instead I start snapping my fingers to a relaxed rhythm, and start singing.

"I don't like you, but I love you, seems like I'm always thinking of you"

His face breaks into a broad grin.

"I was just messing with you guys, I knew you weren't cops. Cops wouldn't be driving round in this piece of shit. What can I do for you gentlemen?"

Andy gets bold now.

"What have you got?"

The dude instantly gets businesslike.

"Hey man, why don't you get out of the car for a minute so we can take a little walk to the corner? It don't look good standing here like this."

Andy complies instantly. I start to get out of the passenger's side, but the dude doesn't like it.

"No, just one of you, man. You stay in the car, Ringo."

Now I do feel exposed, and Andy is clearly even more so. I've seen dope deals go down before, but I'll be glad when we're out of here. I'm looking around, and I don't see anyone dancing in the street. A couple of very long minutes later and he's back, deftly pushing a small package into the glove compartment with one hand while turning the ignition with the other.

"I think I got some good stuff" says Andy, and with that we're away. Twenty five minutes later we're home free, and back in the world of white fences and white Colonel Sanders.

Whether I was hungry or not, and I was, as we had been driving all day, Andy's grandma was going to feed me. Thick vegetable soup with crusty bread, potato cakes, pork and dumplings, followed by Andy's favourite, apple dumplings. I know for sure I've lost a few pounds since I left home, but last night it felt as though I had put them all back in one sitting. Then she persuaded me to let her do my laundry. Usually I'm private about stuff like that, but Granny Kazmierczak has a way about her that made me feel it would be rude not to, like I would be depriving her of something. The offer came at the right time. My southern practice of washing stuff out in hot water, leaving it on the shower rail overnight, rinsing it out in cold water the next morning, and then putting it straight on and allowing it to dry on my body wasn't to be advised up in Canada. In Texas it took fifteen minutes. My new underwear from Frisco was now well christened, so I gratefully accepted her kindness in the spirit with which it was given.

It was apparent that Andy doted on his Grandma and with good reason, but we were at the house a couple of hours before his dad got a mention. He was in Indiana selling insurance and would be back Friday, said Grandma. I sensed a feeling of disappointment about the man from both parties. Well at least he was working.

Andy got some beers from the fridge, but it wasn't long before both of us realised we were ready for an early night.

"Tomorrow I'll take you into Detroit and show you around the city" he yawned.

Well he was true to his word there, and no mistake.

Friday morning I'm idly flicking through the local newspaper, on account of there being nothing else to do and Andy having given me no indication of today's plan of action, when a picture of Elvis Presley catches my eye and leads me to the not particularly big caption above it.

"The King comes to Detroit."

The picture is at least ten years old, and the slight story beneath it is just as lazy.

"Elvis Presley, the self-styled king of rock and roll, visits Detroit this weekend. Presley, now thirty nine, appears in concert at the Olympia

Stadium this Sunday, September 29th. As we went to press tickets were still available at the box office."

"Hey Andy." I'm awake now, my idleness gone in a flash.

"Yeah?" Andy's most assuredly hasn't.

"Where's the Olympia Stadium?"

"That's the hockey stadium downtown. Why, do you want to catch a game?"

"No. Elvis is playing. I'm thinking maybe we can get tickets."

Andy slowly looks up from his stock car racing magazine.

"Elvis Presley?"

No Andy, Elvis Murphy. Elvis Cohen. Elvis Muhammad. Jesus, Andy.

"Yes! Elvis Presley!"

Andy picks up on the excitement in my voice. I'm making no effort to conceal it.

"You want to go and see Elvis Presley?"

He sounds puzzled. Incredulous, even. Like I was suggesting we go and see Pat Boone.

"Why?"

Why!

"Because all that stuff you listen to and you think it's so cool, none of it would exist if it wasn't for Elvis Presley. You'd be listening to Bing Crosby and Perry Como."

I know enough about the history of music to know this isn't completely true, but there's more than a grain of truth there, and it gets my point across. Andy doesn't get it, as I knew he wouldn't.

"Well I can take you down there if you want to get a ticket. We can go now if you want. But if you really want to go I think you'll have to go on your own. I don't know anybody who would want to see Elvis Presley. Maybe Grandma will go with you."

"Ready when you are" I say, not rising to the bait.

Back in the Pinto, and we're off into Detroit again. For a while I'm thinking that the hockey stadium must be somewhere near the scene of yesterday's adventure, which can't really be Elvis territory, but we turn off Gratiot before it hits the inner city, and then we're on the Detroit freeway system, and within minutes we're miles away and swooping down to the hockey stadium.

"Here we are" says Andy. "This is an old stadium. They're talking about pulling it down, which would be too bad. I saw Yes here last year, they were great."

283

I don't know what's worse, the prospect of this impressive looking big brick building being bulldozed, or the fact that Andy would pay to go and see the worst kind of English prog rock group, but scorns Elvis. I quickly conclude that they are both equally barbaric. To the ticket window, and amazingly they have tickets. The best tickets are gone, what they call the floor seats, but I get myself one up on the side, about halfway back from the stage, for ten dollars.

Ten dollars to follow that dream as far as that dream will lead me. Elvis in concert is all it says, no surname necessary. I'm surprised to find that it's an afternoon show. I'm not a fan of matinees, but there is no evening performance, so there'll be no reason for him to hold back. As we head back to the suburbs I keep fingering the ticket as if it may magically disappear. No one I know has ever seen Elvis play. He's never played outside the States because the Colonel won't let him. As far as I know he's never even left the States except for when he was in the army. His plane touched down in Scotland and he may or may not have walked around the tarmac for a bit. When I go home and announce that I've seen Elvis it's going to give me definitive been there, done that, seen everything status. So feel free to mock as much as you like, Andy.

"Are you happy now?" He asks.

"Andy" I reply truthfully, "I was happy before, but I'm even happier now."

Friday evening Rick comes round. Conveniently Andy's grandma goes to bingo. I didn't even know they had bingo in America, but they do, and Granny Kazmierczak goes every Friday the same as Granny Downes. The only difference between the two is that one of them drives there in her own Cadillac. Andy's Dad called to say he wouldn't be home until tomorrow.

Andy laughed. "He's got a girlfriend in Ypsilanti" he explained. He looked a little sad. "Him and my mom split up last year. She's in Grand Rapids."

"That's too bad."

A much used phrase this side of the pond. I quickly learned that it's a suitable riposte whether someone's family has been wiped out by an earthquake or if they're just out of cigarettes.

"That's where President Ford comes from."

"Double too bad."

284

Apart from filling each other in on our ethnic backgrounds we hadn't discussed families. I liked Andy well enough, Rick also, they were both generous and straightforward guys, but I had quickly come to realise that the almost manic camaraderie we had shared that night in Canada could only exist in its own moment. I know now that my road buddies were just that. I'll always remember the four days we spent travelling. I won't remember hanging around the bourgeois suburbs. Andy doesn't ask me about my parents and I don't tell him. So Rick shows up about eight, and we've got the house to ourselves. Rick's got some news.

"I split up with Diane."

"Again?" says Andy.

"She got mad because I didn't call her as soon as I got home."

"It's not the first time. She'll be back."

"I guess so."

It doesn't appear to be the end of Rick's world.

"We're having a cookout tomorrow night at our house. You guys coming? You've got to come, Frank. I've told everyone about you."

"You're having a what?"

It turns out that a cookout is a barbecue. They have the word barbecue, but they use it differently to us. Barbecue is the actual food you eat at the cookout, not the event itself. This keeps us going for twenty minutes, about ten times longer than was allocated to Rick's girl trouble.

"Hey guess what?" Andy's already laughing. "Frank got himself a concert ticket for Sunday."

"Oh yeah? Who's playing? Why didn't you tell me?"

"Elvis Presley. He's going to see Elvis Presley."

Rick stares in disbelief. "Jesus Christ! Is Elvis Presley big in England?"

"Bigger than you could possibly imagine Rick" I tell him, and he shakes his head in wonder. Then we get down to the main business of the evening.

"OK. So what have you got?"

"I got some hash oil."

I had been wondering when we might see the results of yesterday's transaction, as it hadn't been mentioned since. Andy goes to his bedroom to get the dope, and when he returns Rick pulls out some greenbacks. I think back to Andy's remark about him being on the wrong side of the tracks, and get a flash on how Rick really is higher up the chain than he is. Rick will happily pay for the gear, but he wouldn't risk going down to the ghetto to score.

Andy prepares the dope. It's a new one for me. Not much to it. Pour the liquid hash into some silver paper, light a flame underneath, and inhale the smoke through a straw.

"I'm glad you've got the straws Andy" I say. "I was worried you might have to drive down to Gratiot and buy some more."

Not that funny, but they think it's hilarious. They're already in the mood. I'm curious. I don't pretend to have done this before, so I watch what they do and then take a hit myself. Looks like the dude sold us some good gear. I get an almost immediate rush without the dry mouth and throat I usually get from inhaling a joint. Andy puts on Dark Side of the Moon, which wouldn't have been my choice, but I'm not about to do anything other than surrender myself to it now. The boys are already stoned, laughing about anything and nothing, and I must look the same, as Rick says "Hey look at your eyes man. You're high."

I don't need a mirror to know that.

"Elvis Presley!" Shouts Andy, and they both collapse in near hysterics. I'm laughing too.

They're laughing at Elvis, and they're laughing at me in a friendly fashion, but I'm laughing because we're back living in the moment the same as we were up in Canada. We smoke the silver paper dry, and have a beer and a cigarette, which tastes better than any cigarette I ever smoked, even the post coital ones. Grandma comes home happy because she's won sixty five dollars, which sets us off again, so she bids us a fond if slightly puzzled good night and leaves us to it. Andy cuts off some more silver paper and cooks some more oil, and starry eyed and laughing we stay up till dawn.

I wake up Saturday lunchtime and make for the kitchen, where I find a man I don't know eating lunch. Hello, Andy's dad. Bald, and wearing cardigan and slippers, he could be anybody's dad. He looks to me to be one of those men in their late forties or early fifties who has worked too hard for too long a time. Once the necessary formalities have been exchanged he tries to sell me some insurance. For a while he has the upper hand, as I have a serious case of the munchies, and he has control of the frying pan. I don't know where Andy is, or Granny. Once I've got some eggs, sausages and coffee inside me, and my wits more about me, I return his serve.

"Well that's a real coincidence Mr Kazmierczak, you being in that line of business, as my dad is too."

Warming to the task, I tell him how the old man has worked for the Prudential for twenty five years and how rewarding he finds it, making a living while helping people to provide for the future, and I realise as I'm talking that he wasn't really expecting to sell me anything. He just has a need to convince this total stranger, and more than likely himself at the same time, that his life has some validity. I'm rescued by Andy, who has been to the grocery store with his gran.

"Me and Frank are getting on like a house on fire. I think you could do with some more friends like him."

Andy gives me a questioning look.

"He hasn't been trying to sell you insurance has he? Have you Dad?"

"No. I'm well covered for that. We were just having a chat."

Andy shrugs, and well he might. A chap who doesn't know what he's doing beyond next week is not a good customer for insurance. Still, me and the old fella are buddies sure enough, and I join him in the living room to watch sport on television. It's either that or go to Andy's room and listen to music, and I've already heard quite enough of the kid's record collection, thank you. Emerson Lake and Palmer, Jethro Tull, Wishbone Ash even. If our friendly drug dealer hadn't mentioned it I could easily forget I'm in the Motor City, the home of the hits. You sure don't hear it round these parts, not on the radio or anywhere else. I think for a moment of so many million bright, well dressed, English working class kids with good haircuts who brought themselves up digging the ultra sharpness of Tamla Motown. For that one split second I feel almost homesick. Then I remember that Detroit isn't really Motown any more. They moved out to LA. Marvin and Stevie are still great and getting greater, but they could work out of any studio they pleased now. Don't forget the Motor City. How could we?

Mr Kaz, as he likes to be known, fetches me a beer, and to my surprise informs me that he will be joining us at the cookout. Turns out it's going to be much more of a family affair than I had thought. By the time we are ready to leave me and Mr Kaz have shared more than a few cans of some nameless fizzy brew, and are almost family. Andy is amused, but also slightly irritated in equal measure.

Rick's house is altogether grander than the Kaz's, complete with large garden, deck, and pool, although there is no suggestion of anyone going in. Detroit is still hot by day, but the nights are chilly.

"This will be our last cookout of the year" Rick's dad tells me. The man seems perfectly pleasant, but that's about all he says to me all night on account of there being business contacts there who he needs to look after. On a Saturday night. In his own house. I'm thinking I would rather live in Stanley's world, distant as it seems now, than live my life like that. The boys got me high like they said they would, but the promise of a girlfriend would appear to be hot air as they don't seem to be having any success providing for themselves, never mind me. Rick's girl is here, blonde and vacuous, but she's making a point of not speaking to him. Andy, who is still without, seems happy catching up with his college buddies. So me and Mr Kaz drink more beer and eat steak sandwiches, and I smoke Marlboros because I don't feel like drawing attention on myself. Mr Kaz tells me he has to go to Pittsburgh on Tuesday if I want a ride. I know there has to be an overnight Greyhound from Pittsburgh to New York, so I accept gratefully.

The party, such as it is, winds up at midnight so as not to disturb the neighbours. Not the most exciting social gathering I've ever been to, but I enjoyed it far more than the posing, preening, peacock parade I ran out of in the Hollywood Hills. Maybe I'm getting old and naturally gravitate more towards the cardigan brigade these days.

"Don't you feel kinda weird going to a concert by yourself?" asks Andy as we approach the Stadium. I'm two hours early. I didn't want to take up too much of Andy's time by getting caught in traffic, and I also want to take in the atmosphere. Well to be honest Andy, no I don't, I never did. Anyway I'm not going by myself; I've got a special friend with me.

"Thanks pal, I appreciate it" I tell him.

I don't answer his question, because he will know the answer if he thinks about it for more than one second. If I can stand out by the highway in Manitoba on my own and not feel weird, I can sure go to a concert. I tell him I'll see him later.

"Enjoy it, man" says Andy, not getting it like he never will get it. So come on Ma, it's down to you and me now. This is our day.

Look at these people here early, Ma. Some of them are your age. Some of them are older. Some of them would have bought those old records at the same time you did, but none of them bought them at the same shop we did, did they Ma? None of them sang let me be your teddy bear to our Joey when he was a baby either. So even though we're way ahead of time, let's check out the arena and find our seats.

Well this isn't bad, is it? It's a big place, I'd guess maybe one and a half times bigger than Wembley Pool. We're halfway back up on the side, but we've got a clear view down to the stage. We're just a little bit too far back for you to be throwing your knickers at yer man, but then you would never be one for doing that anyway, would you Ma? There's plenty of room between the seats, so you can stand right here in front of me Ma, no one is going to bother you. This one has been a long time coming.

Thirty minutes to show time, and it looks as though the King can't do any better than half fill this old sports stadium, but no, twenty minutes to go, fifteen minutes to go and the place is packed. From what I can see and hear some of these fans are tour veterans, because Elvis has been on the road for five years solid now, and some of them are first timers like you and me, Ma. You know what I'm thinking, maybe this is what made me get off that train in Canada, some primal instinct calling me on. But I can't be thinking too much about that now, that dark night of the soul was more than a week ago now, and we've come a long way since then, and even though there must be at least fifteen thousand people in, we're not going to have to wait much longer before it's going to be just you me and Elvis, Ma, and it doesn't get any better than that. What do you think he's going to be wearing, Ma? Remember the great comeback, the TV special of 1968, and how great he looked in his black leathers, especially in the section when he was sitting down playing the guitar.

Look, the lights are going down and there's an MC walking onto the stage, and I was forgetting that Elvis isn't going to be playing a three hour show, he isn't exactly the Grateful Dead, and let's all be grateful for that, ha ha, so we're going to have a support act. And guess what, the support act isn't a band, because after all, what band could possibly support Elvis, but it's a comedian. I don't really need the comedian Ma, and I know you don't either, and neither does anyone else. If the idea is to put everyone in a good mood before the show starts, well you don't need to be the Brain of Britain or anywhere else to know that we all are anyway, which is why he gets a polite ripple of applause at the end and then the lights go back on.

It's three thirty and we've been waiting for three hours now, but finally the lights are going down again and the theme to 2001 is playing, just to give it some drama, as if we needed any. Now the stage lights go on and we see the musicians, all dressed in white like some unholy band of angels. Now the drummer is giving it some welly, and the spotlight is fixed stage left, and now, look, yes it's him Ma, it couldn't be anyone else, and women are on their feet, and you can shout and scream as much as you like Ma, this is your day. He's at the mike now, and the band go into a shuffle beat, and he's singing, see, see see rider, won't you see what you done done, and if he walked off stage right now we could at least say we were here.

Listen Ma, you can run down the front for a while if you like, because you're the only person here who is allowed to do that, just so long as you make sure you come back. You go on and live the dream for the moment while I check the reality. He's not wearing the black leathers. I can see that he wouldn't have been able to for quite some time. He's wearing this loose fitting, white judo outfit decorated with gold Chinese figures, and OK it does look a little like something a black belt fifth dan might wear, but it also looks like something you might wear around the house before breakfast Ma, especially if it was after Christmas and you were trying to conceal a few pounds. Nothing can disguise the fact that the King is now well and truly king size. Now he's singing I got a woman way across town she's good to me, one of the very first songs he cut when he signed for RCA, and I remember how Elvis played acoustic rhythm on that track, and how the record just attacked right from the start. There's little or no attack here, and he doesn't sing all the song, going into the old Amen song that Otis used to do. There's not one, but two groups of backing singers onstage, white male for the Jordanaires type stuff, and black female to sing the gospel, and it's the girls who let loose on this one.

If you're down at the front I hope you can control yourself Ma, cos' now he's singing treat me like a fool, treat me mean and cruel but love me, and there's a woman in the row in front who I think is going to melt, although Elvis might beat her to it 'cos he's sweating up a storm already. Then he goes into Blue Suede Shoes, and it should be one of the greatest moments of my young life, but instead it's the moment when it hits me that this is all wrong. You can still enjoy it Ma, but for me it's one of those times when I think I know too much about music for my own good. The sound is great for an arena, but it's not the sound, it's what I'm hearing that's not right. Everything is messed up, the horns and backing vocals fighting for space, the drummer playing a relentless shuffle when this song above all others should be a straight down the line rocker. There's nothing wrong with the players, I'm fairly sure that it's the great James Burton on guitar, but there's too many of them, and the sad thing is that it's meant to sound like this, you can tell that the whole show is rehearsed like clockwork. For the old material all you need is Elvis on acoustic guitar and shaky leg, plus three others.

A ballad I don't know, a limp version of Fever and a sloppy Big Boss Man, and then Elvis speaks. I can't really catch what he's saying, but he mumbles something about a new album and goes into a song that I remember hearing down in Lafayette when Molly Malone played it on the radio. If you love me let me know, if you don't let it show. I can't stand another minute of a day without you in it. It's a nice enough tune, but why the king of rock 'n roll should want to cover an Olivia Newton John record is a mystery to me. Then it's Love Me Tender, and I can see that Elvis isn't really singing the song which was so simple but so effective when he did it right, he's acting his way through it. How is Elvis' acting? No one needs to ask. I know nothing is going to spoil if for you Ma, because there's gals of your age all round me in tears at the wonder of it all, touched by the Elvis who lives inside of them as much as by the man on stage, and Elvis is laughing at it and milking it at the same time.

We get about forty five seconds of Hound Dog and then he introduces the band, which seems to take for ever complete with indecipherable private jokes and solos. A bit of Lawdy Miss Clawdy, and then he goes into Teddy Bear, and he's slurring the words, and as poor as it is I still find myself getting a little choked up thinking about you singing it to little Joey, and you had better come back and sit with me now Ma, 'cos I know you'll be thinking about that too, and look Ma, some of the women are bringing teddy bears to the front of the stage, teddy bears and other stuffed animals, and Elvis is smiling and saying "thanguverrmuch" as only Elvis can.

"Well since my baby left me I found a new place to dwell. It's down at the end of lonely street at heartbreak hotel."

Just for a moment I sense there's a spark trying to escape from two hundred pounds of lard as Elvis casts his mind back to nineteen fifty six. His first single after he left Sun for RCA, his first hit nationwide. For kids in England like John and Paul and Mick and Keith, it would almost certainly have been the first time they ever heard him. In nineteen fifty six there were no teenagers in the UK, there were thirty year olds who had been born fifteen or sixteen years earlier, wearing suits identical to their dad's demob issue. I've tried many times to imagine what that must have been like, to stumble on something that great blasting out of the Bakelite on a dull fifties English Sunday, the like of which they could never possibly have heard before, destined to change their lives irrevocably in less than three minutes. Elvis showed them what was possible.

There are many purist fans who believe that Elvis' best work was already behind him when he walked into the RCA studio for the first time. Elvis came alive for the first time when he sang in public and realised he had it, and not only did he have it, he had it like precious few if any had ever had it before. The life force that was in him came bursting out like a dormant volcano when he stepped inside Sam Phillip's studio at Sun, and then burnt gloriously for all to see when he hit the road with Scotty and Bill.

I didn't really get it myself until nineteen sixty eight. I entered my teens when Elvis was in his post army phase, making singles that were OK but nothing more, the Return To Sender period, you might say. In sixty seven he put out a great single called Guitar Man, one of those songs that I was always a sucker for back then because it listed a whole load of exotic sounding places like Panama City and Mobile, and it was backed up by the funkiest acoustic guitar picking you could ever wish to hear. He followed up with something similar called the US Male, in which Elvis sounded mean and threatened violence, announcing to the world that he was back and he meant business. Then came the TV special.

Swinging London, nineteen sixty eight. The Beatles were in India with the Maharishi, the Stones were hanging out with tribesmen in Morocco, and Elvis Presley was about as unhip as a soul could be. Still, there had been a buzz about this programme for weeks ahead. It had already aired in the States, and rave reviews had preceded it across the pond. For someone like me, who had a knowledge of musical history and saw beyond the latest craze, it was a must see.

It started with Elvis looking directly into the camera and proclaiming "If you're looking for trouble you've come to the right place, if you're looking for trouble just look in my face" and he looked the business at thirty three, and he knew it too. The show wasn't perfect even if the star himself was. Some of it was over choreographed and schmaltzy, but all in all it was far better than anyone had any right to expect. For the faithful it was a stunning return to form. For the uninitiated it was a revelation. For me the highlight was the jamming section, Elvis seated on a tiny stage with a small group, playing an electric Gibson with limited technique but an exquisite sense of timing, and playing songs twice when he had played them perfectly the first time, playing them again for the sheer joy of it. Looking back at it now I'm wondering if he did some of those songs twice because he sensed it might have been the last moment of real freedom he was likely to enjoy for a long, long time.

Six years on and the man is singing the Hawaiian Wedding Song, and looking little more than a bloated parody of himself. Elvis has made some good records mixed up with the dross during the last five years, but we don't get to hear many of them. No Suspicious Minds, no Always On My Mind, no American Trilogy. Instead we get Johnny B Goode. On any given night in England you will find two hundred bands in pubs across the land doing versions of Johnny B Goode, and I would bet the rent that one hundred and ninety eight of them will be better than this one. A couple of years back I was at home watching television when this fellow called Tony Joe White appeared on the screen. He did the original of Polk Salad Annie. Elvis did a cover, but it was nowhere near as good. Tony Joe plays his own mixture of blues and country on guitar, either on his own, or backed up simply with bass and drums. He writes songs about Louisiana mostly, which he sings in a deep southern drawl. Flashing on that sixty eight special again, I'm thinking that's what Elvis should be doing now, not this. He couldn't be as good a player as Tony Joe, but if he worked at his chops he might get close.

But no, it's a leaden version of James Taylor's Steamroller Blues which completely misses the irony of the original version, on to Funny How Time Slips Away, and then he's slowly making his way from the stage. He returns to sing Can't Help Falling in Love, and this time I suspend all critical faculties because I know this is the only time in my life I will ever see the man, so I force myself to live in the moment and enjoy it for its own sake, and you enjoy it too Ma, because I can't say when you and me are likely to meet up again.

Then the band are playing him off stage, and I can see that the hard core fans aren't making a lot of noise like you would get at a real seventies rock concert because they know that's all there is, and then the MC is telling us "Ladies and gentlemen, Elvis has left the building" and then without further ado everyone is heading for the exit sign.

293

I get a cab back to Mount Clemens. It costs me fifty bucks, but I don't want to hang around. I don't tell Andy that, I tell him I met some people who lived nearby and gave me a ride.

"So how was it?" he asks.

If it was Elvis himself posing the question I would tell him that even if he didn't know it, he was the one who showed us we could have it all, and tonight he showed us how easy it is to lose it all. It's not Elvis that's asking though, it's Andy.

I give him the look which says if I told you how it really was you would never forgive yourself.

"It was great, man" I tell him. "It was just great."

Later I think of Elvis, and whether he's on his on his way to the next town, or in his suite, and once again I hear Ma's words.

"Be careful of what you wish for, Son. One day you just might get it."

Chapter Seventeen: Take Out Some Insurance

Mr Kaz comes home from the office on Monday evening and tells me there's a change of plan; he's not going to Pittsburgh tomorrow, he's going to Grand Rapids instead, and I wonder for a second whether he might get back with Andy's mum. It's a question I'm sure I'll never know the answer to, like so many slightly more important ones. One of Mr Kaz's colleagues is going to Pittsburgh in his place, and he's going to be my ride, at seven o'clock sharp. Bob's a young guy, I'll like him, so Mr Kaz says. My extremely limited experience with this particular profession tells me that if anything, young insurance salesmen are worse than their seniors, but a ride is a ride, as the actress once said to the bishop. Granny Kazmierczak, who had given me back my sparkling laundry earlier in the day, makes more apple pancakes as a farewell treat. Rick calls to say goodbye, and I tell him most sincerely I hope things work out for him with Diane.

In the morning Andy surprises me by getting up at six thirty to bid me goodbye. It's not that much of a sacrifice, as he can go straight back to bed, but it's still a nice gesture. The door bell rings at seven precisely. There's a chilly wind blowing. It's the first of October.

"Come and stay again" says Andy. "You're welcome anytime."

I give him a self-conscious hug, and remind myself not to be doing this when I get home. "Sure I will." I reply. We both know I won't.

"It's been a lot of fun" I say. We both know that it has. I kiss his Grandma on the cheek, and shake his father's hand.

"Promise me that when you get home you'll ask your dad to get you a job at Prudential. It sounds like a fine company, and you're a fine young man."

I've never been called that before, so I quit while I'm ahead, and then I'm shaking hands with Bob and we're getting in his regulation blue Dodge. Bob looks a little hipper than I would have imagined. Suit and tie, but hair coming over the ears, and a big blonde moustache. The rush hour traffic is already building up as we get on the freeway clear through the centre of Detroit and take the interstate heading south. The radio's playing Led Zep and Deep Purple, both of whom have their place, but not at seven am, at least not in my world. Bob seems to agree, as he turns it down.

"That's all you get in this city. Heavy, heavy, heavy. I'll put a tape on when we get out of the city. So how's the music scene in England? Anything we need to know about?"

You seem like a nice guy Bob, but I hope you're not one of those fellows in their mid-thirties who feels the need to reassure everyone how hip he is. I tell him he will be familiar with most of them already.

He nods in agreement. "That's the way it is now. No apprenticeship. Fame overnight. I'm more of a folk buff. I used to play myself. I don't tell many people, but I'm guessing with you coming from England you might know what I'm talking about."

I think I do know what you're talking about Bob. I think you're trying to tell me that although you may have a job which requires you to play the part of being a certain kind of person, underneath it you are not that person at all, and I can understand that, because there have been many times in the past when I've felt exactly that.

"Professional?" I ask.

"Sure" he pulls out a Byrds cassette.

"I used to play with McGuinn in Chicago. That's where he started out. He was still called Jim McGuinn then. Then he decided he wanted to be a rock and roll star, and it was goodbye Skinny Jim."

"So you didn't wanna be a rock and roll star?"

Much as I try, I find it difficult not to reveal just a little sarcasm, but if he picks up on it then he's too polite to show it.

"I didn't really have that kind of talent, you know. I played around Chicago till sixty eight, then I thought it was time to get a real job. Sixty eight. That's when it all went sour."

I feel I'm expected to ask. "So what happened in sixty eight?"

"If you had been in Chicago then, you wouldn't need to ask."

"Oh, right." I was thinking he meant his career went sour, when what he meant was that the dream did. Martin Luther King. Bobby K. Democratic convention in Chicago. I tell him about my sixty eight.

"I was eighteen, I was in London. We marched on the American embassy in Grosvenor Square. We found out later the marines were on the first floor. They had orders to shoot if anyone made it as far as the stairs."

"That would have been interesting. Good for you, Frank."

He looks genuinely impressed. I take this as an opportunity to ask something.

"Do you mind if I smoke, Bob?"

There is nothing in the car to suggest that he indulges. He smiles.

"Sure. What's your brand? Marlboro, huh? Congratulations, you're working for two governments. You're paying American sales tax on those suckers, and you're near as damn it guaranteeing that you're gonna shorten your life span and save your own country on retirement benefit down the line. But don't let me spoil it for you man, light up and enjoy."

I do just that, while Bob puts on the Byrds tape. It's got the long version of Chestnut Mare, and we fall silent for a while, while Lake Erie occasionally reveals itself through the left hand window. It takes little more than an hour before we cross into Ohio, another new state for the list, and drive straight through the chemical factories and oil refineries of Toledo, a town which on the surface appears to be as far removed from the exquisite Spanish city which bears the same name as it is possible to be. Then we're slowing down for a toll booth, and we're on the Ohio Turnpike going east towards Cleveland, and we're away from the factories and back among the farms.

"So" I ask, "why insurance?"

This time I don't betray any traces of sarcasm as I'm genuinely interested.

"Well I saw how important it appeared to be for most people to hold on to what they've got, so I figured insurance was always going to be a secure line of work. It didn't take me too long to figure out most of the hippies were as selfish as everyone else, if not more so. It was always about my drugs, my right to do what I want, my right not to get up in the morning."

I realise that I'm going to be listening to Bob, listening to him and not just humouring him, all the way to Pittsburgh. I'm no hippie, but all the same I feel like he's talking directly to me now, with my right to go wherever I want, my right to leave when I want, and take what I want and to hell with the consequences. Bob's just getting warmed up.

"They would have done better to have got jobs and joined the union. That's the biggest freedom under attack in this country. All the rights that men fought for back in the twenties, and women, are going to go. They've all got too damn complacent. That's another reason I'm sitting in this car shooting the breeze instead of being on the line at Ford's or GM. Are you familiar with Lennon?"

"Of course."

"Good. So you will know then that Lennon understood that the battle was lost as soon as the people thought the revolution was won. That's why they have to have a constant enemy, counter revolutionaries in their midst, and so on."

I was confused for a minute before I realised he didn't mean Lennon, he meant Lenin.

"That just leads to paranoia. Then Stalin came after Lenin and took it to extremes. That's why communism doesn't work. Back in the real world it's not really any different. A working man has to get up every day and fight for his rights. Too many guys now come home, take a beer out of the refrigerator and switch on the TV, and they don't think about too much else."

"Are you familiar with Lennon?"

I pronounce it Len On for Bob's benefit.

He grins. "Sure."

"Len On said they keep you doped with religion and sex and TV."

Bob sings the next line.

"And you think you're so clever and classless and free."

He's got a good voice, which doesn't sound unlike McGuinn singing Working Class Hero. We sing the next line together.

"But you're still fucking peasants as far as I can see."

Bob knows he has his audience of one in his hand, and he's enjoying himself now. "All right! I don't think John Lennon is a prophet or a poet, but he nailed it with that one, sure enough."

I tell Bob I went to see Elvis. He laughs, but I can tell he's interested.

"So how was he?"

"Well I think he might have been better a few years back."

Much as I'm enjoying listening to Bob, I don't want to tell him what I really think about Elvis. It would be disloyal to Ma, for one thing.

"I'm sure he would have been. You believe Elvis Presley thinks he's like everyone else? I know a fellow who played bass on a session for him once. He said he thought he might have been a nice guy, but it was hard to tell on account of him being surrounded by servants the whole time. Even in the studio there was one guy to light his cigarette, another to mop his brow."

Bob shakes his head in sadness and disbelief. "You think John Lennon thinks he's like everyone else? We've destroyed these people as human beings."

298

Not for the first time since I left LA the frightened face of Keith Moon passes before me.

"No, Frank. Elvis is history. So's Dylan. The Beatles were great, but as solo artists they sound pretty average to me. The Rolling Stones seem to be in it just for the money these days. I got no time for The Eagles or any of those groups, they're in it strictly for the bread as well. Give it a year or so and they'll all be gone. You think the kids in fifth grade now are going to be content with the Doobie Brothers? Something's going to come along and sweep it all away. Wish I knew what it was, then I wouldn't be doing this. Remember what Dylan said when he was great, the old order is rapidly ageing. You think that was just then? You think that's not happening all the time?"

I disagree with him in that I think Dylan is still great, but I realise it's an argument I can't win, so I change tack slightly.

"You were on the front line in Chicago back in sixty eight. Do you think the music helped stop the war?"

Good question, even if I say so myself, and Bob does it the honour of giving it serious consideration.

"It may have helped a little bit. One, two, three, what are we fighting for, all that stuff. What I know is the war wouldn't have ended if it didn't suit the people who really run the country, the people you never see. To be honest, I'm beginning to think that music may have been more of a distraction than anything else. Folk music, Woody Guthrie and Pete Seeger, and Dylan when he first started, they were singing about reality and how to make it better. Rock and roll is more about escaping reality. In the sixties we thought things were changing for the better. We thought it was the natural order of things. Now I'm more of the opinion that isn't necessarily so. We can build planes that can fly halfway round the world in three hours or something, but so what."

"We can invent new ways to kill each other." I interrupt.

"Exactly. And that's why there are plenty of more Vietnams out there waiting to happen. We don't know where they are, but somebody does. Some Churchill is getting ready somewhere."

"South America?" I offer, as much for something to say as for any other reason.

"We've been there for the last hundred years" he snorts. "We just make a better job of keeping it quiet. They elected a Marxist government in nineteen seventy three, and there was no way Uncle Sam was going to stand for that. The army took over last year, helped no end by the USA, and in no small part by your own country.

I know it. That's one march I didn't go on. I had other things on my mind.

"As for all the little countries, Bolivia, Nicaragua, Guatemala, we just own them. Always have. Here's a question for you. I'm tootling down this turnpike, locked in at fifty six miles an hour like a good citizen, because of the actions of a bunch of Arabs. How long do you think the west is going to tolerate that? The only reason we do is because the Russians want the same thing we want. One of these days Sam and Ivan are going to team up. That's when things will get really scary. So things aren't going to get better by themselves. We're all going to have to take responsibility. We're all going to have to stand up and be counted."

I ponder on that one for a while as the Dodge tootles down the turnpike, and then we're seeing signs for Cleveland, but we are spared the delights of that city as the road skirts around the edge of town in the direction of Youngstown. We pass a sign saying twenty miles to Akron, Ohio, home of the Firestone Tyre Company. Firestone, who for a British outpost, built themselves an art deco palace in Brentford. Sometimes you could smell the rubber burning a mile away. I imagine the whole town of Akron being like that. I ask Bob if he's been there.

"Only when I've had to, believe me. Hey I need gas. You want something to eat?"

Bob orders a grilled cheese sandwich, and I take the fried option. Over coffee I find myself telling him about the Firestone factory in Brentford.

"You miss home?"

"If I was missing home Bob, it wouldn't be the Firestone factory I'd be talking about."

"So what are you going to do when you get home?"

I tell him I'm planning to spend some time considering my options.

He laughs, as he should at such a bullshit line.

"Did you get a degree?"

I explain how things work in England. Bob shakes his head. He finds it difficult to believe I left school at sixteen.

"See, you're having a great time right now. You're seeing the world, you're going to all these different places. After a while you're going to start wondering, am I going to places or am I going from places? Someday you're going to have to deal with things right here, right now, right where you are. But you know what? I think you already know that. What you possibly haven't acknowledged yet is that you're going to die someday. One day you wake up and that hits you. That's when everything changes. Then when you get kids you see the changes every day. One minute you're learning how to change diapers, next thing you know they're in first grade."

Then I click with something Gino said to me once.

"You're no different to anyone else Frank, you're going to end up six feet under one day. Think about what you're going to leave behind."

I can't think about it now Gino, because Bob hasn't finished.

"So once it sinks in that you're not going to be around forever, what do you think you're going to think about the most? I'll tell you. The past. You think about the past. What you did, what you didn't do, what you should have done. Then the older you get the more past you got. The trick is to learn to live with it, not in it."

I hear what you're saying Bob, but I can't really think about what I should have done or anything like that, because I'm too busy staring into my coffee thinking about being six feet under. Thankfully he breaks the spell.

"Hey, let's get moving. I need to be in Pittsburgh by two."

Back in the car and unconstricted by possible eavesdroppers, Bob is immediately into full flow.

"All those kids at Berkeley and Michigan and Wisconsin and Kent State, which incidentally is about ten miles from where we are now, were out marching, but there weren't too many people out demonstrating at Yale or Harvard Business School. They're the people who are going to be running this country in twenty years time. Yours too, more than likely. Not to mention all the kids at West Point. Some of them will probably end up in the Pentagon without ever seeing any action. Now, they are the people who start wars."

"So are you going to be running this insurance company?"

"No chance of that, pal, but I do all right."

Suddenly serious now, more serious than when telling me about how the world might end. It's important to him that I know he's good at his job.

"I do OK at this job. You know why? Some people don't like the hard sell. I tell them what's on offer, and there's enough of them will take it. Some of them tell other people, and without pushing it too hard I'm doing good business. It doesn't always work. Some people only go for the hard sell. That's when we send somebody else in."

301

"Mr Kazmierczak by any chance?"

"Yeah, old George Kaz, boy he never stops. Did he hit on you? Yeah, thought as much. You see, he's got that immigrant thing, you can never stop because you're never going to be secure enough no matter what you do. He won't stop until he's in an early grave."

"I don't doubt it." I don't either.

Bob turns the dial and finds a country station.

"Did you catch any of that bible radio down south?"

I think of old Jethro for a moment, and laugh, nodding in agreement.

Bob's still serious. "It's funny, sure it is, but it's kind of worrying at the same time."

"They're harmless enough aren't they?"

"No, they're not. Used to be you would only find those stations down in cracker country. You might put it on for a while just to get a little local colour so to speak, like you might put on a Mexican station in Texas. These days they're cropping up all over the place. You could probably find one here if you looked."

To my relief he doesn't.

"There's a lot of money in religion, Frank. Some of them are even buying their own TV stations. I'm not sure where it's heading, but I don't like it, I don't like it one bit. For one thing they're all as right wing as hell, if you pardon the phrase. You know what I heard one of them say the other day? If people are rich it's because it's God will. Taxation is evil. Get that? Taxation is evil."

"What was that about a camel passing through the eye of a needle?"

"Exactly."

"There are a lot of people in England who would be only too happy to embrace that philosophy."

"Yeah but it's different. This is America. Everything is more extreme. The country was built on the idea that there will always be some new frontier to conquer. We reached California a long time ago. There's no more gold in them thar hills. We've ravaged the earth in the process, as you saw in Detroit and Toledo, and as you will most surely see in good old Pittsburgh. We've won the space race, we've conquered the fucking Moon, where do we go next? Simple. Let's go with God. Let's go to Heaven. That's got to be the ultimate frontier."

I'm wishing old Jethro was sitting in the back. It would be even better if he had his tongue talking grandaddy with him.

"This is still a young country. An immature one in many ways. You can't have helped but notice that, with all this Watergate business on

302

every radio and TV every day. I don't even want to talk about that now, I've had enough of it."

I'm not about to encourage you to Bob, don't worry.

"In a lot of ways this country is afraid to grow up. When it does it's going to happen real fast, and it's going to be a real shock to a lot of people."

As if to emphasise the point he kicks down on the gas to overtake a mobile home. We're losing the country station, and he puts on a Buffy Saint Marie tape which I last heard when I was at school. It's many a mile I've been on this road, which is true enough now. I'm half thinking about what Bob was saying, and half about Harry Chapin travelling on ten thousand miles and staying right where he is. Is that escape Bob, is it reality, or is it both? Is it going to be my reality? Only I will ever be able to answer that, someday maybe. We're slowing down for a tollbooth, and we are leaving Ohio without me having set foot in it, other than the diner. Welcome to Pennsylvania. I like Bob, but he appears to have spoken his piece and I suddenly feel alone. The sign says Pittsburgh seventy miles.

Chapter Eighteen: Spirit In The Night

So I board the Greyhound in Pittsburgh just like Paul and Kathy did, but I find those visions which resurfaced as we bypassed Saginaw are gone now. I'm counting different cars on the turnpike, and every one of them is taking me home. The bus is half empty, so I compensate for not having a female companion to innocently while away the hours with by spreading out and catching a little sleep. I've finally found out how to sleep on a bus, a skill I have no idea when I will next put to use.

Bob dropped me off at the bus station shortly before two as he said he would. Bob just about talked himself out crossing Ohio. By the time we reached Pennsylvania his thoughts had switched from the state of the world to the state of the insurance business and his upcoming meeting, and few words were said as we drove into the Sheffield of the Americas. He bid me goodbye with a smile, and a sincere sounding good luck. I wished him the same, and told him I had enjoyed talking to him, which was true enough, and he switched back on for a moment.

"Hey, Woody Guthrie said let me be remembered as the man who told you what you already knew. Think of me the same, Frank."

"Thanks again Woody" I told him before he drove away, his attention turned once again to soft selling business cover to some lucky punter.

Well Bob, you told me I was going to die one day, which is one thing I already knew, as much as I know anything, although I didn't particularly need to be reminded of it, not today anyway. But thanks, it was an education.

It's an eight hour ride from Pittsburgh to New York City. There was a bus leaving at three, but this time I wanted to come in to the apple in daylight, and I had a hankering to ride the hound overnight just one more time. I bought a ticket for the one a.m. bus, and allowed myself a couple of hours to take in the sights of my Celtic cousin Carnegie's fair city, which was about ninety minutes more than was necessary. There was nothing for it but to hit the bars. They're big on sports in

Pittsburgh, sports and drinking beer, same as they are in Newcastle, Hamburg, Marseilles or any other city where men work, really work, that is. I moved from one football, baseball, ice hockey pennanted joint to another, soaking up the beer with Italian sausage on Italian bread. It must have been that which kept me in reasonable shape, even though I finished off the final session with a couple of shots of Four Roses. So that's how you sleep on a bus.

I'm awoken by the sound of the traffic echoing in the tunnel, and we're beneath the Hudson and minutes away from the Port Authority Bus Terminal. I feel much better than I have any right to. At the hotel booking agency I conjure up Lord Snooty one more time to request a good hotel, stressing the good, which is convenient for the Village. They give me the Gramercy Park on 21st St and Lexington. Perfect. Check in at one pm. Out on the street it's cool and cloudy, just the ticket for walking around. I set my compass for 7th Avenue, and head downtown. There's a coffee shop I know does a great 99c breakfast.

It's late afternoon when I walk into the White Horse to find Seamus holding court behind the bar. It feels as familiar and comfortable as an old pair of shoes. I know how easy it would be to kid myself I know this city well, almost as well as I know my own, if I had a couple more weeks. Still, it feels like home well enough, a thousand times more than LA ever could. Los Angeles, the city you could never get to know because it isn't a city at all, populated by people you can never really get to know either as they spend most of their time in cars, by swimming pools, or having meaningless conversations in the dark.

I'm soon reminded that much as I might want it to be, New York is not my home and this bar is not my local, when Seamus makes it clear that he doesn't know me from Adam. I wait till I'm on my second pint before I engage him in conversation.

"Have you seen Robyn?"

I had hardly thought about the girl for weeks. As soon as I stepped off the bus the sweet taste of her last kiss came fresh to my mind, quickly followed by the even sweeter taste of what had passed in her walk up brownstone a few days before that.

"Robyn?"

Oh, come on man.

"About five feet, brown hair, glasses, artist. Vodka and grapefruit."

"Oh, Robyn. She went to California. Went a couple of weeks ago. Gone for good, I believe."

Robyn? California? Robyn, who thought the world extended from 52nd St to Coney Island? Seamus notes my surprise and obvious disappointment. He shrugs. "They come and they go."

Then he's away to the other end of the bar and reciting his pint of plain piece.

The thing about a village is that you are always likely to bump into someone you know, and this village is no exception. The White Horse had temporarily lost its appeal, and I preferred to reacquaint myself with the old familiar neighbourhood in the early evening dusk, the summer nights long consigned to the past. On 4th St I saw a vaguely familiar face come towards me, one that instantly registered recognition.

"Hi Frank, how are you?"

"Hi Neil. I'm fine thanks."

I don't want to go anywhere with Neil you understand, much less his absent friend, but I'm unexpectedly pleased that he recognises me, even more so after being blanked by Seamus. We only spent one evening in each other's company. I ask him the same question I asked the Irishman, hoping that Seamus may have got it wrong.

"Oh, you're just back in the city? Robyn went to California."

So it's true.

"She met a guy. A musician. It all happened very quickly."

"Robyn went off with a guy?"

The words come out of my mouth with unplanned righteous indignation. Any passer by on 4th St this evening will think I'm gay for sure. Neil grins.

"I always had my doubts about that kid. Like I said, it all happened very quickly. I think it may have been you who set the wheels rolling, Frank. Robyn was restless ever since you left."

Neil is laughing, but I can tell he's serious at the same time.

"No one has seen Shannon since, but if you see her I would advise you to run. She was seriously pissed off."

"Sure. I'll bear that in mind."

I'm standing here nodding stupidly.

"So, did you get to Texas?"

I'm still nodding.

"Were there many faggots down there?"

"One or two."

At least one, anyway.

"I'm sure there were."

That's about as much as we have to say to each other, so we're just saying an awkward goodbye when Neil remembers something, and pulls out his wallet as if he wants to give me ten bucks or something.

"You remember in the pizza parlour we were talking about that guy Springsteen?"

"Sure. I've heard him since then. He's good."

"That's what I wanted to hear. Somebody in the theatre gave me a couple of tickets, and like I said, it's really not my thing. He's playing uptown Friday at the Lincoln Center. Take 'em. I'm sure you'll enjoy it. The word is he's going to be big."

Neil puts the tickets in my hand, and then he's gone.

Back to the Gramercy Park, which makes a virtue of its faded elegance. Sitting on the end of the bed I feel the need to talk to someone, someone who isn't Neil and isn't Seamus. I scramble around in a bag which although bruised and battered is still in one piece, and pull out a crumpled Hershey bar wrapper.

A voice which sounds not unlike Rod Steiger playing Al Capone answers the phone.

"Who is this?" Gruff is not the word.

"Is Patti there?" Despite myself I sound about twelve. He says nothing to me, but I hear him bark out her name.

"Hello?" Curious, like someone who doesn't get too many calls.

"Hi Patti. It's Frank, from England."

"Oh hi, Frankie! I was really hoping you might call some time!"

She sounds like she was too.

"See, I told you I would. I kept your number safe" which is true, but it's more by luck than judgement.

"So how was your trip? Did you get to California?"

"Sure I did. California, Texas, you name it."

"Jeez, Frankie. I've been to the Catskills a few times, and that's about it."

"Well it's good to be back in New York."

Said sincerely, because it is.

"I really enjoyed that day we spent, Frankie. I enjoyed it a lot."

"Me too. Been to Nathan's lately?"

"No I haven't. You know what, Frankie? I'm on a diet. Seriously. That was my last hot dog. I've lost thirty pounds, Frank. What do you think of that?"

I think there might be a little more room for me on the ferris wheel.

"I'm thinking I might not recognise you."

"It would be great to see you, Frank." Her voice jumping out of her throat, and almost down the phone. I wasn't sure if I was going to do this when I made the call, but now I have no doubt.

"What are you doing Friday?"

"Friday I'm free."

Thought you might be somehow.

"So Saturdays you charge, right?"

"Oh, you English guys."

"Us blokes, right?"

"You blokes, huh."

Patti's never heard of Bruce Springsteen, but she says it sounds great anyway. She likes old music, The Beatles and The Four Seasons. We have to find a place to meet. Patti doesn't know the White Horse, never heard of it. That figures. Robyn and Shannon may have dipped down into her world now and then, but no way would they bring her into theirs. Turns out she doesn't know Manhattan well, she's a Brooklyn girl through and through, but by chance she does know where the Lincoln Center is, and that it has its own subway stop. We arrange to meet there on Friday at seven thirty.

Friday evening I have a few drinks early, partly because I always like to get a little loose before a concert, and how I wish I had before the Elvis show, and partly so I won't be too embarrassed to be seen with big Patti if it turns out she's been a little economical with the truth about the weight loss. I'm a terrible man I know, but if I've learnt one thing in life it's that seeing is believing. This means I'm late, not seriously so, because I don't want to miss the show, but fifteen minutes, which hardly constitutes being late at all in my book. Walking up to the ticket hall it occurs to me that there are so many exits to these stations I might not even find her, and if she's on the level about the diet I might not recognise her, but I don't have to worry, if worry is the right word, because she sees me first, which is just as well because no, I probably wouldn't have recognised her.

"Hey, it's good to see you. I was thinking maybe you weren't going to show."

I'm sorry I'm late now. The kid probably got there early, and had been standing around for the best part of half an hour thinking another humiliation was on the cards. She wasn't lying about the thirty pounds, either. She can surely shift a few more, don't get me wrong, but she's definitely heading in the right direction. She's dressed in black, which my Ma might have called a sensible choice. Her skirt and blouse clearly did not come from the five and dime, and she's wearing a black suede jacket with leather buttons, not dissimilar in design to my brown one. My expensive brown one.

"I'm sorry, I don't know my way round that well yet."

It sounds about as lame as it is. She fixes a pair of warm brown eyes on me, and smiles. She's got a nice face, pretty even, with a solid bone structure which is now able to reveal itself.

"Well you're here now. Let's go and enjoy the show."

It's a little confusing at first, as there's a lot of other stuff going on at this Lincoln Center place, but we latch on to what would appear to be the concert crowd. A lot of leather jackets, not bikers exactly, but greasier than you would expect to find in uptown Manhattan. An out of state crowd with a few hipsters. A lot of the chicks are dolled up in leathers as well, although they are outnumbered by the guys roughly two to one, which in my experience is a good sign. Too many girls indicates teeny bop stuff, all boys and you know you're likely to be in for ELP Yes Genesis bollocks. This is a healthy crowd. I've still only ever heard one song by this guy, but I'm starting to get the buzz. I don't need another drink now. This is not the Hammersmith Odeon, where you might manage five minutes before closing time after the show if you're lucky, and the very thought of that reminds me why I haven't felt homesick once since I left. I tell Patti there will be plenty of time afterwards, and I mean it too. There's plenty of ways you can accidentally get separated from your date on the way out of a concert, but I know now I'm not going to do that, I'm going to find the gentleman who hides in me and emerges only on rare occasions. Patti gets herself something called a diet tab. The girl's on a mission. Don't get too carried away girl, or in six months time you might end up looking like Leah or any one of those skinny girls at Stanley's. Well, maybe not.

Patti finishes her calorie free concoction as the five minute call comes, so we file into the auditorium and find our seats. Old Neil must have good connections because we're in second row centre, and the beers are kicking in now, not enough for me to make a fool of myself and embarrass my date but enough to set me up for a rocking good time, and I'm feeling good to be here and good to be with Patti. Then the lights go down and the band are on stage and playing, and it's not what I'm expecting because the light is on this bearded, balding type at the piano playing a slow classical kind of piece, and then another light shines on this hippy gypsy chick playing long sweeping notes on the violin, and then after about a minute another light fixes on this skinny guy wearing a vest and an oversized cap, and he steps up to the microphone and sings, or breathes more like it, "Spanish Johnny drove in from the underworld last night", and the regulars who clearly follow this guy around and make up three quarters of the audience explode, and just that one line tells me immediately that I'm going to love this. I don't get all the words of this first song because I'm taking in the whole scene, but I pick up enough on it to know that it's a story about a kid who gets tempted to make some easy money on the side, and it's a real hot night, and he likes to spend a lot of his time sitting out on the fire escape like I always pictured all the cool cats do in the New York summer, and his girlfriend's called Puerto Rican Jane, and I put my arm round Patti to share it with her and because it seems the natural thing to do, and I know that I'm going to surrender myself to every story this guy is going to tell tonight.

Then the song is over and the rest of the band ambles on to the stage. They look like a bunch of guys you might see in a bar, apart from this big black guy with a saxophone and a white suit who looks so sharp and so cool that he makes the singer look even skinnier and scruffier than he already is. The band go straight into this jazzy type thing, with the saxophone honking, and people are up and dancing, and the band are singing the chorus and so are the crowd, and I'm not because I don't know the song, but I get it the second time round, like a spirit in the night, all right, and Patti's squeezing my arm.

"This bus never stops", cue for another number they all know, and it feels like a private party as they goes off into a song about a bus driver that has way too many words for me to take in, but sounds great all the same. Then they slow it down for a cover, and I love people who respect rock and roll history enough to slip great cover versions into their set, and it's Cupid draw back your bow, and I look at Patti, and she knows this one, and I can tell she's loving this as much as I am. Next up is a song about how hard it is to be a saint in the city, which makes me feel as if the man is singing it just for me, as I know that as much as anyone and more than most.

This fellow isn't Elvis. He's not up on that stage to put himself in a palace or a gilded cage, and I would bet the contents of my money belt that he's not the type of guy to let any Colonel Parker put him in one either. I don't even believe he's in it for the fame and fortune, although if I know anything at all I would stake my life that's exactly where he's heading. No, he does this because it's what he does, and he's living his dream up on stage every night, and more important than that he takes the audience with him and allows them to live theirs. So rock and roll does still matter when it's performed with this amount of passion and conviction, and I'm wishing for a moment that Bob the insurance man could be here to see it, and Zaria and Railroad Phil, and anyone I've ever met that I felt to be any kind of kindred spirit. Even Julie would admit to being impressed by this.

Now the drummer's laying down a Bo Diddley groove, and the singer is telling us how somebody discovered this beat about twenty years ago and how it makes good girls bad and bad girls worse, and it's another song with a riotous chorus, and I'm soon howling it out with the rest of them, "Oh, She's the One". Then we get a long epic tale about street gangs crossing the Jersey line, and an hour has flown by, and the band stretch out on a couple of jazzy pieces that last at least half an hour for the two of them, and I switch off from the words for a while to dig the musicianship of the whole ensemble.

Then the regulars are on their feet and running down to the front, and I'm thinking this must be the last number, and it's a wild latin type celebration about this chick called Rosalita, with the sax player blowing up a storm, and there's a line near the end where he tells the girl that her father shouldn't worry because the record company just gave him a big advance, and the whole theatre rejoices with him in his good fortune. Sure enough the band leave the stage, but they're back soon enough, and I've got my wish because he's doing the one song I know, the one called Sandy. Watching him living it out on stage, I understand that it's a song about loss and triumph in equal measure, and when he reaches the line about chasing all the silly New York virgins by the score he looks a little coy about singing it here, but he needn't be because the whole crowd roar their approval. I'm thinking this must surely be the end, but no, there's another song, an old rocker, we danced till a quarter to three, and the whole place is going crazy, and after five minutes there is no indication that this song is going to end any time soon, but when it does it comes abruptly as half the stage collapses, and there are speakers falling onto people at the end of the row, and the seats are tumbling down, and that's the end of the show for sure, and the whole place is erupting, and we're making for the exit pronto in case the whole damned building falls down around us.

So we're back on the street, and I'm shaking my head, and I ask Patti if she's ever seen anything like that in her life, and she shakes her head too and says unbelievable Frank, just unbelievable, and any wariness we might have felt about each other has long evaporated into the night. I want to sit down with her and drink and talk, but not around here, I want a neighbourhood type place and I know she won't feel comfortable in the Village. I pull her down the subway steps.

"Come on, babe. You're taking me back to Brooklyn."

The train rattles south through places I'm familiar with, Houston Street and Canal.

"Are you sure you want to come back to my neighbourhood? It's a long ride back to the city."

I am fully aware that any kind of love action is out of the question as her old man is probably sitting at home cleaning his semi-automatic as we speak, but I don't care about that. The adrenaline is pumping from the show, and I want to carry on celebrating life like we've been doing for the last two hours, and as for my intentions towards Patti, well on this occasion I just want to be nice, because sometimes it's nice to be nice.

"It's no problem, really. I know Brooklyn."

Patti looks at me questioningly, probably realising for the first time that she knows some things that I don't. A few stops down the line she tells me we're in Brooklyn already, and at the next station she motions for us to get up, and I'm thinking this is a piece of cake, but this isn't home. Instead we have to change for the D train.

"Where do we get off?"

"86th Street."

She's right, it is going to be a long way back, but I've got a fair few thousand miles under my belt these past three months, and a few more ahead of me I don't doubt, so I'm hardly going to worry over a few miles of subway. The train soon emerges above ground, and I remember now that this is the way we came to Coney Island way back when. When we finally reach 86th Street I recognise it as one of those wide thoroughfares I looked down on from the train and wondered what lives were going on down there. Now I'm about to find out.

It's past midnight as she leads me into the bar. I take an instant liking to it, as it's crowded enough to have some atmosphere, but not so as you can't get a drink or sit down. This may be near Patti's house, but she doesn't appear to know anyone here and no one knows her. The girl is really stepping out. I'm relieved to find that she'll take a vodka and seven. I make it a double, and I get myself a couple of beers, as I know the first one won't touch the sides. We take a seat, and I notice that the walls are covered with black and white photographs of famous Italian Americans, Frank Sinatra and Tony Bennett, Dion and Frankie Valli, Jake La Motta and Joe Di Maggio.

"This an Italian neighbourhood?"

I get that look again which says she knows some things I don't. Don't start doing a Julie on me now.

"Sure."

"So are you Italian yourself, Patti?"

"Sure."

Like Teresa. Zaria too, on her dad's side. What is it with you and the Catholic girls, Downes? God's little joke, perhaps? I don't want to be thinking of Zaria now, but I do recall her saying her brother was in the music business here, and I wonder if he was at the concert. So while I'm thinking about that, Patti's asking how I managed to get such great tickets.

"I guess it's because of your job, huh?"

My job? What? Oh yeah, I fed them that line about the NME last time. Still, I don't want her thinking I've been hanging out with Neil or anything like that.

"It comes in useful sometimes. To tell you the truth, it's not a line of work I intend to pursue further. It's not real."

Which it clearly isn't, as far as I'm concerned anyway, which could be why I'm not likely to pursue it any further.

"This" I say, and I gesture with my hands the way that Gino used to, "this is real."

"What about that great concert? Wasn't that real?"

"That was as real as it gets, Patti. That was the exception that proves the rule."

I realise as I say it that I'm always going to remember every single detail of that concert, which means I am always going to remember Patti.

"So have you seen Robyn?" I ask innocently.

"Oh my God, wait and I'll tell you."

I laugh despite myself, because that's what the Irish girls say, wait and I'll tell you.

"You won't believe this."

She moves forward a fraction, like women of every land, clime, colour and creed will if they think they've got something juicy to share.

"Robyn met a guy."

So it's true.

"Would you believe it?"

Well yes I would, actually.

"It all happened really quickly. She went to her office one Friday, and the music publishers in the same building were having a party for this band from Queens. Robyn hit it off with the lead singer. Three weeks later they've gone to Los Angeles to make a record and Robyn's gone with them. What do you think of that?"

I'm thinking that it's nine thirty in Hollywood, and it's not beyond the bounds of possibility that Robyn is sitting at the bar in Stanley's ordering vodka and grapefruit as we speak.

"Well" I say. "So what's the name of the band?"

Like I want to know the name of the band.

"The Astorias. Robyn says they're going to be big."

Well she would, wouldn't she?

"So what happened with Shannon?"

Patti looks sad for the first time.

"She's disappeared. Gave up the apartment, and hasn't been seen in Brooklyn."

That will allow me to breathe a little easier around these parts.

"Maybe she'll meet a nice young man as well."

Patti doesn't look too convinced. Time to change the subject. I don't want her getting down, and anyway I don't want her thinking I'm too bothered about Robyn, let alone Shannon.

"I had a dream about you Patti. I dreamt that we were in Paris."

By the way she's looking at me I can tell she's hurt.

"Are you making fun of me, Frankie?"

It was a stupid thing to say. Patti's idea of Paris would be one of total sophistication, and her image of herself is the total opposite. Without thinking, I take her hand.

"I did, too. I went into a cafe for a beer, because that's what they do in France, they drink beer in cafes, beer or wine, and you were in there waiting for me. It was a surprise, a nice surprise. We were talking just like we are now, and it wasn't all that different to being here except that we were in Paris and not Brooklyn."

"Then what happened, Frankie?"

"We talked for a while, I can't remember what about, and then I woke up. Do you know what? I've been trying to get that dream back ever since."

I'm going too far now, my mouth running away with me like it always does. Patti's not seeing it that way though, she's with me every step of the way.

"I'll give you your dream back Frankie" and I feel like I should kiss her, but there's too many people here, so I squeeze her hand and jump up to the bar for some more drinks. Don't hurt her, Frank. I return with more vodka and beer, and Patti's got a question for me.

"So when are you going home, Frankie?"

Just the one lie. Just one lie to stop a chain of them.

"Sunday."

Patti looks disappointed, but soon takes it in her stride, like a person for whom disappointment has been a way of life.

"If you had been staying an extra day I was going to ask you to meet my family on Sunday. My Mom is a great cook, and my Dad really isn't as bad as he sounds on the phone."

His bark is worse than his bite, huh?"

Have to stop saying things like huh in three days time.

"Exactly."

Tell one lie to prevent a chain of them. If I were to go round for Sunday lunch and start bonding with the old fellow, the next thing is he's going to be asking me what I do, what I plan to do, and I know I would start making stuff up like I always do, and it would get way out of hand. Best to tell the lie now, just the one.

"I'll be coming back to New York."

That's true.

"Sooner than you think. I promise"

That's true also, because she's thinking never. The clock on the wall has worked its way around to closing time. I take a final drag of a Disque Bleu and put it out.

"Can I ask you something, Frankie?"

"Sure you can."

"Why do you smoke so much?"

Good question. It occurs to me that probably the only two people I've met in this whole country who didn't smoke have been Bob and Patti, and they are more than likely the wisest.

"I don't know really. I smoke more when I'm travelling. You go into a bar and light one up, it's like a companion."

Patti looks at me like I'm being downright silly.

"You don't need to do that."

"I know. I'm going to give up soon, when I get home I reckon."

Well maybe two lies. Two white ones.

The bartender makes the last call for alcohol, but I don't get another round because I know that if I do it will be hard to leave, and I want us to go while we're still welcome. I walk Patti to the end of her road, a long row of respectable wooden houses just like I pictured. She tells me I don't need to walk her to her door, meaning that she doesn't want me to. Too many curtain twitchers, and her old fellow is probably waiting up for her anyway. I kiss her on the lips, gently, chastely, and she responds tenderly and affectionately.

"I'll call you." I whisper. I will too.

"Goodnight Frankie."

She smiles, and then turns and walks away. She walks about a hundred yards, and it's only then that she looks to see if I'm still waiting. She waves, and then her key is in the lock and she's back in her own world.

I know the subway runs all night, but I could do without it at this hour. A perfect evening gets even better when a yellow cab with its light on comes cruising down the avenue just as I reach the corner. The euphoria of the concert is still upon me, and so is the taste of Patti's lips. I think about how I kissed her on the cheek like a sick child less than three months ago, and how she's a different person now, and maybe I am too. As the cab crosses the East River I'm thinking that it wouldn't be impossible for me to live right here in Brooklyn. Get a job, go home every night to my not so fat wife, and sit in my vest and eat veal parmigiano and drink Chianti. Manhattan and its treasures are just a cab ride or the D train away, and we could buy a second hand cherry red Camaro and follow Bruce Springsteen at weekends if he's playing round the New York and New Jersey area. I'm still thinking on that as I slide between the crisp sheets of the Gramercy Park Hotel.

The top of the Empire State Building is crowded on a Saturday morning in October, but not like it must be in summer. The tourist season is over now, as much as it ever is in this city, and I'm joined on the viewing platform mainly by daytrippers from Connecticut and New Jersey, Queens even. It's cool and cloudy, so I can't see much further than across the river, and I'm wondering what I'm doing up here with these people, but then miraculously the clouds part and the Sun appears, and I'm looking miles out across the big country, and it brings home to me what I know anyway, which is that I could spend the rest of my life rambling around from state to state and town to town, and still only scratch the surface. What would Uncle Michael make of it? Michael, who has hardly left Tipperary other than to go to Dublin a time or two, a place he has no time for. Mike knows every blade of glass in every field within fifteen miles of his home, and if there is a wiser man on the planet I've yet to meet him. Who's to say he doesn't know more than anyone. That will never be my road; I found that out a long time ago.

Somewhere out there old Jethro, who isn't called Jethro at all, and is no more than a year or two older than me, but will always be old Jethro to me, is trampling all over a speed limit with a big grin on his face and pussy on his mind. I wonder if sometimes the grin turns a little puzzled, and he shakes his head and wonders what happened to old Frank from England. Goddamn. I can't deny that there are crazy women out there who think Paris is in England and their dog is their brother, and twisted racists who hate everyone especially themselves, but they are more than outnumbered by the good. JW and Don, Railroad Phil and Ernie, all of whom could have become lifelong pals if we had met in different circumstances. Instead I was privileged to know all of them for a few hours and no more, time enough for each of them to cause me to reveal the best of myself without even thinking about it. The Detroit boys, who turned a meal in a draughty pizza joint into an evening to remember just when I needed it the most. Bob the insurance salesman, who appeared to know everything including how to live with the knowledge. Lynnie, poor Lynnie. I wish I had her address or phone number. Still, maybe she will learn from it. You'll frighten the good ones away if you carry on like that girl, you surely will. Debbie the Georgia peach, the one who got away. Pamela Jo, long back home in Minneapolis, and who has probably forgotten all about me by now. On second thoughts no, I can picture her out with her friends on a Friday night, getting drunk and telling them how she went to New Orleans and slept with an English guy, can you believe that?

Somewhere out there Patty Hearst is running wild and free, while teenage rich kids in California borrow their Mom's car so they can go and paint TANIA on a wall, and Nixon is free too, sort of, holed up in an ivory tower somewhere down San Diego way. I don't suppose there's much chance of him ever popping out to the little cafe where Bruce Springsteen is after taking Rosalita.

Three thousand miles from sea to shining sea, did it both ways, and north to south and back up on the other side, that's at least eight thousand and more like ten, and now I'm thinking of the places I didn't go. Memphis, where I would surely have found more of Elvis, the real Elvis, than I did in Detroit. The Mississippi delta, where there must still be old men playing who travelled down to Rosedale with Robert Johnson, and who are still singing songs about their Friars Point mamas. Chicago, where I could have easily made a detour to, and maybe even sat at the feet of Muddy Waters in a Southside lounge. Boston, where I must have more long lost cousins. Missouri, home of Huck and Tom and my childhood dreams. Kentucky, Tennessee, Oklahoma and Colorado, all of them stretched out waiting for me the next time round. The alluring sounding Jersey shore just down the coast, where there might be more guys like Bruce Springsteen playing those seaside bars. Kansas, where the Wichita lineman is always going to be on the line, putting off his vacation and worrying about that stretch down south. Dallas, where someone and something died in sixty three, and where creepy Jerry now makes the scene. Maybe not Dallas.

JFK was nearly eleven years ago. I can recall exactly what I was doing like everyone is supposed to. It was a Friday evening in late November, and I was watching Harry Worth with Ma when the news flash came on. I remember Ma started crying, and although she wasn't one of those holy water sprinkling, hail Mary reciting Catholics, she'd escaped all that, she managed to find a candle to light. Ma wasn't greatly bothered with politics, she was upset because he had young children, although him being Irish and handsome with it never did him any harm in her eyes either. I remember the BBC went straight back to old Harry standing on one leg by a shop window. It would take an earthquake to rock their world, and a big one at that.

Looking out from this platform a hundred and two floors up, I'm not thinking about Kennedy, I'm thinking about me. Eleven years ago and it seems like last week. They say the years go by faster as you get older. Eleven years forward and I'll be thirty five. Halfway to my three score and ten. Elvis Presley will be fifty. Will he be putting on the same old act? Will I?

Over breakfast I picked up the New York Times and read about the big fight coming up in a few weeks time. Muhammad Ali, now thirty two, taking on the fearsome George Foreman. Foreman, unbeaten and never even seriously challenged. Ali, majestic, magnificent, once supreme and all powerful. Now many of those who know boxing fear for his life.

I heard a new Rolling Stones track on the radio while I was in the shower. Time waits for no one, and it won't wait for me. What was that Railroad Phil said? Don't stay on that road too long. One day you might find it's all you got.

On Sunday I walk across the bridge to Brooklyn. I'm not about to go far. I don't want to bump into Patti when I'm supposed to be at the airport, although it's hardly likely. This is a big borough. That much I know now. I go into a bar which turns out to be Irish, although you wouldn't know it from the outside, it not being one of the shamrock and blarney tourist traps you find across the river. It feels like a Sunday lunchtime, with good natured banter a plenty up at the bar, but I'm not in need of that right now. I get a beer and find a seat in a dark corner. Already I feel like I'm half way where I'll be tomorrow. I put my jacket on the seat beside me, but the visitors come like a whole string of ghosts of Christmas past.

Julie. I could write and apologise. What good would that do? I feel her green eyes gazing at me in a cool and reproachful fashion.

Teresa. Looking like she did the last time I saw her in Park Royal only older now, innocence gone, a woman of the world. When you're a kid you think things will always be the way they are. Then one day you find out. She found out. Sipping her drink and looking at me as if to say, what have you got to say for yourself?

Then a real ghost. Gino. Can you at least tell me what was going through your mind on your last day on earth? No you won't, because you can't, you're just going to sit there and look at me as long as I allow you to, and no you don't have to say it, and don't you think I'm

319

disappointed in me as well when I stop and think about it, which I do more than I could ever tell you. I've never been one for the confession, me, it always seemed like kicking your dog and then putting a quid in the RSPCA box, but if I did, I know I'd have plenty of sins to fess up to.

I try and think of the seven deadly ones, and how many of them I've fallen foul of. Sloth. No, I've never been too lazy to get up off my arse. Envy, absolutely not. This world is big enough to find your slice of pie easily enough, though sometimes you have to go looking for it. Gluttony, no not that one either. I wouldn't be travelling in this country if I was that bothered what I stuff my face with. Lust. Well I'll have to hold my hands up to that one. It's a fair cop guv, and no mistake. If I think about it, everywhere I've ended up since the day I discovered it wasn't for stirring my tea with is a direct result of the lust.

Greed. That's the one I'm most ashamed of. I'd never been greedy, which is why I pass with flying colours on the gluttony. Then I met Gino and bit the hand that fed me. At the end of the day, it's lust that makes the world go round and it's greed that will most likely destroy it.

Pride? I haven't worked that one out. I know that if you build a house, or build a bridge or a railway you're entitled to be proud, same if you bring up a family in a rightful fashion. But then there's false pride, the pride that comes before a fall. The thing is, I don't know what that kind of pride is yet. Maybe when I do it will provide the key.

So that's two out of five I'm bang to rights, and the more I think about the pride I'm sure I must fall foul of that one too, because every time I say to myself I'm Frank Downes, that's who I am, then that's not exactly being humble. So three out of six, and I can't remember what the seventh one is, and it's starting to bother me, because if I know that then I'll know if I have a winning score and whether I'm beyond redemption or not. I'm sure there must be someone in this bar who would know, what with it being an Irish place and all, but I'm not about to ask anyone. I would bet my bottom dollar that Seamus would know, but Seamus is on the other side of the Brooklyn Bridge. I'm sure that when I get back to London I'll be waxing lyrical about the White Horse, but I don't want to be there today, my last day. I know I would only conjure up more recent ghosts.

Robyn. The first friend I made, who took in the wayfaring stranger like the statue of Liberty for no reason other than generosity. Well now

I'm thinking there may have been some lust involved on her part, but there's me with the pride again. Neil suggested I might have turned her, not that he would put it like that, but I have to admit the idea of it gives me a bit of a glow, and there I go with the pride again, and oh no, there's some envy creeping in now as well, envy of the skinny dude from Queens who reaped my harvest, and what kind of name is the Astorias for Christ's sake, sounds like a chain of cinemas, and I'm thinking that if he starts hitting the scene in LA, as he surely will, there's a good chance he might run into Zaria and more than likely hit on her too, and that really would be my comeuppance, not that I'd ever know about it, but the possibility of it ever happening is punishment enough. Then I feel anger welling up, and that's it, anger, that's the other deadly sin, so now I'm guilty as charged of five out of seven.

Then I've got another visitor, and stone me if it isn't blue eyed Tel from Acton Vale, who I've seen twice in my life. Once when he was driving along the High Street like a king, and once in a windowless bar where he wished me luck as though he meant it, and spoke to me like my Uncle George would. He's turning into Budgie right in front of me with a movement of the shoulders.

"Don't be too hard on yourself. You've got a good heart. If you didn't none of this would trouble you."

Tel sits there flashing his Budgie smile, and now Ma is there with him.

"He's right son. Your heart's in the right place. But remember what I used to tell you Frank. Be careful of what you wish for, one day you might just get it", and I know this is all too much now, and I need to get back to the hotel and start packing.

It's Zaria's voice I'm hearing as I make my way back across the bridge.

"You need to go home Frank. There's things you need to do. You know it."

Sunday night. My last night. I wander the streets of the Village, careful to stay away from anywhere I'm likely to have any adventures. I've had enough of those for a while. Back at the hotel I realise I've spoken to no one all day other than bartenders, waiters and desk clerks. I go to sleep quickly, only to find myself in a dream. I'm making my way back to England on foot across the icy wastes of Greenland. On a glacier I find an empty 747 parked on the ice like the Mary Celeste. I awake from the dream, and then lie awake for hours wondering what it might be about.

So then I find I've got Gino and Teresa to deal with again, right when I'm not in a room full of people drinking beer and whisky as a distraction, right when I was hoping they might stay away at least until I got home. Not that I deserve to be let off so easily.

I'm sorry for what I did to Teresa, not that it isn't partly her fault for playing with fire and leading me on like that on a fateful Saturday morning. She'll get through it. Since word got out that she is wherever she is, there's probably been a line of Vespas following her down the street every time she's taken her evening stroll, as I believe they do over there. For all I know she might settle down with some Romeo who thinks it a good idea to take his English speaking wife across the water. She could end up in Bensonhurst living around the corner from Patti. The more I step out to see how big the world is the more I find the opposite.

I know I hurt Gino, but one thing just lead to another. Gino never learned, he kept on turning people into the children he never had. Mario. Teresa. Me.

I don't think I'm a bad person. I know I can be better. Perhaps I'll put the suit on next week and get a job. There are plenty of opportunities for sales reps. I could get that yellow Capri, no bother. Spend a year or so zipping up the M1 and work my way up to be area manager and then an exec. I'll pull a few in the course of my duties, how could I not, but I'll always be honest with them.

Who am I kidding? That's not being a better person, just a different one.

I make a vow never to help myself to anything again that isn't mine, be it a man's business account or a woman's heart, and go back to sleep.

At JFK I buy postcards, and write identical messages to Don Hargreaves and JW Pope.

"Had a great trip. Thanks again for your hospitality. Best wishes, Frank Downes."

Then I address another one to Miss Zaria D'Amato, c/o Stanley's Bar, Sunset Boulevard, Los Angeles, California.

"Going home. There's things I need to do."

Then I find a payphone and call Patti.

"Hi Frankie! Are you home?"

"I'm nearly home." That's true enough.

"What's all that noise? Are you calling me from the airport, Frankie?"

Patti thinks I've just landed at Heathrow and I couldn't wait to phone her, God bless her.

"No one ever called me from across the ocean before."

"Well there's a first time for everything."

"I wish you were still here, Frank."

"I wish I was still there myself, Patti. I went all around the country, and I can tell you that New York is the place for me." Ain't no mistake about it. "Right now there's things I need to do, stuff to take care of. Family stuff."

"Nothing's more important than family, Frank."

"I'll be back. I promise."

"Well I really hope so, Frank."

Sad now, like she's heard it all before, but still hopeful.

"Will you send me a postcard of Big Ben? That would be neat."

"Sure I will. And I'll do more than that, Patti, I'll write. Real letters, let you know what I'm doing and what's going on in England. Then one day I'll come back."

Write. Me. I never write.

"Oh that would be so great, Frankie. I really hope you do."

And you know what?

Maybe I will. Maybe I will.

THE END

Thanks again to all those too numerous to mention by name whose friendship, encouragement and advice helped bring this novel to publication.

Many thanks to you also, dear reader, as it would appear you made it to the end

You can contact the author by email at

htrf74@gmail.com

Milton Keynes UK
Ingram Content Group UK Ltd.
UKHW011807231023
431193UK00001B/46